A Hungarian Nabob

A Hungarian Nabob

MAURUS JÓKAI

Authorized Edition, Translated from the Hungarian by
R. NISBET BAIN

ÆGYPAN PRESS

From the edition published by Doubleday & McClure Co. in 1899.

A Hungarian Nabob
A publication of
ÆGYPAN PRESS
www.aegypan.com

Preface

This noble novel, now translated into English for the first time, was written nearly fifty years ago. On its first appearance, Hungarian critics of every school at once hailed it as a masterpiece. It has maintained its popularity ever since; and now, despite the manifold mutations of literary fashion, in Hungary as elsewhere, has reached the unassailable position of a national classic.

It is no light task to attempt to transplant a classic like "Egy Magyar Nábob." National tastes differ infinitely, and then there is the formidable initial difficulty of contending with a strange and baffling non-aryan language. Only those few hardy linguists who have learnt, in the sweat of their brows, to read a meaning into that miracle of agglutinative ingenuity, an Hungarian sentence, will be able to appreciate the immense labor of rendering some four hundred pages of a Magyar masterpiece of peculiarly idiomatic difficulty into fairly readable English. But my profound admiration for the illustrious Hungarian romancer, and my intimate conviction that, of all continental novelists, he is most likely to appeal to healthy English taste, which has ever preferred the humorous and romantic story to the *Tendenz-Roman,* or novel with a purpose, have encouraged me to persevere to the end of my formidable task.

I may add, in conclusion, that I have taken the liberty to cut out a good third of the original work, and this I have done advisedly, having always been very strongly of opinion that the *technique* of the original tale suffered from an excess of episode. This *embarras de richesse* would naturally be still more noticeable in a translation, and I am particularly anxious that "A Hungarian Nabob" should attract at first sight. Let this, therefore, be my apology to Dr. Jókai and, as I trust, my claim upon his forgiveness.

– R. Nisbet Bain
August, 1898

Chapter I

AN ODDITY, 1822

It is nasty, dirty weather outside there on the *puszta*;* the sky is cloudy, the earth muddy, the rain has been falling for two weeks incessantly, as if by special command. There are inundations and submersions everywhere; rushes are growing instead of wheat, the stork is plowing, the duck is fishing all over the precious sealike expanse. "This judgment weather began on St. Medardus' Day, and will last now for forty days longer, but if it does last, I know not where we are to find the Noah to save man and beast from a partial deluge."

This melancholy reflection was made by the noble Mr. Peter Bús, whom a cruel fate had called to be a perpetual wrangler with guests on the cross-roads of the famous county of Szabolcs, for he was the innkeeper of the "Break-'em-tear-'em" *csárda* there. That worthy inn owed its name, not to its ancestors, but to its own peculiar merits, for no traveler could possibly reach that sweet haven till he had had endless spills and been nearly torn to pieces. This was especially the case at such times when the floodgates of Heaven were open, and it naturally occurred to a man's mind how much better it would have been to have had floodgates on the earth instead, for then you would not be brought to a standstill on the dike between two ponds, with the ground so soaking wet beneath your feet that there seemed nothing for it but to stick there till you grew old, or carry your wagon away with you on your back.

It was drawing towards evening. Mr. Peter Bús was coming home from his fields on horseback, grumbling to himself, but softly, for he grudged taking his pipe out of his mouth merely for the sake of what he was saying, which goes to prove that pipes were invented in order that man may have something to stuff his mouth with, and thus stop

* For the meaning of this and all other Hungarian words used in the text, see the glossary at end of book.

from swearing so much. "All the hay has gone to the devil already," he muttered, "and he'll have the wheat too! The whole shoot has gone to the deuce!" For the innkeeper of the *csárda* does not live by only doling out wine, but is a bit of a farmer besides, and his business is no sinecure.

While he was thus murmuring to himself, a dubious-looking being of the feminine gender, of whom it was difficult to judge whether she was a spouse or a scullery-maid, appeared at the extreme end of the dike, which led towards the River Theiss.

"Isn't there a coach coming along there?" she said.

"So I'm to be saddled with guests on an infernal day like this, eh! It only needed that," said Peter Bús, grumbling still more. He did not look in the direction indicated, but hastened into his pothouse to strip off his saturated pelisse before the fire, and swear a little more. "When our store of bread is gone, I don't know where I am to get anymore from, but I don't mean to starve for anybody."

At last, however, he condescended to look out of the window, drying the sweat from his brow the while, and perceived a carriage a good distance off, drawn by four post-horses, struggling along the dike. He made a gesture of satisfaction towards it with one hand, and said, pleasantly, "It won't get here today." Then he sat him down in front of his door, and, lolling his pipe out of the corner of his mouth, looked on in calm enjoyment, while the coachman cursed and swore at the four horses on the far-extending dike. The lumbering old vehicle on its high springs swayed to and fro from time to time, as if it were on the point of toppling over, but a couple of men kept close to it on each side, and, whenever a jolt came, they clung heavily on to the steps to keep it steady, and when it stuck fast in mud up to the axles of the wheels, and the horses came to a standstill, they would, first of all, shout till they were husky at the horses, and then, buckling to, dig the whole conveyance out with sticks and staves, raise the wheels, clean out the spokes, which had been converted into a solid mass of mud, and then proceed triumphantly a few paces further.

Mr. Peter Bús regarded the dangers of others in the spirit of a true predestinarian. Frantic cries and the cracking of whips reached his ears from time to time, but what business was it of his? It is true he had four good horses of his own, by the aid of which he might have dragged the coming guests out of the mud in the twinkling of an eye, but why should he? If it were written in the Book of Fate that the carriage would safely arrive at the *csárda,* it *would* arrive, but if it were preordained to stick fast in the mud and remain there till dawn, then stick fast it must, and it would be wrong to cut athwart the ways of Providence.

And at last all four wheels stuck so fast in the mud in the middle of the dam that it was impossible to move either backwards or forwards. The men were hoarse with shouting, the harness was rent to pieces, the horses lay down in the mud, and the weather began to grow beautifully dark. Mr. Peter Bús, with a lightened heart, knocked the ashes of his pipe-bowl into the palm of his hand. Thank God! no guest will come today, and his heart rejoiced as, passing through the door, he perceived the empty coach-house, in which his little family of poultry, all huddled up together for the night, was squabbling sociably. He himself ordered the whole of his household to bed, for candles were dear, put out the fire, and stretching himself at his ease on his *bunda,* chuckled comfortably behind his lighted pipe, and fell reflecting on the folly of people traveling anywhere in such dripping weather.

While Mr. Peter Bús was calmly sleeping the sleep of the just, danger was approaching the house from the other, the further side. In the direction of Nyiregyháza there was no dike indeed, and the water was free to go up and down wherever it chose. A stranger venturing that way might just as well make his will at once, but those who knew the lie of the land, could get along more easily than if there had been a regular road; indeed, there were coachmen who had loafed about the district so long and learnt to know all its boggy and hilly turnings and windings so thoroughly, that they could make their way across it late at night in any sort of vehicle.

It must have been close upon midnight, for the cocks of the "Break-'em-tear-'em" *csárda* had begun to crow one after the other, when a light began to twinkle in the twilight. Twelve mounted men were approaching with burning torches, with a carriage and a wagon in their midst.

The wagon went in front, the carriage behind, so that if a ditch presented itself unexpectedly the wagon might tumble into it, and the carriage might take warning and avoid the spot.

The bearers of the torches were all heydukes wearing a peculiar uniform. On their heads were tschako-shaped *kalpags* with white horse-hair plumes, on their bodies were scarlet dolmans with yellow facings, over which fox-skin *kaczagánys* were cast as a protection against the pouring rain. At every saddle hung a *fokos* and a couple of pistols. Their *gunyás* only reached to the girdle, and below that followed short, fringed, linen hose which did not go at all well with the scarlet cloth of the dolmans.

And now the wagon comes in sight. Four good boorish horses were attached to it, whose manes almost swam in the water; the reins were handled by an old coachman with the figure of a *betyár.* The worthy fellow was sleeping, for, after all, the horses knew the way well, and he only awoke at such times as his hands closed upon the reins, when he would give a great snort and look angrily around him.

The interior of the wagon presented a somewhat comical sight, for though the back seat did not appear to be occupied, in the front seat two ambiguous looking individuals were sitting with their backs to the coachman. Who or what they were it was difficult to make out, for they had wrapped themselves up so completely in their shaggy woolen mantles, or *gubas,* and drawn their hoods so low down over their heads, that they had no resemblance to anything human. Moreover, they were sleeping soundly. Both their heads were jig-jogging right and left, and only now and then one or the other, and sometimes both at the same time, would be thrown backwards by the jolting of the wagon, or they would bump their heads together, and at such times would sit bolt upright as if determined to say, "Now, I really am *not* asleep!" and the next instant off they were nodding again.

The body of the wagon was fenced about with large baskets, whose rotundity warranted the suspicion that they must be stuffed with plenty of all sorts. The basket on the back seat moved slightly now and then, and, therefore, might fairly have been assumed to contain some living creature, which the two gentlemen held in high honor or they would not have given up the best seat to it. Presently a more violent concussion than usual tilted the basket over, when, after a desperate struggle, the mysterious something poked out its head, and revealed to the world a beautiful greyhound. So it was to him that precedence belonged! And this he seemed to be quite conscious of, for he sat up on his haunches in the wagon, gaped majestically for a moment, then condescended to scratch his aristocratic ears with his long legs, shook his steel-chain collar, and when an impertinent nocturnal gadfly attempted to cultivate his acquaintance by force, plunged into a determined contest with it, and snapped at it vigorously with his teeth. Tiring at last of this diversion, he turned his attention to his sleeping companions, and being in a condescending humor, and observing that the lankiest of the two sleepers was nodding at him, the humorous greyhound raised his front paw and passed it over the face of the slumberer, who thereupon murmured heavily, "Pah! don't taste it, your honor!"

And now let us have a look at the carriage. Five full-blooded stallions were harnessed to it, and all of them were tossing their gaily decked heads proudly. Two of them were beside the shafts and three in front, and each of the three had jangling bells around his neck, to warn all whom they might encounter to get out of the way. On the box sat an old coachman in an embroidered *bekes,* or fur-pelisse, whose sole instructions were that wherever he might go, he was not to dare to look into the carriage behind him under pain of being instantly shot through the head. We, however, who are in no fear of having our heads blown off, may just as well take a peep inside.

Beneath the hood of the carriage sat an aged man wrapped up to the throat in a wolfskin *bunda*, and with a large astrakhan cap on his head drawn down over his eyes. Inside it one could make out nothing but the face. It was a peculiar face, with eyes that looked strangely at you. An errant spirit seemed to dwell in them; they spoke of a mind that had been destined for great, for amazing things. But fate, environment, and neglect had here been too much for destiny, and the man had grown content to be extraordinary in mere trifles, and seemed quite surprised at the wonderful expression of his own eyes. The whole face was fat but colorless, the features were noble but puckered up in bizarre wrinkles. This, with the heavy eyebrows and the neglected moustache, caused repulsion at the first glance; but if the man looked at you long enough, you gradually got reconciled to all his features. Especially when he shut his eyes and sleep had smoothed out all the lines and creases of his face, he wore such a patriarchal expression that one involuntarily thought of one's own father. But what made him look still more remarkable was the peculiar circumstance, that crouching up close beside him sat two peasant girls; two chubby little wenches, from the seriousness, not to say anxiety, of whose faces it was possible to conclude that no mere idle freak had lodged them there by the side of the old gentleman. The cold wet night froze the blood in the veins of the aged man, his wolfskin *bunda* could not keep him warm enough, and, therefore, they placed close beside him two young peasant girls that his dilapidated organism might borrow warmth from their life-giving magnetism.

All night long he had been unable to get any rest, any pastime in his distant castle, so at last he had hit upon the idea of knocking up the landlord of the "Break-'em-tear-'em" *csárda,* and picking a quarrel with him at any price. The insult would be all the more venomous if he woke him in the middle of the night, and demanded something to eat and drink immediately. If the fellow cursed and swore, as he was pretty sure to do, he should have a good hiding from the heydukes. As the innkeeper was himself a gentleman, the whole joke would possibly cost about a couple of thousand of florins or so, but the fun was quite worth that.

So he called up his serving-men, and made them harness horses and light torches, and set off through the pathless darkness with twelve heydukes, taking with him everything necessary for eating and drinking, in order to have a banquet in honor of the jest as soon as it was accomplished, not forgetting to carry along with him the three personages who chiefly ministered to his amusement, and whom he sent on before him in a separate wagon, to wit, his favorite greyhound, his gypsy jester, and his parasitical poet, all three of whom made a nice little group together.

Now, worthy Mr. Peter Bús was famous far and wide for his peculiar sensitiveness to insult; the merest trifle was sufficient to lash him into a fury. A heyduke, therefore, was sent on in advance, who rattled at his windows like a savage, and bellowed at the top of his voice –

"Get up there, you innkeeper fellow! Get up, get up! You are required to wait upon your betters, and look sharp about it!"

At these words Peter Bús bounded to his feet as if he had been shot from a gun, snatched up his *fokos*, looked out of the window, and perceiving the brilliant array of serving-men, who lit up the whole house with their torches, instantly guessed with whom he had to do. He now grasped the fact that they wanted to make him fly into a rage for their especial amusement, and resolved for that very reason not to fly into a rage at all. So he hung his *fokos* up nicely on its nail again, thrust his head into his sheepskin cap, threw his *bunda* over his shoulders, and stepped out.

All the newly arrived guests were already inside the courtyard. In the center, surrounded by his bodyguard, was his lordship, in a large *attila* with gold buttons, reaching down to his knee; the circumference of his body constrained him to hold his head a little thrown back, and he supported himself with a gold-headed Spanish cane. It was now quite evident how ill that scornful, mocking expression of his became his face, and wholly distorted its naturally jovial character.

"Come nearer, sirrah!" he called to the innkeeper in a loud imperious voice. "Throw open your apartments, and make ready for our entertainment. Give us wine, tokay, and *ménes*; give us also pheasants, artichokes, and crab salad."

The innkeeper humbly took off his hat, held it in his hand, and replied with the utmost calmness and *sangfroid* –

"God hath brought your lordship to us; I will serve you with everything you command. I would only beg of you to pardon me for not possessing either tokay or *ménes*. My pheasants, too, have not yet been fattened up; and as for my crabs, they have all been drowned in this great deluge, as you may see for yourself. And I suppose your lordship will not give me for my kitchen the two crabs I see here?"

This last sally was directed at the scarlet uniforms of the heydukes, and diverted his lordship's attention. He was pleased to find the innkeeper rising to the level of the joke. He had not expected it, and was all the more amused.

Meanwhile, the gypsy jester had poked out his black phiz, which vied with that of any nigger, and, flashing a row of white teeth at the innkeeper, began to tot up on his fingers what he wanted.

"All I want," said he, "is a dish of bird of paradise eggs, served with the fat of a sucking deer, and a brawn of pickled salmon spawn. I never eat anything else."

"Then I am sorry for that lordly belly of thine. A little gypsy-ragout is at your service, however," replied Peter Bús.

"I beg your pardon," cried the gypsy, "but that is my kinsman, and you are not allowed to roast him."

His lordship fell a-laughing at this insipid jest. Such witticisms formed no small part of his amusement, and because the innkeeper had humored him, his intentions towards him had completely changed.

"Then what *can* you give your guests?" he resumed.

"Everything, my lord. Only, unfortunately, what is mine is all gone, what will be mine is far off, and what should be mine is nowhere."

His lordship was so pleased with this circumlocution of "nothing" that he burst out laughing, and, wishing to immortalize it, exclaimed –

"Where is Gyárfás? Where is that poet fellow skulking now?" And yet the worthy fellow was standing close beside him with his hands folded behind his back, and with his pale, withered, parchmentlike face peevishly regarding the whole entertainment. "Look alive, Gyárfás! Quick! Make a verse upon this inn, where people can get nothing to eat!"

Mr. Gyárfás cast down his eyelashes, drew his mouth up to his nose, and, tapping his brow with the tip of his finger, delivered himself of this extemporized verse –

"If thou bring not to eat with thee hither,
All empty the plates stand before thee.
The fast of this house is eternal;
The Turk will not visit this shanty."

"What's the man talking about! What has the Turk to do with this *csárda?*"

"He has a great deal to do with it," responded Gyárfás, placidly, "inasmuch as the Turk needs to eat, though he does not always get the chance, and therefore would not be likely to come here where he would find nothing, so the verse is perfect."

The Nabob now suddenly turned towards the landlord.

"Have you a mouse on the premises then?"

"They are not mine, my lord. I only rent the house. But as there are plenty of them, I don't suppose the ground landlord will begin an action at law if I take one or two."

"Then roast us a mouse!"

"Only one?"

"Plague on such a question! Dost thou take the belly of a man for the abyss of hell, to think that one such beast is not quite enough for it?"

"At your service, my lord," said the innkeeper; and he immediately called the cats into the room to assist him, though he had only to move a few stones away in order to be able to pick and choose his mouse quite as well as any cat could have done it for him.

And here I may say, by the way, that a mouse is such a nice pretty little animal, that I cannot conceive why folks should hold it in such horror. It is very much the same thing as a squirrel or a guinea-pig, which we keep in our rooms and pet and play with; nay, it is cleverer far than they. What a delicate little snout it has, what sweet little ears, what wee little pets of feet! And then its comically big moustache, and its quick black eyes like sparkling diamonds! And when it plays, when it squeaks, when it stands up to beat the air on its hind legs, it is as clever and as comely as any other animal in the world. Nobody is horrified at a crab being cooked, nobody flies in terror when snails are served up at table, yet they are both far more horrible animals than a mouse. What, then, is there so horrifying in the idea of cooking a mouse? Why, in China, it is the greatest of delicacies, a lordly dish for epicures, and they feed it up in cages with nuts and almonds, and serve it up as the choicest of savories!

Nevertheless, the whole company was persuaded that the very idea of such a thing was the most exquisite of jokes, and everyone laughed aloud in anticipation.

Meanwhile, while Mr. Peter Bús threw open a large barnlike room for his guests, the heydukes had unpacked the wagon, and dragged into the light of day cushions, curtains, camp-stools, and tables; and in a few moments the empty, resonant room was changed as if by magic into a sumptuous apartment. The table was piled high with silver goblets and dishes, and, reposing among the ice in large silver pitchers, flasks of carved Venetian crystal with long necks seemed to promise something seductive.

The Nabob himself lay down on the camp bedstead prepared for him, his heydukes drew the large spurred boots from his feet, one of the peasant girls sat by his head stroking continually his sparse grey hairs, while the other sat at the end of the bed rubbing his feet with bits of flannel. Gyárfás, the poet, and Vidra, the jester, stood before him; a little further off the heydukes; the greyhound was under the bed. And thus, surrounded by gypsy, heydukes, jester, peasant-girls, and greyhound, lay one of the wealthiest magnates of Hungary!

Meanwhile, the mouse was a-roasting. The innkeeper himself brought it lying in the middle of a large silver dish, surrounded by a heap of horseradish shavings, and with a bit of green parsley in its mouth, the usual appurtenances of a very different animal.

Down it was placed in the middle of the table.

First of all, the Nabob offered it to the heydukes one by one. They did not fancy it, and only shook their heads.

Then it came to the poet's turn.

"Pardon, gratia, your Excellency! I am composing verses on him who eats it."

"Well, you then, Vidra! Come, down with it, quick!"

"I, your Excellency?" said Vidra, as if he did not quite catch the words.

"Yes, you. What are you afraid of? While you were living in tents, one of my oxen went mad, and yet you and your people ate him!"

"True; and if one of your lordship's hogsheads of wine went mad I would drink it. That's another thing."

"Come, come, make haste! Do the dish honor!"

"But my grandfather had no quarrel with this animal."

"Then rise superior to your grandpapa!"

"I'll rise superior to him for a hundred florins," said the gypsy, scratching his curly poll.

The Nabob opened the pocket of his dolman, and drew forth a large greasy pocketbook, which he half opened, displaying a number of nice blood-colored banknotes.

The gypsy squinted with half an eye at the well-crammed pocketbook, and repeated once more –

"For a hundred florins I don't mind doing it!"

"Let us see then!"

The gypsy thereupon unbuttoned the frock-coat which it was his master's whim he should wear, contracted his rotund, foolish face into a squarish shape, twitched the mobile skin of his head up and down once or twice, whereby the whole forest of his hair moved backwards and forwards like the top-knot of a peewit, and then, seizing the horrible animal by that part of its body which was furthest from its head, and thereby raising it into the air, pulled an ugly, acidulous face, shook his head, constrained himself to a desperate resolution, opened his mouth, shut his eyes, and in an instant the mouse had disappeared.

The gypsy could not speak, but one of his hands involuntarily clutched his throat, for it is no joke to swallow a four-legged animal at a gulp; but his other hand he extended towards the Nabob, gasping with something like a sob –

"The hundred florins!"

"What hundred florins?" inquired the humorous gentleman. "I said I'd give you a hundred florins? Nonsense, sir. You should thank me for providing you with such a rare dish which your grandfather never ate, I'll be bound to say, and would have paid for the chance of it."

It was a screaming joke, no doubt; yet suddenly the merriment ceased, for the gypsy all at once began to turn blue and green, his eyes threatened to start out of his head, he sank down on his chair unable to speak, but pointed convulsively to his distended mouth.

"Look, look, he's choking!" cried several voices.

The Nabob was terribly alarmed. The joke had taken a decidedly serious turn.

"Pour wine into his throat to wash it down," he exclaimed.

The heydukes speedily caught up the flasks, and began to fill up the gypsy's throat with half a bottle at a time to assist the downward progress of the worthy mouse. After a long time the poor fellow began to breathe hard, and seemed to recover slightly; but his eyes rolled wildly, and he was gabbling something unintelligible.

"Well, take your hundred florins," said the frightened Nabob, who could scarcely contain himself for terror, and wished to comfort and compensate the gypsy on his return from Charon's ferry-boat.

"Thank you," sobbed the latter, "but there's no need of it now. It is all up with Vidra; Vidra is dying. If only it had been a wolf that had killed poor Vidra; but a mouse – oh, oh!"

"Don't be a fool, man! You'll take no harm from it. Look! here's another hundred. Don't take on so; it has quite gone now! Hit him on the back, someone, can't you? Bring the venison on now, and make him swallow some of it!"

The jester thanked them for the thump on the back, and when they set the venison before him, he regarded it with the doubtful, ambiguous expression of a spoiled child, who does not know whether to laugh or to cry. First he laughed, and then he grumbled again, but finally he sat him down before the savory cold meat, which had been basted with the finest lard and flavored with good creamlike wine sauce, and began to cram himself full with morsel after morsel so huge that there was surely never a mouse in the wide world half so big. And thus he not only filled himself, but satisfied the Nabob also.

And now, at a sign from the Nabob, the heydukes carried in all the cold dishes they had brought with them, and shoved the loaded table along till it stood opposite the couch on which he lay. At the lower end of the table three camp-stools were placed, and on them sat the three favorites, the jester, the greyhound, and the poet. The Nabob gradually acquired an appetite by watching these three creatures eat, and by degrees the wine put them all on the most familiar terms with one another, the poet beginning to call the gypsy "my lord," while the gypsy metaphorically buttonholed the Nabob, who scattered petty witticisms on the subject of the mouse, whereat the two others were obliged to laugh with all their might.

At last, when the worthy gentleman really believed that it was quite impossible to play anymore variations on the well-worn topic of the mouse, the gypsy suddenly put his hand to his bosom, and cried with a laugh, "Here's the mouse!" And with that he drew it forth from the inside pocket of his frock-coat, where he had shoved it unobserved, while the terrified company fancied he had swallowed it, and in sheer despair had soothed him by making him eat and drink all manner of good things.

"Look, Mat!" said he to the dog, whereupon the greyhound immediately swallowed the *corpus delicti.*

"You good-for-nothing rascal!" cried the nobleman, "so you'd bandy jests with me, would you! I'll have you hanged for this. Here, you heydukes, fetch a rope! Hoist him upon that beam!"

The heydukes immediately took their master at his word. They seized the gypsy, who never ceased laughing, mounted him on a chair, threw the halter round his neck, drew the extreme end of the rope across the beam, and drew away the chair from beneath him. The gypsy kicked and struggled, but it was of no avail; there they kept him till he really began to choke, when they lowered him to the ground again.

But now he began to be angry. "I am dying," he cried. "I am not a fool that you should hoist me up again, when I can die as I am, like an honest gentleman."

"Die by all means," said the poet. "Don't be afraid. I'll think of an epitaph for you."

And while the gypsy flung himself on the ground and closed his eyes, Gyárfás recited this epitaph over him –

"Here liest thou, gypsy-lad, never to laugh any longer,
Another shall shoulder the fiddle, and death shall himself fiddle o'er thee."

And, in fact, the gypsy never moved a limb. There he lay, prone, stiff, and breathless. In vain they tickled his nose and his heels; he did not stir. Then they placed him on the table with a circle of burning candles round him like one laid out for burial, and the heydukes had to sing dirges over him, as over a corpse, while the poet was obliged to stand upon a chair and pronounce his funeral oration.

And the Nabob laughed till he got blue in the face.

While these things were going on in one of the rooms of the "Break-'em-tear-'em" *csárda*, fresh guests were approaching that inhospitable hostelry. These were the companions of the carriage that had come to grief by sticking fast in the mud of the cross-roads, for, after the men and beasts belonging to it had striven uselessly for three long hours to move it from the reef on which it had foundered, the gentleman sitting alone inside it had hit upon the peculiar idea of being carried to the *csárda* on man-back instead of on horseback. He mounted, therefore, on to the shoulders of his huntsman, a broadly built, sturdy fellow, and leaving his lackey in the carriage to look after whatever might be there, and making the postillion march in front with the carriage lamp, he trotted in this humorous fashion to the *csárda*, where the muscular huntsman safely deposited him in the porch.

It will be worth while to make the acquaintance of the newcomer, as far as we can at least, as soon as possible.

From his outward appearance it was plain that he did not belong to the gentry of the *Alföld*.

As he divested himself of his large mantle with its short Quiroga collar, he revealed a costume so peculiar that if anyone showed himself in it in the streets in our days, not only the street urchins but we ourselves should run after it. In those days this fashion was called the mode *à la calicot*.

On his head was a little short cap, somewhat like a tin saucepan in shape, with such a narrow rim that it would drive a man to despair to imagine how he could ever catch hold of it. From underneath this short cap, on both sides, there bulged forth such a forest of curly fluffy hair that the rim of the cap was quite overwhelmed. The face beneath was clean-shaved, except that a moustache, pointed at each end, branched upwards towards the sky like a pair of threatening horns, and the neck was so compressed within a stiffly starched cravat, with two sharply-pointed linen ends, that one could not so much as move one's chin about in it. The body of this gentleman's dark green frock-coat lay just beneath his armpits, but the tails reached to the ground, and the collar was so large that you could scarce distinguish its wearer inside it. He also had double and triple shirt frills, and while the brass buttons of his coat were no larger than cherry pips, the monstrously puffed sleeves rose as high as his shoulders. The wax-yellow waistcoat was almost half concealed by the huge projecting ruffles. The whole costume was set off by hose *à la cosaque*, which appeared to amplify downwards, bulged over the boots, and were slit up in front so as to allow them to be stuffed therein. Above the waistcoat dangled all sorts of jingling-jangling trinkets, but the boots were provided with spurs of terrible dimensions, so that if a fellow did not look out he might easily have had his eyes poked out. Such was the martial mode of those days, at the very time when no war was going on anywhere. The finishing touch to this get-up was supplied by a thin tortoiseshell cane with a bird's head carved in ivory, which a beau with any pretensions to *bon ton* used regularly to twiddle in his mouth.

"Eh, ventre bleu! eh, sacré bleu!" exclaimed the newcomer (so much, at any rate, he had learnt from Béranger), as he kicked at the kitchen door and shook his saturated mantle. "What sort of a country is this? Hie, there, a light! Is there anyone at home?"

This marvel brought forth Peter Bús with a light, and after gaping sufficiently at the newcomer and his servant who had thus broken into his kitchen, he asked, with an alacrity to oblige by no means corresponding to his amazement, "What are your commands, sir?" His face showed at the same time that he meant to give nothing.

The stranger murdered the Hungarian language terribly, and he had a distinctly foreign accent.

"Milles tonnerres!" he cried, "can't you speak any other language here but Hungarian?"

"No."

"That's bad. Then where's the innkeeper?"

"I am. And may I ask, sir, who you are, whence you came, and where you live?"

"I own property here, but I live at Paris, and what devils brought me hither I don't know. I would have gone on further if the mud of your roads hadn't stopped me. And now give me – comment s'appelle ça?" And here he came to a stop because he could not find the word he wanted.

"Give you what, sir?"

"Comment s'appelle ça? Tell me the name!"

"My name, sir? Peter Bús."

"Diable! not your name, but the name of the thing I want."

"What *do* you want, sir?"

"That thing that draws a coach, a four-legged thing; you strike it with a whip."

"A horse, do you mean?"

"Pas donc! They don't call it that."

"A *forspont?*"*

"That's it, that's it. A forspont! I want a forspont immediately."

"I have none, sir; all my horses are out to grass."

"C'est triste! Then here I'll remain. Tant mieux; it will not bore me. I have traveled in Egypt and Morocco. I have spent the night in as deplorable a hut as this before now; it will amuse me. I will fancy I am in some Bedouin shanty, and this river here is the Nile, that has overflowed, and these beasts that are croaking in the water – comment s'appelle ça? – frogs? oh yes, of course – these frogs are the alligators of the Nile. And this miserable country – what do you call this department?"

"It is not a part of anything, sir; it is a dam, the dam of the cross-roads, we call it."

"Fripon! I am not speaking of the mud in which I stuck fast, but of the district all about here. What do they call it?"

"Oh, I see! They call it the county of Szabolcs."

"Szabolcs, eh? Szabolcs? C'est parceque, no doubt, so many *szabos*† live in it, eh? Ha, ha! That was a good *calembourg* of mine, c'est une plaisanterie. Dost understand?"

"I can't say for certain, but I believe the Hungarians so called it after the name of one of their ancient leaders who led them out of Asia."

"Ah, c'est beau! Very nice, I mean. The worthy magyars name their departments after their ancient patriarchs. Touching, truly!"

"Then, may I ask to what nationality you yourself belong, sir?"

"I don't live here. Bon Dieu! what a terrible fate for anyone to live here, where the puddles are bottomless and a man can see nothing but storks."

Peter Bús turned to leave the room; he was offended at being treated in this manner.

"Come, come, don't run away with the light, signore contadino!" cried the stranger.

"I beg your pardon, but I am of gentle birth myself. My name is Peter Bús,‡ and I am well content with it."

---

* Relay of horses: Ger. *Vorspann.*

† Tailors.

‡ Pronounced *Bush.*

"Ah, ah, ah, Monsignore Bouche, then you are a gentleman and an innkeeper in one, eh? That's nothing. James Stuart was of royal blood, and at last he also became an innkeeper. Well, tell me, if I am to remain here, have you some good wine and pretty girls, eh?"

"My wine is bad – 'tis no drink for a gentleman – and my serving-maid is as ugly as night."

"Ugly! Ah, c'est piquant! There's no need to take offence; so much the better! 'Tis all the same to a gentleman. Tomorrow an elegant lady of fashion, today a Cinderella, one as beautiful as a young goddess, the other as villainous as Macbeth's witches; there perfume, here the smell of onions. C'est le même chose! 'tis all one; such is the streakiness of life."

Mr. Peter Bús did not like this speech at all. "You would do better to ask yourself where you are going to lie tonight, for I am sure I should very much like to know."

"Ah, ça, 'tis interessant. Then is there no guest-chamber here?"

"There is, but it is already occupied."

"C'est rien! We'll go halves. If it is a man, he need not put himself out; if it is a dame, tant pis pour elle, so much the worse for her."

"It is not as you think. Let me tell you that Master Jock is in that room."

"Qu'est-ce-que ça? Who the devil is Master Jock?"

"What! have you never even heard of Master Jock?"

"Ah, c'est fort. This is a little too strong. Folks lead such a patriarchal life in these parts that they are only known by their Christian names! Eh, bien, what do I care for Master Jock! Just you go to him and let him know that I want to sleep in his room. I am a gentleman to whom nothing must be refused."

"A likely tale," observed Peter Bús; and without saying another word, he put out the light and went to lie down, leaving the stranger to seek out for himself the door of the other guest's room if he was so minded.

The darkness was such as a man might feel, but the merry singing and howling served to guide the newcomer to the chamber of the mysterious Nabob, who went by the name of Master Jock; why, we shall find out later on. The fun there had by this time reached its frantic climax. The heydukes had raised into the air by its four legs the table on which the jester lay, and were carrying it round the room, amidst the bellowing of long-drawn-out dirges; behind them marched the poet, with the tablecloth tied round his neck by way of mantle, declaiming d – d bad Alexandrine verses on the spur of the moment; while Master Jock himself had shouldered a fiddle (he always carried one about with him wherever he went), and was dashing off one *friss-magyar* after another with all the grace and dexterity of a professional gypsy fiddler, at the same time making the two little peasant girls dance in front of him with a couple of the heydukes.

At this moment the stranger burst into the room.

"Good evening, ladies and gentlemen," he cried, "I have the honor to salute you!"

The tumult instantly subsided. Everyone gazed open-mouthed at the stranger who had suddenly appeared in their midst, and saluted them with such affability. Master Jock let his fiddle-bow fall from his hand, for though he loved a practical joke to excess, he did not like strangers to see him at it. But the newcomer was not a stranger for long, for the jester, surprised at the sudden silence, looking up, and perceiving a gentleman attired not altogether unlike himself, thought fit to come to life again, and, springing from his bier, rushed towards the stranger, embraced and kissed him, and exclaimed –

"My dear brother, Heaven has surely sent you hither!"

At this mad idea the laughter burst forth anew.

"Ah! ce drôle de gypsy!" said the stranger, trying to free himself from the gypsy's embraces. "That's quite enough; kiss me no more, I say."

Then he bowed all round to the distinguished company, wiped away all traces of the gypsy's kisses with his pocket-handkerchief, and said –

"Do not derange yourselves on my account, ladies and gentlemen; pursue your diversions, I beg! I am not in the habit of spoiling fun. I am a true gentleman, who knows how to prendre son air in whatever company he may find himself. I have the pleasure of introducing myself to your worships as Abellino Kárpáthy, of Kárpát."

And with these words he whistled into the hollow end of his cane, flung himself with a noble nonchalance into one of the camp-chairs, and threw one of his heavily spurred feet over the other.

This speech fairly astonished the company. Even Master Jock now sprang from his seat, and, resting the palms of both hands on his knees, regarded the newcomer with amazement, while the gypsy went down on all fours and began sniffing around him like a dog.

At length Master Jock, in a solemn, drawling voice, exclaimed –

"What! that gentleman a Kárpáthy? Do you know what it means to bear the name Kárpáthy? That name which has a line of thirty ancestors behind it, all of whom were *főispáns* and standard-bearers; that name which is as sonorous as any in the kingdom! Bethink you, therefore, of what you are saying, sir! There is only one Kárpáthy in the world besides myself, and him they call Bélá!"

"Le voilà! That's just myself," said the stranger, protruding one of his legs in front of him, and beating time with the other to an operatic tune, which he whistled through the hole in his stick until he had quite finished it. "I was born in this barbarous land, and the father who bore me – ah, ça! not my father! comment s'appelle ça? – that one of my parents who was not my father, I mean."

"I suppose you mean your mother?"

"Yes, yes, of course! My mother, that's it! Well, my mother was a noble dame, and well-educated, but my father was a bit of an oddity who dearly loved his joke. But the greatest joke he ever perpetrated was when he christened me, his eldest son, Bélá, and made me learn Hungarian. Bélá, forsooth! Now, *is* that a proper name for a gentleman? Luckily for me, my father died betimes, and I went with my mother to Paris. My name displeased me, and as the most fashionable name just then happened to be Abellino, I changed my name Bélá into it. On the other hand, I could not forget the Hungarian language. But it does not matter. I know the nigger lingo just as well. It is no disparagement to a real gentleman."

"Then why, may I ask, are you traveling about here?"

"Ah! venir ici de Paris, c'est tomber du ciel à l'enfer! ('To come hither from Paris is to fall out of heaven into hell!') C'est merveilleux, wonderful, that men can live here at all. Ah, mon cher heyduke, sure I see something cooked. Be so good as to bring it nearer; put it on the table, and fill my glass for me. A votre santé, messieurs et mesdames! And to your health in particular, Monsieur Jock!"

Jock had listened patiently to this harangue. His eyes followed attentively every movement of the stranger, and a sort of resigned melancholy gradually stole over his features.

"Then what brings my lord hither – out of heaven into hell?"

"Hélas!" sighed Abellino, drumming a march on his plate with his knife and fork. "An unavoidable piece of business. A gentleman who lives abroad has many necessities, and my father only left me an income of a moldy four hundred thousand francs. Now, I ask you, how can a man live decently on that? If a man wants to do honor to his nation, he must, before all things, cut a decent figure abroad. I keep going one of the first houses in Paris; I have my own meute and écurie; my mistresses are the most famous dancers and singers. I have traveled in Egypt. In Morocco I abducted the most beautiful damsel of the Bey from his harem. I spend the season in Italy. I have an elegant villa on the shores of the Lake of Como. I have whole folios written of my travels by the best French authors, and I publish them as if I had written them myself. The Académie des Sciences has elected me a member in consequence. At Homburg I have lost half a million francs at a sitting without moving a muscle of my face. And so my moldy four hundred thousand francs have all gone, interest and capital alike – where?"

And here, with hand and mouth, he intimated in pantomime that it had all dissolved itself into thin air.

Master Jock continued to regard the juvenile *roué* with a look that grew stonier and stonier, and involuntarily, unconsciously, a deep sigh escaped from his breast.

"Nevertheless, that was nothing," continued the young dandy, with a self-satisfied voice. "So long as a man has a million he can easily spend two millions; 'tis a science readily learnt. All at once ces fripons de créanciers, those villainous creditors of mine, took it into their heads to ask me for money, and when one began the others were not slow in following. I cursed them; but that did not satisfy them, so they went to the courts about it, and I had to leave Paris. C'est pour brûler la cervelle! It was enough to make me blow my brains out. Mais v'la! Fortune favored me. It chanced that a kinsman of my father's, a certain John Kárpáthy, who was very much richer than my father –"

"Aha!"

"A mad, doating old fellow, of whom I could tell you a thousand follies."

"Really?"

"Oh yes. He never budges from his native village; but he has a theater in his castle, in which they play his own comedies; he sends for the leading prima donnas, simply that they may sing boorish peasant ditties to him; and he keeps a whole palace for his dogs, who eat with him from the same table."

"Anything else?"

"Then he has a whole harem of farmyard wenches, and *betyárs* similar to himself dance with them and him till dawn. Then he sets the whole company by the ears, and they fight till the blood flows in streams."

"Nothing more?"

"And then his conduct is so very eccentric. He can't endure anything that comes from abroad. He does not allow peas to appear on his table, because they don't grow on his estate. They are for the same reason not allowed to bring coffee into the house, and he uses honey instead of sugar. Mad, eh?"

"Certainly. But do you know anything else about him?"

"Oh, I could tell you a thousand things. His whole life is an absurdity. He only did a wise thing once in his life. When I was at the very last gasp, and nothing in the world could save me but a rich uncle, this Hungarian Nabob, this Plutus, one night crammed himself up to the very throat with plover's eggs, and died early in the morning. I was immediately advertised of the fact."

"And so I suppose you have come hither to take over the rich inheritance without delay?"

"Ma foi! nothing else were capable of bringing me back into this detestable country."

"Very well, my pretty gentleman, then you may just clap your horses into your carriage, and drive back to Paris, or Italy, or Morocco if you like, for *I am* that half-crazy uncle of yours, that rich *betyár* of whom you speak, and I am not dead yet, as you can see for yourself."

At these words Abellino collapsed; his arms and legs grew limp and feeble, and he involuntarily stammered in his terror –

"Est-ce possible? Can it be possible?"

"Yes, sir, it can. I am that John Kárpáthy whom the country folks jokingly call Master Jock, and who likes to be so called."

"Ah, if only I had thought a little!" cried the young gentleman, leaping to his feet and hastening to grasp his great-uncle's hand. "But, indeed, evil-minded persons described my only uncle to me so differently that I could not picture him to myself in the shape of such a gallant, noble gentleman. Milles tonnerres! let nobody in future dare to say in my presence that my dear uncle is not the finest cavalier on the continent! I should have been inconsolable if I had not made your acquaintance. Capital! I was looking for a dead uncle, and I have found a living one. C'est bien charmant! The Goddess of Fortune is not a woman for nothing. I protest that she has quite befooled me!"

"Enough of this sort of flummery, my sweet nephew; I don't like it. I am used to rough, plain speaking, even from my heydukes. I prefer to have it so. You, my good nephew, have come hither from a great distance to inherit my estate, and your creditors no doubt will be marching after you in regiments, and now you find me alive. A little aggravating I take it, eh?"

"Au contraire, as I find my dear uncle alive, it will be all the easier for him to show himself amiable towards me."

"How? Explain yourself!"

"Well, I do not ask you for a yearly allowance, ce serait bien fatigant for us both. My proposal is that you pay my debts in a lump sum, and there shall be peace between us."

"Hum! Most magnanimous! And if I do *not* pay them, I suppose war will be declared?"

"Come, come, my dear uncle! You are pleased to be facetious! Not pay, do you say! Why, 'tis only a matter of one or two hundred thousand livres or so, a mere bagatelle to you."

"Well, my dear Mr. Nephew, I much regret that you think so lightly of the estate which was won by the valor of your ancestors, but I am quite unable to help you. I also am in want of cash. I also squander it on follies, but on follies of purely home growth. I have a whole mob of comrades, heydukes and ne'er-do-weels, at my heels, and anything over and above what I spend on them, I scatter among the bumpkins who till my fields, or, if a foolish whim seize me, I build me a bridge from one hill to another. But I certainly do not waste my substance on opera-dancers, nor am I given to abducting Moorish princesses, or clambering up pyramids. If you like eating and drinking, you shall always have as much as you like of both at my house, and you may also choose you there pretty girls to your heart's content, who will look every bit as picturesque as your Morocco princesses, if only you trick them out finely enough. Moreover, if you have a mind to travel, this kingdom is quite big enough. You can ride in your carriage for eight days at a stretch without getting to the end of my property. But send money abroad I will not; we don't carry water to the Danube."

The young gentleman began to lose patience during the course of this lecture, turning incessantly in his chair and wriggling backwards and forwards.

"I don't ask for a gift, you know," he exclaimed at last, "but only for a payment in advance."

"What! a payment in advance! You want me to part with my very skin, I suppose?"

"Eh!" cried Abellino, impatiently, and his face began to wear an impertinent, contemptuous expression. "'Tis mine, you know, practically, or at least will be one day. I suppose you don't want to carry it away with you in your coffin?"

"In my coffin!" shouted the old man, deeply agitated, and his face suddenly turned pale. "What! In my coffin! Do you speak of coffins to me?"

"Of course I do. Why, you've one leg in your coffin already, and banquets, parties, and peasant-girls are dragging the other one in too, and thus all will be mine, and I shan't owe you a thank you, for it."

"Hie! my coachman!" thundered old Kárpáthy, springing from his chair, and at that moment his face wore an almost heroic expression, "get ready my conveyance. We'll depart – depart this instant. Let nobody breathe the air of this room any longer."

Abellino laughed aloud at the old fellow's impotent rage.

"Come, come, don't be so furious," he said. "Why échauffer yourself? You only give the apoplexy a quicker chance. Come, come, my good old boy, don't be waxy. I can wait, you know. I am quite a juvenile." And with that he stretched himself at full length across three chairs, and began to whistle a fragment of some vaudeville ditty that occurred to his mind.

The heydukes, packing up the things, would have pulled the chairs from under him, but the old man cried –

"Leave everything where it is; I'll touch nothing that that fellow has had aught to do with. Landlord! Where is the man? Everything in this room is his!"

The last words were spoken in so hoarse a voice as to be scarcely intelligible. The jester took his master's hand to prevent him from falling, while the poet led the way.

"You see, it is of no use kicking up a row," said Abellino, with ironical sympathy. "Don't go so quickly or you'll fall, and that won't be good for your health. Put on your fur pelisse lest you catch cold. Where are his lordship's leg-warmers? Hie! you fellows! Put a warm brick under my dear uncle's feet! Watch over every hair of his head!"

All this time John Kárpáthy said not a word. It was the first time in his life that anyone had dared to anger him. Ah, if anyone else had dared to do such a thing, what a scene there would have been! The heydukes, the coachmen, stood before him trembling. Even Mr. Peter Bús himself was speechless as he looked upon that dumb listening countenance staring fixedly at him with bloodshot eyes. With great difficulty the heydukes hoisted him into his carriage. The two little girls took their places by him, one on each side. Then he beckoned the innkeeper to approach, and murmured something in his ear in a low hoarse voice, whereupon Bús nodded with an air of approval. Mr. John then handed him his pocketbook, and signified that he was to keep its contents, and after that the carriage rumbled off with its escort of mounted torch-bearers.

The *roué* in a mocking, strident voice, sent an irritating farewell after it with a lavish accompaniment of resounding kisses – "Adieu, cher oncle! adieu, dear Jock *bácsi!* My respects to the little girls at home, and to the little dogs also. Au revoir! To our next merry meeting!" And he kept on sending after him whole handfuls of kisses.

Meanwhile the innkeeper had begun to drag out of the room one by one all the beds and tables which Sir John had left him.

"Ah, cher ami! won't you leave the furniture till morning? I shall want to use it."

"Impossible. The house has to be burned down."

"Que diable! How dare you say such a thing?"

"This house belongs to the gentleman who has just gone out. What is inside it is mine, and has been paid for. He has ordered that this inn shall be burned down, and that no other inn shall ever be built on this spot again. To everyone his fancy, you know."

And thereupon, with the utmost phlegm, he neatly applied his candle to the rush-thatched eaves of the house, and with the utmost coolness watched to see how the flames would spread. By the light of the fire he could the more comfortably calculate how much money he had got for this illumination. He found he could hire three good houses for it in the neighboring town of Szeged, and he was quite satisfied.

As for the young gentleman, if he had no wish to be burned, he had nothing for it but to huddle himself in his mantle, whistle for his long-legged steed, mount on its back, and allow himself to be taken back to his carriage.

"You have driven me out of this inn; I'll drive you out of the world," he murmured between his teeth, as his human steed with squelching boots tramped along with him through the endless mud. By the light of the fire the two men, one on the back of the other, resembled a half-submerged giant.

And thus ended the fateful encounter of the two kinsmen at the "Break-'em-tear-'em" *csárda.*

Chapter II

A BARGAIN FOR THE SKIN OF A LIVING MAN

One of the richest capitalists in Paris at this time was Monsieur Griffard. Not so very long ago, somewhere about 1780, Griffard was nothing more than a pastry-cook in one of the suburbs of the city, and his knowledge of the science of finance was limited to his dealings with the needy students who ate his wares on credit, and paid for them accordingly. The Mississippi mania whirled him along with it also. In those days every man in Paris meant to be a millionaire. In the streets, alleys, and public squares everyone was either buying or selling Mississippi shares. Monsieur Griffard left his pastry-shop in the charge of his eldest assistant while he himself went in search of millions, and, what is more, found them. But one day, like a beautiful soap-bubble, the whole Mississippi joke collapsed, and Monsieur Griffard found himself out in the cold with but nine sous in his pocket.

Now, when a man who has not been a millionaire finds he has only nine sous in his purse, there's no reason why he should be particularly angry. But when a man has stood on an eminence from whence he can survey his own coaches, horses, liveried flunkies, magnificently furnished rooms, sumptuous table, pretty mistresses, and other agreeable things of the same sort, a relapse into insignificance may be very unpleasant indeed. So poor Monsieur Griffard, frantic with rage, hastened off to a cutler's shop, bought a large knife with seven of his sous, and had it well sharpened with the remaining two; but in the meantime up came a mob of ragged citizens with Phrygian caps on, bawling at the top of their voices, "Down with the aristocrats!" and carrying on a pole by way of a banner the last number of Marat's newspaper, whereupon it occurred to Monsieur Griffard that he might make a better use of his well-sharpened knife than applying it to his own throat, so he mingled with the crowd, and cried, "Down with the aristocrats!" as loudly as anybody.

How or where he was pitched and tossed about during the next few years he himself probably could not have told you; but when, a few years later, we come across him again under the Directory, we find him attached as commissary of stores to the army of the Rhine, or the army of Italy, and dodging from one to the other, according as this or that general showed a disposition to shoot him. For army commissaries are of two classes, those whose business makes them beggars and those who become millionaires; the former generally shoot themselves, while the latter are shot by others. But the last case is much the rarer.

Fortunately for himself, Monsieur Griffard belonged to the class who are not shot, but become millionaires. He managed to acquire some of the neat little estates which the *emigré* magnates had left to the care of the State, and when they came home again in the days of the Restoration, Monsieur Griffard was one of the lucky men who watched the gorgeous pageant of the march of the allied armies through Paris from his own balcony. Several of the *emigrés*, who came in batches in the rear of the triumphant hosts, beheld with amazement the splendid five-storeyed palace in the Boulevard des Italiens, which was not there at all when they last saw Paris, and when they inquired after its owner, the name they heard was quite unfamiliar to them.

But it did not remain unfamiliar for long. The owner of millions has very little difficulty in acquiring distinctions which will admit him into the very best society. In a short time Monsieur Griffard's name became one of the most harmonious of passwords. An elegant *soirée*, a genial *matinée*, a horse race, an orgy, an elopement, were not considered complete without him, and Monsieur Griffard never remained away, for all such occasions were so many opportunities to an able business man for learning all about the passions, the follies, the status, the extravagance, or the necessities of other people, and building safe calculations upon what he learnt.

Monsieur Griffard was one of the boldest speculators in the world. He would lend large amounts to ruined spendthrifts whom their own servants summoned for their monthly wages, and yet, somehow or other, he always made his money by it. When I say "his money," I mean that he got back about twice as much as he expended. He did not risk his money for nothing. Amongst all the villas and pavilions on the Île de Jerusalem, Monsieur Griffard's pleasure-house was the most costly and the most magnificent. It was built on a little mound, which human ingenuity had exalted into a hill, and its parade looked into the waters of the Seine. In point of style it owed something to almost every age and nation – a great point with the architects of the day, who, equally rejecting all pedantic classicism, and all rococo prettiness, strove instead to make everything they put their hands to as complicated, bizarre, and incongruous as possible. It was not enough that the garden itself should stand on an island, but it was surrounded by an artificial stream meandering in the most masterly style in every direction, and with all sorts of bridges thrown across it, from an American suspension-bridge to a rustic Breton bridge, composed of wood and bark, and covered with ivy. And each of these bridges had its own warden, with a halberd across his shoulder, and the wardens had little sentry-boxes to correspond with the style of the bridges, some like hermitages, others like lighthouses, and their own peculiar trumpets to proclaim loudly to approaching guests over which of the bridges they ought to go to reach the castle.

Beyond the bridges extended the winding ways of the English garden, which in those days had quite thrown into the background the earlier taste for stony, wall-like, rectilinear alleys. A man might now wander helplessly about for hours among densely foliaged trees without being able to find his destination. He would see the beds beside him everywhere thickly planted with flowers in full bloom, and at every turn he would come upon arcades of jasmine with idyllic benches underneath, or marble statues of ancient divinities overgrown with creeping gobæas, or pyramids of modish flowers piled one on the top of the other. In one place he would behold masterly reproduced ruins, with agaric and cactus monsters planted amongst them. In another place he would observe an Egyptian tomb, with real mummies inside, and outside eternally burning lamps, which were replenished with oil early every morning, or a Roman altar with vessels of carved stone and Corinthian vases. Here and there, in more open places, fountains and waterfalls plashed and gurgled in marble basins, throwing jets of water into the air, and enabling merry little goldfish to disport themselves, whence the stream flowed among Oriental reeds into artfully hidden lakes, where, on the tranquil watery mirror, swam beautiful white swans, which did not sing as sweetly as the poets would have us believe, but made up for it by eating no end of Indian corn, which was then very much dearer than pure wheat.

Supposing a man to have safely run the gauntlet of all these obstructions and admired all these marvels, he would, at last, somehow or other, stumble upon the terrace leading to this Tusculum, every stage of which was planted thickly with orange trees, some in bloom, while others were weighed down by loads of fruit. Among these orange trees today we perceive that young gentleman we have already been fortunate enough to meet. Nevertheless, as a whole twelve months has elapsed since then, and the fashion has changed completely, we must look at him pretty hard before we shall recognize him.

The calicot season is at an end. The young dandy now wears a long overcoat reaching to the knee, buttoned by broad pendant gewgaws, with stiff, inexpressibly high-reaching boots. There is no longer the trace of a moustache; it has been supplanted by whiskers, of a provocative description, extending from the ears to the nose, and quite changing the character of the face. The hair is parted, smoothed in the middle, and pressed down from the top by a frightful sort of thing, which they called *chapeau à la Bolivar,* a hat with so broad a rim that it could serve just as well as an umbrella.

This was Abellino Kárpáthy.

The banker's staircases and antechambers are swarming with hosts of lazy loafers strutting about in the silvered liveries of lackeys, who hand the arriving guests on from one to the other, and deprive them on entering of their overcoats, sticks, hats, and gloves, which they have to redeem on their return in exchange for liberal *pour-boires.* These worthy bread-wasters know Abellino of old, for Hungarian magnates are well aware that it is especially necessary in foreign lands to keep up the national dignity in the eyes of domestics, and here is only one way of doing this, *i.e.* by scattering your money right and left, parting with your guineas, in fact, every time you have a glass of water or drop your pocket-handkerchief. You know, of course, that a really elegant cavalier never carries any sort of money about with him short of guineas, and these, too, must be fresh from the mint, and well sprinkled with eau de Cologne or some other perfume, so as to be free from the soil of vulgar hands.

In an instant Abellino's cloak, cap, and cane were wrested from him, the servants rang to each other, and ran from apartment to apartment, and the cavalier had scarce reached the last door when the first courier came running back with the announcement that Monsieur Griffard was ready to receive him, and with that he threw open the wings of the lofty mahogany folding-door which led into Monsieur Griffard's confidential chamber.

There sat Monsieur Griffard surrounded by a heap of newspapers. In front of the banker, on a little china porcelain table, stood a silver tea-service, and from time to time he sipped from a half-filled saucer some fluid or other, possibly a raw egg beaten up in tea and sweetened by a peculiar sort of crystallized sugar, made from milk which was said to be a very good remedy against chest complaints, but was extraordinarily dear, for which reason many a bigwig thought it *de bon ton* to suffer from chest complaints, so as to have an excuse for using the sugar. The banker himself was a very respectable-looking old gentleman of about seventy, with a face gracious to amiability, and at first sight certainly most taking. Not only the dress, but the whole manner of the man, vividly suggested Talleyrand, one of whose greatest admirers he actually was. His hair was of a marvelously beautiful white, but his face quite red and clean-shaved, and therefore all the fresher and more animated; his teeth were white and even, his hands extraordinarily smooth and delicate, as is generally the case with men who have had much to do with the kneading of dough.

No sooner did the man of money perceive Abellino at the open door than he put down the paper which he was reading without the aid of an eyeglass, and, advancing to meet him to the very threshold, greeted him with the most engaging affability.

"Monseigneur," exclaimed the young Merveilleux (such was the title of the dandies of those days), "I am your servant to the very heel of my shoe."

"Monseigneur," replied Monsieur Griffard, with similar pleasantry, "I am your servant to the very depths of my cellar."

"Ha, ha, ha! Well said, well said! You answered me there," laughed the young dandy. "In an hour's time that *bon-mot* will be repeated in every salon of the town. Well, what's the news in Paris, my dear money monarch? I don't want bad news – tell me only the good!"

"The best news," said the banker, "is that we see you in Paris again. And still better news than that is seeing you here."

"Ah, Monsieur Griffard, you are always so courtly!" cried the young man, flinging himself into an armchair. "Well, Monsieur Griffard," he continued, regarding himself at the same time in a little pocket-mirror to see whether his smooth hair had been rumpled, "if you have only got good news to tell me, I, on the other hand, have brought you nothing but bad."

"Par exemple?"

"Par exemple. You know I went to Hungary to look after a certain inheritance of mine, a certain patrimony which would bring me in a clear million and a half."

"I know," said the banker, with a cold smile, and one of his hands began playing with a pen.

"Then you also know, perhaps, that in the Asiatic kingdom where my inheritance lies, nothing is on such a bad footing as the land, except it be the king's highways. But no, the law is much the worse. The highways, if the weather be dry, are tolerable, but the law is always the same whether there be rain or sunshine."

Here the young Merveilleux stood up as if to allow the banker an opportunity to congratulate him on this *jeu d'ésprit,* but the other only smiled calmly.

"You must know, moreover," continued Abellino, "that there is a vile expression in the Hungarian language, 'Intra dominium et extra dominium,' which may be expressed in French by 'In possession and out of possession.' Now, whatever right anybody may have to any property, if he be out of possession he is in a hobble; while he who happens to be in possession, let him be the biggest usurper in the world, may laugh at the other fellow, and spin the case out indefinitely. Now, here am I, for instance. Just fancy, the inheritance, the rich property, was almost in my hands; I hasten to the spot in order to enter into my rights, and I find that someone has been before me, and sits comfortably in possession."

"I understand," said the banker, with a cunning smile, "some evil-disposed usurper is in actual possession, Monseigneur Kárpáthy, of the property that was so nearly yours, and will not recognize your rights, but stupidly appeals to that big book, among whose many paragraphs you will also find these words written, 'There is no inheriting the living.'"

The young dandy stared at the banker with all his eyes.

"How much do you know?" he cried.

"I know this much – the evil usurper who makes so free with your inheritance is none other than your uncle himself, who is so lacking in discretion as to sufficiently come to himself again after a stroke of apoplexy, with the aid of a hastily applied lancet, to do you out of your property, and place you in such an awkward position that you cannot find a single article in that thick code of laws of yours which will enable you to bring an action against your uncle, because he had the indecency not to die."

"Then it is a scandal," cried Kárpáthy, leaping from his seat. "I have everywhere been proclaiming that I intend to bring an action."

"Pray keep quiet," remarked the banker, blandly. "Everyone believes what you say, but I must know the truth, because I am a banker. But I am accustomed to keep silence. The family relations of the Rajah of Nepaul in the East Indies are as well-known to me as is the mode of life of the greatest Spanish grandee, and it is as useful to me to know of the *embarras de richesses* of the one as of the splendor-environed poverty of the other. I know the position of every stranger who comes to Paris, wherever he may come from, or whatever racket he may make. During the last few days, two Hungarian counts have arrived here, who are on a walking tour through Europe; another is returning from America, and he traveled third class the whole way; but I know very well that the properties of these three gentlemen at home are in such excellent condition that they could lend me money if I wanted it. On the other hand, there rode through the Porte St. Denis quite recently, in a gilded carriage, drawn by white horses, and escorted by plumed outriders, a northern prince, whose name is on everyone's lips; but I know very well that the poor devil carries about with him all the money he has, for his property has been sequestered on account of some political scandal."

Kárpáthy impatiently interrupted the banker's speech.

"Well, well! – but why should I be forced to listen to all this?"

"It may serve to show you that there are and will be secrets at the bottom of the heart and the pocket, that the men who control the money market know things that they keep to themselves, and that although I am well aware of your delicate circumstances, you may tell the world quite another tale, and you'll find it will not doubt your word."

"Enfin, of what use is that to me?"

"Well," replied the banker, with a shrug, "I know very well that it would not trouble you much if the whole world knew of you what I know, if only I did not know it. You naturally come to me, intending to describe to me the symptoms of a disease entirely different to that from which you are actually suffering; but I am a practical doctor, who can read the symptoms of my patients from their faces. Suppose, now, I were able to cure you?"

The bitter jest pleased Abellino. "Hum! feel my pulse then," he said jestingly, "but put your hand, not on my pulse, but in my pocket."

"There is no necessity for that. Let us consider the symptoms. Are you not suffering a slight indigestion in consequence of an undigested debt of some three hundred thousand francs or so?"

"You know I do. Give my creditors something to go away with."

"But that would be hard on the poor fellows. You would not choke off your upholsterers, your coach-makers, and your horse-dealers because you can't pay them, I suppose? Would it not be juster to pay them up in full?"

"How can I?" cried Abellino, furiously. "If only, like Don Juan de Castro, I could raise money on half of my moustache by sending it to Toledo! But I can't even do that, for I have cut it off."

"And what will you do if they keep on dunning you?"

"Blow my brains out; that's soon done."

"Ah! don't do that. What would the world say if an eminent Hungarian nobleman were to blow his brains out for a matter of a paltry hundred thousand francs or two?"

"And what would it say if they clapped him in jail for these same paltry francs?"

The banker smiled, and laid his hand on the young dandy's shoulder; then, in a confidential tone, he added –

"Now we will try what we can do to save you."

This smile, this condescending tap on the shoulder, revealed the *parvenu* most completely.

The banker now took a seat beside him on the ample sofa, and thus obliged him to sit straight.

"You require three hundred thousand francs," continued Monsieur Griffard, in a gentle, soothing voice, "and I suppose you will not be alarmed at the idea of paying me back six hundred thousand instead of that amount when you come into your property?"

"Fi donc!" said Kárpáthy, contemptuously. A feeling of noble pride awoke within him for an instant, and he coldly withdrew his arm from the banker's hand. "You are only a usurer, after all," he added.

The banker pocketed the affront with a smile, and tried to smooth the matter over with a jest.

"The Latin proverb says, *'Bis dat qui cito dat'* – 'He gives twice who gives quickly.' Why should I not wish to double my money? Besides, money is a sort of ware, and if you are at liberty to expect a tenfold return from grain that you have cast forth, why may you not expect as much from money that you have cast forth likewise? Take into consideration, moreover, that this is one of the hardiest speculations in the world. You may die before the kinsman you hope to inherit. You may be thrown from your horse at a fox-hunt or a steeplechase and break your neck; you may be shot through the head in a duel; or a fever or a cold may seize you, and I shall be obliged to go into mourning for my dear departed three hundred thousand francs. But let us go further. So far as you are concerned it is not enough that I pay your debts. You will want at least twice that amount to live upon every year. Good! I am ready to advance you that also."

At these words Kárpáthy eagerly turned towards the banker again.

"You are joking?"

"Not in the least. I risk a million to gain two. I risk two millions to gain four, and so on. I speak frankly. I give much and I lose much. At the present moment you are in no better a position than Juan de Castro, who raised a loan on half his moustache from the Saracens of Toledo. Come now! an Hungarian gentleman's moustache is no worse than a Spaniard's. I will advance you on it as much as you command, and I'll boldly venture to doubt whether there is anyone except myself and the Moors of Toledo who would do such a thing? I can answer for nobody imitating me."

"Good! Let us come to terms," said Abellino taking the matter seriously. "You give me a million, and I'll give you a bond for two millions, payable when my uncle expires."

"And if your uncle's vital thread in the hands of the Parcæ prove longer than the million in your hands?"

"Then you shall give me another million, and so on. You will be investing your money well, for the Hungarian gentleman is the slave of his property, and can leave it to nobody but his lawful heir."

"And are you quite certain that you will be the one lawful heir?"

"None but me will bear the name of Kárpáthy after John Kárpáthy's death."

"I know that; but John Kárpáthy may marry."

Abellino burst out laughing. "You imagine my uncle to be a very amiable sort of cavalier."

"Not at all. I know very well that he stands at the very brink of death, and that his vital machinery is so completely out of order that if he does not change his diet immediately, and give up his gluttonous habits, of which there is but little hope, I regret to say, he will scarcely live another year. Pardon me for anticipating so bluntly the decease of a dear relative!"

"Go on, by all means."

"We who have to do with life assurance transactions are in the habit of appraising the lives of people, and I am regarding your uncle's life just as if it had been insured in one of these institutions."

"Your scruples are superfluous. I have no tender concern whatever for my uncle."

The banker smiled. He knew that even better than Abellino.

"I said just now that your uncle might marry. It would not be a very rare occurrence. It often happens that elderly gentlemen, who for eighty years have regarded matrimony with horror, suddenly, in a tender moment, offer their hands to the very first young woman they may chance to cast their eyes upon, even if she be only a kitchen wench. Or it may be some old inclination which, after years and years, suddenly springs into life again, like some tenacious animal that has lain imprisoned for centuries in a coal-seam, and the ideals which at sixteen he was unable to make his own, possibly because he had other ties, he turns to again at seventy when he finds himself free again."

"My uncle has no ideals. He does not know such a word. Besides, I can assure you that such a marriage could not possibly have the usual results."

"I have no uneasiness on that score, otherwise I should scarcely venture to make you an offer. But there is another point on which I shall require a satisfactory assurance from you."

"A satisfactory assurance from me? Now it is the turn of my beard, I suppose," murmured Abellino, smoothing down his black whiskers.

"The assurance I want from you," said the banker, cheerfully, "is that you will live long enough."

"Naturally, lest I die before my uncle."

"It might so happen. I will, therefore, not only give you money, but will take care that no harm happens to your life."

"How?"

"I mean to say, so long as old John Kárpáthy is alive, you must fight no duels, go to no stag or boar hunts, undertake no long sea voyage, enter into no liaison with any ballet-dancer; in a word, you must engage to avoid everything which might endanger your life."

"And I suppose I must also drink no wine and ascend no staircase, as the drink might fly to my head, and I might fall down and break my neck?"

"I won't bind you too strictly. I admit that you may find the enumerated prohibitions somewhat grievous, but I know of a case which would free you from them all."

"And that is – ?"

"If you were to marry."

"Parbleu! Rather than do that I would engage never to mount a horse or handle a weapon."

"Look at it in this way. Suppose you were to honor an elegant young gentlewoman with your hand. The first year you would be able to pass happily enough; for surely in all Paris you would be able to find a lady capable of making a man happy for at least a whole year! At the end of that year the Kárpáthy family would be enriched by a vigorous young scion the more, and you would be absolved from your onerous engagement, and be quite free to blow your brains out or break your neck, according as the fancy took you. But if, on the other hand, you preferred to enjoy life, why, then, Paris is large enough; and there's the whole world beyond. That's not such a very terrible affair, I'm sure."

"We'll see," said Abellino, rising from his seat and smoothing his ruffled shirt-front with the tips of his nails.

"How?" inquired the banker, attentively. He had foreseen that if he showed himself ready to help Kárpáthy out of his financial difficulties, the latter would at once grow coy.

"I say we will see which of the paths before me is the most practicable. The money you offer I will accept in any case."

"Ah! I hoped as much."

"Only the assurances you require somewhat complicate the matter. I will try, first of all, if I can put up with the restrictions you have laid upon me. Oh! don't be afraid. I am accustomed to ascetic deprivations. Once I cured myself homœopathically, and for five weeks I was unable to drink coffee or perfume my hair. I have a great deal of strength of mind. If, however, I can't stand the test, I'll try matrimony. But it would be best of all if someone would neatly rid me of my uncle."

"Sir, sir!" cried the banker, leaping to his feet, "I hope this is only a jest on your part!"

"Ha, ha, ha!" laughed the young dandy. "I am not thinking of murder or poison. I am only thinking that the poor old fellow's health may be shattered by peasant-girls and fat pasties. There are, I must tell you, pasties so jolly heavy that they call them 'inheritance pasties.' There's no poison in them, but lots of goose-livers and other delicacies. Eat your fill of 'em, and throw in some good red wine, and apoplexy will be waiting for you round the corner."

"I can't say: I never made such things," said the ex-pastry-cook, gravely.

"Nor did I mean to say that I would have them made for my uncle. I am capable of killing, I am capable of shooting or cutting down the man I hate; but it is not in me to kill a man in order to inherit his property. But so much I may say, that if only I chose to take the trouble, I could accelerate his departure from the world a little."

"That would be a shame. Wait till he departs of his own accord."

"There's nothing else to do. Meanwhile you must make up your mind to be my banker. The more money I borrow, the better it will be for you; for you will get back as much again. What do I care? Whoever comes after me will have to shut the door."

"Then we are agreed?"

"Tomorrow morning, after twelve, you can send your notary to me with all the documents ready, so that no time may be lost."

"I will not keep you waiting."

Abellino took his leave, and the banker, rubbing his hands, escorted him out to the very door of the saloon.

And thus there was a very good prospect of one of the largest landed estates of Hungary falling in a few years into the hands of a foreign banker.

Chapter III

THE WHITSUN KING

And now we are home again in poor dear Hungary.

It is the red dawn of a Whitsun Day, and a real dawn it is. Very early, soon after the first cock-crow, a band of brown musicians began marching along the roads of Nagy-Kun-Madaras, and in front of them, with a long hazel-wood wand in his hand, strutted a sworn burgher of the town, whose face seemed full of angry dignity because he was engaged on an important official function before ever a drop of *pálinka* had crossed his lips.

The worthy sworn burgher was honorably clad in blue, which well becomes a man in his official capacity; his spiral hat was adorned by a couple of large peonies in full bloom; in his buttonhole was a posy of pinks and vine leaves; his silk vest had silver buttons; his face was red, his moustache pointed, his boots shaggy and spurred. He kept raising his feet as gingerly as if he were walking on eggs, and not for all the world would he have looked on either side of him, still less upon the gypsy minstrels behind his back; only when he came in front of the door of any burgher or town councilor he would signify, by raising his stick, that they were to walk more slowly, while the trumpets blared all the louder.

Everywhere the loud music aroused the inhabitants of the streets. Windows and blinds were thrown open and drawn up, and the young women, covering their bosoms with aprons, popped their heads out and wished Mr. Andrew Varju a very good morning. But Mr. Andrew Varju recognized nobody, for he was now the holder of a high office which did not permit of condescension.

But now he reached the houses of the civic notabilities, and here he had to go indoors, for he had particular business with them. This particular business consisted of a drink of *pálinka,* which awaited him there, and whose softening effect was visible on his face when he came back again.

This accomplished, the most important invitation of all remained to the last, to wit, that of his honor the most noble Master Jock, which had to be given in due order.

Now, this was no joke, for Master Jock had the amiable habit of keeping tame bears in his courtyard, which devour a man without the slightest regard to his official position; or the poor man might stray among the watchdogs, and be torn to ribbons. Fortunately, however, on this occasion a red-liveried menial was lounging about the gate, from whom it was possible to get a peaceful answer.

"Is the most noble Master Jock up yet?"

"Deuce take it, man! What are you shivering at? Why, he hasn't lain down yet!"

Mr. Varju trotted on further. He had now to report himself to their worships at the community-house, which he accomplished without any beating about the bush by simply saying, "I have done everything."

"It is well, Mr. Varju."

And now let us take a look at these famous men.

In the worshipful community-room, hanging in long rows on the walls, were the painted effigies of the local and civic celebrities, with room enough between for the arms of these defunct patrons, baillies, curators, and charity-founders also. On the table were tomes of tremendous bulk, pressed down by a large lead inkstand. The floor beneath the table was nicely covered with ink-blots – it was there that the pens were usually thrown.

The bell of early dawn was only now beginning to ring, and yet their worships were already assembled in the room, with their elbows planted in a circle all round the long table. The judge presided – a worthy, stout man.

Near the door stood a group of young men in short, strong, baggy knee-breeches and broad-buttoned pelisselike dolmans. Everyone of them had a bright kerchief in his buttonhole, and spurred boots upon his feet.

Prominent amongst all the youths stood the Whitsun King of the year before. He was a tall, lanky stripling, with a large hooked, aquiline nose, and a long moustache triply twisted at the ends and well stiffened with wax. His neck was long and prominent and burned black by the sun where it was not protected by his shirt. Below his shirt it looked as though it had been cut out of another skin. His dress was different to that of the common folks. Instead of linen hose, he wore laced trousers tucked into boots of Kordovan leather from which long tassels dangled down. The sparkling copper clasp of his broad girdle was visible beneath his short silken vest. A bright kerchief peeped out from every pocket of his dolman, and was tied at one corner to his buttons; and his fingers were so swollen with hoop and signet-rings that he could scarce bend them. But what distinguished the youth more than anything else was a large umbrageous wreath on the top of his head. The young girls had twined it out of weeping-willow leaves and flowers in such a way that the pretty chains of pinks and roses flowed a long way down the youth's shoulders like long maidenhair, leaving only his face free, and thus forming a parting on both sides.

Will he win this wreath again? Who can tell?

"Well, Martin," said the judge, "so here we have red Whitsun-Day again, eh?"

"I know it, noble sir. Tomorrow I also shall be in church, and will listen."

"Then you intend to remain Whitsun King this year also?"

"I shall not be wanting to myself, noble sir. This is only the sixth year that I have been Whitsun King."

"And do you know how many buckets of wine you have drunk during that period, and how many guests you have chucked out of feasts, sow-dances,* and banquets?"

* A dance given at sow-slaughtering time.

"I cannot say, noble sir. My one thought was not to miss one of them, and so much I may say, neither man nor wine has ever floored me."

"Mr. Notary, read to him how many pitchers of wine and how many broken heads stand to his account!"

And it appeared from the register that Martin, during the year of his Whitsun Kingship, had cost the community seventy-two firkins of wine, and more than a hundred heads broken for fun. He had also made an innkeeper quite a rich man by smashing all his glasses every week, which the town paid for.

"And now, answer me further, little brother: How many times have your horses come to grief?"

"I have not troubled myself about them. I leave all that to my underlings."

"How many girls have you befooled?"

"Why should they let themselves be befooled?"

"How much of ill-gotten goods has passed through your hands?"

"Nobody has ever caught me."

"But thy Whitsun Kingship has cost the town a pretty penny."

"I know this much, that it does not come out of the coffers of the town, but out of the pockets of our dear father, the noble John Kárpáthy, whose worthy phiz I see hanging up on the wall yonder. He it is who has presented a sum of money to the community to keep up our old customs, and to improve the breed of our horses by gathering together all our young riders, in order that they may run races with one another. I also know that whoever proves to be the victor on that occasion has the privilege of getting drunk gratis at every hostelry in the town, while every landlord is bound to look after his horses, and whatever damage they may do they are not to be impounded, but the sufferer has to make good the damage for not looking after them better. Besides that, he has the free run of all festivities and junketings that may be going on; and if sometimes, in the exuberance of high spirits, he knocks anyone about a bit, he is not to be punished either by corporal chastisement or imprisonment."

"Bravo, little brother! you would make an excellent advocate. Where did you learn to speak so fluently?"

"For the last six years I have remained the Whitsun King," answered the youth, haughtily sticking out his chest, "and so I have had plenty of opportunities of learning my rights."

"Come, come, Martin!" said the judge, reprovingly. "Bragging does not become a young man. You have now got so accustomed to this sort of life that you'll find it a little difficult to fall into the ranks again, drink wine that you've paid for, and be punished for your offences if today or tomorrow you are deposed from your Whitsun Kingship."

"The man is not born who will do that," replied Martin, lifting his eyebrows, twiddling his thumbs, and hitching up his trousers with great dignity.

The councilors also perceived that the Whitsun King had made a mistake in answering so rashly, but as it would have been unseemly to have offended the dignity of so considerable a personage, they devoted themselves exclusively to the preparations for the entertainment.

Four barrels of wine, each of a different sort, were piled upon wagons; another wagon was full of freshly baked white rolls; fastened behind the wagons by their horns were the couple of yoke oxen that were going to be slaughtered.

"That's not the right way of going about it!" cried Martin. It was not his natural voice, but he was so accustomed to a peremptory tone now that he could use no other. "We want more pomp here. Who ever heard of the festal oxen being tied to a cart's tail? Why, the butcher ought to lead the pair of them by the horns, one on each side, and you ought to stick lemons on the tips of their horns, and tie ribbons round them!"

"Bravo, little brother! He knows how it ought to be done."

"And then four girls ought to sit on the top of each barrel, and dole out the wine from where they sit in long-eared rummers."

"Anymore commands, Martin?"

"Yes. Let the gypsy musicians strike up my tune as we march along; and let two heydukes hold my horse when I mount."

These commands were punctually obeyed.

The people, after a short religious service, made their way towards the fields. In front trotted two sworn burghers with ribbon-bedizened copper axes in their hands; after them came a cart with the gypsy musicians, roaring out Martin's song as if they meant to shout the heavens down. Immediately upon their heels followed two gaily tricked-out oxen, led by a couple of bare-armed butcher's lads; and then came the provision-wagons; and last of all the wine-carts, with sturdy young bachelors astride every barrel. Then followed Mr. Varju. Fate had raised him still higher, for he was now sitting on horseback, holding a large red banner, which the wind kept flapping into his eyes every moment. From the satisfied expression of his face he evidently thought to himself that if Martin was the Whitsun King, he himself was at least the Whitsun Palatine.

Last of all came the Whitsun King. His horse was not exactly beautiful, but it was a large, bony beast, sixteen hands high, and what it wanted in figure was made up to it in gay trappings and ribbons woven into its mane; its housings too were of fox-skin. Martin did not ride badly. He rolled about a bit, it is true; but this was due, not so much to anything he had taken at breakfast, as to his usual habit of swaggering; indeed, for the matter of that, he sat as firmly in his saddle as if he had grown to it.

On both sides of him trotted a couple of burghers with drawn swords, who had to look well after themselves all the time, for Martin's horse, whenever he perceived any other horse half a head in front of him, would bite at it till it screamed again.

After him, in a long row, came the competing youths. In every face was to be seen a confident gleam of hope that he, perhaps, would be the winner.

The rear was brought up by a crush of carriages and carts, raising clouds of dust in their efforts to overtake the horses in front, adorned with green branches and crammed with merry holiday-folks with bright, streaming neckerchiefs.

At that moment the report of a mortar announces that the prime patron of the festivities, the rich nabob, Master Jock, has departed from his castle. The crowd takes up its position in the cemetery and the gardens adjoining. The wary horsemen stand out in the open; some of them make their horses prance and curvet to show their mettle, and lay bets with one another. Shortly afterwards a cloud of dust arising from below the gardens declares that Master Jock is approaching. No sooner are the carriages visible than they are welcomed by a thundering huzzah, which presently passes over into peals of merry laughter. For Master Jock had hit upon the joke of dressing the gypsy Vidra in a splendid costume of cloth of gold, and making him sit in the family state-carriage drawn by four horses, while he himself came huddled up in a common peasant-cart immediately afterwards, and the honest country-folks loudly applauded the gold-bedizened costume till they perceived that there was only a gypsy inside it, whereupon the laughter grew louder still, which greatly amused the good gentleman.

With him came, besides his court jesters, those of his boon companions whom he liked the best. Number one was Miska Horhi, the owner of an estate of five thousand acres or so at the other end of the kingdom, who would skip over to his crony in March and stay till August, simply to ask him who he thought would be the next vice-lord-lieutenant of the county, leaving word at home that the crops were to be left untouched, and nothing was to be done till he returned. Number two was the famous Laczi Csenkö, the owner of the finest stud in the *Alföld*, who, rather than tire his own beautiful horses, preferred to go on foot, unless he could drive in somebody else's conveyance. Number three was

Lörincz Berki, the most famous hunter and courser in the county, who told falsehoods as glibly as if he lied from dictation. Number four was Friczi Kalotai, who had the bad habit of instantly purloining whatever came in his way, whether it were a pipe, a silver spoon, or a watch. Nevertheless, this habit of his was not without its advantages, for whenever his acquaintances lost anything, they always knew exactly where to look for it, and would simply seize him by the neck and turn out his pockets, without offending him the least bit in the world. Last of all came Bandi Kutyfalvi, the most magnificent tippler and swash-buckler in the realm, who, in his cups, invariably cudgeled all his boon companions; but he had the liquid capacity of a hippopotamus, and nobody had ever seen him dead-drunk in his life.

On the arrival of these distinguished guests, the brown musicians blew a threefold flourish with their trumpets, and the principal jurors measured the racecourse, at one end of which they stationed Mr. Varju with a red flag: this was the goal. At the other end the horsemen were arranged in a row, having previously drawn their places by lot, and so that the gentry might survey the race from their carriages in the most comfortable manner possible. The course was a thousand paces in length.

Master Jock was just about to signify, by a wave of his gold-headed cane, that the mortars were to be fired – the third report was to be the signal for the race to begin – when far away on the *puszta* a young horseman was seen approaching at full tilt, cracking his whip loudly, and galloping in the direction of the competitors. On reaching the two jurors – and he was not long about that – he reined up, and, whipping off his cap, briefly expressed the wish to compete for the Whitsun Kingship.

"Don't ask me who or what I am. If I am beaten I shall simply go on my way, but if I win I shall remain here," was all that the jurors could get in answer to their questions. Nobody knew the youth. He was a handsome, ruddy young fellow of about six and twenty, with a little spiral moustache twisted upwards in *betyár* fashion, flowing curly locks gathered up into a top-knot, black flashing eyes, and a bold expressive mouth, slight of build, but muscular and supple. His dress was rustic, but simple almost to affectation; you would not have found a seal on his white bulging shirt, search as you might, and he wore his cap, with a tuft of meadow-sweet in it, as gallantly as any cavalier.

Wherever he might have got the steed on which he sat, it was a splendid animal – a restive Transylvanian full-blood, with tail and mane long and strong reaching to the ground; not for an instant could it remain quiet, but danced and pranced continually.

They made him draw lots, and then placed him in a line with the rest.

At last the signal-guns were fired. At the first thundering report the steeds began to rear and plunge; at the second they grew quite still, alertly pricking up their ears; one or two of the old racers slightly pawed the ground. Then the third report sounded, and the same instant the whole row plunged forward into the arena.

Five or six immediately forged ahead of the rest. These were the more impetuous horsemen, who are wont to spur their horses to the front at the outset, only to fall behind afterwards: among them was the last-comer also. The Whitsun King was in the center group; now and then he snapped his fingers, but as yet he had not moved his whip. Only when three hundred paces had been traversed did he suddenly clap his spurs to his horse's flanks, lash out with his whip, utter a loud cry, and in three bounds was ahead of the others.

Then, indeed, began a shouting and yelling and cracking of whips. Every horseman lay forward on the neck of his horse, caps fell, capes flew, and in mid-course everyone fancied he was going to win. One steed stumbled beneath his rider; the rest galloped on.

From the carriages it was easy to see how the Whitsun King was galloping along among the rest, his long chaplet of flowers streaming in the wind behind him. One by one he overtook those who were galloping in front of him, and as often as he left one of them behind he gave him a crack with his whip, crying derisively, "Wire away, little brother!"

By the time three quarters of the course was traversed he had plainly left them all behind, or rather all but one – the stranger-youth.

Martin hastened after him likewise. His horse was longer in the body, but the other's was as swift as the wind. And now only two hundred paces were between them and the goal. The youth looked back upon his competitor with a confident smile, whereupon the gentlemen in the carriages shouted, "Hold fast!" which warning applied equally to both competitors. Master Jock actually stood up to see better, the contest had now become exciting.

"And now he's laying on the whip!" cried he. "Something like, eh! And now he gives his horse the spur! One lash, and it flies like the storm! What a horse! I'd give a million for it; and how the fellow sticks on! Well, Martin, it will be all up with your Whitsun Kingship immediately. Only a hundred paces more. 'Tis all over; he'll never be able to catch him up!"

And so, indeed, it proved. The stranger reached the goal a whole half-minute before Martin, and was already standing there in front of the flag when he came up. Martin, however, as he came galloping in, quickly snatched the flag out of Mr. Varju's hand, and cried triumphantly to the youth –

"Don't suppose, little brother, that you have won; for the rule is that whoever seizes the banner first, he is the Whitsun King, and you see it is in *my* hand."

"Indeed!" said the youth, serenely; "I did not know that. I'll take care to remember that at the second race."

"Really, now," cried Martin. "You appear pretty cock-sure that you'll get in before me again. I tell you, you'll not. You only managed it this time because my horse got frightened and shied. But just you try a second time, and I'll show you who is the best man."

Meanwhile the other competitors had come up, and Martin hastened to explain how it was that the stranger had got in quicker than himself. He had a hundred good reasons for it at the very least.

The stranger allowed him to have his say in peace, and, full of good humor, returned to take his place again in the ranks of the competitors. His modest self-reliance and forbearance quite won for him the sympathy of the crowd, which was disgusted at the arrogance of Martin, and in the carriages of the gentry wagers began to be laid, and the betting was ten to one on the stranger winning all three races.

The mortars were again loaded, the youths were once more placed in a row, and at the third report the competing band again plunged forward. Now also the two rival horses drew away from the other competitors. In the middle of the course they were a length ahead of the foremost racers, and side by side urged their steeds strenuously towards the goal. Almost to the very end of the course neither was able to outstrip the other; but when they were scarce fifty paces from the flag, the stranger suddenly gave a loud smack with his whip, whereupon his steed, responding to the stimulus, took a frantic bound forward, outstripping Martin's steed by a head, and this distance was maintained between them unaltered to the very end of the race, though the Whitsun King savagely laid about his foaming horse with his whip-handle. The stranger was at the banner before him, and so vigorously tore it out of the hand of Mr. Varju, that that gentleman fell prone from his horse.

Martin, beside himself with rage, lashed at the ravished flag with his whip, and made a great rent in its red center. Useless fury! The umpires hastened up, and, removing the floral crown from the head of the Whitsun King, who was quivering with passion, placed it on the head of the victor.

"I don't want that!" cried the vanquished horseman, huskily, when they offered him a cap. "I mean to win back my wreath."

"You had better let it rest where it is," came a voice from the carriages.

"No need of that," replied Martin, defiantly. "Neither I nor my horse is tired. We will run, if we die for it. Eh, Ráró?"

The good steed, as if he understood what was said to him, pawed the ground and arched his head. The sworn umpires placed the youths in line again. Most of them, however, seeing the uselessness of competing with these two horsemen, fell out of the line and mingled among the spectators, so that scarce six others remained on the ground with the two rival heroes. All the more interesting, therefore, the contest; for there will be nothing to distract the attention of the onlookers.

Before engaging in the contest for the third time, the stranger-youth dismounted from his horse, and cutting a supple willow sapling from a tree in the cemetery, stripped it of its leaves, and thrusting it into his whip-handle, mounted his horse again. Hitherto he had not once struck his steed.

But now, when the noble animal heard the sharp hiss of the thin willow wand, it began to rear. Standing on its hind legs, it fell to savagely worrying its bit, and careering round and round. The spectators began to fear for the youth, not that he would fall from his horse – that was out of the question – but that he would be too late for the contest, for the second report had now sounded, and the others were all awaiting the signal with loosely held reins, while his horse was curveting and pawing the ground.

When the third report resounded, the stranger suddenly gave his horse a cut with the willow switch, and let the reins hang loosely.

The smitten steed scudded off like a tempest. Wildly, madly, it skimmed the ground beneath its feet, as only a horse can fly when, panic-stricken, it ravishes its perishing rider along with it. None, no none, could get anywhere near it; even Martin was left many yards behind in mid-course. The crowd gaped in amazement at the fury of the steed and the foolhardiness of the rider, especially when, in the midst of his mad career, the long chaplet of flowers fell from the youth's head, and was trampled to pieces beneath the hoofs of the other horses panting after him. He himself did not notice the loss of his chaplet till he reached the goal, where he had to exert all his strength to rein up his maddened steed. He had reached the goal; but he had lost his crown.

"Look! he has lost his crown: he cannot therefore be the Whitsun King!" cried many voices.

But who was to be the king, then? The crown was irrecoverably trampled to pieces in the dust.

"That is not fair!" exclaimed the majority. Many proposed a fresh race.

"I am ready for anything you like," said the strange youth.

"Stop, little brother!" replied Martin, in a subdued, husky voice, which quivered with rage. "We want to prove which of us two is the better man. I confess that on level ground you go quicker than I. You have the better horse, and a fool may win if his horse be quick enough. But, come now, show us whether you are a man where standing one's ground, not running away, is the great point. There's a nice lot of people here, you see, and for all these folks they have only brought hither two bullocks – and little enough too. If you're a man, come with me and fetch a third. We shall not have to go far. Among the reeds yonder is a stray bull, which has been prowling in these parts for the last fortnight, killing people, scattering flocks and herds, destroying the crops, overturning the carts on the high-road, and chasing the laborers out of the fields into the town. Not one of the drovers, or *gulyás*, in the place can cope with him single-handed. Let us go after him together, and the one that drags him hither shall be the Whitsun King."

"There's my hand upon it," said the strange youth, clapping the palm of his rival without even taking time for reflection.

Those who happened to hear this proposal showed signs of retiring precipitately. "They must be fools to bring a mad bull among the people on a holiday like this," murmured these waverers.

"You need have no fear," said Martin. "By the time we bring him here he will be as gentle as a lamb, or else we shall be lying where he is now."

Quick as wildfire spread the rumor of this mad idea. The more timorous part of the crowd tried to get behind the nearest fenced and ditched places; the bolder spirits took horse and rushed to follow and see the hazardous enterprise. All the gentlemen present began betting on the issue forthwith, and Master Jock himself hastened after the youths in his rustic cart. Possibly he thought that even the wild animal would know how to treat a Kárpáthy with due respect.

Scarce half an hour's journey from the town began the enormous morass which extends as far as Püspök-Ládany and Tisza-Füred, in which not merely a wild bull but a hippopotamus could make his home comfortably. On one side of it extended rich wheat-fields, on the other side the rich, dark green reeds marked the water-line, only a narrow dyke separating the meadow from the swamp.

It was easy to learn at the first of the shepherd huts scattered along the border of the morass where the errant bull happened to be at that moment. Amongst the shrubs of the little reedy island opposite he had made his lair; there you could see him crouching down. All night long he would be roaring and bellowing there, only in the daytime was he silent.

First of all, however, you must know what sort of a character the beast known as an "errant bull" really is.

When there are two bulls in a herd, especially if one of them be only a growing calf, they are quiet enough, and even timid all through the winter. If they meet each other they stand face to face, rubbing foreheads, lowing and walking round and round each other; but if the herdsman flings his cudgel between them they trot off in opposite directions. But when the spring expands, when the spicy flowers put fresh vigor and warmer blood into every grass-eating beast, then the young bulls begin to carry their horned heads higher, roar at each other from afar, and it is the chief business of the *gulyás* to prevent them from coming together. If, however, on a warm spring day, when the herdsmen are sleeping beneath their *gubas*, the two hostile chiefs should encounter each other, a terrible fight ensues between them, which regularly ends with the fall or the flight of one of them. At such a time it is vain for the herdsman to attempt to separate them. The infuriated animals neither see nor hear him; all their faculties are devoted to the destruction of each other. Sometimes the struggle lasts for hours on a plot of meadow, which they denude of its grass as cleanly as if it had been plowed. Finally, the beast who is getting the worst of it, feeling that his rival is the stronger, begins with a terrific roar to fly away through the herd, and runs wild on the *puszta*; with blood-red eyes, with blood-red lolling tongue, he wanders up and down the fields and meadows, frequently returning to the scene of his humiliation; but he mingles no longer with the herd, and woe betide every living animal he encounters! He begins to pursue whatever meets his eye in the distance, and he has been known to watch for days the tree in which a wayfarer has taken refuge, until casually passing *csikóses* have come up and driven the beast away.

From the information given by the *gulyáses,* it was easy to trace the lair of the bull. Two distinct paths led to it among the tall reeds, and the two youths, separating, chose each of them his path, and waded into the thicket in search of the furious beast. Meanwhile, the horsemen, who had come to see the sport, scrambled on to the high dyke, from whence they could survey the whole willow wood.

Martin had scarce advanced a hundred paces among the reeds when he heard the snorting of the bull. For a moment he thought of calling to the stranger youth, who had taken the other path, but pride restrained him. Alone he would subdue the beast, and he boldly sought the spot from whence the snorting proceeded.

There lay the huge beast in the midst of the reeds. He had buried himself up to the knees in the swamp, and, whether from rage or for amusement, had trampled down a large area of rushes all round about him.

When he heard the clatter of the approaching hoofs, he raised his head. One horn, prematurely developed, bent forwards, the other stood up straight and pointed. His sooty black forehead was covered with prickly water-burrs, across his snout was the scar of a large and badly healed wound.

On perceiving the approaching horseman, he immediately raised himself on his fore feet and uttered a wild prolonged roar. Martin, who wished to entice the beast on to solid ground, where he could grapple with him better than in the midst of this unknown morass, and also, by way of provocation, cracked his long whip loudly. Maddened still more by this exasperating sound, the wild beast arose from his resting-place and rushed upon the horseman, who immediately turned his horse and fled out of the swamp, enticing after him the infuriated bull.

When the wild beast came out into the plain, looked about him, and saw all the people standing on the dyke, as if guessing what they wanted to do with him, he suddenly turned tail again, and snorting as he went, angrily lay down again on the border of the swamp. Martin followed after him, and again cracked his whip over the beast's head.

The bull roared at him, but did not budge from the spot. On the contrary, he burrowed with his snout among the reeds, and however much the young man might crack his whip, he only responded by beating the air with his tail.

This supreme indifference irritated Martin, and, creeping closer to the wild bull, he gave it a cut with his whip. The hooked steel wire plaited round the end of the whip cut out a whole patch on the skin of the savage beast, but it did not move. Another cut reached its neck, chipping away the skin with a sharp crackle. The bull only grunted, but did not stand up, and buried its head among the reeds to avoid being lassoed by the halter-line which the horseman held handy.

But now it was the huntsman's turn to grow angry, and he kept on flicking away at the obstinate animal without being able to move it from the spot, and presently a whole mob of horsemen began to assemble around him, profoundly irritated by the cowardice of the bull, and tried to arouse it by making as great a din and racket as possible.

Suddenly a flick from the whip chanced to hit the bull in the eye. Quick as lightning the beast leaped to its feet, shook its head, and frantic with rage, rushed upon the horseman, and before he had had time to escape, struck him sideways, and with frightful force hurled him to the ground, horse and all, and began trampling them both in the dust.

The other horsemen scattered in terror. The overthrown charger made frantic efforts to regain its feet; in vain! The savage beast transfixed its loins with his horn. Never again will the noble animal run races in the fields. Bleeding profusely, it falls back again, crushing its rider, who, with his feet entangled in the stirrups, was unable to liberate himself.

The baited bull stood on the plain roaring terribly, and tearing up the ground with his hoofs, while the blood from his cutout eye trickled down his black breast. He did not pursue the fugitives, but, turning back, and seeing the overthrown horse and rider still wallowing on the ground, he began taking short runs at them, like goats often do, throwing up the earth here and there with his horns. God be merciful to the poor youth beneath him!

At length Martin succeeded in extricating himself from his steed. No sooner did the bull perceive that his enemy was on his feet again, than, in a fresh access of rage, he rushed straight at him. A shriek of horror filled the air; many hid their faces. In another moment all would be over.

At that instant, when the savage beast was not more than a yard's distance from its victim, it stopped suddenly, and threw back its head with a jerk. A skillfully thrown noose had gripped it round the neck, and the end of that noose was in the hands of the stranger youth, who now emerged from among the reeds. Hearing a sound like bull-baiting, he had hastened to the spot, and did not arrive a moment too soon. Another second and his rival would have been trampled to death.

The bewildered beast, feeling the suffocating pressure of the lasso about its neck, turned towards its new opponent, but he also now turned his horse's head, and throwing the lasso-line across his shoulder, set off at the top of his speed across the plain.

That was something like a gallop! The heavy wild beast was constrained to run a race with the swiftest of steeds. The cord was pressing tightly round its neck, and blindly, helter-skelter, it had to go in a perfectly straight direction till it dropped.

The youth galloped with it straight towards the racecourse, and then suddenly sprang to one side. The bull bounded away right on, and now the horse remained behind, while the bull flew on in front. By this time it had lost all count of where it was.

The horseman now drew forth his long whip, and began to cut and lash out from behind at the bull, which rushed on even quicker and quicker. The trampling of the horse's hoofs, the cracking of the whip, the shouting of the people, confused it into utter stupidity. It could only run on and on, the blood trickling from its nose and mouth, its whole front flaked with foam, its tongue lolling forth, till, on reaching the racecourse, which was covered with a roaring mob, its strong legs gave way beneath it, and, unable to hold itself up any longer, it collapsed in a ditch, and, rolling a good distance, rooted up the ground with its snout, then stretched itself out at full length on the sward, and ceased to breathe.

Shouting and huzzahing, the mob escorted the new Whitsun King along all the streets of the town, for he was in duty bound to stop before the houses of the chief magistrate and town councilors, and there drink their healths in a good bumper, which admirable custom goes to prove that the Whitsun King had need to be not merely a good runner, but a good drinker too; and this latter quality was all the more necessary, owing to the circumstance that, when he had done with the rest of them, he had, last of all, to go up to John Kárpáthy's castle in the company of all the sworn jurors, and drink again there.

Now, when the sworn jurors brought in the new Whitsun King to introduce him to Squire John, the great man ordered everyone to leave the room incontinently, so that they two might be quite alone together.

Master Jock was sitting in an armchair, with his feet in a large tub of water, chewing a couple of bitter almonds. All this was by way of preparation for the evening's debauch.

"What is your name, little brother?" he inquired of the Whitsun King.

"Michael Kis, at your service, your honor."

"Well, Mike, you are a fine young fellow. You please me greatly. So now you are going to be Whitsun King for a whole year, eh? What will you do with yourself all that time?"

The youth twisted his blonde moustache upwards, and steadily regarded the ceiling.

"I really don't know. I only know that I shall be a bigger man than ever before."

"And if at the end of the year you are deposed?"

"Then I shall go back to my stable at Nadudvár, from whence I came."

"Have you neither father nor mother?"

"I have no belongings at all. I have never seen either father or mother."

"Then stop where you are, Mike. What if I make a bigger man of you than you yourself have any idea of; make you take your place in genteel society here; give you as much money as you like, to drink and play cards with; and turn you into Michael Kis, Esq., lord of the manor of Nadudvár?"

"I shouldn't mind, but how to conduct myself so that they may take me for a gentleman, I don't know."

"The bigger blackguard you are, the greater gentleman they'll take you to be. It is only our rustics who are modest and respectful nowadays."

"If that be all, I am ready."

"I'll take you with me everywhere. You shall drink, dice, bully, brawl, cudgel the men, and befool the women to the top of your bent. At the end of twelve months your Whitsun Kingship will be over, you will doff your genteel mummery, and become the leader of my heydukes. You shall then don the red *mente*, and wait upon those very gentlemen with whom you have been drinking and dicing for a whole year; you shall help into their carriages the same little wenches with whom you used to make merry. I consider that a very good joke. I don't know whether you think so, too? How the gentlemen will curse and the ladies blush when they find out who you were!"

The youth reflected for a moment; but then he threw back his head, and cried –

"All right! I don't care."

Master Jock looked at his watch. "It is now a quarter to four. Remember that. At a quarter to four twelve months hence your gentility, your nobility, will cease. *Till* then you are just as much a gentleman as the rest of us. Every month you will receive from me a thousand florins plunder money. The first thousand is in this reticule. Now be off! My heydukes will dress you. When you are ready, come down to my drinking-room. Be rude to the servants, especially as they know you to be but a boor, and call the gentry by their nicknames only – Mike, Andy, Larry, Fred, Ned, for instance. Me they call Jock, remember."

Half an hour later Mike was back again, dressed as a gentleman.

In the drinking-room there was fun enough going on already even without him; for there the rule was, Welcome everybody, and wait for nobody. The master of the house introduced the newly arrived guest as Michael Kis, Esq., lord of the manor of Nadudvár, who, "like a jolly good fellow," had come disguised as an ostler to the Whitsun Kingship competition, and there acquitted himself like a man.

Everyone thought this a most original joke. It was plain to every eye, moreover, that he was a gentleman and no boor. All his movements, whether he lolled back on a chair, or leaned his elbows on the table, or chucked his cap in a corner – *betyár* tricks everyone of them – was proof positive that he must have been brought up in good circles. A real *betyár* would never have dared to lift up his head here; but this fellow, metaphorically speaking, buttonholed everybody. In a few moments, in fact, Mike had drunk good-fellowship with the whole company, and become as familiar as if he had lived among them all his life.

Meanwhile the eternal bumper began to circulate, and Mike fell to singing a new drinking-song which none of them knew, and the company took it up with spirit; and, more than that, it was better than any they had ever sung before.

Within an hour Mike had become a perfect hero in that genteel circle. In his cups he far outstripped them all; and when it came to card-playing, he won whole heaps of money from all and sundry without moving a muscle of his face, raking the dollars in with as much *sangfroid* as if he had sacks of them at home. Nay, he even lent a lot to Franky Kalotai, thereby obviously displaying an utter contempt for money, for it was notorious that Franky never paid anything back.

And now the heads of most of the gentlemen engaged in this drinking-bout began to loll about unsteadily. Everybody had got beyond the limit where the good humor begotten of good wine ends and drunkenness begins; when a man no longer tastes his wine, and is only sensible of a giddy hankering for more. At such times Bandi Kutyfalvi was wont to exhibit his ancient *tour-de-force,* which consisted in swallowing with outstretched neck a whole bumper of wine at one gulp or, to use his own technical expression, without a single hiccough. Now, such a feat naturally requires for its performance an extraordinarily concave and well-practiced throat, and, with the exception of Bandi, there were not above one or two others who could successfully accomplish it.

"Why, that's nothing at all!" cried Mike Kis, accomplishing the feat without the slightest exertion. "But now, let anyone try and do what I can do – sing a song and at the same time drain a bumper without leaving off singing."

Now, this was an entirely new trick, and an extremely difficult one to boot; for, to be properly performed, it required not only that the glottis should remain immovable during the passage of the vinous torrent down the throat, but also that the throat should give forth at the same time a clear, uninterrupted voice. Yet Michael Kis performed this feat with masterly dexterity, to the general astonishment, and gave back the bowl for the next man to imitate him.

Naturally they all came to grief. Every bumper of wine was a fresh occasion of shame, and the drinkers laughed heartily at one another, for everyone of them was obliged to interrupt his song while he drank.

Michael Kis had to show them once more how it was done.

"A bumper here!" cried Bandi at last, and gallantly buckled to the attempt; but the song only proceeded a little way, and then a drop of wine managed to get into his windpipe, and immediately, like a whale rising to the surface of the sea to blow, or like a stone triton spouting forth the water of a fountain, a violent upward rush of imprisoned breath discharged through every aperture of the suffocating wretch the wine that filled his throat.

The whole table arose, the company bursting with laughter, while Bandi, gasping and coughing, shook his fists at Mike during every brief respite his lungs allowed him, and cried, "I'll kill you I'll kill you!" And at last, when he began to feel better, he rolled the sleeves of his shirt up his big bony arms, and yelled hoarsely, "I'll kill you! I'll kill you! Look out, I say, for I'm going to kill the whole company."

At these words there was a general rush for the door. Everyone knew Kutyfalvi's way of going to work, and it was just as well, at such times, either to fly before him or to lie down, for he had this in common with the bear race, that he never hurt anyone whom he found lying on the ground. The heydukes hastily removed Master Jock outside also. All the rest who had still the slightest command over their legs crept under the table.

Kutyfalvi was a big, strong brute of a man. He could take up three bushel sacks of wheat with his teeth and fling them over his head; he could bite a thaler piece in two; he could pull a wild horse to the ground single-handed – all of which feats inspired his comrades with such a respect for him that a very advanced stage of drunkenness was necessary before even the strongest of them would venture a bout with him, especially as all such foolhardiness generally resulted in the monstrous Cyclops mangling his weaker antagonist out of all recognition.

No wonder, then, if every living soul in the room sighed, "Woe to thee, Mike Kis!" when they beheld him draw down upon his devoted head the wrath of this giant, who, infuriated at the failure of the wine-swallowing experiment, now rushed upon him with open arms, in order to pound him to pieces, pitching all the chairs out of his way as he rushed along.

But the ennobled ostler was used to such encounters, and when his antagonist had come quite close to him, he deftly ducked beneath his arms, and then gave him a lesson in the stable dodge. With one hand he caught hold of his opponent's collar, twisting it so tightly that he gasped for breath, at the same time tripping up his legs, and then, with the other hand, he threw him over his knee. That is the stable dodge, which can be safely employed against even the strongest rowdies.

Meanwhile those of his cronies who ventured to peep back through the doorway, heard a great bang as Bandi Kutyfalvi's huge carcass smote the floor, and saw the big, powerful man lying motionless beneath his opponent, who kept him down with his knee, and pummeled him from head to foot, as he had been wont to pummel others when they quarreled with him in their cups. Everyone was delighted that his turn had now come, and when at last Mike Kis let go his collar and left him lying at full length on the floor, they carried the avenger of their long years of contumely round the room, and drank his health in bumpers till break of day.

Kutyfalvi, however, whom, after this little joke was over, the servants removed from the room and tucked up nicely in bed, dreamt that he fell down from the top of a high mountain into a quarry, the jagged stones of which smashed all his limbs into little bits, and, on waking, was greatly astonished that he should still feel the effects of his dream.

From that day forth Mike Kis became Master Jock's prime favorite, and the sworn comrade of every gentleman who lived in the neighborhood. Nay, even when the Hungarian Diet assembled at Pressburg in 1823, and Master Jock, with great reluctance, forsook his dogs, his cronies, his zanies, his heydukes, and peasant-wenches, in order to attend to his legislative duties, he could not find it in his heart to part with Mike, so he took the lad along with him to Pressburg. This, however, may only have been part of the joke. How comical it would be, for instance, to introduce the pseudonymous young gentleman to the various noblemen and gentlemen assembled there! Nay, better still, some young countess or other might fall over head and ears in love with the handsome youth, and what a capital jest it would then be to exhibit the fellow in the scarlet livery of a heyduke, whose duty it is to climb up behind the carriage when his master goes out for a drive!

So Michael Kis made his appearance in the midst of the elegant society of Pressburg, and his merry humor and handsome, manly figure, backed up by the best letters of introduction, made him a general favorite. Polite society had a peculiar phraseology in those days. Rudeness used to be called frankness; bad language, originality; violence, manliness; and frivolity, nonchalance. To Mike, therefore, was attributed a whole host of good qualities, and the only alteration required of him was that he should wear an *attila* instead of a *mente.* He was a gentleman by birth, and that was enough. Everyone admired, not his mind, indeed – they troubled themselves very little about that in those days – but his manly bearing, his rosy cheeks, his muscular figure, his sparkling eyes, his black moustache, which are of far more account than any amount of learning. And all the while Master Jock was laughing in his sleeve, for the red Whitsun Day was drawing near, and most of the young noblemen were hail-fellow-well-met with Mike Kis; and here and there you might even hear dear, thoughtful mammas making inquiries about the circumstances of the fine young fellow whom they were by no means indisposed to see hovering around their darling daughters; nay, more than one of them confided in a whisper to her bosom friends that she had good cause to suspect that the fine young fellow in question had serious intentions.

Such secrets have a way of spreading like wildfire, and old Kárpáthy began to suffer from the drollest paroxysms. Sometimes, in the gravest society, he would commence ha-ha-ha-ing at the top of his voice. At such moments he was reflecting that in a very few days the much-befêted cavalier would turn out to be nothing but his heyduke! Many a time he would sit up in bed to laugh; nay, once, in the House itself, in full session, when the galleries were filled with the *élite* of society, and the protocols were being read, the old gentleman, observing how the ladies were regarding the handsome figure of Mike, as he stood amongst a group of young nobles, with all their eyes – the old gentleman, I say, was so overcome thereby that he burst into an irrestrainable fit of laughter on the spot, for which he was called to order and fined. He paid the fine immediately, but he had to pay it over double before the day was over, for he could not restrain his laughter when he bethought him of the near-approaching *dénoûment* of this humorous masquerade.

And at last rosy Whitsun Day, most comical of days, arrived. Kárpáthy had ordered a great and costly supper to be laid in the park beyond the Danube, to which he invited everyone who was at all intimate with Mike. What a splendid joke it will be to present the hero of so many a triumph to the company as – a lackey! Master Jock would not have parted with his joke for an empire.

The clock had just struck a quarter to four. According to the compact, the Whitsun King ought now to be waiting there in the antechamber, and Master Jock ordered him to be shown in.

"What new sort of manners do you call this?" cried Mike as he entered the room, flinging himself into an armchair; "why do you keep an honorable man waiting ten minutes in your antechamber?"

There was a pipe in Master Jock's mouth, and he was engaged at that moment in filling it with tobacco.

"Halloa! Mike my son!" said he with infinite slyness, "just you get out of that chair and light my pipe for me – d'ye hear?"

"Light it yourself!" replied Mike; "the flint and steel is close beside you."

Master Jock stared at him with all his eyes. The lad himself had clearly forgotten what day it was. All the more piquant then to startle him out of his insolent security.

"Then, my beloved little brother, are you not aware that today is red Whitsun Day?"

"What's that got to do with me? I am neither a parson nor an almanac-maker."

"Eh, eh! Recollect that at a quarter to four your Whitsun Kingship ceases!"

"And what then?" inquired Mike, without the slightest perturbation, polishing the antique opal buttons of his *attila* with his silken handkerchief.

"What then?" cried Jock, who was beginning to get warm; "why, from this instant you cease to be a gentleman."

"What am I then?"

"What are you, sirrah? I'll tell ye. You're a boor, a *betyár*, a good-for-nothing rascal, a runaway ragamuffin, that's what you are! And you'll be glad enough to kiss my hand, and beg me to make you one of my lackeys, to save you from starvation or the gallows."

"Excuse me," replied Mike Kis, deftly twisting his moustache, "but I am Michael Kis, Esq., proprietor of Almasfalva, which I purchased the day before yesterday from the trustees of the estate of Kázmér Almásfalvi, for 120,000 florins, with the full sanction of the Court, wherefore my title thereto is unexceptionable."

Master Jock fell back in astonishment. "One hundred and twenty thousand florins! When and where did you pick up all that money?"

"I got it honorably," said Michael Kis, smiling. "I won it at cards one evening, when I and a few of my gentlemen friends sat down to play together. To tell you the truth, I won a good deal more than that, but the balance will do to build up a splendid castle on my estate, where I can reside during the summer."

To Master Jock this part of the matter was quite intelligible; much larger sums than this used to be lost and won during the sessions of the Diet at Pressburg. But one thing he could not understand at all.

"Pray how did you get your diploma of gentility?" he asked; "you are not a gentleman by birth."

"That was a very simple matter. When Whitsun Day was only a week off, I strolled into one of the trans-Danubian counties, and there advertised that a prodigal member of the Szabolcs branch of the noble Kis family was in search of his relations, and if there were any noble Kises who remembered that branch of the family, and had certificates of nobility in their possession, which they were willing to transfer to the undersigned in exchange for one thousand florins, would they be kind enough to communicate with him. In a week's time fifteen members of the Kis family remembered their Szabolcs kinsmen, and brought me all kinds of certificates of nobility. All I then had to do was to select the one which had the prettiest coat of arms; whereupon we kissed each other all round, and traced out the genealogy. I paid down the thousand florins; they recognized me as their kinsman, and advertised the diploma throughout the county; and so now I am a landed gentleman. Look, here on my signet-ring is my crest."

This joke pleased Master Jock even more than his own. Instead of being angry, he covered with kisses the astute adventurer who had more foresight than anyone else, had got the better of those who thought they were getting the better of him, and had accepted in good earnest the part which had been thrust upon him by way of a joke.

Chapter IV

A FAMILY CURSE

In those days there lived at Pressburg a famous family, if the sad fate of becoming a by-word in the community can be indeed considered fame. They called themselves Meyer, a name borne by so many people that nobody would care to adopt it unless obliged to.

The father was a counting-house clerk in a public institution, and blessed with five beautiful daughters. In 1818 two of the girls were already grown up – the queens of every ball, the toasted beauties of every public entertainment. The greatest dandies, nay, even magnates, delighted to dance with them, and they were universally known as "the pretty Meyer girls."

How their father and mother rejoiced in their beauty! And these pretty girls, these universal *belles*, were brought up in a manner befitting their superiority. No sordid work, no domestic occupations for them! No, they were brought up luxuriously, splendidly; their vocation was something higher than the dull round of household duties. They were sent to first-class educational establishments, instead of to the national schools in the neighborhood, where they were taught to embroider exquisitely, sing elegantly, and acquire other ladylike accomplishments. And all the time their father hugged himself with the thought that one of his daughters would become a famous *artiste*, and another would grow rich as a milliner *à la mode*, and the whole lot of them would be married by some of those rich squires and bankers who were continually trampling the ground around them. Perhaps he had read of such cases in some of the old-fashioned romances of the day.

Now, such an elegant education presupposes an elegant income; but, as we all know, the salary of a cashier in a public establishment is nothing very remarkable. Housekeeping cost much more than Mr. Meyer could afford to give to it. Papa knew that only too well, and he would lie busy all night long thinking of some way out of the difficulty without ever being able to find it. And he could not call his girls away from the great world, for fear of spoiling their prospects.

Just at that very time a country squire was courting the eldest, whose acquaintance he had made at last year's dances. He was pretty sure to marry her, as any other connection with the daughter of a man of good repute would not be honorable; and then no doubt the bridegroom would advance "papa" a couple of thousand florins or so to relieve him from his embarrassments.

But the acquaintance of these squires was certainly very costly. Public entertainments, frippery, and splendor made frightful inroads; and when the domestic table was spread, the invisible shapes of tailors, bootmakers, milliners, mercers, and hairdressers sat down and helped to consume poor pater-familias' dinner.

As for the mistress of the house, she was the worst manager it is possible to imagine. Understanding nothing herself, she left everything to the servants. Whenever she was in a difficulty she ran up debts right and left (it never entered into her calculations that she would one day have to pay them back), and often when there was only just enough money left to pay for kitchen requisites for another couple of days, she had a pleasant little trick of posting off to the fruiterer's and bringing back a pine-apple.

One day it happened that the directors suddenly, and, as is their wont, without any previous notification, visited and examined the cashier's department, and Meyer was found to be six thousand florins short in his cash – the natural result of papa's frivolity. Meyer was incontinently dismissed from his post, and the little property he possessed was seized; there was even some talk of locking him up. For a whole fortnight this catastrophe was the sole talk of the town.

Now, Meyer had an elder sister living in the city, an old maid who had withdrawn from the world, and in happier times had been the butt of the family's sarcasms. She did nothing all day but go to church, say her prayers, and caress her cat; and whenever she and her cronies came together they would gossip and abuse the younger generation, possibly because they themselves were past enjoying what their juniors liked. But towards nobody was she so venomously spiteful as towards her own family, because they walked about fashionably dressed, lived well, and went to balls, while she herself had to crouch beside the fire all the winter, wear the same dress for twelve years at a stretch, and had nothing better to eat than a light pottage flavored with caraways, with a wheaten loaf broken up in it. The Meyer girls, whenever they wanted to make each other laugh, had only got to say, "Shall we go and have dinner with Aunt Teresa?"

Now, when this partly ridiculous, partly malevolent old lady heard of her younger brother's sad case, she immediately called in what little money she had out at interest – the fruits of many years of pinching and sparing – converted it into florins, and, tying them up in a bright pocket-handkerchief, went up to town, and paid into the public coffers the amount of her brother's defalcation, and would not be quiet till, by dint of much weeping and supplication, she had induced all the great gentlemen concerned (she visited them one by one) to promise not to put her brother in jail, and to abandon criminal proceedings against him.

Meyer, on hearing of his sister's good deed, hastened to seek her out, and kissing her hand repeatedly, sobbing and weeping bitterly all the time, could not find words adequate to express his gratitude. Nay, he even prevailed upon his daughters also to come and kiss his sister's hand; and could the good girls have shown a greater spirit of self-sacrifice than by condescending to bring lips like theirs, veritable roses and strawberries, into immediate contact with the old lady's withered hands, and looking without a smile at the old maid's old-fashioned garments?

Meyer swore by heaven and earth that his whole life would henceforth be devoted to showing his gratitude to his sister for her noble deed.

"You will do that best," replied the aged spinster, "by bringing up your family honorably. I have given my all to preserve your name from a great reproach, you must now take great care to preserve it from a still greater, for here below there is even a greater degradation than being thrust into prison. You know what I mean. Get something to do yourself, and accustom your children to work. Don't be ashamed of offering your services as a book-keeper to any tradesman who will have you; you will, at least, earn enough that way to make both ends meet. As for your girls, they are now old enough to help themselves. God guard them from accepting the help of other people. One of them might earn her bread as a milliner's apprentice, for she can do fine needlework. Another can go as a governess into some gentleman's family. God will show the others what to do in His own time, and I am sure you will all be happy."

Worthy Meyer returned home from his sister's thoroughly comforted. He thought no longer of suicide, but very quickly found himself a place as assistant in a merchant's office; counseled his daughters to adopt some wholesome mode of life, and they, weeping sorely, promised to obey him. Eliza got a situation with a sempstress; but instead of trying to get a governess's place, Matilda preferred to go in for art, and as she had a nice voice, and could sing a little, it was easy for her to persuade her father that a brilliant future awaited her on the stage, and that that was the easiest and most glorious way to riches; and he at once bethought him of the names of several celebrated actresses who had also sprung from ruined families and, taking to the stage, had amply provided, by their own unaided efforts, for the wants of their growing families.

So Meyer allowed his daughter to follow her bent and adopt an artistic calling. At first she was only employed as a chorus-singer, but then, as everyone knows, the most famous artistes have begun in that way.

Naturally enough, nothing of this reached the ears of Aunt Teresa, who fancied that Matilda was a governess. The worthy spinster herself never entered a playhouse, and if anyone should whisper to her that one of the Meyer girls was employed in the theater, it would be easy to say that it was another Meyer and not her kinswoman, Meyer being such a very common name. So poor Meyer really began to believe that now the whole family was going to lead a new and orderly life, that everyone would do his and her duty, and prosperity would flow into the house through door, window, and chimney.

Mrs. Meyer had now to accustom herself to cooking, and Mr. Meyer to burned dishes, and the whole family slaved away all day long. Meyer was occupied in his counting-house from dawn to dusk; Mrs. Meyer during the same period was in the kitchen; the children sewed and stitched; while the bigger ones worked out of doors on a larger scale, one of them turning out a frightful quantity of hats and bonnets, while the other was mastering her noble profession, or so at least they made each other believe. As a matter of fact, however, Mr. Meyer lounged about the coffee-houses pretty frequently, and read the newspapers, which is certainly the cheapest way of taking one's ease; Mrs. Meyer confided the pots and pans to the nursemaid, and gossiped with her neighbors; the children read books surreptitiously or played at blind-man's buff; elegant dandies diverted the elder girl who was in the employment of the milliner, and it will be better to say nothing at all about the arduous artistic labors of the chorus-singer. The family only met together at dinner-time, and then they would sit round the table with sour, ill-tempered faces, the younger ones grumbling and whining at the meager food, the elder girls with their appetites spoilt by a surfeit of sweetmeats, everyone moody and bored, as if they found each other's company intolerable, and all of them eagerly awaiting the moment when they might return to their engrossing pursuits again.

There are certain happy-minded people who never will believe what they don't like. They won't believe that anyone is angry with them until he actually treads on their corns; they fail to observe whether their acquaintances snub them in the street; they never notice any change, however nearly it concerns them, even if it be in the bosom of their families, unless somebody calls their attention to it; and they will rather invent all sorts of excuses for the most glaring faults than put themselves to the trouble of trying to correct them.

Providence, as a rule, endows those people who have to live by their labor with a beneficial instinct, which makes them find their pride and joy in the work they have accomplished. When the whole family meets together in the evening, each member boasts of how much he has done in the course of the day; and how good it is that it should be so! Now, the Meyers lacked this instinct. The curse of the expulsion from Paradise seemed to rest upon *their* labors. None of them ever boasted of having made any progress. None of them ever inquired how the others had been getting on. All of them were very chary how they opened a conversation, as if they feared it would be made a grievance of; and is there anything in the world so dreadful as a family grievance!

And grievances there are which speak even when they are dumb. Indoors, every member of the family began to wear rags, and this is what every family must come to that can only look nice in new clothes. Such people, unless they are able to sit before the mirror all day long, look draggle-tailed and sluttish, even if the clothes that hang about them are not very old, and so betray their poverty to the world. The girls were obliged to get out and do up their last year's dresses. Carnival time came round again, and big balls were advertised, but they were forced to sit at home, for they had no money to go anywhere.

Meyer, in whatever direction he looked, saw nothing but ill-tempered, dejected, sullen faces around him; but after a while he did not trouble himself much about them. Only on Sunday afternoons, when a little of the wine of Meszely had soothed his nerves, would his tongue be loosened, and a fine flood of moral precept would pour forth for the edification of his daughters. He would then tell them how happy he was at having preserved the honor of his name, although he was poor and his overcoat was ragged (which latter fact, by the way, was not very much to the credit of his grown-up daughters), but he was proud of his rags, he said, and wished his daughters to be equally proud of their virtues, and so on. As for the daughters, they were, naturally, out of the room long before this sermon was over.

Suddenly, however, a better humor and a more cheerful spirit descended upon the family. Mr. Meyer, whenever he returned from his office or from goodness knows whence, would find his daughters boisterously singing. His wife, too, bought new bonnets; their dresses began to look stylish again, and their food grew decidedly better. Mr. Meyer, instead of having his modest measure of Meszely wine on Sunday afternoon only, now met that pleasant table companion at dinner every day. He would have taken the change as much as a matter of course as the sparrows take the wheat from the fields without inquiring who sowed it, if his wife had not whispered to him one day that Matilda was making such delightful progress in her profession that the manager had thought well to very considerably raise her salary, but that the matter was to be kept secret for a time, lest the other chorus-girls should come to know of it, and demand a rise of salary likewise. Mr. Meyer considered this to be quite natural.

It is true he was a little surprised to find Matilda appearing in finer and finer clothes every day, and wearing continually the most stylish shawls and bonnets, which she passed on to her younger sister when she had worn them a bit; he frequently noticed, too, that when he entered the room, the conversation was suddenly broken off, and when he inquired what they were talking about, they first of all looked at each other as if they were afraid of giving contradictory answers, and once or twice his impatience went so far that he asked his wife, "Why does Matilda wear such expensive dresses?"

And the good lady thoroughly satisfied the anxious pater-familias. In the first place, she said, the material of the dresses was not very expensive, after all; it was made to look like *moiré*, but it was only watered taffety. In the second place, Matilda did not buy them at the original price, but got them from the prima donna for next to nothing, after she had worn them once or twice; the things were as good as given away. It was a common practice at the theater, she said.

Mr. Meyer found that he was learning a great deal he had not known before. But he considered it all quite natural.

From henceforth the whole family did their best to keep him in a good humor. They consulted his wishes, inquired after his tastes, and were always asking if there was anything he fancied or had a particular liking for.

"What good girls these girls of mine are!" said this happy pater-familias to himself.

On his birthday, too, they had pleasant surprises in store for him in the shape of presents.

Matilda, in particular, delighted him with a valuable meerschaum pipe on which hunting-dogs were carved. The whole thing, not including the silver stopper, cost five and twenty florins in hard cash.

Moved partly by the fullness of his joy and partly because he thought it the proper thing to do, Meyer resolved to visit Aunt Teresa that very day, and was the more disposed to do so because a new velvet collar had recently been sewn on to his overcoat, so he stuck the beautiful meerschaum pipe in his mouth and went to Teresa's dwelling, which was situated at the other end of the town.

The worthy spinster was sitting by her fireside, for she had a fire lighted though the spring was fine. Mr. Meyer greeted her without taking his pipe from his mouth.

Teresa made him sit down. Her demeanor towards him was most frosty; she coughed thrice for every word she spoke. Mr. Meyer was only waiting for her to say, "Where did you get that nice pipe?" and behind this expectation was the afterthought that, perhaps, when she knew of the festive origin of the present, Teresa also would hasten to gratify him with birthday gifts. At last, however, he was forced to begin the conversation of his own accord.

"Look, sister, what a handsome pipe I have!"

"It's all that," she replied, without even looking at it.

"My daughter bought it for me as a birthday present. Look!" and with these words he handed the beautiful artistic masterpiece to Teresa.

She took the pipe by the stem and dashed it so violently against the iron foot of the stove that it flew to pieces in every direction.

Mr. Meyer's mouth fell at both corners dismally. This was a pleasant birthday greeting if you like!

"Sister! what does that mean?" he cried.

"What does that mean? It means that you are a stupid, a fool, a blockhead! All the world knows that one of your daughters is the mistress of a nobleman, and you are not only content to live with her and share her shameful earnings, but you actually come here to me and make a boast of it!"

"What! Which of my daughters?" exclaimed Meyer.

Teresa shrugged her shoulders. "If I did not know you for a credulous simpleton," said she, "I should take you for an abandoned villain. You thought me fool enough to believe that you were bringing up your daughter as a governess when she was on the stage all the time. I don't want to tell you what my views are as to choosing a profession – I admit that they are old-fashioned, and out of date – but will you tell me how it is possible for a girl with a salary of sixteen florins a month to expend thousands on extravagant luxury?"

"Pardon me, Matilda's salary has been raised," said Meyer, who would very much have liked others to believe something of what he believed himself.

"That is untrue. You can find out the real state of the case from the manager if you like."

"And then, too, her clothes are not as expensive as you fancy, sister. She wears cheap dresses which she bought second-hand from the prima donna."

"That also is untrue. She bought everything brand new. This very week she purchased three hundred florins' worth of lace from Messrs. Flesz and Huber alone."

To this Mr. Meyer knew not what to say.

"Don't sit staring at me there like a stuck pig!" cried Teresa, with a sudden access of temper. "Hundreds, aye thousands, of times have I seen her sitting with a certain gentleman, in a hired carriage. 'Tis only a blockhead like yourself that can't see what all the world sees! You are a stupid dolt, made to be taken in. I wonder it has never entered into the head of some play-writer to put you into a farce! What! a pater-familias who, when he is half-tipsy, on Sunday afternoons preaches moral sermons to daughters, who are laughing in their sleeves at him all the time, and who brags about the meerschaum pipe which the seducer of his own daughter gives him as a birthday present! Why, if I thought that you had had any idea of this abomination, I would sweep you out of this room with the very broom with which I now sweep up the fragments of your pipe."

Mr. Meyer was very much upset by this language. He got up without answering a word, put on his hat, and went, first of all, to the shop of Messrs. Flesz and Huber, to find out how much his daughter had spent there. It turned out to be considerably more than three hundred florins. Aunt Teresa was certainly well-informed.

Thence he proceeded to the theater, and inquired what his daughter's salary was. The manager had no need to consult his books about it. He told Mr. Meyer straight out that his daughter was paid sixteen florins, but she did not earn it, for she was very backward in learning – in fact, she made no progress at all; nor did she seem to care very much, for she never appeared at any of the rehearsals, and her salary went for the most part in paying fines.

This was a little too much. Mr. Meyer was beside himself with rage. He rushed wildly home. Fortunately, he made such a row when he burst into the house that the other members of the family had time to get

Matilda out of his way, so that he had to be content with disinheriting his abandoned daughter on the spot, and forbidding her, under pain of extermination, ever to appear beneath his roof again. A tiger could not have been more furious, and in the pitilessness of his rage he commanded that her accursed name should never be mentioned in his presence, and threatened to send packing after the minx whoever had the audacity to defend her.

His merciless humor lasted for a whole week. Very often his tongue itched to ask a question or two, but he stifled the rising words, and still kept silence. At last, one day, as they all sat together at dinner, not a single member of the family could touch a thing – then Mr. Meyer could stand it no longer.

"What's the matter with you all?" he cried. "Why don't you eat? What's the meaning of all this blubbering?"

The girls raised their handkerchiefs to their eyes, and blubbered more than ever; but his wife, loudly sobbing, replied –

"My daughter is dying!"

"Naturally!" replied her husband, thrusting such a large spoonful of pudding into his mouth that he nearly choked. "'Tis easy to say that, but it is not so easy to die!"

"It would be better for the poor thing if she did die; she would not suffer so much then, at any rate."

"Then, why don't you send for the doctor?"

"Her sickness is not to be cured by any doctor."

"Hum!" said Mr. Meyer, beginning to pick his teeth.

His wife waited for a little while, and thus continued in a tearful voice –

"She is always thinking of you. All she wants is to see her father. She says if she could kiss his hand but once, she would die of joy."

At these words the whole family in chorus sent up a piping wail like an organ. Mr. Meyer pretended to blow his nose.

"Where is she, then?" he inquired in a constrained voice.

"In the Zuckermandel quarter, in one poor room which she has hired for a month, abandoned by everyone."

"Then she is *poor!*" thought Mr. Meyer. "Perhaps, therefore, all that Teresa said about her is not quite true?"

Perhaps she had loved someone, and accepted gifts from him. That was not such a great crime, surely, and it did not follow from that, that she had sold herself. Those old spinsters, who have never experienced the world's primest joys, are so jealous of the diversions of young people.

"Hum! Then that bad girl speaks of me sometimes, eh?"

"She fancies your curse rests upon her. Since she departed –"

Here the conversation was again interrupted by a general outburst of weeping.

"Since she departed," continued Mrs. Meyer, "she has never risen from her bed, and leave it I know she never will, unless it is to be put into her cof-cof-coffin."

"Well, well, bring her home this afternoon," said Mr. Meyer, thoroughly softened at last.

At these words the whole family fell upon his neck and kissed and fondled him. Never was there a better man or a kinder father in the whole world, they said.

They scarce waited for the table to be cleared in order to deck out the worthy pater-familias in his best, and, putting a stick in his hand, the whole lot of them accompanied him to the Zuckermandel quarter, where Matilda lay in a poor garret, in which there was nothing, in the strictest sense of the word, but a bed and an innumerable quantity of medicine-bottles.

The heart of the good father was lacerated by this spectacle. So Matilda had nothing at all, poor girl!

The girl would have risen when she beheld her father, but was unable to do so. Mr. Meyer rushed towards her with a penitent countenance, just as if he had sinned against her. The girl seized his hand, pressed it to her bosom, covered it with kisses, and in a broken voice begged for his forgiveness.

A father's heart must surely have been made of stone to have resisted such an appeal! He forgave her, of course, and a coach was immediately sent for in which to convey her home. Let the world say what it liked, blood is stronger than water; a father cannot slay his offspring for the sake of a little tripping!

And besides, as a matter of fact, there was not the slightest reason why he should punish her so severely, for that very same day he received a letter (it was brought to the house by a liveried servant), which the nobleman so frequently alluded to wrote him with his own hand, and in which he expressed his grief that his innocent, well-meaning advances should have occasioned such a misunderstanding. He declared, moreover, that he regarded the whole family with the greatest respect, and as to his intercourse with Matilda, it was simply dictated by his enthusiasm for art. Nay, he was prepared, if necessary, to furnish the most incontestable proofs, under his own hand and seal, that the young lady's virtue was fenced about by absolutely impregnable bulwarks.

Ah! an honest, honorable gentleman, indeed!

"Well, that's all right," said Mr. Meyer, whom this letter perfectly satisfied – "quite another sort of thing, in fact. But, at any rate, he ought not to try and make Matilda go out with him, or try and see her behind the scenes. That might so easily compromise her. If his intentions are honorable, let him come to the house."

Imbecile, to give bread to the rats that they might not disturb him in the night-time, instead of keeping a cat!

Naturally, in a couple of days, Matilda was as rosy as an apple just plucked from the tree, and her squire now came to the house to visit her quite nicely. In a few months' time he departed, and after him came a young banker, and then another squire, and a third and a fourth, and goodness knows how many more. And all of them were great votaries of art, worthy respectable gentlemen everyone of them, who were never known to utter an improper word, who kissed mamma's hand, and talked on sensible topics with papa, and bowed as decorously to the girls as if they were young countesses at the very least. And among them were such merry, amusing young fellows, who would make one die of laughter with their jokes, and teased mamma by going into the kitchen and tasting the dishes, and pocketing the pancakes. Oh, they were such funny, quizzical young fellows!

Four of the Meyer girls were now tall and stately, and all of them as beautiful as could be, and not a year's difference between them. As they grew up, and their virginal charms developed, Mr. Meyer's house became more and more noisy and frequented. The old luxury, frivolity, and extravagance returned, and a perpetual jollity took possession of it. The most select company, moreover, assembled there – counts, barons, gentlemen of high degree, bankers, and other bigwigs.

It is true that it struck Mr. Meyer as somewhat peculiar that when he met these counts and barons in the street they did not seem to see him, and if his girls were with him, they and these friends of theirs did not even exchange looks; but it was his way not to trouble himself about anything unpleasant; besides, he fancied that great folks always behaved like this.

And now his youngest daughter also was growing up; she was already twelve years old, and she promised to be more beautiful than any of her sisters. At present she was in short frocks, and her long thick hair, twisted into two pigtails, dangled down her back. The guests who honored her father's house with their presence had already begun to ask her, in joke, when she was going to wear long dresses like her sisters.

One day Mr. Meyer had an unusual and surprising visitor. A bevy of good-humored youths were flirting with his daughters just then, while papa was smashing flies on the wall at intervals, smiling complacently whenever one of his daughters, startled by an extra loud bang, gave a little shriek, when a knocking was heard at the door. As nobody answered the door, the knocking was repeated twice, much louder each time, and at last one of the jovial young fellows aforesaid jumped up and opened the door, imagining that it was some other merry wag who wanted to surprise them all – and behold! a dry, wrinkled old maid in a shabby black dress stood before the brilliant assembly!

Papa was so frightened by this apparition that his knees knocked together. It was Aunt Teresa!

The old spinster, without deigning to bestow the least attention on the company assembled there, made straight for Mr. Meyer with the utmost composure.

The worthy pater-familias was in the most unspeakable confusion. He knew not whether to ask the old lady to take a chair, or whether to introduce her to the gay throng as his sister, or whether to deny that he knew her. But Teresa herself relieved him from his embarrassment. With a calm and cold look, she said, "I have a few words to say to you, and if you have leisure to quit your guests for a moment or two, be so good as to take me where we may not disturb the company."

Papa Meyer at once accepted this proposal, and, opening the door before her, led her into one of the remoter rooms. They had scarcely closed the door, when a merry laugh arose from the midst of the company which they had just quitted. Papa Meyer thereupon drew Aunt Teresa still further away. Even he was not quite so simple as not to know why the young people in there laughed so uproariously at this old-fashioned spinster of a bygone generation.

Papa Meyer, when he did address Aunt Teresa, tried to assume his most friendly air.

"Won't you take a seat, my dear kinswoman? Oh, what a pleasure it is to see you at last!"

"I have not exactly come here to bandy compliments," replied Teresa, dryly, "and it is not necessary to sit down for the sake of the few words I have come to say. I can say them just as well standing up. For two years we have not seen each other. During that time you have placed a pretty considerable distance between us, and your mode of life has been such as to make it impossible for all eternity for us ever to approach one another again. This I fancy will not very greatly astonish you, and the knowledge that this is so has given me the courage to say it. You have chosen for your four daughters, one after the other, the same career. Don't speak. It is better to be silent about such things, and I beg you will not interrupt me. I shall not reproach you. You are the master of your own actions. You have one daughter who is twelve years old; in a short time she will be a marriageable girl. I have not come to this house to make a scene, nor do I wish to preach about morality, or religion, or

God, or maidenly innocence, subjects which great men and grand gentlemen simply sneer at as the stock-in-trade of hypocrites. I will therefore tell you in a couple of words why I have come. All I ask is that you deliver over to me your youngest daughter. I will engage to bring her up honorably as a respectable middle-class girl should be brought up. Her mind is still uncorrupted, she is still in the hands of God, and I will undertake to the day of my death to preserve her reputation. All I require of you is that neither you yourself, nor any member of your family, ever think of her again. God will help me to carry out my good resolution. And one thing more, in case you reject my offer I shall petition the highest authorities to favor my request which may have very unpleasant consequences for you, for I am prepared to go to the Prince Primate of Hungary himself, and explain to him the reasons which have induced me to come forward in this manner. My proposition does not require much consideration. I'll give you till early tomorrow morning to make up your mind. If by that time you have not brought the girl to my house, you can reckon me as your most irreconcilable enemy, and then the God who remits sins have mercy upon you!"

With these words the old spinster turned her back upon him and left the house.

Mr. Meyer escorted his sister to the door, and so long as he saw her before his eyes, his mind stood still, he was not the master of a single thought. Only when she had crossed his threshold did he come to himself again. The girls and the young dandies commented on the appearance of the venerable virgin in the most amusing manner, and their jokes put some heart into papa Meyer again. He began to tell them what had brought the ancient spinster there.

"She actually wants to take away Fanny," he cried, "and keep her forever."

"Ho! oh! ah!" resounded on every side.

"And why? I should like to know why? Have I not always brought her up respectably? Can anyone say anything against me? Can anyone reproach me with anything? Do not I treasure my daughters as the very light of my eyes? Has anyone ever heard an ill word fall from my mouth? Am I a swindler, perhaps, who give my daughters such a bad example that the State feels bound to step in and take them out of my hands? Well, gentlemen, say what you know of me! Am I a thief, or a brigand, or a blasphemer?"

And all the time he strode rapidly up and down the room like a stage hero, while his guests stood still and stared.

What he said, however, made a great impression, for all the young gentlemen now vanished from the house. There was something in Aunt

Teresa's threats which might have unpleasant consequences even for them.

When the family was alone again, there was a violent outburst of wrath against that meddlesome Aunt Teresa, and Mr. Meyer himself waxed so wroth that he felt bound to pour forth his grievances outside as well as inside the house. He still possessed two or three acquaintances whom he had learnt to know in his official days: they were now leading counsel in the supreme court, eminent jurists whose opinions he could safely follow. He had not seen them for a long time, but it now occurred to him that he might just as well look them up and be beforehand with Aunt Teresa in case she put her threat into execution.

His nearest acquaintance was Councilor Schmerz, a bachelor of about forty, a smooth-faced, quiet sort of man, whom he found in his garden grafting his pinks. To him he confided his grievance, telling him all about Aunt Teresa and the shabby trick she threatened to play him – reporting him to the Prince Primate, forsooth!

Mr. Schmerz smiled once or twice during this speech, and now and then warned Mr. Meyer, who was quite carried away by the force of his declamation, not to trample on his flower-beds, as they were planted with cockscombs and larkspurs. When, however, Mr. Meyer had finished his oration, he replied very gently –

"Teresa will not do that!"

"Teresa will not do that?" thought Mr. Meyer. "That's not enough for me." He wanted to be told that Teresa *could* not – was not allowed to do it; and if she tried it on, so much the worse for Teresa.

Mr. Schmerz had evidently made up his mind to graft an endless series of pinks that afternoon, so Mr. Meyer thought it best to carry his complaint to another of his acquaintances, in the hope that he would and must give a more definite reply.

This other acquaintance was Mr. Chlamek, a famous advocate, one of the most honorable of characters, and withal an exceedingly dry man – practical shrewdness and commonsense personified. He, too, was a pater-familias with three sons and two daughters.

Mr. Chlamek listened to the matter laid before him with all an advocate's patience, and answered the question quietly and frankly –

"My dear friend, never quarrel with a relation for showing a disposition to relieve you of one of your daughters. Thank God that you have still daughters left and to spare. I know from experience that one girl gives more trouble than three boys. I should not refuse this offer if I were you."

Mr. Meyer said not a word. This advice pleased him even less than the other. So he went to his third acquaintance.

This third acquaintance was a really excellent fellow, and by profession a judge of the criminal court. He was always frightfully rude to those with whom he was in any way angry, and if the whole penal code had been his ring, he could not have twisted it round his finger more easily.

Mr. Meyer found the eminent criminal lawyer in the midst of a heap of dusty papers. Mr. Bordácsi, for that was his name, had an extraordinary faculty for so identifying himself with any complicated case he might take up as to absolutely live and breathe in it. Any attempt at sophistry or chicanery made him downright venomous, and he only recovered himself when, by dint of superior acumen, he had enabled the righteous cause to triumph. He was also far-famed for his incorruptibility. Whoever approached him with ducats was incontinently kicked out-of-doors, and if any pretty woman visited him with the intention of making her charms influence his judgments, he would treat her so unceremoniously that she was likely to think twice before visiting him again on a similar errand.

No sooner did Bordácsi perceive Mr. Meyer than he took off his spectacles and put them on the page of the document before him, so as not to lose his place; then he exclaimed, in an extraordinarily rough voice –

"Well, what's the matter, friend Meyer?"

Mr. Meyer was glad to hear the word "friend," but this was a mere form of expression with his Honor the Judge. He always said "friend" to lawyers' clerks, lackeys, and even to the parties to a suit whom it was his duty to tear to ribbons. Meyer, however, set forth his grievance quite confidently. He even sat down, though he had not been invited to do so, as he was wont to do in the bygone happy days when they were official colleagues together. It was Meyer's custom never to look those whom he was addressing in the face, which bashfulness deprived him, of course, of the advantage of being able to read from their countenances what impression he was making upon them. He was therefore greatly surprised when, on finishing his speech, his Honor Judge Bordácsi roared at him in the angriest of voices –

"And why do you tell me all this?"

Mr. Meyer's spirit suddenly grew cold within him; he could not answer a word, only his mouth moved weakly up and down, like the mouth of a puppet that you pull with a string.

"What!" cried Judge Bordácsi, with a still more violent exertion of his lungs, rushing upon his unfortunate client and fixing him with frightfully distended eyes.

In his terror the unfortunate man leaped from the seat in which he had sat down unasked, and murmured tearfully –

"I humbly beg your pardon. I came here for advice and – and protection."

"How? Do you imagine, sir, that I shall take your part?" bawled the judge, as if he were speaking to someone who was stone deaf.

"I fancied," stammered the unfortunate pater-familias, "that the old kindliness which you formerly showed to my house –"

Bordácsi did not let him finish. "Yes, your house! In those days your house was a respectable house, but now your house is a Sodom and Gomorrah which opens its doors wide to all the fools of the town. You have devoted your four girls to the bottomless pit, and you are a scandal to every pure-minded man. You are the corrupter of the youth of this city, and your name is a by-word throughout the kingdom wherever dissolute youths and outraged fathers are to be found."

Here Mr. Meyer burst into tears, and murmured something to the effect that he did not know anything about it.

"With what a handsome family did not God bless you! and, sir, you have made it the laughingstock of the world. You have traded with the innocence, the love, and the spiritual welfare of your daughters; you have sold, you have bartered them away to the highest bidder; you have taught them that they must catch passers-by in the street with an ogle or a stare, that they must smile, laugh, and make love to men whom they see for the first time in their lives, that they must make money by lying!"

The wretched man was understood to say, amidst his sobs, that he had done none of these things.

"And now, sir, you have one daughter left, the last, the prettiest, the most charming of them all. When I used to visit at your house, sir, she was a little child no higher than my knee, whom everyone loved, everyone fondled. Don't you remember, sir? And now, sir, you would abandon her also. And you are angry, you storm and rave when a respectable person wants to save the unfortunate child from having her innocence corrupted, save her from withering away profitlessly in the claws of a pack of gross, rowdy, street-lounging, rake-hell young profligates, from living a life of wretchedness and shame, from dying abandoned and accursed, to say nothing of the fire of hell after death. And you even raise objections, sir! But, of course, I understand, they would be depriving you of a great treasure, of something you can sell at a high price, something that you can calculate upon making a handsome profit out of, eh?"

Meyer gnashed his teeth with rage and horror.

"Let me tell you, sir, if you are still able to follow good advice," continued the judge, in the same pitiless voice, "that if that respectable person, your kinswoman Teresa, is still willing to take charge of your daughter Fanny, surrender her unconditionally, renounce all your rights to her now and forevermore, for if you raise any further objections, if the matter comes before the courts, so help me God! I'll have you locked up myself."

"Where?" asked the terrified Meyer.

This question took the judge somewhat aback at first, but he soon found an answer.

"Where? Well, in the house of correction, in case the things that are done in your house, sir, are done with your knowledge and consent; and in a madhouse if they are done without your knowledge."

Mr. Meyer had got a sufficient answer at last; he took his leave and departed. He could scarce find the door by which he had entered, and he had to grope his way down to the street. The loafers there who saw him nudged each other with a grin and said, "That chap has had a good skinful somewhere!"

So he had to learn from others that he was not a respectable man; he had to learn from strange lips that people looked down upon him, laughed at, cursed him, sneered at him as the man who made money out of his daughters' love affairs, and whose house was a place where young men were corrupted.

And he had always fancied that he was the best man in the world, whose house was honored and respected, and whose friendship was sought after!

In his confusion of mind he had wandered out of his way as far as the Malomligeti pond. What a nice pond! he thought. How many wicked girls could be suffocated there! A man, too, might easily leap into it, and be at rest! Then he turned back again and hastened home.

At home they were still chattering and exclaiming at the pretensions of Aunt Teresa. The youngest girl was passed from hand to hand, and kissed and embraced as if some great misfortune awaited her.

"Poor Fanny, it would be better for you to be a servant with us than to live with Aunt Teresa!"

"Oh, what a pleasant time you'll have, sewing and knitting all day long, and in the evening reading devotional books to aunty till she dozes off!"

"I know she will always be running us down; you will never see us, and we shall become quite strangers to you."

"Poor Fanny, the old faggot will beat you, too."

"Poor Fanny!"

"My poor girl!"

"Poor little sister!"

They quite frightened the child with all these lamentations, and it was at last determined that if Fanny would say to papa, if he pressed her, that she did not want to go to Aunt Teresa, they would all take her part.

At that same moment Meyer's steps were audible upon the staircase. He rushed into the room with his hat on – but, indeed, in such a house as that it was not usual to take off one's hat at all at any time. He knew that everyone was looking at his face, but he also knew that his face was distorted enough to frighten anyone who looked at it.

Without bestowing a glance on anyone, he simply said to Fanny –

"Put on your hat and cloak, and look sharp about it!"

"Why, papa?" asked Fanny. Like all badly-brought-up children, she always said, "What for?" before doing anything she was told to do.

"You are to come with me."

"Where?"

"To Aunt Teresa's."

Everyone present affected an air of astonishment. Fanny cast down her eyes, and twisting a ribbon round her finger, "I don't want to go to Aunt Teresa," she faltered timidly.

A disjointed embroidering frame was lying on the table.

Fanny stole a glance at her mother and sisters, and meeting with looks of encouragement, repeated, this time in a bold, determined voice –

"I don't want to go to Aunt Teresa!"

"What? You don't want to go, eh?"

"I want to stay here with my mother and sisters."

"With your mother and sisters, eh? and become what they are, I suppose?" and seizing the girl with one hand, he snatched up with the other one of the sticks of the embroidering frame, and, before Fanny had time to be frightened, he thrashed her in a way that made his own heart bleed for her.

The sisters tried to interfere, and got their share also, for papa Meyer broke all the remaining sticks of the frame over their shoulders, so that when it came to his wife's turn, he had to pummel her with his fists till she collapsed in a corner.

A few years sooner a moderate dose of this discipline might have been of use, now it only caused physical pain. And all the time Mr. Meyer never said a word; he simply gratified his rage, like a wild beast that has escaped from its cage.

After that he seized Fanny by the hand, and without taking leave of anyone, dragged her along with him to Aunt Teresa's. The child wept all the way.

The chastised damsels wished, in their wrath, that their departing father might never return again. And their wish was gratified, for Mr. Meyer never did return home again. From henceforth he vanished from Pressburg. Where he went or what became of him nobody ever knew. Some maintained that he had jumped into the Danube, others that he had emigrated; and years afterwards distant travelers sent word home from time to time that they had seen a man greatly resembling him, some said in England, some in Turkey.

Chapter V

THE TEMPTER IN CHURCH

Three years had passed since Fanny went to live with Aunt Teresa. Those three years had a great influence upon her youthful and pliable disposition. At first Teresa was severe and stony-hearted towards the child; her obstinacy, like a thorny hedge, had to be broken down. The smallest fault was chastised, every moment of her time had its allotted task, of which she had to give an account, not a single contradiction, not the slightest sulkiness was put up with. Then, too, she was never able to escape detection, a far-seeing, austere pair of eyes was ever upon her, making falsehood impossible, looking through her very soul, seizing and pruning down every thought as it arose. The weeds had to be extirpated before the seeds of nobler flowers could be sown.

When, however, she had at last brought under the child's unruly disposition and convinced her that it was of no use to play the hypocrite or tell lies, inasmuch as there is a Being Who sees behind all our thoughts, Who is everywhere present and watchful, Whom nothing escapes, and Who watches over us even when we are asleep, so that we are bound from very necessity to be just and honest; when she had brought her charge as far as this, I say, Teresa began gradually to teach her how conversion could have its pleasant side likewise. Teresa's confidence grew proportionately with Fanny's candor. She frequently left the child to herself, ceased to supervise her allotted tasks, showed her that she believed what she said, and thereby gradually exalted and purified her whole disposition. Perceiving that her rigorous mentor trusted her, Fanny began to discover what self-respect means. And what a precious treasure that is! and what a pity more attention is not paid to it!

Teresa never alluded to the child's relatives; on the contrary, whenever her thoughts seemed to be turning that way she would divert them into a different direction. And gradually, as Fanny's notions of right and wrong grew clearer and firmer, she felt less and less of a desire to inquire after the members of her own family. At last it came to this – that when, one day, having obtained Teresa's permission to go somewhere, she suddenly came face to face in the street with Matilda, who was riding in an open carriage, she fled terror-stricken into the courtyard of the house where dwelt a lady of her acquaintance, in order that her sister might not see her.

Teresa heard of this, and ever afterwards treated Fanny much more tenderly.

One day, while sitting at her work, the girl sighed heavily. Teresa knew at once that she was thinking of her relatives.

"Why do you sigh?" she asked.

"Poor Matilda!" said the girl; and she spoke with quite genuine emotion, for she really did pity her sister who rode in a carriage and wore Brabant lace, while she herself was so happy at home over her sewing.

Teresa made no reply, but, full of emotion, she clasped the child to her breast. God had at last rewarded her for all the labors and anxieties of the last three years, for Fanny was now saved, and doubtless reserved for a happier future.

And, indeed, poverty in itself is not such a very great calamity, after all. Those who have a close acquaintance with it will tell you that it possesses joys of its own which are not to be bought with heaps of gold pieces. Besides, Teresa was not absolutely destitute. She received five hundred florins a year from an insurance office for life, with one half of which she not only supported the pair of them comfortably, but even left a margin for a little recreation. The other half she carefully put by, that Fanny might have something when she herself was gone. And the girl made a little money as well; she earned something by her needlework. Oh, ye men and women who swim in luxury, you do not know what delight, what rapture it is when a young man or woman receives the reward of his honest labor for the first time; you know nothing of the proud consciousness of being self-sufficient, of being able to live without the compassion, without the assistance, of other people!

And Fanny's work was very well paid, too!

In the house where they lived there was an Hungarian cabinet-maker, who owned several houses in Pressburg, John Boltay by name. This rich artisan, long, long ago, when he had only just served his apprenticeship, was tenderly disposed towards Teresa, and offered her his hand. But Teresa's relatives would not give him the girl, although she loved him; their family belonged to the official class, and looked down upon a mere workman. So Boltay went away and married someone else, and the marriage turned out unhappy and childless; and by the time his wife died both he and Teresa had grown old. Teresa had never married at all. For forty years she had been growing old and grey, but she had never forgotten her first love. In the meantime her family had gone down in the world, and she had been obliged to live in a house in the suburbs, where she had remained for five-and-twenty years. Boltay meanwhile had become a rich man, and had purchased the house in which Teresa lived, and this gave him an opportunity of doing little kindnesses to Teresa, which she could not very well refuse. Thus, he turned the yard into a garden, gave the noisier of his tenants notice to quit, and charged her a purely nominal rent. And yet, for all that, they never exchanged a word together. Boltay himself lived at the opposite end of the town, over his shop; but he knew very well, all the same, what was going on at Teresa's. He knew, too, that she had adopted Fanny, and about this time he frequently sent over his head journeyman (a worthy, honest young fellow, and his favorite, whom he meant to make his heir, so people said, for he had no relatives) to purchase Fanny's handiwork, for which he paid very handsomely. He would not have dared to offer Teresa any direct assistance; but Teresa, for the girl's sake, felt bound to accept what he offered in this way.

Maybe both she and Boltay thought what a pretty pair the two young people would make. Alexander (to give the young journeyman his name for the first time) was a tall, muscular, well-built fellow, with blonde curly locks, ardent blue eyes, and a bold, manly face. There was nothing slovenly or commonplace in his bearing, nor, on the other hand, did he affect gentility; but there was that quiet self-confidence about him which belongs to the man whose mind and body are equally developed. The girl was a slender, ideal creature, with languishing black eyes and a rosy, chubby face so full of color that even round her eyes one could not detect a spot of pallor – just such a beauty, in fact, as the world is apt to make much of. They contrasted prettily enough – blonde and brunette, blue eyes and black; he so bold, vigorous, and sedate, she so overflowing with tenderness and feeling; yet who can tell what is written concerning them in the stars?

Amongst Teresa's acquaintances was a dapper little man who was generally known, not by his real name, but by his official title – the precentor. One evening the worthy precentor happened to hear light-hearted Fanny sing the snatch of some song or other, and, surprised, connoisseur as he was, by the music of her pretty voice, suggested that he should teach her an air from the "Stabat Mater," that she might sing it in the choir at church.

Teresa trembled at the thought. Matilda at once occurred to her mind; yet, after all, it is one thing to sing frivolous love ditties on an open stage in fancy costume, face to face with a lot of lazy young loungers, and quite another to sing in the Church of God, behind a closed screen, sublime and edifying hymns for the benefit of devout worshippers, although, of course, the Evil One, who is always seeking his prey, may find his victim in the Church of God itself. Teresa, therefore, felt bound to allow Fanny to go to the precentor, who instructed her with great enthusiasm, and was never weary of praising her. The girl, indeed, rarely went there alone. Either Teresa herself, or a worthy crony of Teresa's, Dame Kramm by name, regularly accompanied Fanny to the precentor's dwelling, and in an hour's time returned to fetch her away again. That the rumor of Fanny's beauty and virtue should not have spread through the town was too much to expect. There are always a number of unoccupied young gentlemen about, whose sole mission in life seems to be to make such discoveries, and the number of these pleasure-hunters was considerably increased on the occasion of the assembling of the Diet at Pressburg, when many of our younger conscript fathers spread the report of newly found female virtue as far as possible. Who did not know of the Meyer girls in those days? – and those who did, could not help knowing likewise that there was a fifth sister. Now, where was this last little sister hiding? Why, it was the most natural question in the world.

The girls themselves made no mystery of the matter. They explained with whom Fanny was, and where and when she might be seen. Ah! and this was much more than mere giddiness; it was shamelessness, jealousy, hatred! Matilda could not forgive Fanny for avoiding her in the street, and the others could not pardon her for possessing a treasure which they possessed no longer – innocence! What a dish for the fine palate of a connoisseur! What a rare fruit of paradise! A child of fifteen or sixteen, whose diamond soul has been cleansed from mud and filth, who is still conscious of God, and capable of pure delights, whose tender loving heart, perhaps, is in the safekeeping of some honest, romantic youth – what a fine thing to root her up unmercifully, to tear off her budding leaves one by one, hurl her back again into the mire from which she has been plucked, and make her acquainted with that new, that withering, consuming fire of infernal passion begotten among the souls of the nether world!

So the chase was let loose after the tender roe that had emerged from the garden of paradise. Swarms of those knight-errants who have nothing else to do waylaid and accosted her in the streets and byways, and offered her their flattery, their homage, their gifts, but above the head of the fairy roe rested a star, which suffered not the darts of the huntsmen to hit their mark. That star was the star of purity.

The discomfited youths, more and more angry every day, used to meet at the Meyers' and deride one another at the failure of their endeavors. Very often, too, heavy bets on the issue of the event were offered and taken, just as if it were a horse-race or a coursing-match. At length a well-known dandy, Fennimore by name, resolved to try the effect of an open direct attack; it was, he opined, the best way of conquering the sex. So one day, when he had ascertained that Fanny was alone at home, he sent her a splendid bouquet of hothouse flowers, in which was concealed a *billet-doux* of the following purport: If Fanny were inclined to reward the devotion of a loving heart, she was to leave the back door of the garden open in the evening. There are cases, he argued, in which similar proposals lead most rapidly to the end desired.

The inexperienced girl, in the innocence of her astonishment, accepted the proffered bouquet. This was adroitly calculated upon by the sender. Any other missive might have aroused her suspicion and made her more cautious, but flowers harmonize so well with a young girl's disposition that how could she refuse them?

Only when the bearer of the missive had withdrawn did Fanny observe a letter concealed among the flowers, and immediately, just as if she had caught sight of a venomous spider, she threw away the bouquet, and ran weeping to Dame Kramm, and sobbing bitterly, related the incident. She fancied she was disgraced already.

Shortly afterwards Teresa returned home, and she and Dame Kramm held a consultation over the sealed letter. Fanny was inconsolable when Dame Kramm confided to her its contents. She seriously believed that the bare receiving such a letter had dishonored her forever and ever, and despite the consolations of the two worthy old spinsters, she lay in a fever the whole night.

Meanwhile the two old ladies were concocting a plan of vengeance against the originator of all this trouble, and, believe me, ancient spinsters know how to be revengeful! They left the back door of the garden wide open, laid in wait till the cavalier had entered, and then closed it again. Then they took it in turns to watch from the garret window how the valiant young woman-hunter, the would-be seducer, who had himself fallen into the pit, cooled his heels for hours in the mouse-trap they had prepared for him, and when at last the rain began to fall, they went to bed full of malicious joy, with the house-keys tucked snugly beneath their pillows, and listening with delight to the rain pattering against the windowpanes.

This very considerable defeat only raised the ardor of the huntsman still higher. What, to surrender to an inexperienced child! to be worsted by a pair of old women! Why, *l'esprit de corps* could not let matters rest there; and Abellino, who was the leader of the band, took upon himself to rehabilitate their *renommée*, as he called it, and with proud self-confidence laid a bet to a very considerable amount that, within twelve months' time, he would induce this beauty to quit her paradise and come and live with him – naturally not as his consort.

On the following Sunday Fanny sang the "Stabat Mater Dolorosa" in the cathedral sublimely, and the heart of every worshipper was filled with devotion. Dame Kramm, decked out in all her Sabbath finery, was sitting by one of the side altars, enjoying in her own way the child's beautiful singing, when she heard an enraptured voice close beside her sigh, "Oh, what splendid, what sublime singing!"

She immediately felt bound to turn round and see who it was that was pouring forth the rapture of his soul so abundantly.

She saw before her a modestly attired gentleman, who wore mourning on his hat, and had just dried a tear from his upturned eye. It was Abellino Kárpáthy.

"She sings beautifully, sir, does she not?" said the good spinster, proudly.

"Like an angel! Ah, madam, every time I hear such singing the tears start from my eyes." And the sensitive youth put his handkerchief to his eyes again. Then he departed without saying another word to Dame Kramm.

The whole week through Dame Kramm was tortured by curiosity. What could be amiss with this mysterious youth? Would he come again on the following Sunday?

And come again he did, and now they greeted one another like old acquaintances.

"Look ye, madam," said the young gentleman, with a mournful countenance, "ten years ago I had a sweetheart, a betrothed, who used to sing the 'Stabat Mater' with just such a beautiful voice; it makes me actually think that I can hear her now. She died on the very day fixed for our wedding. On her deathbed she made me promise that if ever I found a poor young lady who could sing these divine canticles with just such a beautiful voice as she had, I was, in memory of her, to devote every year the sum of three thousand florins to enable such young lady to cultivate to the utmost her noble art, and thus secure for herself a happy future. I only imposed one condition before consenting to my betrothed's desire: I insisted that the young lady in question should be just as pure, just as innocent, as was my beloved, my never-to-be-forgotten Maria!" And the young man again applied his pocket-handkerchief to his eyes.

"What genuine grief!" thought the old lady to herself.

"I must regretfully confess, madam," pursued the young dandy, in a shaky voice, "that I have not been able to carry out the desire of my deceased bride. So far as natural gifts are concerned, there were heaps and heaps of candidates, but in the way of virtue they all failed me. I think of them with shame, and yet there are some among them whom the world has loaded with its applause. And every fresh attempt has proved a fresh illusion."

And here he again broke off the conversation, and left Madam Kramm to cogitate upon this strange story for another week. She said not a word about it to anyone.

On the following Sunday, Abellino again made his appearance. He kept silence till the singing was quite over, but it was clear from his face that there was something he would very much have liked to ask, had he not been too shy to do so. At last, however, he constrained himself to speak.

"Pardon me for troubling you with such a question, madam, and do not take it ill of me; but do you not know the singer personally? I have so many times been deceived in my benevolent intentions that I scarce dare to approach anyone without making preliminary inquiries. I have heard the most astonishing reports of this young woman's family, which seem to prove that virtue is in no very great request there."

At this Dame Kramm also became loquacious. "Whatever this young woman's relations may be, sir, she has had absolutely nothing to do with them since she was a child. Her heart is as pure as a child's, and her education has been so austere that, even if she were now to be abandoned entirely to herself, not the shadow of a vice could possibly find admittance in her breast."

"Ah, madam, you have made me altogether happy!"

"How so, sir?"

"The soul of my Maria will at length be able to rest in peace."

And off he went again, leaving Dame Kramm to think the matter over for another week.

On the following Sunday he honored the worthy spinster with his entire confidence.

"Madam," said he, "I am convinced that your young charge is quite worthy of my protection. That girl will one day become a famous *artiste,* and her rare virginal modesty will raise her far above all her fellows. But a strict watch must be kept upon her. I am well aware that sundry rich young men are lying in wait for her. Be careful, madam, and warn the young woman's guardians to look well after her! Excessive light blinds the greatest characters; but I have determined to save her from their nefarious intrigues. She *shall* be an *artiste.* In her voice she possesses such a treasure that, if only it be properly cultivated, all these cavaliers, with all their wealth to boot, will seem but beggars beside her; and then, if she preserve within herself the source of her riches, she will escape the danger with which wealth always threatens innocence."

Madam Kramm thoroughly believed him. Her thoughts now began to turn from the church to the theater, and she looked forward to the day when she should applaud Fanny's singing.

"A couple of years will make a thorough *artiste* of her. Great care, and a very trifling expenditure is all that is wanted. I will take upon myself the rest, for my dead bride's sake. I will make no presents, I will give nothing gratis; what I advance will be only as a loan. When she has grown rich she shall repay me, so that I may be able to make others happy also. I will give you three thousand florins every month, that the young woman may be able to pay for the necessary tuition; but pray do not let her know that the money comes from a young man, or she might possibly refuse it. Use the name of my dead bride, Maria Darvai, to designate the mysterious benefactor; and, indeed, she does send it, even if it be from Heaven. I impose but one condition: she must remain virtuous. If I should ascertain the contrary, my patronage will instantly cease. Be so good, then, as to now accept from me the first monthly installment, and employ it conformably to my wishes; and, once more, I beg of you to say nothing about me. I ask it simply for the girl's sake. You know what an evil tongue the world has."

Dame Kramm took the money. Why, indeed, should she not have taken it? Anyone else, in her place, would have done the same thing. The secret benefactor had given her no cause for suspicion. He remained unknown to her, and insisted on remaining unknown; but he had forewarned her of the machinations of others, and acted himself as the guardian of defenseless virtue. What more could he do?

Madam Kramm took the money, I say, and secretly hired music and singing masters for Fanny, to whom alone she told anything about the matter. Of course, it was a mistake on her part not to have admitted Teresa into her confidence; but, perhaps, she surmised – and no doubt her surmise was correct – that that austere old lady would have incontinently pitched the money out of the window, with the remark that a virtuous girl ought, under no pretext whatever, to accept money which she has not honestly earned. And then, too, that other point – an artistic career? That would certainly have encountered vigorous opposition on the part of Teresa. Why, it was a subject which could not even be broached in her presence.

But the affair was no secret to Teresa, after all. From the very first she noticed the change that had taken place in Fanny's disposition. In the girl's mind the idea that she possessed a treasure which would raise her far above her competitors on the path of glory had already taken root. She had no longer any heart for the simple tasks, the humble pastimes, in which she had rejoiced heretofore. She no longer conversed as openly as before with the young journeyman. She would sit and brood for hours together, and after such broodings she would frequently say to her aunt that one day she would richly requite her for her labor and trouble.

How Teresa used to tremble at these words!

The girl was dreaming of riches. The Evil One had shown her the whole world and said, "All this I will give thee: worship me." And it never occurred to her to reply, "Get thee hence, Satan!"

The huntsman had laid his snare right well.

A feeling of gratitude often urged the girl to beg Dame Kramm to take her to this unknown benefactor, that she might express her burning thanks to her, and take further counsel of her. She also wished to tell her aunt of the unselfish kindness of which she was the object. These repeated entreaties drove the worthy old spinster at last into such a corner that she, one day, suddenly blurted out that this mysterious benefactor was not a woman, but a man, who wished to remain forever in the background.

This discovery at first terrified Fanny greatly; but subsequently it tickled her fancy all the more. Who could this man be who wished to make her happy without ever appearing to have a hand in it, and who was so anxious, so fearful, lest his honest gifts should cast the slightest slur on her reputation that he would not so much as allow his name to be mentioned?

What more natural, then, that the girl should draw, in her imagination, an ideal picture of her unknown defender? She represented him to herself as a tall, gloomy, pale-faced youth, who never smiled except when doing good, and his gentle look frequently followed her into her dreams.

Whenever she went for a walk in the streets and encountered young cavaliers there she would steal glances at them and say to herself, "I wonder if that one is he, or that?" But not one of them fitted into the place that she held vacant in her heart.

At last, one day, she did meet with a face with eyes and features and looks similar to the ideal of her dreams. Yes, she had pictured him just like that. Yes, this must be her secret tutelary deity, who did not want himself to be known to her. Yes, yes, this was the hero she was wont to dream of, with the beautiful blue eyes, the noble features, and the handsome figure!

Poor girl! That was not her benefactor. That was Rudolf Szentirmay, one of the noblest and most patriotic of the younger noblemen of Hungary, already happily married to the lady of his choice, the Countess Flora. He had no thought of her whatever. But she had got the idea into her head that he *was* her benefactor, and nobody could drive it out again.

She begged and prayed Dame Kramm repeatedly to show her, if even at a distance, the man who had so mysteriously taken charge of her fate. But when, at last, the good-natured lady had resolved to satisfy her desire, it was not in her power to do so; for Abellino no longer appeared in church on Sundays. Nay, he had not, as usual, given her the three thousand florins for the coming month personally, but had sent it to her in advance by an old lackey.

What fine calculation!

Dame Kramm could only believe that the unknown gentleman was determined at all hazards not to approach the girl, and that an effort would have to be made to find him. She therefore humbly asked the lackey whether it was not possible to catch a glimpse of his master in a public place, even if only at a distance and but for a moment.

The lackey replied that his master would be visible at the public session of the Upper House of the Diet on the morrow, and that he would be sitting opposite the fifth pillar.

Oh ho! So he was a great nobleman, then – one of the fathers of the Fatherland who are occupied day and night with the thought of how to make the realm and the nation happier! And still greater confidence arose in her heart. He to whom the destiny of the realm is entrusted could scarcely be a fribbler!

Dame Kramm informed Fanny that she would be able to see her unknown benefactor on the morrow in the Diet; that she could pick him out from among the throng without anybody being the wiser, and that the whole affair would only take a moment or two.

So Fanny went to the gallery of the Diet, where Dame Kramm pointed out to her her mysterious benefactor.

Fanny fell down from heaven forthwith. She had expected to see someone quite different. The face which Dame Kramm pointed out had no attraction for her. On the contrary, it filled her heart with a feeling of distrust and consternation. She hurried Dame Kramm away from the gallery, and carried her poor disillusioned heart home. There she took her aunt into her confidence, and revealed everything – her dreams, her ambitious longings, and her disappointment. She confessed that now she loved – yes, loved – a man who was her ideal, whose name she knew not, and she begged to be defended against herself, for she felt tottering on the edge of an abyss. She was mistress of her own heart no longer.

Next day, when Dame Kramm came for Fanny to take her to the singing-master, she found Teresa's house deserted. The doors and windows were shut, and the furniture had been removed. Nobody could tell where she had gone.

She had taken it into her head to flit in the night-time. Her rent she had deposited with the caretaker, unknown porters had removed everything, and she had left no address behind for kind inquirers.

Chapter VI

PAID IN FULL

And whither, then, had Fanny vanished so suddenly, so untraceably, with her aunt?

It was with a feeling of despair that Teresa had listened to her niece's confession. The girl had told her honestly that she was in love, in love body and soul, with all the fervor of her nature, with an ideal whom she had believed to be identical with the benefactor whose benefits she had one day meant to repay with a love stronger than death; and now, discovering that her secret patron was not he whom she had dreamed of, he whom once she had actually seen, and could never again forget, her heart was full of horror. She now felt that she had acted improperly in accepting money from that other man under any pretext whatsoever, for by so doing she had placed herself under an obligation, and she trembled at the thought of it, and feared to show her face in the street lest she should meet him. A distrust of that face grew up in her heart, and she shuddered at the idea that *that* man was thinking of her, perhaps. Ah, that was indeed a thorn in her soul! And the other, the ideal, there was no reason for thinking of him at all now; and yet cast him out of her heart again she could not. She knew him not, she knew not even his name, yet she felt that she would love him henceforth to the last moment of her life.

Poor Alexander!

So Teresa saw the labors of these many years all in ruins, and in the bitterness of her despair she brought herself to take a step which, at one time, the greatest misery would have been powerless to make her do – she went to Boltay, told him everything, and entreated him to defend, to protect the girl, for this was a case where female protection was insufficient.

Boltay accepted the guardianship with joy. The coarse-handed artisan's big face turned dark red with rage, and he did not go to his factory that day, lest he should pitch into someone; but he gave orders that Teresa's belongings should be carried into his house that very night. Alexander, who heard everything, became very sorrowful, but was doubly attentive to Fanny. It was a case of hopeless love all round. He loved the girl and the girl loved another, and both were very unhappy.

Everyone in the family knew the secret, but nobody said a word about it. The two old people often laid their heads together, and sometimes Alexander was admitted to this family council.

The good old people tried to find out the name of the unknown nobleman, as they wanted to send back to him the whole of the money that he had forwarded to Fanny. A debtor under such an obligation could not feel free. They wanted to pay him back as soon as possible, in just the same coin, florin for florin, three thousand down in one lump, lest anyone should say he did not get back exactly what he had given.

Yes, but how were they to find out his name? Fanny herself did not know it, and she would not have pointed him out in the street if she had had to die for it. Boltay took the trouble to frequent the coffee-houses and the meetings of the merchants, and listened with all his ears in case he might hear any talk of a shop-girl who had accepted earnest money from a rich gentleman as the price of her virtue. But there was no such talk anywhere. This was reassuring in one way, as tending to show that nobody knew anything about it, and therefore the trouble was not so great as it might have been; but the name, the name?

At last Abellino himself came to help them in their search.

Alexander used to go every Sunday to the church which Dame Kramm frequented, and, leaning against a column, would watch to see with whom the spinster conversed.

On the third Sunday Abellino appeared upon the scene also.

The worthy spinster told him the marvelous story of how Fanny and her aunt had unexpectedly disappeared one night without telling her whither they had gone, which was not very nice of them; but she suspected that they had flitted to Mr. Boltay's house, and Teresa had kept it quiet, no doubt, because there had been certain relations between her and Boltay in their younger days, or perhaps she went to see him because Boltay's adopted son wanted to marry Fanny. As for herself, she did not mean to trouble her head about them anymore.

Abellino bit his lips till the blood came, he was so angry. Could these Philistines smell a rat, then?

"What sort of an artisan is this Boltay?" he inquired of Dame Kramm.

"A carpenter," was the reply.

"A carpenter!" and in a moment Abellino had a new plan already in his head.

"Well, God be with you, madam!" said he; and, having no further use of her, he hurried out of the building, with Alexander at his heels. So at last, then, he had found the tempter in church.

Abellino marched rapidly to the corner of the street, with Alexander after him all the way. There he got into a carriage which was awaiting him. Alexander threw himself into a hackney-coach and trundled after him. He overtook him at the Michael Gate, and here the gentleman got out, while the carriage clattered into the courtyard. A big porter in bearskins was standing at the entrance.

"Who was that gentleman who went in there just now?" inquired Alexander of the porter.

"The Honorable Abellino Kárpáthy, of Kárpáth."

"Thank you."

So his name, then, was Abellino Kárpáthy! Alexander hastened home with his discovery.

On that day the whole family had such a vicious expression of countenance that everyone who came to see them was positively afraid of them.

The following day was a work-day, so everybody went about his own business. Mr. Boltay, with his sleeves tucked up, worked away with a will among his apprentices; but in vain was all the noise and racket – every tool he took up seemed to repeat one name continually in his ear, Kárpáthy, Kárpáthy!

Meanwhile Teresa and Fanny were sitting at one of the windows overlooking the street, occupied with needlework. They spoke not a word to each other; it was a way they had got into lately.

Suddenly a handsome carriage turned into the street, and stopped in front of Boltay's house.

Fanny, young girl as she was, peeped out of the window. The person sitting in the carriage was just about to get out. Terrified, all trembling, she drew back her head; her face was pale, her eyes looked feverish, her hands hung down by her side.

Presently the footsteps of the visitor were audible on the staircase. They heard someone outside making inquiries in an arrogant tone, and then the antechamber also was invaded. Would he presume, then, to come into their room also?

Fanny leaped from her chair, and, rushing despairingly to her aunt, knelt down before her and hid her face in her bosom, sobbing loudly.

"Don't be afraid! don't be afraid!" whispered Teresa; but every muscle in her body trembled. "I am here."

But at that moment the outer door also opened, and Mr. Boltay entered the antechamber in time to receive the newly arrived guest.

"Ah, good day!" cried that gentleman with friendly condescension, as he caught sight of the artisan. "Mr. Boltay, I presume? Ah, I thought so, my worthy fellow! You have a great reputation everywhere; they praise your workmanship to the skies, my good, honest fellow. Fresh from your workshop, eh? Well, that, now, is what I like to see. I hold industrious citizens in the highest esteem."

Mr. Boltay was not the sort of man to accept indiscriminate laudation from anyone, so he somewhat curtly interrupted this eulogistic flux of words.

"To whom have I the pleasure of speaking, pray? and what are your honor's commands?"

"I am Abellino Kárpáthy," replied the stranger.

It was only the armory behind him that prevented Mr. Boltay from falling flat. On such a surprise as this he had not counted.

The great gentleman did not condescend to observe the expression of the artisan's face, opining, as he no doubt did, that an artisan's face has no business to have any expression whatever; but he continued as follows: –

"I have come to you to bespeak an order for a whole *établissement,* and I have come personally because I hear that you draw very fine, artistic specimens of furniture."

"Sir, it is not I who draw, but my head apprentice, who lives at Paris."

"That doesn't matter. I have come myself, I say, that I may choose from these patterns, for I should like something particularly neat, and at the same time a simple middle-class production, quite in the middle-class style, you understand. And I'll tell you why. I am about to marry, and my future wife is a young girl, a citizen's daughter. Does it surprise you that I am going to make a middle-class girl my actual, lawful wife? Why do I do this? you may ask. Well, I have my own special reasons for it. I am a bit of an oddity, you must know. My father before me was an oddity, and so is every member of my family. Now, I had resolved to marry, and my sweetheart was a small tradesman's daughter, who used to sing beautifully in church."

Aha! the old story!

"And marry her I would have done," continued the fluent dandy, "but the poor thing died. I then determined that I would never marry until I had found another middle-class girl who should be just as beautiful, just as virtuous, as she was, and who could sing the 'Stabat Mater' just as nicely. And now I have been knocking about in the world these nine years without being able to find what I seek; for either she whom I found sang well and was not beautiful, or she was beautiful but not virtuous, or she was virtuous but could not sing, and therefore could not be mine. And now, sir, in this little town, I have actually found at last the very thing I seek – a girl who is beautiful, virtuous, and can sing; and her I am going to take to wife. So now I want your advice as to what sort of furniture I am to give her as wedding-present."

All these words were plainly audible in the adjoining room. Teresa involuntarily covered Fanny's head, which was hidden in her breast, as if she feared that this artless tale would win her credence, and so deceive her youthful mind, for young girls are so very credulous. Why, they even inquire of the flowers, "Does he love me, or does he not love me?" What will they not do, then, if anyone looks straight into their eyes?

Mr. Boltay had gradually pulled himself together during the course of this speech, and all the answer he gave when it was quite finished was to step to a writing-table, search diligently for something, and begin to write rapidly.

"I suppose he is looking up his patterns and making out his account," thought Abellino to himself; and meanwhile he began looking about him, wondering in which of the rooms this Philistine kept his little sugar-plum, and whether the girl had heard what he had just been saying.

The master-carpenter had by this time finished his scribbling and rummaging, and he now beckoned Kárpáthy to the table, and counted out before him a bundle of hundred-florin notes in six lots, together with four florins in twenty-kreutzer pieces, and thirty red copper kreutzers besides.

"Look here!" said he; "count. There are one, two, three, four, five, six thousand florins in notes, twenty florins in silver, and thirty copper pieces" – and he indicated the money with a wave of his hand.

"What the deuce does this Philistine mean by showing his dirty halfpence to me?" thought Abellino.

"And now be so good as to sit down and write me a receipt."

And he thrust into the young gentleman's hand a form of receipt for six thousand florins, with four florins thirty kreutzers interest, which amount was declared to have been a loan to the undermentioned "Miss Fanny Meyer," but was now discharged in full on the date indicated.

Abellino was immensely surprised. That these dull Philistines with fat, fleshy cheeks should see through his whole design – for this he was not in the least prepared. On the other hand, he could not have had a better opportunity for playing the injured gentleman.

With silent, grandseignorial, superciliousness he surveyed the artisan from head to foot, cracking his horse-whip once or twice by way of expressing that language was here superfluous, then he turned to go.

All this time there was deep silence in the room, and the trembling women in the adjoining chamber hung upon this silence with beating hearts, well aware what a storm of passion was brooding within it.

Boltay, perceiving that the dandy was preparing to withdraw, spoke once more in a voice all the more emphatic because of its visibly suppressed emotion.

"Take that money, sir, and subscribe that receipt, for I assure you you will be sorry if you do not."

Kárpáthy turned contemptuously on his heel and, banging the door to behind him, withdrew. Only when he was already sitting in his carriage did the thought occur to him – "Why did I not box that man's ears?" And yet, somehow, he could not help feeling very thankful that he had omitted doing so.

Abellino durst not recount this scene to his comrades. He felt that whatever turn he might give to the affair, the artisan could not fail to appear triumphant.

But the matter did not end here.

Master Boltay did not put back in his pocket the money lying on the table, but swept it up, sent it to the editor of the *Pressburger Zeitung*, and the next day the following notice was to be read in the columns of that respectable newspaper: "A pater-familias residing in this town presents through us six thousand florins thirty kreutzers to the civic hospital, which amount the honorable Abellino Kárpáthy was pleased to offer as a gift to the daughter of the donor in question, who, however, thought the sum more suitably applied to charitable purposes."

The affair made a great stir. The name advertised was well known in the highest circles. Some were amused, others amazed at the comic announcement. A couple of wits belonging to the opposition complimented Abellino in front of the green table in the name of suffering humanity. As for Abellino, he strutted up and down the town all day on the offchance of calling someone out; but as nobody gave him the opportunity, he and the other young elegants finally held a conference at the Meyers' house, and it was decided that a challenge should be sent to this advertising pater-familias.

"What, Master Boltay? The master-carpenter! Why, that would be a mere jest. Suppose he refused to come out? Why, then he shall be insulted all over the place till he is forced to leave Pressburg."

"But why?"

"Why, to frighten the Philistine, of course. Cow him, tame him, take all the pluck out of him. Why, there's not a more amiable fellow in the world than a thoroughly cowed and tamed foe, for he will always be trying to make up for his earlier misdeeds. And then? Why, then the enchanted maiden, her guardian dragon once subdued, will fall an easy prey."

As to whether it was becoming for a person of quality to fight a duel with an artisan who perhaps was no gentleman, or, if he was, had forfeited the respect due to a gentleman by engaging in manual labor in order to live thereby, such a question never once arose. We all know what these honest Philistines are, and how they shake with terror even when they have to fire off their own guns on the occasion of the solemn procession on Corpus Christi Day! He'll never accept the duel, but will give explanations and offer apologies, and we'll drink a toast together with the pretty little fugitive, as Hebe, pouring wine into our glasses and love into our hearts. That will be the most natural termination to such an affair.

So in the afternoon Abellino sent his seconds to the carpenter. The first was named Livius. In all affairs of honor his opinion was a veritable canon to the *jeunesse dorée* of the day. The other second, Conrad, was an herculean, athletic-looking fellow, whom, on that very account, every challenger tried to secure in those cases when a little judicious bullying might be necessary. This swash-buckler had, moreover, a most imposing countenance, and a voice capable of frightening even a bear back into its den.

These two estimable gentlemen then, having, *pro superabundante*, written out the challenge, in case the Philistine should deny himself or hide away from them, sought out the house of Mr. Boltay and made their way into his workroom.

The master was not at home. He had got into a cart very early in the morning with Teresa and Fanny, and from the nature of his arrangements there was reason to suspect that he would be absent for some time.

Alone in the room sat Alexander drawing patterns on a piece of paper fastened to the table.

The two gentlemen wished him *bon jour*. He responded in a similar strain, and, approaching, asked them what were their commands.

"Hem! young man!" began Conrad, in a thunderous voice, "is this Master Boltay's house?"

"It is," replied Alexander. There is surely no need for much growling, thought he.

Conrad, snorting violently, glanced round the room like one of those fairy-tale dragons that scents human flesh, and then roared –

"Let the master be sent for!"

"He is not at home."

Conrad glanced at Livius, murmuring, "Didn't I say so?" Whereupon he planted one fist on the table, flung the other behind his back, and thrusting forward his chest, regarded the youth with a savage stare.

"Then where *is* the master?"

"He did not so far honor me with his confidence as to tell me," replied Alexander, who had sufficient *sang-froid* to assume an expression of utter indifference.

"'Tis well," said Conrad, and he drew from an inner pocket a sealed letter. "What's your name, young man?"

Alexander began looking at his interlocutor with surprise and annoyance.

"Come, come!" said Conrad, "don't be afraid. I don't mean to frighten you. I only want to know your name."

"My name is Alexander Barna."

Conrad took a note of the fact in his pocketbook, and then ceremoniously holding the letter by the edge of the envelope, he said –

"Then listen to me, my dear *Mr.* Alexander Barna." He laid particular stress upon the word "Mr." that the lad might be duly sensible of the honor done to him thereby. "This letter tells your master –"

"You may give it me, sir. I am Mr. Boltay's confidential agent, and during his absence he has entrusted me with the transaction of all his business."

"Then take this letter," remarked Conrad in voice of thunder; and was on the point of adding something of a very imposing character, when Alexander completely disconcerted him by indiscreetly tearing open the letter addressed to his master, and approaching the window that he might be able to read it better.

"What are you doing?" cried both the seconds at the same time.

"I am authorized by Mr. Boltay during his absence to open all letters addressed to him, and discharge all debts or claims that may come in."

"But this is a purely personal matter which does not concern you."

Meanwhile Alexander had been glancing through the letter. He now came straight towards the two seconds.

"Gentlemen, I am at your service," he said.

"How! What business is it of yours?"

"Mr. Boltay has empowered me to satisfy any claim whatever that may be made upon him."

"Well, what then?"

"Why, then," said Alexander, smoothing out the letter with his hand, "I am ready to settle this account also whenever and wherever you please."

Conrad looked at Livius. "This lad seems disposed to joke with us," said he.

"I am not joking, gentlemen. Since yesterday I have become Mr. Boltay's partner, and all the obligations of the firm are binding upon both of us equally. The credit of the establishment demands it."

Conrad began to doubt whether the youth was in his right mind or knew how to read.

"Have you read what is in that letter?" he roared.

"Yes. It is a challenge."

"And what right have you to accept a challenge which is meant for someone else?"

"Because my partner, my foster-father, is not present, and everything, be it ill or good fortune, disaster or annoyance, which touches him, touches me equally. If he were present he would answer for himself. Now, however, he is away, and he has his own reasons, no doubt, for not telling me whither he has gone or how long he will be absent; and therefore, gentlemen, you must either take away this challenge or let me give you satisfaction."

Conrad drew Livius aside to consult him as to whether this was regular according to dueling rules. Livius recalled similar cases, but only as between gentlemen.

"Hark ye, Alexander Barna," said Conrad, "what you propose is only usual among gentlemen."

"Well, gentlemen, I am not the challenger; the challenge comes from you."

This was unanswerable.

Conrad folded his terrific arms over his immense chest, and roared this question almost down the young man's throat –

"Can you fight?"

Alexander could scarce refrain from smiling. "I can fight with either swords or pistols, gentlemen," said he; "'tis all one to me. Let me tell you that I was at Waterloo and there won a decoration."

"Who are your seconds?" asked Livius, coldly. "Give me the names of two of your acquaintances."

"My acquaintances are all peaceable working men, who would have nothing to do with so risky an affair. I might possibly shoot down the challenger, and in that case, I should not like to make exiles of two innocent men; but if you will be so good as to choose for me two seconds from your own honorable circle, I will accept them whoever they may be."

"We will let you know the time and place of the meeting at once," said Livius; and with that they took up their hats and withdrew.

"It seems to me," said Livius to Conrad, as they went away, "that that young fellow has as stout a heart as any gentleman could have."

"We'll see what he's made of early tomorrow morning," returned the other.

That same evening a gorgeous silver-laced heyduke might have been seen looking for Master Boltay's workshop, and making inquiries for Alexander Barna. There was a letter in his hand.

"Be so good as to tell me," said the heyduke in a courteous voice (a sure sign that he was accustomed to polite treatment from his superiors), "whether you used to work in Monsieur Gaudehoux's *atelier* at Paris?"

"Yes, I did."

"And three years ago you met three Hungarian gentlemen in the Ermenouville Forest, did you not?"

"Yes, I did meet them," replied Alexander, surprised that anybody should bear in mind such *minutiæ* of his past life.

"Then this letter will be meant for you," said the heyduke, delivering the letter. "Be so good as to read it. I await a reply."

Alexander broke open the letter, and, as was his wont, looked first of all at the signature. A cry of astonishment burst from his lips. There stood two names written one beneath the other which every Hungarian, who accounted himself a good patriot and a man of honor and enlightenment, held in the highest veneration — Rudolf and Michael.

What could such as they have to write to a poor orphan like him, they the great men, the idols of the nation, the popular heroes of the day, to a poor unknown artisan like him?

The letter said —

"You worthy young man, you have acted quite rightly. In your place anyone of us would have done the same thing. If you will accept our assistance, for old acquaintance sake, we are ready to place our service as gentlemen at your disposal."

Alexander folded up the letter with great satisfaction. He had a vivid recollection of the two young noblemen who had met him by accident at Paris, and treated him as a friend.

"I am much honored by their lordships' offer," said he, turning to the heyduke, "and will accept it in any case."

The messenger respectfully bowed and withdrew.

In half an hour's time Rudolf and Michael appeared, and the former said that a written authorization on Alexander's part was necessary, lest Conrad and Livius should give him seconds that he did not like.

"Then there are others, also, who would offer their assistance?"

"Oh, no end to them! There is quite a competition among these young lions as to which of them shall be present at the tragicomedy, as they call it."

"It will not be a tragicomedy; I can tell them that."

"That is principally what induced us to offer you our services. We do not see any particular glory in hounding men on against each other, and making them fight duels which our age, unfortunately, considers such an excellent pastime. On the other hand, we regard it as our duty as gentlemen to offer you our assistance, and thereby put a stop to what might become a senseless and insulting jest, which if our feather-brained friends had their way might even have a very serious termination."

Alexander thanked them for their kindness, and early next morning the two young men appeared again in a hired coach. Alexander was ready waiting for them. He had only to seal a few letters which he had written overnight, one to his master, reporting in what state he had left the business, and the other to Fanny, begging her to do him the favor to accept as his heir the little property which his thrift had accumulated.

These letters, enclosed in a third envelope, he gave to the caretaker of the house, with the request that if he, Alexander, did not return by twelve o'clock, the envelope was to be opened and the documents inside forwarded to their respective addresses. Then he got into the carriage where Rudolf and Michael were awaiting him; a surgeon followed them in another carriage.

The youths were surprised to observe that the young artisan's face showed no signs of anxiety or trouble, nay, he bore himself as calmly and nonchalantly as if he were used to such situations.

It was still very early when they crossed the bridge leading into the park, where a freshly erected tent was standing. The youths then told the coachman to stop, and asked Alexander whether he would not like a little breakfast first of all.

"No, thank you," he replied. "People might say I wanted something to put pluck into me. Let us say afterwards – if an afterwards there be!" he added lightly, and in the best of humors.

They proceeded onwards through the wood to the spot agreed upon, and they had not waited more than a few moments before their antagonists also arrived upon the ground.

It was a cloudy, gloomy morning, and there was an expression of gloomy *sang-froid* on the faces of the young men which suited very well with the morning.

The enemy, smiling, and with nonchalant haughtiness, came strolling arm in arm through the silver poplar woods – Abellino, the large-limbed Conrad, and Livius. A surgeon and a servant brought up the rear.

The four seconds went apart and conversed together in a low voice; they were evidently arranging the details of the affair. They soon came to an agreement. The extreme retiring distance was fixed at five-and-forty paces, the barriers at five-and-twenty.

During this negotiation, Abellino produced a pair of good flint-locked Schneller pistols, and exhibited his skill before the company. He ordered his lackey to throw linden leaves up into the air in front of him, and riddled them with bullets three times running. This he did simply to fill the adversary with terror. Michael, fathoming his object, whispered confidentially in the young artisan's ear –

"We are not going to fire with those pistols, but with ours, which are quite new, and it will not be so easy to show off with them."

Alexander smiled bitterly. "It is all one to me. My life is no more precious to me than those linden leaves."

All the necessary formalities having been arranged, the seconds attempted to reconcile the combatants. Abellino thereupon offered to withdraw his challenge under two conditions: (1) If the challenged, in the name of the firm he was defending, publicly declared that there was no intention to insult in the advertisement complained of, and (2) if Mr. Boltay caused to be inserted in the same newspaper in which the offensive advertisement had appeared a notification to the effect that Kárpáthy had given the amount in question to the girl's guardian from purely artistic motives of the noblest description.

Alexander's seconds laid these conditions before him.

He immediately sent one of them back. Did they wish to insult him? He meant in the plainest, most unmistakable manner, and with the fullest knowledge of what he was doing, to take all the responsibility of the alleged insult on his own shoulders, and he had nothing to retract.

Ah! he had far better reasons for fighting than the mere love of swagger. There was nothing for it, therefore, but to fight.

Conrad thereupon turned towards the surgeon whom they had brought with them, and roared in a stentorian voice –

"Have you your instruments with you? Then, mind you hold them in readiness. There will not be much need of blood-letting, I fancy. What! not brought your bone-saw with you, eh? My friend, your thoughtlessness is disgraceful! It happens in duels sometimes that a man is not shot through the head or the heart straight off; but the bullet may hit him in the arm or leg, and then if the bone is injured and he has to wait for an amputation till he is carried into town erysipelas may set in."

"Take your places, gentlemen! take your places!" shouted Rudolf, putting an end to this cruel prolonging of the agony.

Abellino thereupon pierced his fourth linden leaf at twenty-five paces.

"Those pistols must be put aside, as they are evidently old acquaintances," said Rudolf. "Mine are new."

"We agree," replied Conrad; "only you must take care," he continued, turning towards Abellino, "that when you prepare to take aim you do not lower your arm from your shoulder downwards, but raise it from your hip gradually upwards, so that if you aim at the chest, and the pistol kicks downwards, you may be able to hit him in the stomach, but if it kicks upwards you may hit him in the skull."

Meanwhile they were loading the pistols, dropping the bullets into the barrels in everyone's sight. The challenged party then chose one of them.

Then the antagonists were placed at the two extremities of the ground, and the barriers were indicated by white pocket-handkerchiefs.

The seconds stepped aside, forming two separate groups. Conrad placed himself behind a huge poplar, capable of shielding even his bulky frame.

A clapping of hands, thrice repeated, was the signal for the opponents to advance.

Alexander remained standing in his place for some seconds, holding his pistol in his hand pointed downwards. A cold calmness was written on his face – regret you might even have called it, were not regret under such circumstances somewhat akin to cowardice. Abellino, holding himself sideways, advanced with little mincing steps, frequently pointing his pistol as if he were on the point of firing. He meant to torture his adversary by holding him in suspense as long as possible without firing. And you should have seen the malicious smile, the expression of teasing, provoking scorn, with which Abellino tried to throw his adversary into confusion. Why, a man who can pierce a falling leaf with a bullet, may be pretty sure of his man in a duel!

"Poor young fellow!" sighed Rudolph to himself, while his fellow-second was just about to call out to Abellino that such tricks were not permissible in encounters between gentlemen, when Alexander suddenly started from his place and walked with firm, unfaltering steps right up to his barrier, there stopped, raised his pistol, and took aim. His eyes sparkled with a strange fire, and his hand was perfectly steady.

This was an unheard-of audacity. Before the first shot it is most unusual for anyone to walk right up to his own barrier, for, in case of ill luck, he gives his adversary a great advantage. This boldness, however, had the effect of making Abellino stop short six paces from his own barrier, and move away his thumb from the trigger of his pistol, where he had hitherto held it.

What happened the next moment nobody was able to exactly explain.

A report rang out, and half a minute afterwards another. The seconds hastened to the spot, and found Alexander standing erect in his place; but Abellino had turned right round, and his hand was over his left ear. The surgeons came running up with the others.

"Are you wounded?" they asked Abellino.

"No, no!" said he, keeping one hand continually over his ear. "Deuce take that bullet, it flew so damned close to my ear that it has almost made me deaf. I can't hear a word of what I am saying. Curse the bullet! I would much rather that it had gone through my ribs."

"I wish it had with all my soul!" roared Conrad, who now came rushing up. "You are a damned fool, for you shot me instead of your opponent! Look, gentlemen! You see that tree by which I was standing? Well, the bullet burrowed right into it. What! fire at your own seconds? Do you call that discretion? If that tree had not been there, I should have been as dead as a ducat – as dead as a ducat, I say!"

So this is what must have happened. At the very moment when Alexander's bullet whizzed past Kárpáthy's ear he must have been so startled by the shock as to have involuntarily wheeled round and clapped one hand to his ear, and the same instant the loaded pistol in his other hand must have gone off sideways. At any rate, Kárpáthy was found standing, after the shot was fired, *with his back to his opponent.*

He himself heard none of Conrad's reproaches, and the blood slowly began to trickle in little drops from his ear. He did not show it otherwise, but from the paleness of his face it was plain that he was suffering torments. The doctors whispered, too, that the membrane of the ear was ruptured, and that all his life long he would be hard of hearing.

Kárpáthy had to be conducted to his carriage. But for his sufferings he would have sworn. He would much rather have had a bullet in his lungs.

Rudolf and Michael then approached the seconds of the opposite party, and asked whether they considered the satisfaction given sufficient.

Livius admitted that everything was now perfectly in order, but Conrad declared that he was so completely satisfied with this duel that he would deserve to be called thief and robber if ever he took part in another as long as he lived.

"Then be so good, gentlemen, as to receipt this bill," said Alexander, turning to the seconds, and producing the written challenge which they had addressed to his master. "Kindly write at the bottom of it, 'Discharged in full.'"

The seconds laughed immensely at the idea, and, procuring a pen and ink from the first shanty they came to, they duly wrote at the bottom of the challenge the words, "Paid in full."

The young man thereupon thrust the attested document into his pocket, thanked his own seconds for their kind services, and returned on foot to town.

Chapter VII

THE NABOB'S BIRTHDAY

Squire John's birthday was approaching, and a famous, notable day it always was for the whole county of Szabolcs. The clergymen in all the surrounding villages ordered new frock-coats from Debreczin or Nagy-Kun-Madaras a month beforehand, at the same time directing the tailors to make the pockets "extra large;" the Lemberg firework-makers collected hay and straw far and wide for the rockets; the students of Debreczin learnt nice congratulatory odes, and set fine old folk-ballads to music; the gypsy *primas* bought up all the resin in the shops he could lay his hands on, and the Strolling Players' Society began, in secret, to plan how they could best escape from Nyiregyháza.*

In more distinguished circles, where prudent housewives are wont to take their unfortunate husbands in hand, and exercise towards them that office which guardian angels perform in heaven, and police-constables perform on earth, the advent of Squire John's birthday festival was the signal for domestic storms. The festival itself used to last for a week. On the first day thereof every well-ordered female being fled from the place, and on the last day thereof those of the nobler masculine race who had remained behind, came tottering home – some half-dead, others wholly drunk, and all of them more or less battered and penniless.

Squire John himself was so much accustomed to the delights of that day, that he would have considered the year lost in which he did not duly celebrate it; and any of his acquaintances who should have neglected to appear before him on the day itself would have been thenceforth regarded by him as his mortal enemies. Death was regarded as the one legitimate excuse.

The festivities were this year to be celebrated at the Castle of Kárpátfalva, Squire John's favorite residence, where nobody ever lived but his cronies, his servants, and his dogs; and he obtained special permission from his Highness the Palatine to absent himself for a fortnight from

* The county town, where they had a standing engagement.

his legislative duties at Pressburg, in order that, as a good host, he might devote himself entirely to his guests.

As the day approached, an unwonted piety used to take possession of Squire John. The buffoons and the peasant wenches were excluded from the castle, and his reverence the village priest took their place, and was closeted long and frequently with the squire; the dogs and the bears were locked out of the courtyard, that they might not, as usual, tear approaching mendicants to pieces; and the Nabob and all his retainers went to church to partake of the sacrament, the former vowing on his knees before the altar that he would mark the day by giving all his enemies the right hand of fellowship and forgiveness. Then came the regulation interview between the Nabob and his steward, Mr. Peter Varga, who was such a fool that he not only did not know how to steal, but was by no means willing to even receive presents except for services rendered. Anybody else in his place would long since have become a millionaire; but he had not got much beyond fastening a pair of silver spurs in his Kordovan leather boots, and making use of a ramshackle old *calèche,* to which he attached two horses, trained by his own hand ever since they were colts. This, moreover, was only when he wanted to cut a figure.

And now, too, we see him descending from this venerable conveyance. He forbears to drive right in, lest the cranky wheels of his carriage should cut up the beautiful round pebbles with which the courtyard is covered.

The inside of the carriage was chock-full of longish tied-up bundles of documents, which Mr. Peter first of all crammed into the arms of the two heydukes hastening to meet him, and sent on before him, whilst he, picking his way along, with his spurred feet at a respectable distance from each other, straddled leisurely into the presence of Master Jock, who was awaiting him in the office of the family archives, whose gigantic whitewashed and gilded coffers, in their worm-eaten cases, rose up to the ceiling, filled with the mummies of old deeds and discharged accounts, which, for a long series of years, had been disturbed by nobody except an ostracized mouse or two; and what accursed appetite or hereditary perversity constrained even them to feed upon such meager fare, when the granaries and bacon-larders were in such tempting proximity, Heaven only knows.

Master Jock, on perceiving the approaching steward, leaned forward in his armchair, and held out his hand. Peter, however, instead of advancing straight towards the hand extended towards him, retreated backwards all round the large oak table, to avoid the discourtesy of approaching his honor from the left hand; and, even when he got where he thought he ought to be, he remained standing before him, at three paces' distance, and bowed with deep respect.

"Come, come, man! Draw nearer!" cried the confidential heyduke Palko,* who was also present. "Don't you see that his honor has been holding out his front paw forever so long?"

"Crying your pardon," said the worthy steward, drawing his hands away, "I am not worthy of so much honor!"

And not for the whole world could he have been brought to extend his hand towards Master Jock, to whom he alone of all the world gave his proper title. It was also impossible to ever get him to sit down by the side of his honor. Palko had to hold him down in a chair by main force, but he would always jump up again, and remain standing before his master as soon as the pressure was removed.

And, indeed, his honor, the steward, and the heyduke made up an odd-looking trio between them. Kárpáthy's face, at such moments, was always unusually serene, his great bald forehead shone like the cupola of a temple, the scanty remains of his grey hair curled round his forehead and the nape of his neck in silvery wisps; he was shaved beautifully smooth, save for a well-kept moustache curling elegantly upwards at both ends; the fiery redness of his eyes had vanished, and there was no longer any trace of deforming wrinkles.

Opposite him stood the worthy steward, with the old-fashioned, scrupulously obsequious, and infallibly respectful homage of a former generation writ large on every feature of his bronzed countenance. His moustache was clipped close to save trouble, but all the more care had he bestowed upon his marvelous powdered top-knot – itself a survival – which respectable elevation the worthy fellow revealed to the light of day, neatly bound up with a black ribbon. Behind him stands the old heyduke Palko in a laced dolman. He is just as old as they are. All three have grown up together, all three have grown old together; and now, too, Palko is as familiar with his honor as he used to be in the days when they played and fought together in the courtyard. The old fellow's head is grey now, but not a hair of it has he lost, and its flowing abundance is brushed backwards and kept in its place by a circular comb; his moustache is more pointed than a shoemaker's awl, and waxed to a fearful extent at both ends; his features are so simple that a skillful artist could have hit them off in three strokes, only the coloring would have given him something to think about, for it is a little difficult to paint-in blood-red on scarlet.

* *I.e.*, Little Paul.

"Would his honor," said Peter, standing by the table, "be graciously pleased to cast his eyes over these accounts? I have made so bold as to most humbly make out a brief summary thereof, that his honor may find the examination a little easier." And with that he beckoned to Palko to put down the documents.

The latter venomously banged down the whole bundle on the table, but he could not refrain from observing, "What a shame to spoil such a lot of nice clean paper by scribbling on it!"

"You speak like a fool," growled Master Jock.

"It would be all the same, so far as your honor is concerned, if they put blank paper before your honor; for they don't pay the slightest attention to what your honor says. It is not enough to know that they *do* rob you; I should also like to know how much they rob you of."

"Come, come, my heart's best son, what do you mean by talking to your master like that? Look now! you shall look through all the accounts along with me, from beginning to end, so just stand behind my chair, and hold your tongue."

"I am ready to eat up all that your honor looks through," murmured the old servant to himself.

Thereupon Master Jock, with commendable determination, extended his hand towards the top-most bundle lying before him, which contained the accounts of his agent János Kárláts, and began fumbling about with it till he arrived at the conviction that he could make neither head nor tail of it, whereupon he handed it back to Mr. Peter, who immediately found the schedule he was looking for.

"This is a schedule of the income and expenditure of your Kakadi estate."

And now, reader, let us listen. You may find it a trifle tedious, perhaps, but you could not have a better opportunity of seeing how the estates of the Nabob were administered.

"With your honor's gracious permission, I would beg to call your attention to a few notes in the margin concerning the exact position of affairs, if your honor will listen to them."

Master Jock intimated that he would undertake to do as much as that.

"To begin, then, the Kakadi estate this year yielded twelve thousand bushels of pure wheat, consequently, the richest soil scarcely produced sufficient grain to pay for the expense of cultivating it."

"It was a bad year, you know," objected Master Jock. "The corn was leveled with the ground by hailstorms in the spring, and there was so much rain afterwards that it sprouted in the stack."

"That, indeed, is what your agent said," returned Mr. Peter; "but he could have insured against hail at Pressburg, and there's such an enormously big barn on the estate, that the whole crop could have been safely housed, and then there would have been no fear of its sprouting."

"Very well, Master Peter, go on! Another time things shall be different; you may rely upon me for that."

"The twelve thousand bushels of corn were sold at nine florins the bushel to a corn-dealer of Raab, I see, thus making a total of one hundred and eight thousand florins, although I notice from the newspapers that good wheat was selling all the time at Pest at twelve florins the bushel, and the corn might easily have been transported thither, for, owing to the inundations, the oxen had no work to do."

"Yes; but those very inundations carried away the bridge, so that it was impossible to cross the Theiss."

"It was a pity, truly, that the water carried away the bridge, but if the dyke had been kept in proper repair, the water would not have got at the bridge."

"Never mind; rely upon me in the future. Go on!"

"The millet-seed, it is said, got musty from waiting too long for purchasers, so that we could only get eight thousand florins for it. Now, that is a misstatement. I know as a fact that there was no rain just then; but the agent, in order that he might attend a christening, stacked the crop so hastily that it got black and sour from heat."

"No, really! And would you, as a Christian man, I ask, have the agent postpone the baptism of his son even for the sake of all the millet-seed in the world? Leave that to me, and go on!"

"The water carried away the hay because, just in the middle of harvest-time, your honor required the services of every man capable of holding a hay-fork at a big hunt. Otherwise nice large sums would, as usual, have been entered to your honor's credit under this item."

"Well, then, it is simply my fault this time; the poor fellows are not to blame. Rely upon me in the future."

"On that account, however, the receipts are increased by a new item, to wit, the hides of the sheep and oxen, which fell dead in heaps from want of fodder."

"Ah, you see it is an ill wind that brings nobody any good."

"On the other hand, our receipts are less, so far as the item of wool is concerned, which usually is considerable."

"Yes, I know, the price was low; there was scarce any demand for it."

"Moreover –"

"Let that be, Peter. We know that you are a worthy, honest man, and that everything is in order. What is that other bundle there?"

"That is the account of Taddeus Kajáput, the overseer of the Nyilasi estate."

"Ah! that is generally interesting reading. Any fresh discoveries?"

The gentleman in question was an enterprising soul, who had started model farming on the estate committed to his care, but this model farming cost infinitely more than it brought in. Moreover, amongst other things he had started glass-works, sugar-works, a silk-factory, a post office, laid down fir plantations in drift-sand, not to mention many other wonderful things, all of which had come to grief.

"So that is what comes of your scientific gentlemen taking up economical questions," observed Master Jock, sententiously, when he had laughed heartily over each separate item.

"I humbly crave your honor's pardon," said Peter, "but it is not the scientific but the semi-scientific who do the mischief. Science is one of those poisons of which a good deal cures but a little kills."

"Well, well, let us go on with the rest. What is that slender little bundle over there?"

"That is the report of the lessee of the opal mines. He has paid the four thousand florins rent in precious stones, which we could have bought in the market for a thousand florins, if we had paid cash for them."

"But what is the poor man to do? He must live. I know he has children to support."

"But there was a merchant here from Galicia a little time ago who looked at the mine and offered twenty thousand florins rent for it straight off."

"What? Would you have me give the mine to a man from Galicia – to a foreigner? Not if he paid me for it with the stars of heaven! Let us stick by the old agreement. What is that other bundle?"

"That is the account of the Talpadi Forest."

"The Talpadi Forest! Why, it is now twelve years since I have seen any accounts at all from that quarter. Don't you recollect how you and I were out coursing a little time ago, and the rain overtook us? It doesn't matter, said I. We must be near my Talpadi forest; let us gallop thither and shelter till the storm has blown over. So we galloped thither in hot haste, and when we got there not a trace of the forest was to be seen. At last I asked a maize-reaper I fell in with, where on earth the Talpadi forest was? Over there, said he, pointing to a spot where some fifty birch trees were withering in the sand like so many broomsticks, all set nicely in a row. And that, if you please, was the Talpadi forest which I had planted at a very great cost! You had better tell the man to plant out a few more broomsticks if he wants me to see my forest in the future."

"This, again, is the account of the miller of Tarisa. He always mixes bran with his meal."

"Let him alone; he has a pretty wife."

"Pretty, but bad, your honor."

Upon this moral observation, Master Jock thought fit to make the following philosophical commentary: –

"My friend, bad women are a necessity in this world. For inasmuch as there are dissolute men, it is needful that there should be dissolute women also, for otherwise the dissolute men would of necessity cast their eyes upon the virtuous women. You just leave that to me."

"Yes, you leave the wife of the miller of Tarisa to his honor," observed Paul, from behind his master's chair.

"What, sir, you presume to speak again, eh?"

"I? I never said a word."

"Come, then, Peter, let us make an end of these accounts quickly. Surely, there's no need of so much fussing. What else is there?"

"Your honor's donations and charities."

"Don't undo them. You need only tell me which are paid. Are there any fresh claims upon us?"

"Yes. The college at A——— has not received its annual gift."

"It did not get it because it did not send in a petition on my birthday last year."

"Then if it sends the petition this year you will give the donation, I suppose?"

"Yes, and for last year too."

"There are, besides, a heap of petitions and circulars."

"What for?"

"This is an invitation to subscribe to the foundation of a Hungarian learned society."

"Not a farthing will I give. The kingdom was happy enough till the pedants got into it. We learn quite enough at college."

"Here is the specimen-sheet of a newspaper about to be started."

"Newspaper! – a parcel of lies! I'll not spoil my den with that rubbish, I warrant you."

"Here is a proposal to found a permanent Hungarian theater at Buda-Pest."

"Whoever wants play-acting can come here to me. There's a theater here and lots to eat, and they can stay, if they like, all their days."

"Here is a suggestion for bettering the position of the National Museum."

"I'll wager I have far better collections here than there are in the National Museum."

And this was the way in which the Hungarian magnate examined his accounts every year.

When the worthy steward had withdrawn, the Nabob sent for his *fiskal,* or family lawyer, who found him looking out of the window, motionless, with his hands behind his back.

The *fiskal* stood and waited for his master to turn round. He waited a good half-hour, but the Nabob turned round at last, and said to his man of business, "Pray sit down, sir, and write."

An unusual embarrassment was observable in the Nabob's voice, which would certainly have surprised anybody else but the *fiskal.*

"My dear younger brother," old Kárpáthy began to dictate, "inasmuch as you are living at present in this realm, and I do not wish the name of Kárpáthy to be slighted on this particular day when I have made peace with all who ever angered me, therefore I now, as becometh a kinsman, offer my hand to you also, my younger brother,* in the hope that you will not reject it; and I, at the same time, send you, my younger brother, two hundred thousand florins, which you shall receive from me, so long as I live, from year to year. And I hope that henceforth we shall continue to be good kinsmen."

The old man's eyes were wet while he recited these words, and if a more sympathetic man than the *fiskal* had been present, there might have been something like a tender scene.

"Wrap it up and write on the outside: To the Honorable Bélá Kárpáthy of Kárpát, at Pressburg. A stable lad must mount a horse at once, and deliver this letter personally."

Then he gave a great sigh of relief, as if two hundred thousand stones had been lifted from his heart with these two hundred thousand florins. He had never felt so happy as he was at that moment.

How Abellino received this noble disposition to stretch out the right hand of fellowship and forgiveness, we shall see presently.

Master Jock could scarce await the dawn of St. John Baptist's Day; he was as delighted as a child who knows that some long-wished-for amusement awaits him. He was awakened long before sunrise by the baying of the dogs and the rattling of the baggage-wagons into the courtyard. The huntsmen were coming back from the forest with newly shot game; over the sides of the lofty wains the horned heads of the noble antlered stags bobbed up and down; heaps of pheasants were carried between two poles; well-fattened heath fowl were slung over the

* *Öcse,* a familiar and affectionate salutation from an elder to a younger kinsman.

shoulders of the beaters. The cook came forth to meet them in his white *kantus*, and tapped row after row of the fat game, his face beaming with satisfaction all the time. Master Jock himself was looking down from the latticed-window into the courtyard; even then the day had only just begun to dawn, and the eastern curtain of the sky was aflame with purple, pink, carmine, and saffron hues. The whole plain around was calm and still; and silver mists lay here and there over the fields like fairy lakes.

And now the Nabob lay down for another little snatch of slumber. We know, of course, that early morning dreams are the sweetest. And he dreamt that he was speaking to his eagerly desired nephew Bélá, sitting beside him, and drinking the loving cup with him; and so it came about that the sun was already high in the heavens when Palko shook him out of his slumbers by bawling in his ear: "Get up! Here are your boots!"

Master Jock leaped out of his bed with the vigor of a sprightly lad. The first question he asked was: "Has anyone come?"

"As many as muck," replied the old servant; thereby showing *his* appreciation of the arrivals.

"Is Mike Kis here?" continued Master Jock, as he drew on his boots.

"He was the first of all. His father could not have been a gentleman; no gentleman could have had a son who is up and about two hours after dawn."

"Who else is here?"

"There's Mike Horhi. No sooner had he got to the door than he suddenly recollected that he had left his tobacco-pouch in the inn at Szabadka, and would have gone back for it had I not torn him out of the carriage by force."

"The fool! And who else is there?"

"All the good birds of the order of gentleman have already appeared. Friczi Kalotai is also here, in his own conveyance. I wonder where he stole it?"

"But you're as big a fool as he, Palko. Anymore?"

"More! – more! There's no end to them, of course. How do you suppose I can carry the names of all of them in my head? Come, and look at them yourself; you'll soon have your fill of 'em, I warrant."

Meanwhile the trusty heyduke had dressed his master, brushed him down and smoothed him out, till there was not a spot or wrinkle to be seen on any portion of his attire.

"But is there not some other, some strange, unusual guest, the sort of man, I mean, who is not in the habit of visiting me? Eh?"

Palko regarded his master for a moment with wide-open mouth and eyes, not knowing what to answer.

"I want to know," continued Kárpáthy, in a solemn voice, "whether my little brother Bélá is here?"

Palko made a wry face at these words, and dropped the velvet brush with which he was just preparing to smooth out the collar of his master's *mente.*

"What! that weather-cock?"

"Come, come! None of that! Don't you know that a Kárpáthy should always be spoken of respectfully?"

"What!" cried Palko, "the man who insulted your honor so grossly?"

"What business is it of yours?"

"Oh, no business of mine, of course, not a bit! I am only a good-for-nothing old heyduke. What right have I to poke my nose into your honor's affairs? Make friends with him again, by all means! What do I care. Kiss and hug each other if you like, I don't care. It was not me but your honor whom the worthy man insulted, and if your honor likes that, why, be it so – that's all!"

"Come, come, don't make a fool of yourself, Palko," said Master Jock, more jocosely. "Have the comedians arrived?"

"I should think they had. There's that Lokodi with four others. He himself plays the heroic parts; a spindle-shanked, barber's apprentice sort of fellow, takes the aged father parts; and there's a matron, well advanced in years, who acts the young missies. They are now making ready to give a representation this evening. When your honors are all dining in the Large Room they are going to act the *Marriage of Dobozy* in twelve tableaux, to the accompaniment of Greek fire, in the front room."

"But why in the front room, and not rather in the theater?"

"It is too small."

"But there are only five of them."

"True; but all the heydukes we have must be there too, either as Turks or Hungarians. We have already brought down all the costumes and weapons from our museum of antiquities. The students meanwhile will recite the history of Dobozy; the poet Gyárfás is at this moment writing the verses for it, and the chief cantor is composing the music. It will be fine!"

The old fellow took as much delight in the comedy as any child.

Meanwhile he had finished dressing Master Jock – brushed and combed his hair, pared his nails, shaved him, tied his cravat, and buttoned his coat *comme il faut.*

"And now, sir, you may appear before your fellow-men."

"Where's my pipe?"

"Pipe! Tut-tut! Don't you know that, first of all, you must go to church to pray? nobody smokes till after that."

"You are right. But why don't they ring the bell?"

"Wait! I must first tell the priest that your honor is up."

"And there's another thing you must tell him – a sausage should be long, a sermon short."

"I know," said Palko; and off he trotted to the priest, whose chief defect and peculiarity consisted not in delivering long sermons, but rather in the rebuking of Master Jock roundly, in the name of the Lord, on this the one occasion in the whole year when he met him face to face, to the intense delight of the assembled guests, who kept up the joke afterwards till dinner-time. A particular Providence, however, delivered Master Jock from this bitter jest on this occasion, inasmuch as the reverend gentleman had suddenly fallen so ill that he could not perform his duties.

"The dean is here," added Palko, after communicating the sad intelligence.

"Who never knows when to leave off spouting," commented Master Jock. "If he gets hold of us, we must make up our minds to have dinner at supper-time; and he so bombards the ears of God with my praises that even I am ashamed. Let the *supplikans* complete the service."

The *supplikans*, be it explained, was a five years' student (counting not from his birth, of course, but from the beginning of his academical course) – a student *togatus*, as they called it, who ever since he had been immured at college had never set eyes upon a human being. We can, therefore, picture the terror of the worthy youth when he was informed that, within a quarter of an hour, he must preach an edifying discourse for the special benefit of a whole assembly of genteel backsliders.

He would very much have liked to have crawled away into some hole, but they kept much too good an eye upon him for that, and, perceiving his fear and affliction, the unprincipled mob played all sorts of devilries upon him. They sewed his pocket-handkerchief fast to the pocket of his toga, so that he could not pull it out when his nose required its help; they made him believe that the gypsy Vidra was the cantor; and finally contrived to substitute a book on veterinary surgery for his prayer-book.

The poor *supplikans*, when he perceived that he had carried a cattle-book into the pulpit, was so dumfounded that he could not even remember with what words the "Our Father" began, so he descended from the preaching-stool again without uttering a word. They had, therefore, to fall back upon the dean, after all; but they bound him down not to preach, but only to pray; and pray he did – for an hour and a half at least. The right reverend gentleman heaped so many blessings upon the Kárpáthy family and all its members, male and female, *in ascendenti et descendenti,* both in this world and the next, that, whether they lived or died, no very serious misfortune could possibly befall any of them.

All the guests were present at this pious ceremony, for Master Jock made it a point to speak to nobody on his birthday till he had first lifted up his soul to God, and on such occasions there was not a trace on his countenance of any of the feelings that moved him so strongly on ordinary days. When he knelt down to pray, a deep, unaffected devotion was legible in every feature; and when he heard the recapitulation of his merits, he cast down his eyes as if he considered all that he had done in his life so far but a small matter compared with what he might and must do in the future. "God grant me but one more year over and above the many He has already bestowed upon me," he sighed, "and I will make up for my neglect of the rest." But could he reckon upon another year being granted him? Was he sure of another month, or another day, or even of the morrow?

Deeply affected, he quitted the chapel, and it was only the congratulations of his friends that restored him to his usual self.

Master Jock's unusual emotion did not interfere one jot with the good humor of the waggish company, who laughed and joked all the way from the church to the castle, some repairing thither on horseback, and some on foot. Ordinarily, Master Jock would have been much diverted by their practical jokes, but now he only shook his head at them. Mike Horhi devised every conceivable sort of joke capable of making him roar with laughter. He filched the clergyman's book; he rubbed pitch on the cantor's seat, that he might stick fast there; he substituted gunpowder for poppy-meal in the kitchen, and filled the powder-flasks of the heydukes with poppy-meal instead of gunpowder, so that when they prepared to fire salvoes in honor of their master, on his return from chapel, not a gun would go off, while the poppy-cakes intended for the banquet all exploded on the hearth. But Master Jock not only did not laugh at these funny things, but actually took Miska Horhi to task for making such a blockhead of himself, and bade him divert himself more decently in future. He also made the poet show him beforehand the verses he was to recite at table, in case they might contain any frivolous or improper expression; he told the gypsy that when he got drunk he was on no account to kiss all the guests one after the other, as usual; the dogs were kicked into the courtyard, and not allowed to come into the banqueting-room and pick the fat morsels off the plates of the guests, as they generally did; the gypsies, actors, and students were told to behave themselves decently; and the common people were given to understand that, though an ox would be roasted and wine would run from the gutter for them, they were nevertheless not to attempt to fight or squabble, as it would not be allowed. And everyone asked his neighbor in amazement what was the meaning of this strange phenomenon.

In point of fact, this sudden change of conduct was due to a single idea. He believed that his young kinsman Bélá would infallibly come on his birthday. He might come late, but come he certainly would. He could not have given any reason for his belief, but he expected him, he counted on him; and whenever his cronies began to commit any out-of-the-way absurdity, the thought immediately occurred to him: If the youngest scion of the Kárpáthy family were to see this, what would he say to it? No! Once he had beheld his uncle in the midst of diversions unworthy of him; he should now see him taking his pleasure like a gentleman.

After the usual festive congratulations, the guests of quality descended into the garden, where the assembled peasantry were awaiting their master.

At other times, whenever Master Jock ascended or descended the steps, he had to be supported on both sides, for, like a locomotive, he could only get along on level ground; but now he shoved Palko's hand aside, and easily went down the two and thirty marble steps which led into the garden. No doubt the six months of regular living he had had to submit to while attending to his parliamentary duties at Pressburg had restored somewhat the elasticity of his nerves and muscles.

Below, a host of school children, drawn up in a row, greeted him with cries of "*Éljen!*"* And at the moment when he had descended among the festive mob awaiting him there, all the gypsies present blew three loud flourishes on their trumpets, and two grey-haired retainers advanced towards him, leading after them, by the horns, a young stall ox that had been fattened up for the occasion, and the bolder of the twain, coming forward, took off his cap, coughed slightly, steadily regarded the tips of his own boots, and recited congratulatory verses in his master's honor, without the slightest hesitation or stumbling, which, perhaps, is not to be greatly wondered at, considering that he had now recited the selfsame verses nine years running.

"And God grant your honor long life, which I wish you with all my heart!" concluded the worthy man, as if he doubted what reception the pious verses he had just recited might receive in heaven, and was determined to clinch the matter in prose of his own making.

---

* Vivat!

Master Jock, according to good old custom, had fifty ducats ready, which he gave to the veterans who had brought the ox. As for the ox itself, he ordered that it should be roasted forthwith for the benefit of the assembled peasantry.

After them came the youths of the town, rolling before them a ten-firkin cask full of the wine of Hegyalja. They brought the cask to a standstill at the feet of the Nabob, and set on the top of it Martin, the former Whitsun King, as being the one among them whose tongue wagged the nimblest. He took a beaker and, filling it with wine, thus toasted his honor: –

"God willing, I desire and pray that the Majesty of Heaven may suffer your honor, both today and hereafter, to go about clothed in velvet well patched with gold ducats, and ride a good nag shod with silver shoes. I pray that your honor may not be able to count the hairs of your head, and that as many blessings may be showered upon your shoulders as you have lost hairs from your poll. I pray that all the ministering angels of heaven may have nothing else to do but sweep all earthly cares out of your honor's path. I pray that the golden-spurred *csizmas* of your felicity may never be bespattered by the puddles of tribulation. I pray that the field-flask of your good humor may always be filled with the red wine of Eger. And, finally, when that merciless scytheman cometh who makes hay of every man, and mows down your honor with the rest of them, I pray that the chariots of heaven may not keep your honor's soul awaiting, but that the horses of the other world may arrive speedily, and, with a great sound of trumpets, convey you to that great forecourt where Abraham, Isaac, and the other Jewish patriarchs, side by side with three and thirty red-breeched, heaven-ascended gypsy fiddlers, dance the Kálla duet in velvet pump-hose. God grant your honor many more days! I wish it from the bottom of my heart."

Master Jock handsomely recompensed the youth who had rattled off this odd salutation without missing a word. Yet it was observed that he did not take as much pleasure in it as of yore.

And now a pretty young damsel approached – the loveliest virgin that could be found within the limits of seven villages. She brought him a white lamb as a birthday present, and made him some sort of a speech besides; but what it was all about nobody could tell, she spoke so low. They kept on telling her not to hold her apron before her mouth, as they could not hear a word; but it was of no use.

It was a good old custom on Master Jock's birthday to admit the damsel who made the pretty speech on this occasion among the guests, and seat her beside Master Jock at table; and thus she was the only woman present at the banquet. And rumor added that still worse things befell towards the end of the feast, when the wine had mounted into the heads of the guests, and the lamb-maiden had been caught in the whirl of an unwonted carouse. But she was always married to someone afterwards; for Master Jock used to give her a rich dowry, and she got six oxen from her own father into the bargain to set up with. So the good peasants were not very much alarmed at the prospect of bringing their daughters to Kárpáthy Castle.

Master Jock, with patriarchal condescension, approached the damsel, pinched her cheek, patted her head, and asked her kindly –

"What is thy name, my daughter?"

"Susie," she replied, in a scarcely audible voice.

"Hast thou a sweetheart?"

"No, I have not," replied the damsel, casting down her eyes.

"Then choose thee among all the youths present the one that liketh thee best, for married thou shalt be this very hour."

"Is Master Jock in his right mind?" whispered some of his cronies to one another. "Why, he generally postpones this little ceremony to the afternoon of the following day."

"Well, my lads, who among you has a mind to take this young virgin to wife on the spot?"

Ten of the youths leaped forth, Martin among them. Miska Horhi, by way of a joke, also joined himself to them, but Master Jock shoved him aside with his stick.

"I'll have no goat among the sheep," said he. "Come, my girl, make haste. Canst thou not choose thee a husband from among so many pretty fellows?"

"My dear father –" stammered the girl, without raising her eyes.

"Oh, so thou dost want thy dear father to choose for thee, eh?" inquired Master Jock, interpreting her desire. "Where is the girl's father, then?"

A greyish-haired man lurched forward, holding his cap in his hand.

"Come, sirrah! look sharp and choose your daughter a husband."

The boor seemed inclined, however, to take his time. He began to tick off the candidates one by one.

"One – two – three! Not one of you has much to bless himself with." At last he pitched upon a son-in-law agreeable to him – a short, thickset lout who happened to have a well-to-do father.

"Well, are you content to have him?" inquired Master Jock of the girl.

Susie blushed up to the ears and replied in a scarcely audible voice –

"I would rather have Martin!"

At this the whole company laughed heartily.

"Then why send for your father?" said they.

Martin did not wait to think the matter over, but rushed forward and took the girl's hand. Master Jock gave them his blessing and fifty ducats, and advised Martin to look well after his consort.

"Oh, I'll look after her," cried Martin, and he glanced defiantly in the direction of the gentlemen.

"Why, what's come to the old chap?" murmured the guests among themselves; "he has grown very virtuous all at once!"

Then there was another flourish of trumpets, the noble guests ascended into the castle, the peasants looked after their own pastimes, the youths and maidens played at blindman's-buff, kiss-in-the-ring, and other artless games, for the old men there was wine and spirits, and the old women had enough to do to talk of old and young alike.

On reaching the castle a fresh amusement awaited Master Jock. Bandi Kutyfalvi, whom everyone had given up, had just leaped from his horse, and a few moments later they were in each other's arms.

"So it is only you, then!" cried the worthy old gentleman, involuntarily drying the tears from his eyes.

"Yes, but it is only by the merest chance that another whom you expect least of all has not arrived also."

"Who is that?" asked Master Jock, with a face beaming with joy.

"Come, guess now!"

"My little brother Bélá!" said the old man.

"Why, what the devil is the matter with you?" cried Bandi Kutyfalvi. He had expected the Nabob to be enraged, not rejoiced at the news.

"Where is he? Where is he stopping? Why did you leave him behind?" inquired Master Jock, amazing Bandi still more by the impetuosity of his delight.

"He was with me in the next village; he was coming on to you with a birthday greeting, having only just left Pressburg, but was taken ill on the road, and had to put up at my house. Nevertheless he had brought his present with him, and will send it on this very evening. I would have brought it with me, but I came on horseback, and the present was so large that it would have filled a cart, at the very least."

Master Jock trembled for joy. He had so thoroughly made up his mind that his nephew must come, that he regarded his presence there as an indispensable feature of the entertainment.

"Quick, Palko, quick!" he cried; "get the carriage ready for him! Send four horses on before, that you may have a fresh relay at the Rukadi Csárda waiting for you! Go yourself! Nay, you stay behind, and send a man of a less proud stomach than you are! Send the fiscal! Tell Mr. Bélá that I honor, that I embrace him! Bring him along by main force as quickly as you can! Run! I say, run!"

"Run, eh?" grumbled Palko to himself. "I'll go, of course, but don't suppose that I can fly!"

And not another word did Master Jock say to anybody till he saw the fiscal bowl off in the best state carriage to meet his nephew. Then he began making a little calculation: Four hours there and four hours back, that makes eight hours; it is now two o'clock, he'll be here at ten. No doubt he thought I was angry and sent Kutyfalvi on before. It was very nice of him to show me such respect. Well, I'll not be behindhand in expressing my regret for my hastiness – asking his pardon; and from henceforth we will be good friends and kinsmen, and I shall be able to rest in the Lord with an easy conscience.

"Look ye, my friends!" he cried, turning at last to those standing around him, in the exuberance of his frank delight, "this will be the commemoration of a double festival, inasmuch as on this day the two last surviving male members of the Kárpáthy family, after a long estrangement, will extend to each other the right hand of fellowship, in token of complete reconciliation."

Meanwhile the heydukes had begun carrying round *szilvorium* and *öszibaraczk* liqueur, ten years old, with wheat-bread sippets, which signified that dinner-time was drawing near, and it became everyone to have a good appetite. Half an hour later the bell rang, which told that dinner was actually on the table. Thrice it was repeated, to recall any guest who might, perhaps, have strayed away too far, and then the heydukes threw wide open the large folding doors which led into the banqueting hall.

The vast and splendid room was filled from end to end with long tables, which as usual were spread for as many guests again as there were people actually present, so that any late comers might easily find room.

Every table bent beneath the weight of pies and tarts; the most magnificent fruit – golden melons, scaly pine-apples, whole stacks of them – everywhere exhaled their fragrance; pasties of terrific size and shape towered upwards from the midst of the guests who sat opposite and around them, and huge fish, veritable whales in size, embedded in vine-leaves, filled their would-be devourers with despair. Wreaths and bouquets in porcelain vases stood between all the dishes.

A whole museum of gold and silver plate was piled upon the tables. Even the singing students were to drink out of silver beakers. In the midst of the room stood a silver basin, from whose cunningly devised fountain the pure wine of Tokay spouted upwards in a jet of topas yellow.

Everyone sat down in his place while Master Jock made his way to the head of the table. When he got there he perceived that another cover was standing there beside his own. It used to be there on the other birthdays also, for there, from year to year, the peasant girl who brought the votive lambs was wont to sit. But now, Master Jock, in high dudgeon, shouted to Palko, who stood behind his chair –

"What is this? Whose cover is it?"

"There's no need for so much hallooing, surely! Don't you see that the family goblet has been placed there? I thought that if that other should come, he might have somewhere to sit."

At these words Master Jock's long-drawn face grew beautifully round again. This little attention pleased him. He patted Palko on the shoulder, and then explained to all the guests that the empty place had been left for his nephew Bélá. Then he praised Palko before them all.

"I see you have a good heart, after all," cried he.

"Nothing of the sort," growled the old servant, sulkily.

The soup now, for a moment, reduced the guests to silence. Everyone wished his neighbor a good appetite, and then fell to on his own account. At the head of the table sat Master Jock, with the Dean next to him; at the other end of the table Bandi Kutyfalvi presided, supported by Mike Kis. Nobody durst sit beside Mike Horhi, as he was wont to perpetrate the most ungodly pleasantries – letting off fiery crackers under the table, pouring vinegar into his neighbor's wine-glass when he wasn't looking, etc. The smaller gentry occupied another table.

In the background stood a colonaded peristyle, in the center of which was the decorated stage where, during dinner, Mr. Lakody first exhibited a magic-lantern, and afterwards, with the assistance of the students, acted a play called *Dr. Faust* translated from Goethe by Lakody himself, though Goethe himself would scarce have recognized his own masterpiece. Then came twelve tableaux, amidst Greek fire, representing the flight of Dobozy, and at the end of the last tableau the folding-doors in the background were to be thrown open, revealing a magnificent display of fireworks, which was to terminate the entertainment.

The feast went off capitally. Music, singing, the clinking of glasses, and merry discourse were mingled together into a joyous hubbub. There was not a single guest who, so long as he still had full possession of his tongue, did not call down blessings on the head of the master of the house. And he too was in an excellent humor, and his face beamed, though he drank far less of wine than usual. Evening had now fallen. The heydukes brought in large candelabras, the clinking of glasses went on uninterruptedly. At that moment the rumbling of a carriage was audible in the courtyard.

The fiscal had returned from his mission – but alone.

Master Jock sank back dejectedly in his chair when he learnt from the mouth of the messenger that Abellino really could not come, because he was sick; but he had sent what he had promised, all the same – a birthday gift to his dear uncle, with the hearty wish that he might find his greatest joy therein.

It was as much as six strapping fellows could do to bring in the long box which contained the birthday gift, and they hauled it on to the table so that all the guests might see it.

The four ends of the box were fastened down by strong iron clamps, and these had first to be removed with the aid of strong pincers.

What could be in this box? The guests laid their heads together about it, but not one of them could guess.

Suddenly all four clamps burst asunder, the four sides of the box fell aside in four different directions, and there on the table stood – a covered coffin!

A cry of indignation resounded from every corner of the room.

A pretty present for a seventieth birthday! A black coffin covered with a velvet pall; at the head of it the ancient escutcheon of the Kárpáthy family, and on the side, picked out with large silver nails, the name – J-o-h-n K-á-r-p-á-t-h-y.

Horror sealed every mouth, only a wail of grief was audible – a heavy, sobbing cry, like that of a wild beast stricken to the heart. It came from the lips of old John Kárpáthy, who had thus been so cruelly derided. When he beheld the coffin, when he read his own name upon it, he had leaped from his chair, stretched out his arms, his face the while distorted by a hideous grin, and those who watched him beheld his features gradually turning a dreadful blue. It was plain, from the trembling of his lips, that he wanted to say something; but the only sound that came from them was a long-drawn-out, painful rattle. Then he raised his hands to heaven, and suddenly striking his forehead with his two fists, sank back into his chair with wide-open, staring eyes.

The blood froze in the veins of all who saw this sight. For a few moments nobody stirred. But then a wild hubbub arose among the guests, and while some of them rushed towards the magnate and helped to carry him to bed, others went to fetch the doctors. The coffin had already been removed from the table.

The terrified army of guests was not long in scattering in every direction. Late that night all the roads leading from the castle of Kárpáthy were thronged with coaches speeding onwards at a gallop. Terror and Hope were the only guests left behind in the castle itself. But the rockets still continued to mount aloft from the blazing firework and write the name "Kárpáthy" in the sky in gigantic fiery letters visible from afar.

Now, what more natural than that the mob of breathless, departing guests should lose no time in presenting their respects, and paying their court to the heir-presumptive of the vast possessions of the Kárpáthy family, his Honor Abellino Kárpáthy?

They had all seen John Kárpáthy sink back in his chair, stricken by apoplexy. He had not died on the spot, it is true; yet he was as good as dead, anyhow, and there were many who carried their friendly sympathy with his highly respected nephew so far as to urge him vehemently to hasten at once – yes, that very night – to Kárpátfalva, take possession, and seal up everything, to prevent any surreptitious filching of his property. But the young Squire was suspicious of all premature rumors, and resolved to bide his time, await more reliable information, and only put in an appearance on receiving news of the funeral. Early next morning the Dean arrived to greet him. The very reverend gentleman had remained behind at Kárpátfalva last of all, in order to make sure that Master Jock really signed the codicil in favor of the college in which he was interested. He brought the melancholy intelligence that the old gentleman had not indeed actually given up the ghost, but was certainly very near the last gasp, inasmuch as it was now quite impossible to exchange a reasonable word with him, which signified that the Dean had been unable to get him to subscribe the codicil.

The Dean was followed the same day by a number of agents and stewards attached to the Kárpáthy domains, who hastened to introduce themselves to his Excellency, the heir and their future patron. They brought still further particulars of the bodily condition of the expiring head of the family. A village barber had bled him, whereupon he had somewhat recovered his senses. They had then proposed to send for a doctor, but he had threatened to shoot the man down if he crossed his threshold. The barber was to remain, however. He had more confidence in him, he said, because he would not dare to kill him. He would take no medicine, nor would he see a soul, and Mike Kis was the only person who had admittance to his room. But he could not possibly last longer than early tomorrow morning, of that they were all quite certain.

Abellino regarded the appearance of the agents and stewards as of very good augury: it showed that they already regarded him as their master, to whom homage was justly due. On the following day a whole host of managers, cashiers, scribes, shepherds, tenants, and other small fry, arrived to recommend themselves to Abellino's favor. The moments of their old master, they said, were most assuredly numbered. None of them could promise him so much as another day of life.

On the third day the heydukes and doorkeepers also migrated over in a body to Abellino, who began to be exasperated at so much flattery. So he spoke to them curtly enough, and on learning from them that henceforth they would regard him as their earthly Providence, inasmuch as his uncle was by this time drawing his last breath, he suddenly announced that he was about to introduce a series of radical reforms among the domestics attached to the Kárpáthy estate, the first of which was that every male servant who wore a moustache was to instantly extirpate it as an indecent excrescence. The stewards and factors obeyed incontinently, only one or two of the heydukes refused to make themselves hideous; but when he began to promise the lower servants also four imperial ducats a head if they did their duty, they also proceeded to snip off what they had hitherto most carefully cherished for years and years.

On the fourth day, of all his good friends, officials, domestics, and buffoons, Mike Kis, Martin the former Whitsun King, Master Varga the estate agent, Palko the old heyduke, and Vidra the gypsy, were the only persons who remained with John Kárpáthy as he stood at Death's ferry. Even the poet Gyárfás had deserted him, and hastened to congratulate the new patron.

On the fifth day there was nobody to bring away tidings from Kárpáthy Castle; perchance they were already engaged in burying the unfortunate wretch.

On the sixth day, however, a horseman galloped into Abellino's courtyard, whom they immediately recognized as Martin.

As he dismounted from his horse the steward of the Pukkancs estate, one of the first deserters, looked down from the tower, and, smiling broadly, cried out to him –

"Well, so you have come too, eh, Martin, my son? You're just in time, I can tell you. Had your marriage been celebrated a week later, your new landlord would have revived in his own favor some old customs. What news from Kárpátfalva?"

He had come, of course, to invite the gentlemen to the funeral. That was the most natural supposition.

"I have brought a letter for you, Mr. Bailiff," said Martin, nonchalantly; and, to the great disgust of the steward, he did not even doff his cap before Abellino, who was standing on the balcony.

"Look to your cap, you bumpkin! Why don't you doff it, sirrah? Who sent this letter?"

At the first question Martin only shrugged his shoulders; in answer to the second he replied that the steward of the estate had given it to him.

The bailiff broke open the letter, and green wheels danced before his eyes as he peered into it. The letter, which was in old John Kárpáthy's own handwriting, begged to inform the bailiffs, heydukes, and domestics assembled round Abellino that he had so far recovered as to be able to rise from his bed and write them a letter, and that he was very glad to hear that they had found so much better a master than himself, for which reason he advised them to remain where they were, for on no account were they to think of coming back to him.

The bailiff pulled the sort of face a man would naturally have who was compelled to make merry on a diet of crab-apples, and as he had no desire to keep the joyful intelligence all to himself, he passed the letter on from hand to hand amongst his colleagues, the other bailiffs, factors, doorkeepers, shepherds, scribes, and heydukes, till it had gone the round of them all. Under similar circumstances men often find a great consolation in twirling their moustaches; but now, alas! there was not a single moustache to twirl among the lot of them. They had neither places nor moustaches left. Some of them scratched their heads, some burst into tears, others cursed and swore. In their first fury they knew not which to turn upon first, Abellino for not inheriting, or Master Jock for not dying as he ought to have done. To make such fools of so many innocent men! It was scandalous!

Abellino was the last to whom, with tearful faces, they carried the glad tidings. The philosophical youth, who happened at that moment to be sipping an egg beaten up in his tea, received the intelligence with the utmost *sang-froid.*

"Enfin!" cried he, "I verily believe the old chap means to live forever!"

Chapter VIII

AN UNEXPECTED CHANGE

A month later John Kárpáthy was to be met with once more at Pressburg. It made him angry now when people called him "Master Jock."

A great change had come over the Nabob both externally and internally. His frame had grown so meager of late that he was unable to wear his former clothes; the fiery flush had disappeared from his face, the drunken puffiness from around his eyes; he spoke gravely with his fellow-men, busied himself about political and national matters, looked into the affairs of his own estates, sought out trustworthy stewards and bailiffs, renounced riotous pastimes, spoke sensibly and intelligibly at the Diet; nobody could imagine what had come to him all at once.

He had one favorite, Mike Kis, who was to be seen with him in every public place. Very often they encountered Abellino, and on all such occasions the Nabob and the Whitsun King would look at each other and smile and whisper as if they were planning some design against Abellino, as if they held in their hands some humorous trump card which would turn the tables gloriously upon the waggish coffin-sender. For all the young *roués* were still greatly amused at Abellino's masterpiece. The old bucks, on the other hand, had rather more difficulty in grasping the humor of it.

Meanwhile Master Boltay was residing on a little estate he had somewhere among the hills, whither in his first alarm he had conveyed Fanny, and she had hidden away there along with her aunt. Within a week, however, Abellino, who had by no means abandoned the chase, had discovered where they had stowed away the girl, and a few days later Teresa caught one of the servants in the act of popping a suspicious looking letter into Fanny's reading book. Master Boltay discharged that servant on the spot. Nevertheless, there were fresh rumors and alarms every day. Fashionable gentlemen came a-hunting in the neighborhood of the village near their dwelling, and hit upon a thousand artifices for obtaining admittance. Sometimes disguised lackeys presented themselves in the garb of simple gardeners, but, fortunately, Teresa always recognized their crafty countenances, and let them cool their heels on the doorstep. At other times old gypsy women sneaked into the courtyard whenever they had the chance, and by way of diverting the innocent damsel, showed her in the cards that a terribly great gentleman was in love with her, and would have her, too.

Master Boltay, hearing these things from day to day, became as furious as a bull when the dog-star is in the ascendant. He fumed and fussed and swore he would do dreadful things to anyone he might catch on the premises. But, alas! he could catch nobody! The enemy was an airy, agile, artful, experienced creature who was never at the end of his inventions, and had nothing else to think of but how to make a fool of him; while he, with his dull henchman Alexander, was but a stupid, heavy animal, whose horns had to grow before he could butt with them. It was therefore with a very surly look that Master Boltay, standing outside his door one day, beheld a handsome carriage stop in front of his house, and a heyduke assist an elderly Hungarian gentleman to descend therefrom.

The old gentleman approached Master Boltay with a very amicable air, and, bidding the heyduke remain behind, said to the artisan –

"Sir, is this the house of Mr. Boltay?"

The person accosted was so preoccupied that the only answer he gave was to nod his head.

"Then I suppose I have the pleasure of speaking to the worthy master himself?"

Even now Master Boltay was not quite master of his own thoughts, and he could not get it out of his mind that this gentleman had come to pick a quarrel with him.

"Yes, I am; I don't deny it," he replied.

The elderly gentleman smiled, hooked his arm within Master Boltay's, and, in the heartiest manner, invited him to go with him into the house as they must have a long conversation together.

Master Boltay gave way, led the gentleman into the innermost apartment, made him sit down, and remained standing before him to hear what he had to say.

"First of all," said the old gentleman, regarding the master-carpenter with a comical smile – "first of all, allow me to introduce myself. I will begin by saying that I bear a name which will not be exactly music to your ear. I am John Kárpáthy. Yes! out with the oath that hangs on your lips as loudly and soundly as you like! I know very well that it is not meant for me, but for my nephew, whose name is Bélá, but who, fool as he is, has re-christened himself Abellino. You have good cause to curse him, for he has brought misfortune to your house."

"Not yet, sir," said Boltay, "and I hope to God he will not bring it."

"I hope so too; but, alas! the devil never slumbers, especially when pretty girls are about. My nephew has taken upon himself the glorious resolution of seducing your ward."

"I know it, sir; but I am on my guard."

"My good sir, you know not half the artful tricks of the young bucks who have served an apprenticeship in the great world before engaging in such enterprises."

"Stop, sir! One thing I do know. I know that, all because of your nephew, she is condemned to a cloisterlike life, and cannot so much as step into the street unless I am with her. And when, at last, I have had too much of this persecution, I will leave my workshop, I will go into another part of the world, I will quit my country, which I love as well as, aye, and ever so much better than, many of those who call themselves the fathers of the fatherland. But till then, sir, till then, never let me catch hold of any of these painted butterflies! I am not a gentleman, I will fight no duel; but I'll smash whomsoever comes in my way – I'll smash 'em like a piece of rotten glass. Just tell that to your dear nephew!"

"Pardon me, my friend, but I am not in the habit of carrying messages to my nephew, neither have I come hither merely to gossip, but to carry out a well-devised thoroughly thought-out plan. I hate this man more than you do. You need not shake your head like that, for so it is. Abellino is my mortal foe, and I am his. You will better understand the amicable relations between us when I tell you that he wishes me to die, and I will not consent, and as in all probability my road to death is much shorter than his, the contest is conducted with very unequal weapons. On my birthday he sent me a coffin as a present, in the expectation that I should make use of it as speedily as possible. Now *his* birthday is approaching, and I am going to send him, as a present, a beggar's staff, and I hope he will live a long time to use it."

"Well, sir, that is your business, not mine. I am a table-maker; I don't profess to make staves. If you wish to make a present of a beggar's staff, I can recommend you to a turner who lives hard by."

"Master Boltay, don't be so impatient. The staff I spoke of is only an emblem. I have a plan, I say, which you must know of. It would be better if you came and sat down by me and heard me out. Look now! I want

Abellino to wait in vain for the hour of my death. I want my estates not to go to him, but to another. Do you understand?"

"Of course! You would cut him off with a shilling."

"Why, man, you understand nothing. My estates are hereditary; I cannot leave them to whom I will – that depends on the law of succession, and the law of succession is eternal. And a nice little inheritance it is too. It deserves to be talked about, I assure you. My annual income exceeds a million and a half!"

"A million and a half!" cried the artisan, in consternation; and he gazed wonderingly at the magnate, as if he scarce believed that any man in the world could be worth a million and a half a year.

"Yes, a million and a half awaits my successor, and even under the sod I should be tortured by the thought that my ancestral estates, for which far better men than I shed their blood, were being scattered to the winds by a worthless descendant, were dribbling away piecemeal and passing into the hands of usurers, shopkeepers, and aliens, and all through the very man who, so far from weeping at my death, will be ready to dance for joy at it. I mean to deprive him of that satisfaction."

"May I give you a piece of advice, sir?"

"There's no need of that. You've only got to listen to me." Then, seizing the hand of the artisan, to rivet his attention the better, he thus proceeded: "There is one way of drawing a blood-red cross through all Abellino's calculations – for I want to draw blood, I want to wound him to the very heart, because he has insulted me – and that one way is for me to marry."

Here Kárpáthy stopped, and threw himself back in his chair, as if waiting to see what the artisan would say to that. But he only nodded his head, as if he understood the matter completely.

"If a child were to be born to me," continued Kárpáthy, and, in a sudden outburst of merriment, he banged the table with his fist, "why, it would be enough to make me live my life over again. I am not superstitious, sir; but when I was lying on my deathbed, a heavenly vision gave me the assurance that, to the wonder of my fellows, I should return from the realm of death, though everybody looked upon me as a dead man already; and the mere fact of my recovering my strength and good humor is proof enough to me that that vision was no false dream. I mean to marry. And now you shall hear how that concerns you. You have a young ward – a girl whom Abellino persecutes, and Abellino's associates lay bets with each other as to who shall win her first, as if it were a horse-race. Now, I want to put a stop to this base persecution. I would provide her with a place of refuge so secure, that if all its doors and windows stood right open before him, Abellino would not venture in. That place of refuge is my house!"

"What do you mean, sir?"

"I mean that I demand from you your ward as my wife!"

"What?"

"My lawful consort, I say. For many years the world has known me under the title of 'the good old fool.' I would employ the remainder of my days in excising the word 'fool' from that title."

Master Boltay slowly arose from beside the table.

"Sir, your honor's offer flatters and amazes me. You are a gentleman, with an annual income of a million and a half; you are incalculably wealthy, like the rich man in the Bible. But I know, sir, that wealth is not happiness. I knew a poor girl whose parents last year gave her in marriage to a rich man, and the next day they drew a suicide out of the Danube. I want to make my ward happy, but I will not give her away for riches or treasures."

Kárpáthy remained sitting, and gently grasped the artisan's hand.

"Sit down again, my worthy Master Boltay. When first I saw your face, I was prepared for that answer. You certainly would provide a happy, contented future for your ward, and your intention does you honor. You would leave to her a possession that is not to be despised – a safe business, and, perchance, you have also chosen for her a worthy, honest, hard-working, sensible young man, on whose arm she can wander along life's quiet path to the very end. But her destiny is no longer in your power. The girl, unfortunately, springs from a family in whose blood flightiness may be said to have run from the very beginning. She was educated in a school which encouraged ambition, extravagance, and the love of luxury, and the later and more rigorous years of her life have only suppressed, not extinguished, her earlier impressions and recollections. She was wont to see vice fêted and sobriety ridiculed. That, sir, is a bad apprenticeship, and it requires no ordinary strength of mind to call that which seems so sweet, bitter, and that which seems so bitter, sweet. Have not you yourself observed how suddenly she cooled towards the poor young fellow you chose for her, when she got the idea into her head that she was going to become a beauty whom the world would envy and adore? Before very much longer she will have her times of *ennui*, of passionate desire; the claims of nature will assert themselves. Then will come moments of bitterness and self-forgetfulness, when she will readily listen to evil counselors. And who shall save a damsel from falling who herself wishes to fall?"

"I don't believe it, sir. I don't believe what you say. I feel you have spoken the truth, and still I deny it. In general, what you say is right enough; but my darling will be the exception."

"I will not dispute the point. Look now! I don't want to marry your ward against her will. I simply want you to lay my proposal before her: 'A rich nobleman sues for your hand. The suitor is neither young nor handsome, nor even amiable – he might very well pass for your grandpapa; yet the only demands he makes upon you are that you will swear to be his wife, and will honor him as your husband. If you like, he and you shall live in two separate counties, and you shall only see him when you choose to invite him to come and see you. Will you accept his offer?' If the girl says, 'No,' I will be quite content with her answer. We will say no more about the matter, and I will trouble you no further. You will but have done your duty as a guardian. I will give her a week to make up her mind. In a week's time, my confidential agent, who is cooling his heels outside by my carriage, will be sent here – I don't want to carry my basket home myself* – to inquire if by any chance I left a diamond ring behind me here. If the answer be a rejection, you will send back this ring by him; if, on the other hand, my proposal be accepted, you will answer that I must come for it myself."

And with that the gentleman arose, pressed Master Boltay's hand amicably, and left him in a perfect chaos of conflicting thoughts. Impatiently, Boltay began pacing up and down the room. What was he to do? He felt within himself that Kárpáthy had spoken the truth. The girl would not be able to resist the tempting prospect, and would accept the offer. And thus she must needs be unhappy; and what would be the end of it all? At first he had half a mind to conceal the whole thing from her. But no, that would be unworthy of him; a man really worthy of the name must never conceal the truth.

Suddenly a good idea occurred to him. He had discovered a way out of the difficulty. He hastened to consult Alexander.

That worthy youth had just finished his masterpiece – a splendid writing-table, magnificently carved, with secret drawers impossible to discover. He was quite absorbed in his work.

"Alexander," said his old master, "your handiwork is really a masterpiece."

"I am proud of it myself. I think of it night and day."

"Night and day? And don't you think of anything else, then?"

"I? What else should I think of, pray?"

---

* In Hungarian, as in German, a rejected lover is said to "receive a basket."

"Why, that you will be a full master-carpenter the day after tomorrow. Suppose I say that?"

"Oh, I'm sure of that."

"Well, what would you say if I resolved to hand over the whole of my business to you?"

"Ah, sir, you are jesting. Why should you give it all to me?"

"Because I am weary of the worry of it, as you can see, and should like the care of it to repose on younger shoulders. You shall conduct the concern instead of me, and we'll share the profits. Don't you admire my cunning? I want to have an income without any labor."

"I can go on as before; there's no necessity for us to go shares."

"But suppose I wish it? Look now! I have no son, and you are just the son I should like to have had."

Alexander gently raised the old man's hand to his lips, which he placed on his head, as if by way of blessing.

"And then," continued the master, "how nice it will be if you bring a wife home, and I have the joy of a happy domestic life which I have never had yet!"

Alexander sighed. "We shall have to live a long time before we get to that," said he.

"What? Do you want to remain wifeless all your days? Come, don't pull such a holy mug as that! Would you keep your secrets from me, when you know I can see through you as if you were a glass of water? Do you think I don't know whom you love? Speak out! don't be such a coward! Tell the girl you love her, and cannot do without her. Or perhaps you would like me to woo her for you? I shouldn't mind that, I am sure; I should like to be your best man. Well, and now I'll go and ask the girl to have you, and tomorrow you shall have her, and we'll have such a betrothal that the very angels shall dance for joy."

Alexander never said a word; but he cast down his eyes, turned pale, pressed Master Boltay's hand in silence, and then quitted the room.

So long as the lad had been with him, Boltay was all radiant and jocose, but when he had departed, a couple of tears trickled from the old man's eyes. He himself suspected and feared that Alexander loved in vain.

Boltay thought the matter over for some time, and then resolved to first of all ask for Fanny's hand for Alexander – perhaps the girl might still have some kindly feeling for him. If she rejected the proposal, and declared she did not care for the youth at all, he would lay the second offer before her. What would she say to that? Could she possibly be amiable to an old fellow of over seventy, after coldly shutting her heart against a handsome young man?

So the same day Boltay rode out to his country den, which was situated in a romantic little valley in the Carpathians, to pay his ward a visit.

Fanny rushed out to meet Boltay's wagon when he was still a long way off, dragged him down from the coach-box, and, full of childlike gaiety, conducted him all round her little domain; and Boltay kept pinching her cheeks, which were so firm and round that he could scarcely grip hold of them. It was plain that she did not give so much of her time now to melancholy brooding.

"Why, what a good housewife we shall make of you! There's surely nothing in the world you don't know already. We must look you out a husband now."

"Yes, let's have a husband by all means," laughed Fanny, roguishly clipping Master Boltay round the neck, and kissing his stubbly face with her round red lips. "Daddy Boltay is the husband for me!"

"Go along with you, you rogue!" cried Master Boltay, scarce able to contain himself for joy. "Why, I'm older than your father. Let us look for someone who will suit you."

"All right, Daddy Boltay, the sooner the better. But first go and see Aunt Teresa, and in the meantime I'll run off and get supper ready."

Master Boltay hastened to seek Teresa, and make her acquainted with the interesting situation.

The magnate's proposal overwhelmed her likewise, and she too could promise Alexander very little success. Teresa had often tried the heart of the girl, she had often unexpectedly mentioned the youth's name to her, and the girl had always remained cold. She respected, she praised him, but that is not love.

All through supper Boltay was cracking jokes with his ward, who responded with great alacrity, and gave him back as good as he gave her. At last the servants removed the table, and the three remained together alone.

And now Master Boltay's good humor changed into grave solemnity, and he drew the girl towards him by both hands.

"You have a suitor," said he; "tell me straight out if you suspect who it is."

The girl sighed, but made no reply.

"Your suitor is a worthy young man, an honest, honorable fellow, a good liver, a diligent mechanic, and handsome to boot, and, which is the main thing, he has for a long time loved you truly, loyally, and ardently."

"I know. You mean Alexander," replied the girl.

Master Boltay stopped short, although there was nothing very extraordinary in the fact that the girl knew his secret. Both of them hung upon Fanny's next words.

"Poor Alexander!" sighed the girl.

"Why are you sorry?"

"Because he loves me. Why cannot he find a better, more reliable girl than I, to make him happy?"

"Then you don't want to marry him?" asked the old man, sadly.

"If it would give you any pleasure, I am ready to marry him."

"Give me pleasure, indeed! I want you to please yourself, girl. The lad is such a worthy fellow, that seek as you like you will not find a better. He is no mere blockhead, like the ordinary workman; he has traveled in foreign parts, he can stand up before anybody; and then he loves you so much."

"I know; I admit it. I have always respected him, worthy man that he is; but love him I cannot. I will marry him, I will be faithful to him to the day of my death, but he will be unhappy, and so shall I."

Boltay sighed; and in a few moments he said, in a scarcely audible voice, "Then, don't marry him."

The tears flowed involuntarily from the eyes of the two old people. They loved the young folks as if they were their own children; and oh, how they would have liked to have seen them happy together! And Fate willed otherwise!

At last Boltay brushed the sweat off his forehead with his hand, and said, with a great effort at composure, "Get up, my girl! Overrule your heart I cannot; it would be wrong. He certainly could not accept your hand without your love. No, let us talk of something else. You have another suitor. A great and rich gentleman would make you his wife; he has an illustrious name and an honorable title, it takes him a whole week to ride over his estates, and he has an annual income of a million and a half."

Fanny cast down her eyes and shook her head. Then she answered coldly and sensibly, "That would mean good luck, but not happiness."

"It is true," continued Boltay, "that your second suitor is not young; but, instead of love, he promises you ease and a high position."

"Who is it?"

"His name will not have a very pleasant sound in your ears, for it is a gentleman of the same name who is the cause of most of your troubles; he is John Kárpáthy, the uncle of that tempter at church."

Here the girl burst out laughing.

"Ah, yes! the man like a fat spider."

"His figure has improved since then."

"Whom they consider such a lunatic."

"He is much wiser now."

"And who is always drinking and making merry with peasant girls."

"He has completely changed his mode of life now."

"Ah, my dear guardian, this is only a joke, surely, or, if it be a serious business, you only want to make fun of it. Now, look here, Daddy Boltay, first of all, when I told you to marry and I would be your wife, you said you might be my grandfather, and now you offer me Master Jock as a husband. What do you mean by it?"

Master Boltay was delighted. He laughed till the tears ran down his cheeks. Then the cast-iron truisms of ancient experience were false after all, and it was possible to find one childish soul strong enough to reject the dazzling allurements of wealth, even when it had only to stretch out its hand and find power at the tips of its fingers along with an engagement-ring!

"Look now!" replied Master Boltay; "the gentleman left this ring with me, and I am to send it back in case you reject his offer."

"Did he give you a basket with it?" inquired the roguish damsel.

"No need of that; I knew how it would turn out," replied Boltay, laughing.

And, indeed, he was beside himself with joy. His sorrow for Alexander was quite obliterated by the delight he felt that his ward should have exhibited such strength of mind. He pictured to himself how proud he would feel to be able to say to the magnate, "You promised to give a million and a half for the roses on my ward's cheeks, did you? Thank you, but I'll not part with her even at that price." How high he would hold his head before those young dandies who fancied they could buy Fanny's love for a few shameful thousands of florins, wretched beggars that they were!

So the two old people kissed the girl and bade her good night, and they all went to their several rooms. The night was far advanced; it was time to lie down, and yet it was no time for sleeping. Some unruly spirit was about who chased slumber from everybody's eyes.

Master Boltay's brain was chock-full of all the speeches that he meant to make here, there, and everywhere as if he were preparing to be the mouth-piece of the whole town. Teresa's mind was wandering among the events of the present and the past, trying to throw light upon all the manifold contradictions of a young maiden's heart, and find out how much therein was good or bad, instinct or free will.

But it was from Fanny's eyes that the genius of slumber kept furthest away.

Only one thought, one idea now lived in her heart – the face of that man whom she loved, whose shape she crowned with the flowers of her devotion, whom she pictured to herself as noble, grand, and glorious, with the memory of whom her heart was full, whose smiling figure she always conjured up before her when no living face was near her, and oh, then, how good it was to rest in its contemplation!

She had no longer a thought for the twofold offer presented to her by her guardian, the inspiration of these sublime moments erased from her recollection the gloomy-faced youth and the grotesque old man, both of whom wanted to make her their wife.

Where is he now – the unknown, the unnamable, the unforgettable ideal? Most certainly he has no idea that a heart is pining for him in secret, in tribulation, just as the moon is quite unconscious of the lunatic who pursues her rays and leaps across dizzy abysses in order to get nearer to her!

How blessed the lot of those ladies of the great world who can see him every day, speak to, admire, and honor him! Perhaps one among them is his chosen bride! No, nobody could love him so truly, oh, so truly as she would have done. She would never, never tell him so, but she should love him to the death!

Why was it that she could never hope to even get near him?

Never?

Suddenly a strange thought arose in her mind. It would only cost her a single word, and the doors of the haughtiest, the most illustrious houses would fly open before her, and she would stand in the same rank, in the same atmosphere as those lofty, those envied ladies who were at liberty to behold the face and hear the voice of her adored idol.

A shudder ran through her at the thought.

Yes, this goal would be reached if she gave her hand to Kárpáthy. A single step would raise her at once into this seemingly unattainable world.

She rejected the thought, only for a moment did her soul retain it, and then she brushed it away.

What would her good friends and kinsfolk Boltay and Teresa say, if she refused a fine, manly, noble-hearted youth, and, for the sake of money and splendor, accepted the hand of a dotard she did not love?

But again, there were other kinsfolk whom, if she took this step, she could make happy, whom she could rescue from bitter shame, reproach, and wretchedness – her mother and sisters. If she were rich, she could save them from their horrible fate.

Yes, good damsel, yes; thou wilt have no lack of reasons, but it is no tender regard for thy friends or thy relations which leads thee on. No;

'tis Love that goes before thee with his torch, and he will lead thee through the worlds of good and evil – all the rest is mere fustian. Go, then, towards thy Fate!

At last the whole house slept. Sleep on, for sleep brings with it good counsel.

Next morning a strange surprise awaited the two old guardians. Fanny told Boltay that if old Kárpáthy should send for the ring, it was not to be sent back to him, but he was to come for it himself.

Chapter IX

THE HUNTER IN THE SNARE

Boltay and Teresa said not a word against Fanny's resolution, nor did they talk about the wedding, but in the meantime they began to provide the *trousseau,* for though as the wife of a magnate, she might come to wear far more splendid things, she might nevertheless keep what they gave her as a souvenir, and, amidst the whirl and bustle of the great world, reflect from time to time, when she looked at their gift, on the modest domestic joys that she had left behind her. At the same time the preparations for Fanny's marriage were kept so secret that nobody could possibly have known anything of that interesting event; it was not in their natures either to brag about or lament over it.

Now a very singular thing happened about this time.

One day, when Master Boltay was at home in his factory, there rushed into the place a shabbily, not to say raggedly, attired female whom Master Boltay could not recognize as belonging to the circle of his acquaintances. But there was no need for him to puzzle his head over it, for the miserable creature herself hastened to inform him who she was.

"I am the unfortunate Mrs. Meyer, Fanny's mother," sobbed the woman in the bitterness of her heart, throwing herself at Boltay's feet, and covering first his hands and then his knees, and then his very boots with her kisses, and shedding oceans of tears. Boltay, who was not used to such tragical scenes, could only stand there as if rooted to the spot, without asking her to get up or even tell him what was the matter.

"Oh, sir! oh, my dear sir! most worthy, honorable, magnanimous Mr. Boltay, suffer me to kiss the dust from your boots! Oh, thou guardian angel of the righteous, thou defender of the innocent, may God grant thee many, many years upon earth, and, after this life, all the joys of heaven! Was there ever a case like mine? My heart faints within me at the thought of telling my tale; but tell it I must. The whole world must know; and, above all, Mr. Boltay must know what an unfortunate mother I am. Oh, oh, Mr. Boltay, you cannot imagine what a horrible torture it is for a mother who has bad daughters – and mine are bad; but it serves me right! I am the cause of it, for I have always let them have their own way. Why did I not throw myself in the Danube after my poor dear husband? But, sir, a mother's heart is never entirely lost to feeling, and, even when her children are bad, she still loves them, still hopes and believes that they may grow better. For four mortal years I have stood the shame of it, and it is a miracle I have a hair still left on my head for worry and vexation; but at last it has become too much for me; I can stand it no longer. If I were to tell of the abominations that go on in my house every day, Mr. Boltay, your hair would rise up with horror! Only yesterday I spoke to my daughters, I upbraided them; and the words were no sooner out of my mouth than, like harpies incarnate, they fell upon me, all four of them: 'What do you mean by preaching at us? What business is it of yours what we do? Don't we keep you like a lady? The very dress on your back, the very cap on your head, you got from us! There's not a stick or a straw in the whole house that belongs to you. We earned it all!' I was terror-stricken. Was this my sole reward for so many bitter, sleepless nights, which I had passed at their sick-beds? for taking the very food from my own mouth to give it to them? for humbling myself and going in rags and tatters that they might dress in fine feathers? Then, sir, instead of being ashamed, the eldest of them stood up to me, and told me straight out that if I did not like to live in the same house with, and be kept by them, I might go and shift for myself, for Pressburg was large enough, and turned me into the street. I did not know what to do. My first thought was to make for the Danube; but, at the selfsame instant, it seemed as if some angel whispered in my ear, 'Have you not a daughter whom good, benevolent people are bringing up in all honor and virtue? Go there! These good people will not reject you; they will even give you some corner or other where you may stretch your limbs until it please God to take you away.' And so, sir, I came on here, just as you see me. I have absolutely nothing under heaven I can call my own. I have not tasted a bit of food this day; and if you turn me from your door, and if my daughter will not see me, I must die of hunger in the street; for I would rather perish than accept another morsel from my ungrateful and shameful children."

The part of all this rigmarole which appealed to Master Boltay most strongly was that this worthy woman had eaten no food that day. So he considered it his Christian duty to there and then take a plate of lard-dumplings and a tumbler full of wine from a cupboard, place them before her on the table, and compel her to fall to, so that, at any rate, he might save her from dying of hunger.

"Oh, sir, a thousand thanks; but I am not a bit hungry. I am too put out to eat, and, at the best of times, I have no more appetite than a little bird. The little I ever eat at table would never be missed. But what I should desire more than all the riches in the world would be to hear a kind word from the mouth of my darling Fanny. Is such a thing possible? Do you think she would look at her poor mother? Would she be ashamed at the sight of me? Perhaps she would no longer recognize me, in such misery as I am, in rags and wretchedness, and so old and haggard. Might I see her for an instant, if only once? I do not ask to speak to her, but if I might just see her at a little distance – through a window, perhaps – just catch a peep at her surreptitiously, see her pass before me, hear her speaking to someone else – Oh, then, all my desires would be satisfied!"

Master Boltay was quite touched by these words, though it did occur to him that he had witnessed a somewhat similar scene in some German tragedy.

"Come, come," said he to the weeping mother, "don't take on so! You shall assuredly have your wish. You shall both see your daughter and speak to her. You shall live here too, if you like. It will be very nice for us to all live together, and will do no harm, that I can see."

"Oh, sir, you speak like an angel from heaven. But my daughter? Oh, my daughter! She will not be able to love me anymore. She will loathe me."

"Make your mind easy on that score, madam. Nobody has ever disparaged you in your daughter's hearing; and Fanny is much too generous to spurn her mother in adversity. I'll take you home with me, for I have sent her into the country to be out of harm's way. There she lives with a kinswoman of her father's – a somewhat severe personage, I admit; but I'll reconcile her to you."

"Oh, sir, I don't expect that Teresa will raise me up to her level, but I shall be content to be her servant, her kitchen-wench, if only my daughter be about me."

"What nonsense you are talking, my worthy woman!" blurted out honest Boltay, awkwardly. "I've servants enough of my own, so there's no need for my ward to do manual labor. In half an hour we will set out together, and just leave the rest to me."

Mrs. Meyer would thereupon have kissed Mr. Boltay's boots again, but the worthy man escaped from the sentimental creature in time, and employed the half-hour during which he was absent from her in scouring about the slop-shops and collecting all sorts of ready-made garments, and returned home with a complete suit, which Mrs. Meyer, despite her ladylike squeamishness, was obliged to put on instead of her disgraceful rags.

And here I may mention, lest any of my readers should be blessed with as strong a credulity as Mr. Boltay, that there was not one word of truth in the tragic monologue above described. Mrs. Meyer had *not* fallen out with her daughters; they had *not* turned her adrift; there was no need for her to leap into the Danube. The matter stood simply thus: Abellino, since his late rebuffs, had, full of passionate frenzy, plunged deeper and deeper into his unsuccessful enterprise. He had just demanded from Monsieur Griffard the last hundred thousand florins of the second million promised to him. Abellino was constantly attended by a spy in the service of the genial banker, who had immediately hastened to acquaint his principals in Paris with the latest tidings from Kárpátfalva, notably of what had happened on the night of Squire John's birthday. Monsieur Griffard, learning that Squire John was at the last gasp, had sent Abellino not one, but two hundred thousand florins, for which, of course, he was naturally expected to pay back as much again at the proper time. A few days later, he learnt, from a second letter, that the uncle was still alive, and likely to live; but, by that time, the money was well on its way, and reached Abellino punctually, to his great delight.

So now he had a hundred thousand more florins than he had reckoned upon, and at such times a man is apt to feel confident. He therefore concocted a little scheme whereby Mrs. Meyer (the girl's own mother!) should artfully worm her way into the Boltay family, so as to get at her last daughter, and – we know the rest!

She was to have sixty thousand florins down if the plan succeeded. "Is it possible!" you will cry. Yes, quite possible. Say not that I paint monsters; it is life that I describe.

Mrs. Meyer, no doubt, reflected that sixty thousand florins was a nice little sum, and she meant to deposit thirty thousand of it in the savings bank on her own account, and thirty thousand on Fanny's, and thus the pair of them would be amply provided for for life. And what was to be given in exchange for this nice sum of money? Why, nothing at all, so to speak – a mere chimera, which is no good to anybody while they have it, and only becomes profitable when it is parted with – a woman's virtue.

An hour later, the carriage stood before the door.

Master Boltay did not take his seat beside Mrs. Meyer, but went and sat by the coachman, and, taking the reins and the whip, galloped at full speed from the town, as if it were a question of some great mortal disaster which he wished to prevent.

When they reached the outskirts of the village, he dismounted from the wagon, and, with downcast eyes and much stammering, informed Mrs. Meyer that he had a little job to see to; he had to say a few words to a Jew – he meant a Greek. Would she go on to the house? He would go a quicker way among the gardens, and would be at home as soon as the wagon.

To tell a simple lie was almost more than the worthy man could manage. No doubt it was the first time he had ever told a lie in his life, and only urgent necessity drove him to it now. It was true, however, that he did want to get to the house through the gardens a little beforehand, in order to tell Teresa and Fanny of Mrs. Meyer's arrival, and beg them to treat her as kindly as possible, and not appear alarmed when they saw her. At the same time, he told them the cause of Mrs. Meyer's flight, and all this he explained with such brevity that he had quite finished by the time the coach was heard rumbling along the road outside, and was already standing outside in the gate to receive his guest.

The two women were by this time in the passage. Fanny had just come from the garden, and had taken off her straw hat, which might have impeded her mother's embraces. Teresa, too, had put aside for once that *perpetuum mobile* which women call knitting, lest she might poke out her kinswoman's eye with it.

On perceiving her daughter, Mrs. Meyer would not descend from the coach. Master Boltay and the coachman had to pull her down by main force, and when she did touch *terra firma* it was only to grovel at the feet of Teresa and Fanny till Boltay, who had no desire that she should make a scene in his courtyard for the benefit of the village loafers, raised her to her feet again.

The worthy artisan did his very utmost to keep Mrs. Meyer in an upright position, but all to no purpose, for by the time she had reached Fanny, down she plumped on her knees again, and tried to discover

Fanny's tiny feet that she might kiss them. This greatly alarmed Fanny, for, having been engaged in gardening from an early hour, she had put nothing on her tiny feet but two little old house-slippers, and consequently Mrs. Meyer's strenuous endeavors threatened to reveal to the world, the disgraceful circumstance, that – she had no stockings on. Blushing at the thought of such a scandal, she stooped hastily and raised Mrs. Meyer up in her arms, whereupon the sensitive mother hid her face in her daughter's bosom, wept, sobbed, and kissed and embraced her with all her might. Fanny simply stood still and held her, without being able to make up her mind whether she should return these tears, sobs, and embraces.

At length the united efforts of the whole family succeeded in dragging Mrs. Meyer from the hall into the parlor, where they compelled her to sit down, and made her understand, at last, that she was to live there. At first she insisted upon sleeping on the floor; then, in the kitchen among the servants; finally, she begged and prayed that, if they were determined she should have a room of her own, it must be the tiniest of attics in which she could only squeeze by huddling all her limbs together, a room no larger than a coal-cellar, from which she might now and then get a peep at her daughter. Unfortunately, in Mr. Boltay's house there was no room of that size, except a granary.

So, at last, she had to let them be hospitable to her in their own way, and Teresa and Fanny got ready for her a cabinet next to Fanny's music-room. When all was ready, Teresa took Fanny's two hands in hers, and, looking tenderly into her eyes, said in a confidential tone: "Fanny, be kind, tender, and affectionate towards your mother! So far from avoiding, do your utmost to anticipate, her wishes. You see that she loves you dearly, you love her too. One thing, however, I beg of you: say nothing, before her, of your approaching wedding. Keep it a secret for a time – to please me."

And Fanny promised to keep it secret.

On the appointed day, old Kárpáthy – if it be right to call our intending bridegroom old – sent Palko to Boltay's, and with great delight received the message that he was to come for the ring himself.

He flew – nay, that would be saying too much for him; but he hastened to the house as fast as a pair of legs could carry him. On reaching it, he must needs embrace Mr. Boltay himself willy-nilly, and insisted on being conducted to the bride at once. The thought that this wondrously beautiful damsel was ready to take him for a husband, made him positively love her. Mr. Boltay was obliged to call his attention to the fact that the marriage must be preceded by sundry legal and other formalities, which the magnate, despite the fact of his being a member of the legislature, had clean forgotten, though this only shows how completely he was carried away by the idea of his own wedding. Kárpáthy, therefore, had to content himself with requesting his future father-in-law – who, by the way, was a good score of years younger than himself – to keep the whole affair a profound secret in the meantime, as he had his own peculiar reasons for so doing. Boltay promised, and only after the magnate's departure, did he recollect that Teresa and Fanny had demanded a similar promise of secrecy, so he told Teresa of the coincidence.

This circumstance confirmed Teresa's suspicions. If it was for the interest of both parties to keep the matter secret till the wedding-day, Mrs. Meyer could not possibly know anything about it, and therefore she must have another reason for coming here, for that she had a reason Teresa felt quite certain.

It was only natural too, under the circumstances, that a certain estrangement should gradually arise between Teresa and Fanny. Teresa could not forget that Fanny was now the bride of a millionaire, and Fanny felt ashamed to be as familiar with her aunt and guardian as she used to be. "What will they think of me?" she thought. "They will put it all down to vaingloriousness and affectation." Thus it came about that a sort of cold reserve was observable among the members of the family. Everybody seemed to be upon his guard; and they might have been deaf and dumb for all that they said to each other at meals.

The person who observed this atmosphere of reserve and suspicion with the liveliest attention was undoubtedly Mrs. Meyer. "The girl is not happy," she thought. "They are too severe with her. Teresa is cold and unsympathetic. The girl is bored, and feels wretched, plunged as she is up to the neck in this overbearing rural felicity. All day long she never sees any suitable young fellow of her own age, and the desires of her heart are all the stronger in consequence. Yes, something will come of this, I'm sure."

One day Teresa went to Pressburg to see how the wedding-garments were getting on – all the preparations for the marriage were being made outside the house – and as they were not ready, she felt obliged to remain in town all night, and sent Boltay back to guard the house.

Hitherto, Fanny had never lain alone in her room. Her aunt had always slept in the cabinet, and the door between the two rooms had been left open; and on very stormy nights, when the rain beat against the windowpanes, when the wind slammed the doors, and the dogs were howling in the yard below, it was nice to reflect that near her was resting a good faithful soul who, next to God, was her most watchful guardian.

This particular night, too, was very stormy. The rain poured, the tempest shook the trees, the roaming dogs barked and howled as if they were hunting down someone, and the wind shook the doors as if someone was repeatedly trying to open them from the outside. So Fanny invited her mother to come and spend the night with her.

Mrs. Meyer came, of course, and watched her daughter undress. Why should she not? she was her own mother! She looked at her often, and she looked at her long, in fact, she could scarce take her eyes off her. The girl seemed to fill her with equal astonishment and rapture. At each moment the contours of her virginal figure revealed fresh charms. Ah! in the eyes of real connoisseurs sixty thousand florins were but a bagatelle for such a matchless creature!

At night, in the dark, when the candles are extinguished, old women can chatter their best, especially when they light upon someone who does not easily doze off and is prepared to patiently listen to all they have to say, and even to spur them on from time to time with expressions of amazement, horror, approbation, or other stimulating interjections. Such occasions are the most convenient time for recounting all that has happened ten, twenty, even fifty years ago, beginning from births and christenings, and going right on through engagements and marriages to deaths and burials, till at last a half-snore from one quarter or another puts an end to the discourse. Mrs. Meyer, too, was inclined to be talkative, and she could not have had a better opportunity than when they were both lying in bed.

"Oh, oh! my darling girl!" she began; "my sweet, pretty girl, never did I think I should be so fortunate as to sleep in the same room with you. How oddly things come about, to be sure! Here am I with four foolish girls, each one madder than the other; for if they were not mad, they would not behave as they have behaved. Each one of them had an honorable attachment, and well for them had they stopped there! but no, they were not content, they would have the whole world at their feet, and so they lost their opportunity."

This was the first assault.

Fanny, however, never answered a word. Mrs. Meyer, therefore, left well alone. She had made a move in the right direction, as she thought, so she now passed on to something else.

"How happy you are in this house! I see that everyone loves you. They're a little strict, perhaps, but what good honest people! A thousand times fortunate you are to have found your way hither, where you have everything you can desire. Here you can live in perfect contentment so long as old Boltay lives. God preserve him for many years to come! And yet I fear that he may one day die suddenly, for his blood is very thick, and his father and his two brothers all died of apoplexy much about the same time of life. I know very well that he would not leave you in want – he would provide for you, of course, if he had not got a nephew who is an advocate, to whom, perhaps, he will leave everything. That is family pride, and very natural, after all. Blood, you know, is thicker than water."

This was the second assault. Frighten the girl with the thought of what will become of her if Boltay dies! "Waste your precious youth while Boltay is alive, and then it will be too late to sigh and groan over the reflection, 'How much better it would have been to have sold it for so much!'"

And the horror of it was that Fanny understood everything quite well. She knew what her mother was talking about, what she was aiming at, how she was tampering with and tempting her, and she fancied that, through the darkness, she could see her cunning face, and through that cunning face right into that cunning soul, and she closed her eyes and stopped up her ears that she might not either see or hear, and yet she saw and heard all the same.

"Aye, aye!" sighed Mrs. Meyer, by way of announcing that she was about to begin again.

"Are you asleep, Fanny?"

"No," stammered the girl. She was not even sly enough to leave the question unanswered, in which case Mrs. Meyer would, perhaps, have fancied she had dozed off, and not said anything more.

"Are you angry with me for talking? If you don't like it, say so."

Fanny, involuntarily trembling, uttered, with an effort, a scarcely audible "Go on!"

"I should scarcely have recognized you if I had seen you. If I had met you in the street, I should certainly have passed you by without speaking. Yes, it is quite true. What a tiny little girl you were when they took you away from me! Ah! why did not all my girls remain little! Aye, aye! how poor people's daughters do grow up to be sure! Every time a poor man's daughters grow up he has more cause for sorrow than for joy. What will become of them? who will bring them up? Nowadays nobody cares about marrying. Trade brings in less and less, the expenses of housekeeping increase every day, and if a girl here and there does marry after all, what does she gain by it? Why, a worthless sot of a husband, and a life of misery, care, and anxiety. She'll go from bad to worse, have to slave like a maid-of-all-work, be saddled with a lot of wicked children, and when she gets old they'll pitch her into the street. Aye, aye! the best thing a mother could do for her daughter when it is born would be to bury it!"

Thus she emphasized, for the girl's benefit, all the difficulties of marriage, and laid stress upon the more disagreeable features of domestic life. And the girl knew quite well why she spoke to her in this way, for that one word, "How beautiful you are!" had suddenly enlightened her mind, and she also began to entertain the suspicion which, by the way, Teresa had never dared to communicate, that her mother had come to her as a tempter.

"Are you cold, Fanny?"

"No," stammered the girl, huddling up beneath the bed-clothes.

"I thought I heard you shiver."

"No, I didn't."

"You used to know Rézi Halm, didn't you?"

"Yes," faltered Fanny, in a low voice, wondering what was coming next, and what fresh attack was going to be made upon her.

"What a proud girl she was, eh? The whole lot of them were so proud – you remember, surely? – they were neighbors, you know. There was no speaking to them at all. When that misfortune happened to your eldest sister, they would not even look at us. And now do you know what has happened to those girls? A rich country gentleman fell in love with Rézi and carried her off. At first they cursed her, they rejected her. Later on the gentleman gave the girl a nice little property, and then they were reconciled to her, and went to live with her – yes, the whole lot of them, those stuck-up things who were so quick to judge other folks! And now they say there's nothing to make a fuss about; the girl is happier than any lady, and her lover is more faithful to her than many a husband is to his wife – fulfils all her desires, and gives her whatever she wants. The servants call her 'my lady,' and they are glad to see her in polite society, and ask no questions."

Here Mrs. Meyer paused for a moment, to give Fanny time to take it all in and think it all over. Then she went on again as follows: "I don't know how it is, but I don't feel a bit sleepy tonight. Perhaps it is because I am in a strange room. I am always fancying the window to be where the door is. I say, Fanny," she added suddenly, "can you do embroidery?"

It seemed an innocent question enough, so Fanny answered that she could.

"It has just occurred to me that the last piece of embroidery you did is at home – that sofa-cover, you know, with the kissing doves on it. It stands just below your portrait which that young artist – you remember – painted for nothing. Ah! since then he has become a famous artist; since then he has painted your portrait in at least three hundred different ways, and sent it to all the exhibitions, and there the greatest noblemen pay him large sums of money for that very portrait. Yes, and bid against each other for it, too. I might say that that painter has founded his reputation on that one portrait, for since then his name is familiar in all first-class houses. That picture did the whole thing."

Ah! now she is trying the door of vanity!

"The man himself would not believe it," pursued Mrs. Meyer. "A great nobleman, a very great nobleman, became so enamored of the portrait – naturally he saw it abroad – that he came, post-haste, all the way to Pressburg, to convince himself that the subject of the portrait really lived in our city. He came to our house, and you should have seen his despair when he was told that you lived there no longer. At first he wanted to blow his brains out. He succeeded, subsequently, however, in finding out where you were – saw you, and since then he has been worse than ever. He would come to our house, sit down on the sofa which he knew you had embroidered, and stare at your portrait for hours at a stretch. Your sisters were angry with him because he had not a look for them; but I liked him, because I always used to hear something of you from him. He was always following you, and I could at least learn from him whether you were well or poorly off. Oh! that man was positively mad about you!"

So we've got as far as this, eh?

Fanny now raised herself on her elbows, and listened to her mother's conversation with something of that shuddering curiosity with which Damiens regarded the wounds made in his body for the reception of the burning oil.

"Oh, what absurdities that gentleman perpetrated!" continued Mrs. Meyer, noisily shifting her pillows from one side to the other. "The man was not aware that they were laughing at and making fun of him. Not a day passed without his coming to our house, and he said, over and over again, that if you had been there, he would have made you his wife on the spot. 'Go along with you, sir!' said I. Ah, my dear sweet girl, beware when a great nobleman says he will marry you! It is all nonsense; he wants to make a fool of you!"

Here Mrs. Meyer rested a little, and thus gave Fanny time to complete in her own mind the suggestion insinuated above as follows –

"But if he says, 'I won't marry you, but I'll give you money,' that's reason – listen to him. It is only little clerks and twopenny-halfpenny swells that deceive girls with promises of marriage, and these you must avoid; but a real gentleman always begins by giving something, and him you may listen to."

And the shame, the disgrace? Pooh, such is life!

Fanny, horror-stricken, waited to see what else her mother was going to say. Presently she went on again –

"I didn't know whether to be sorry for or disgusted with the poor man when I saw him so far gone. Suddenly you disappeared from the town. Then he gave way to despair altogether, for he fancied that they had got you married somewhere or other. At any rate, he came to me like a madman and asked what had become of you. 'I don't know, sir,' said I; 'they took her away from me long ago. Possibly she is married.' I had no sooner uttered these words than the young man grew quite pale, and cast himself on the very sofa which you embroidered, on which is a couple of billing doves in the middle of a wreath of roses. I was sorry for the poor man, as he was a fine, handsome young fellow; in fact, I never saw a handsomer man in my life. What eyebrows! And his face, too, so pale and refined, a hand like velvet, a beautiful mouth, and a commanding figure. I cannot get him out of my head. I asked him why he did not make haste about it if his intentions with regard to you were so serious. He said he was only waiting for the death of his uncle, who was greatly against the marriage. 'That's all very well, sir,' I replied, 'but you cannot expect the girl to wait till your uncle dies; she herself would be getting old by then. It is not a fair thing to expect any girl to do.' Then he said he would swear fidelity to you in the meantime. 'Alas, sir!' I said, 'it is hard to believe in that; one cannot trust the men nowadays. You would only make the girl unhappy, and the marriage would remain an eternal secret.' Thereupon he said that if I did not believe his word of honor and his oath, he was ready to deposit with me sixty thousand florins, ready money, and if ever he should be such a scoundrel as to fall short of his word and desert you, he would forfeit the money. Now, sixty thousand florins is a great sum of money. Nobody would be such a fool as to lightly chuck it away. A man would think twice about breaking his word when all that was at stake, especially when he had given his word to such a wondrously lovely girl as my Fanny."

"Good night; I want to go to sleep," stammered Fanny, sinking back again between her pillows; and for a long time afterwards she tossed about in her bed, whilst hatred, horror, and disgust struggled together in her soul. Only the late dawn brought rest at last to her weary eyelids.

The sun was already shining through the windowpanes when Fanny awoke. Mrs. Meyer must have got up and gone out much earlier, for there was no sign of her. Her good humor returned, therefore, and she arose and dressed hastily, scarcely allowing herself time to arrange her hair in the simplest manner possible.

Breakfast was already awaiting her. Mrs. Meyer meanwhile was in the kitchen outside making the coffee and the toast. She would not hear of the servants helping her; such a sweet pretty daughter deserved that her mother should take a little trouble on her account.

Fanny and her mother were alone over their coffee. Fanny had wished her mother good morning and kissed her hand, whereupon Mrs. Meyer gave her back tit for tat by kissing her hand also.

"Oh, what a pretty hand, what an elegant hand! Oh, my darling, my only girl! Ah, how blessed I am in living so near to you! Permit me to give you your coffee. I know exactly how you like it, don't I? – a little sugar and lots of milk, that's it, isn't it? I have forgotten nothing, you see."

The woman was quite loquacious. Whenever Teresa was present she hardly ventured to address the girl at all. Teresa's cold, perpetually watchful eyes, always had a disquieting effect upon her; now she was freed from that restraint.

Fanny primly sipped her coffee, looking from time to time at her mother, who never once ceased praising her beauty and goodness, and would have compelled her to eat up every bit of breakfast if she could have had her way.

"Mamma," said the girl, taking her mother's hand (she was no longer afraid of her), "what was the name of that gentleman who was making inquiries about me?"

Mrs. Meyer's eyes began to sparkle villainously. Ah ha! the timid creature was approaching the snare!

If, however, she had regarded her daughter's face a little more attentively, she would have noticed that in putting the question she did not even blush, but remained cold and pale.

Looking round very mysteriously to make sure that nobody was within hearing distance, she drew her daughter's head down towards her, and whispered in her ear –

"Abellino Kárpáthy."

"Oh, 'tis he, then!" exclaimed Fanny, with a peculiar, a very peculiar smile.

"Then you know him?"

"I have seen him once, a long way off."

"Oh, what a handsome, refined, pleasant man he is! Never in my life have I seen such a figure of a man!"

Fanny began brushing the crumbs off the tablecloth and playing with the coffee-spoon.

"Yes, mother; sixty thousand florins is a lot of money, isn't it?"

Ah, the hunted creature is already in the snare! Quick, quick!

"Yes, my darling, a lot of money indeed; the legal rate of interest upon it is three thousand six hundred florins. A poor man would have to put his nose to the grindstone for a long, long time before he could earn that."

"Tell me, mamma, was papa's income as much as that?"

"Alas! no, my daughter. It was much for him when it came to nine hundred florins, and that is only the fourth part of this. Fancy, four times nine hundred florins!"

"Now say, mamma, has Abellino really said that he would marry me?"

"He said he would give a solemn assurance to that effect any moment you like."

Fanny appeared to be considering. "Well, if he deceives me, so much the worse for him, the sixty thousand florins will be ours in any case."

"Ah, what a prudent girl it is! She is not a feather-brain like her sisters. She will not make a fool of her old mother. She is, indeed, my own true girl!" thought Mrs. Meyer to herself, and she rubbed her hands for joy.

Now the iron is hot, now is the time to strike!

"Ah, my daughter, romance is, no doubt, a very fine thing, but it will soon bring you to starvation if you have nothing else to depend upon. Those poetic gentlemen love to scribble about ideals and such like rubbish, yet they themselves are always looking out for the trees on which money grows. Why, the whole world runs after money, nothing but money, and he who has money has honor into the bargain. A beggar may be as honorable as you like, but nobody takes any notice of him. You are young now, and handsome, and can get something on the strength of it; but how long will your beauty last? In ten years' time it will be gone. Nay, more, your loveliness may not even last so long as ten years if you continue to live as you are living now, for those damsels who stint themselves of the joys of life, wither the quickest —"

"Hush! Mr. Boltay is coming."

The old man entered, wished them good morning, and inquired if they wanted anything brought from town, as the horses were already being put to, and he would be off at once.

"Mamma wants to go away," said Fanny, with the utmost composure; "would you be so good, daddy, as to take her along with you?"

Mrs. Meyer stared with all her eyes, and all her mouth too; she had never said that she wanted to go away.

"Very happy!" replied Boltay. "Where does she want to go?"

"She wants to go home to her daughters (Mrs. Meyer looked frightened). There are some embroideries of mine there which I do not want my sisters to throw away or sell in the rag-market; bring them back to me."

(Ah, what a sage damsel! what a golden-minded damsel!)

"I am thinking especially of a sofa that is there. Mamma knows which it is, for I embroidered the cover; it has two doves worked upon it. I would not let my sisters have that on any account; do you understand?"

Why, of course she understood! This was the girl's way of showing that she accepted the offer of the gentleman who was so fond of sitting on the sofa, and how delicately she conveyed her consent – that blockhead of a Boltay did not suspect anything. Oh, a sage damsel! a golden-minded damsel!

Boltay went out for a moment to tell the coachman to prepare a seat for a lady, and taking advantage of this moment, Mrs. Meyer whispered in her daughter's ear –

"When may I come back for you?"

"The day after tomorrow."

"And what answer shall I give?"

"The day after tomorrow," repeated Fanny.

Here Boltay popped in again.

"Wait a moment, my dear uncle," said Fanny; "I want to write a few lines to Aunt Teresa, which you can take with you."

"All right, though it is a pity to ink your fingers, I think, for I can give her the message all the same, if you tell me what it is."

"Very well, daddy, tell aunty to bring me a ball of *cashmir harras,* a yard of *pur de laine,* or *poil-de-chevre* –"

Boltay was frightened at all those foreign words.

"It will be better, after all, if you write it down," said he; "I can never learn all that."

Fanny, smiling all the time, produced her writing materials and wrote a short letter, which she folded up, sealed, and gave to Boltay.

Mrs. Meyer cast a significant glance at the girl out of the corner of her eye, allowed herself to be lifted up into the cart; the whip cracked, and off they went.

Fanny remained looking after them for some time, and then with a cold, contemptuous expression, returned to her room, watered her flowers, fed her birds, and sang herself back into a good humor again.

On reaching town, Boltay dismounted at the first shop (he pretended he had some indispensable purchase to make), and bade the coachman take Mrs. Meyer to where she wanted to go. He would find his way to his house on foot, he said.

Not very long afterwards Mrs. Meyer found herself once more in the circle of her well-beloved. Abellino had just looked in, and the girls were wild to know how their mother had fared.

It took Mrs. Meyer a good couple of hours to tell them all about her happy adventure: how she had struggled, how much eloquence she had expended till she had compelled the girl to surrender. For the girl was frightfully modest, she said, and she had to make her believe that the gentleman really meant to make her his wife, and had said so all along.

Abellino, in his joy, could scarce restrain himself from embracing the duenna at intervals, during the course of her entertaining narrative, especially when she told him what a splendid picture she had drawn of him to Fanny.

Well, let us leave them all making merry together, and accompany Boltay homewards also. Teresa was already awaiting him in the doorway, for the coachman had arrived first, and told her he was coming. His first care was to give her the letter.

"I have brought you a letter," said he, "but its contents are Greek to me. Why, I couldn't even pronounce the lingo!"

Teresa broke open the letter, read it through, and looked at Boltay. Then she read it through again. She read it through a third time, and again she looked at Boltay.

"It is Greek, indeed," said she. "I don't understand it. You have a look at it."

And she handed the letter to Boltay.

"Hum!" growled the old gentleman, fancying that the letter was full of stupid foreign terms, and, to his amazement, he read these words –

> "My dear Aunt,
>
> "I know everything. Don't let that woman, whom I cannot call mother without a feeling of horror, come to our house again. Send word to Mr. John Kárpáthy, and tell him to come to me at once. I have something very serious to say to him, which admits of no delay. Send immediately.
>
> "Your affectionate kinswoman,
>
> "Fanny"

What was the meaning of it? What had happened? When had there been time for anything to happen? They had had their coffee so nicely and quietly together, whispering so confidentially all the time, and kissed each other's hands at parting. Mr. Boltay did not understand it at all.

But Teresa began to understand.

So they had to send at once to John Kárpáthy. Who was to go? Boltay resolved to go himself. He had good legs, and would be there in a moment. So he went and gave the message to old Palko, who communicated it to his master forthwith. The bridegroom understood it in a moment, and lost no time in getting into his carriage and setting out. Boltay and Teresa sat beside him in the carriage. Nobody saw them through the closed windows, and five fiery steeds carried them along the king's high-road at a gallop, taking but a couple of hours to accomplish the journey, whereas Master Boltay at his more leisurely pace would have taken four at least.

Fanny herself received her distinguished guest with a face even paler than usual; but this pallor rather became her. Squire John was beside himself for rapture. He would not give his fair bride time to approach him, but, putting his hand solemnly upon his breast, addressed her in language very unusual for him –

"My dear young lady, so help me God, the one object of my life will be how to make you happy!"

"And I, sir," said Fanny, in a calm and resolute voice, "shall consider it my highest duty to do honor to your name. And now I would ask you all three, my friends, to grant me a few hours' private interview where we shall not be disturbed."

These words were spoken in such a calm and resolute voice that they felt bound to obey, and all four withdrew into the innermost chamber, locking the door behind them.

A few hours later the door was reopened, and they all four appeared again.

But how every face had changed!

Fanny's face was no longer pale, but as red as the dawn, serene, and open as a half-blown rose.

Master Boltay was twisting his moustache as if he meditated something terrible; but for an occasional chuckle, one would have said that he was very angry indeed.

Even honest Teresa's eyes sparkled, but the sparks of triumphant revenge were in them after all.

And then the bridegroom, Squire John! Where was he, and what had become of the old Nabob? Could anyone have recognized him? Was this merry, sprightly, leaping, smiling, triumphant creature the same man? Why, he had grown twenty years younger at the very least! It was a changeling, surely!

"Tomorrow, then, in the afternoon," said he, with a voice that trembled for joy.

"Yes, tomorrow," replied Fanny. Their eyes flashed with a strange fire as they looked at each other.

Thereupon Squire John rushed to his carriage, opened the door himself, without waiting for Palko to let down the steps, and, turning round, shouted once more, "Tomorrow afternoon!"

"Hush, hush!" said Fanny, putting her index-finger to her pretty little lips.

"Drive into Pressburg!" cried Squire John with impatient celerity, while Palko clambered up on to the box from whence he phlegmatically looked down upon his master.

"What are you staring at, sirrah? Drive on, I say."

"We have left something behind here," said the old servant.

"What have we left behind, eh?"

"Twenty years of your age, my honored young sir," replied Palko, without the suspicion of a smile.

Squire John laughed good-naturedly at the comic rejoinder, and a few moments later a cloud of dust far away on the high-road was all that was to be seen of the carriage.

Early next morning a servant arrived at Boltay's country house by the market cart, with the embroidered sofa which Mrs. Meyer sent to Fanny. The servant whispered secretly that a letter had been thrust into the bottom of the sofa; and so it was.

Fanny searched for the letter till she found it. It was in her mother's handwriting. The rich gentleman was delighted, it said, so delighted in fact, that he had arranged to give a grand party in Fanny's honor at Mr. Kecskerey's rooms; and a beautiful invitation card was enclosed, addressed to – "Mademoiselle Fanny de Meyer avec famille."

Quite a family party, you see!

Fanny sent back the servant with the message that she accepted the invitation to supper, and sent her best greetings to Mr. Kecskerey.

But who was this Mr. Kecskerey you will ask? Well, he was a worthy gentleman who was wont to play no inconsiderable part in the refined society of the day, and supplied one of the most crying necessities of the age. Everyone knew him, everybody, that is, who prided himself upon being somebody, whether he was a great nobleman or a great artist.

His rooms, his suppers, his breakfasts were the usual rallying points of the whole world of fashion.

Eminent damsels, whose enthusiasm for art constrained them to come to closer quarters than usual with this or that famous artist; liberal-minded amazons, who extended their tender relations beyond the chains of Hymen; lively dames, who loved to see around them good-humored, free-and-easy folks, instead of the usual dull and dignified drawing room loungers; foreign millionaires, who desired to be regaled with an exhibition of beauty and enjoyment; *blasé* souls, who infected others with the contagion of their own disgust; crazy poets, who needed but a nod to immediately rise to their feet and declaim their own verses; two or three newspaper correspondents, who describe in their journals everything that they hear, see, eat, and drink at Mr. Kecskerey's suppers, and many others of a like kidney, were the sort of guests who frequented these saloons of an evening, generally twice a week.

It must not be supposed for a moment, however, that there was ever the slightest breach of good manners at Mr. Kecskerey's social evenings. Anyone supposing the contrary would be making the greatest mistake in the world. The most rigorous propriety was the order of the day, or rather of the evening. First of all, the artists and *artistes* recited, sang, and played the piano, and then those who chose might dance a few modest quadrilles and waltzes together. Then everyone went to supper in the most perfect order, the ladies sitting down and the gentlemen standing while they ate and drank. Sometimes a few glasses of champagne were drained to toast the ladies who were present, or, perhaps, some of the celebrities of the day. Then, after a little brief but lively conversation, a few more quadrilles and waltzes would be danced, and at eleven o'clock the ladies would rise and retire, and only a few dandies – the younger and the older men as a rule – would remain behind for a glass or two, or a hand at cards.

From this everyone can easily see that at these evening entertainments there was not the slightest thing that could be considered an offence against good manners or good morals. Oh no! Mr. Kecskerey would never have allowed such a thing; he was too proud of his renown for that. He was no minister of love, not he! He only gave people the opportunity of meeting together if they liked, and that is entirely a personal matter, of course.

An especially grand assembly was to be held at Mr. Kecskerey's on the day fixed for Fanny's appearance by Abellino and his friends. They naturally sent out all the invitations, as the money for the entertainment came out of their pockets, and all the elegant world of their acquaintance was to do honor to the occasion.

On the morning of the critical day Mrs. Meyer, dressed in the self-same garments which Master Boltay had got for her, took her seat in a hackney-coach, and drove out of town. All the way along she was concocting the further details of the great affair. Leaving the coach standing on the outskirts of the wood, she would make her way on foot to Boltay's dwelling, and there she would say that she had brought the things from town. Fanny would then go out for a walk with her under the pretext of looking at the crops, and on reaching the coach they would step in, shut the door, and off they would set at full tilt without asking leave of anybody.

Maturing thus her amiable designs, she safely reached the meadows near Boltay's dwelling. Providence was so far merciful to her that she did not break an arm or a leg on the way. On reaching her journey's end, however, a very cruel surprise awaited her, for in reply to her inquiries about Fanny, the servants informed her that the young lady had driven into Pressburg early that very morning.

She was amazed, and not without reason.

"I suppose the old people took her to town?" said she.

"No; they went away at daybreak. The young lady had departed only a couple of hours ago in a hired carriage."

Alas, alas! What was the girl thinking about? Perhaps she only wanted to steal a march upon her mother, and look after the lucrative business herself unaided? Perhaps someone had explained to her that it was best altogether to dispense with the services of go-betweens in such affairs? Well, it would be a pretty thing indeed if she had wiped her mother out of the reckoning altogether!

Away! Back to the coach! Back to Pressburg in hot haste, if the horses died for it. But where could the girl be? What if she had gone quietly off with Abellino in the meantime; or, still worse, with someone else, and did not turn up at all? Oh, what bitter grief and anguish a mother's heart has to contend with!

Meanwhile, all the guests were assembled in Mr. Kecskerey's saloons. One after another bevies of charming women alighted at the entrance with delicate coquetry, permitting the eye-glassed cavaliers to catch glimpses of their tiny beribboned feet as they dismounted from their equipages. In the hall, liveried footmen distributed tickets for shawls and slippers. The master of the house, the honorable Mr. Kecskerey, with dignified condescension, received the arrivals in the doorway. Everybody knows that Kecskerey's money does not pay for the evening's entertainment, and he himself knows that they know it. And yet, for all that, they bow and scrape to one another as politely as if he were a real host and they were real guests. Mr. Kecskerey's shrill nasal voice resounded above all the din and bustle.

"I am so delighted that you have not rejected my modest invitation. Your excellency has, indeed, honored my poor house by your presence. Mesdames, so kind of you not to forget the most sincere of your servants. Sir, it is really too good of you to neglect your important studies on my account! Countess, your siren song is generally acknowledged to be the gem of the evening, etc."

The amiable host laid himself out to make the diversion of his guests as free and unconstrained as possible. Those who did not know and wished to know each other were immediately introduced, though it is possible that they had known each other of old, without his or anyone else's intervention. He gave the poets printed sheets, in which they could read their own works. He made the musicians sit down before the piano, and placed behind their backs someone to praise them, and he possessed the art of saying something obliging, something interesting, to everyone; he scattered freshly done-up gossip and piquant anecdotes amongst the thronging crowds, he knew how to make tea better than anyone else, and his eye was upon everybody, so that nobody felt neglected. A model host, indeed!

At last Abellino arrived. It was not in his power to be punctual. An elderly foreign gentleman was leaning on his arm, and he led him straight up to the host, and introduced him.

"Friend Kecskerey – Monsieur Griffard, the banker."

Fresh bowings and scrapings and shaking of hands.

"Pardon me, honored host, for my indecent haste in introducing among the *élite* of your distinguished guests as if he were a bosom friend, such a cosmopolitan celebrity, who, only this very hour, has unexpectedly arrived here from Paris."

Oh, as for that, Mr. Kecskerey, so far from granting his pardon, expressed himself obliged and gratified a thousand times over at having been afforded the felicity of an introduction to such a distinguished personage. And all this took place with as much solemnity as if Abellino was not in reality the host of the evening, and as if everybody did not know it!

As a matter of fact, the worthy banker had come all the way from Paris (and there was no railway communication between the two places then, remember) on purpose to convince himself with his own eyes, whether the old Nabob, on whose skin he had staked such a pile of money, was really going to die or not?

Mr. Kecskerey lavished his most delicate attentions upon the eminent stranger, conducting him into the society of the most charming women, his principal object therein being to relieve Abellino of this incubus. As for Abellino, he withdrew, meanwhile, with a few young bucks of his own age, into the card-room, where he was likely to pass the time most agreeably until the arrival of Fanny.

A good many people were already seated round the green table, amongst them being Abellino's rival, Fennimore, at the sight of whom Abellino burst into a noisy impertinent laugh.

"Ah, Fennimore!" cried he. "You certainly ought to have mighty good luck at cards today, for, so far as love is concerned, everything is going against you. Diable! you will have to win a jolly lot, for you've lost a thousand ducats to me already. You laid a wager that I would not win the girl, eh? You shall see presently. And perhaps you all fancy that the expenses of this evening will come out of my pocket? You are very much mistaken, I can tell you. It is Fennimore who will have to pay. Here, give me an inch of room at the table, and I'll try my luck."

Fennimore said not a word; he was keeping the bank just then. A few moments later the bank was broken. Abellino won heaps and heaps.

"Ah, ah, my friend! the proverb 'Luckless at cards, lucky at love,' does not seem to apply to you. Poor Fennimore, God help thee!"

Fennimore arose; he would play no more. He was livid with rage. He had lost his wager (he had bet Abellino a thousand ducats that he would never seduce Fanny) – he had lost his money, and he had to bear, besides, the stinging sarcasms of his triumphant rival. His heart was full of gall and venom. More than once he was on the point of making a vigorous demonstration with a heavy candlestick; but he thought better of it, and at last got up and quitted the room.

Abellino went on playing and winning, and in his teasing, tormenting way stung those who lost to the very quick. He was stupefied by the day's good luck. He could not restrain his laughter.

"Well," cried he at last, sweeping into his pocket the banknotes piled up before him, "Fennimore's twofold ill luck has given the lie to the proverb. I am going to contradict it with my twofold good fortune."

In the very next room he came face to face with a lackey who had long been looking for him. Mrs. Meyer was waiting for him, the man said; she was in the antechamber, but could not come in, for she had only just returned from a journey, and had not had time to change her dress.

Ugh! that was not a good sign. Abellino immediately hastened out to have a word with her. She said that she had not come across the girl, but she was sure to come, as otherwise she would not have accepted the invitation.

Abellino received the pleasant tidings very angrily, and left Mrs. Meyer alone in the antechamber. Diable! if they should make a fool of him, after all!

There, however, he could not afford to display his anger; no, there he had to carry it off with a joyous, triumphant, provocative face to the very end. He would rather lose all his money than be left in the lurch by the girl now.

Presently he went out again to ask Mrs. Meyer whether she had not told the girl that he meant to make her his wife.

Oh yes; and the girl seemed greatly delighted at the idea.

And again he cheered up a bit, and returned to the assembly room, and did his best to amuse Monsieur Griffard.

They were handing round the tea, and the Countess X—— had just begun to sing the "Casta Diva," when Abellino's lackey sidled up to his master and whispered in his ear –

"I have just seen Miss Fanny Meyer descending from a carriage."

Abellino pressed into the servant's hand as many ducats as he happened to have about him, pulled himself together, and got up and looked at himself in a mirror. He was elegant and genteel, at any rate, that everybody would be bound to allow. His whole get-up was unexceptionable – his chin was clean-shaven, his moustache and whiskers were downright picturesque, his cravat was ravishing, and his vest magnificent.

And now the flunkey whose duty it was to announce the arrivals, entered the room (Abellino caught sight of him in the mirror), and announced in his ceremonious *salon* voice, "Madame Fanny de Kárpáthy, *née* de Meyer!"

"The deuce!" thought Abellino; "the wench is making pretty free with my name. Can she be taking me seriously? Well, she may do so if she likes. It doesn't matter much."

"Ah, a wedding!" exclaimed Mons. Griffard. "Then you are marrying, eh?"

"Oh, it is only a left-handed marriage," said Abellino, jocosely.

Some of the guests, full of curiosity, pressed forward to meet the new arrivals. The host, I mean Mr. Kecskerey, went towards the entrance; the lackey threw open the folding-doors, and a young lady entered, accompanied by a gentleman. For a moment the whole company was dumb with amazement. Was it the sight of the young lady that amazed them so? She was beautiful, certainly. A simple but costly lace mantle floated, wavelike, round her superb figure; the rich tresses of her hair were covered by a slight veil of Brussels lace, which allowed her long curls *à l'Anglaise* to sweep down on both sides over her marble-smooth shoulders and ravishingly beautiful bosom. And then that face, that complexion like a faintly blushing rose, that look worthy of a goddess, those burning black eyes so full of vivacity and passion, and contrasting so strangely with the childlike lips suggestive of sleeping innocence, but harmonizing on the other hand with the dimples on her rosy chin and cheeks, set there surely for the undoing of any human soul who saw a smile upon them!

And there was a smile upon them now, as Mr. Kecskerey came forward without exactly knowing what to say.

Fanny greeted him.

"I was very pleased to accept your honored invitation," said she, "and I have brought my family with me also, as you see. I mean, of course, my husband, Mr. John Kárpáthy;" and she indicated the gentleman by her side.

Mr. Kecskerey could only say that his delight was infinite, but all the time his eyes were anxiously searching for Abellino in the most evident embarrassment.

As for Abellino, he remained standing before the mirror and looking just like Lot's wife at the moment when she was turned into a pillar of salt.

But meantime John Kárpáthy, the good-humored, merry, radiant Squire John, pressed the hand of the master of the house as if he were an old acquaintance, at the same time keeping his wife's little hand safely tucked under his arm.

"Congratulate me, my worthy friend," said he. "I have won today a treasure, a heavenly treasure. I am blessed indeed. I have no need of any other paradise, for this world is now a paradise to me."

And laughing aloud, and with a beaming countenance, he mingled with the company, presenting his wife to the most distinguished persons present, who overwhelmed him with congratulations.

And Abellino was obliged to look on all the time!

To think that this girl, whom he had pursued so ostentatiously with his love, should have become his uncle's wife, and consequently, henceforth and forevermore, inaccessible to himself!

Why, if she had been carried up to the heights of heaven or down to the depths of hell; if she had been fenced about in a rock-girt fortress, or if wrathful archangels had guarded her with flaming swords, she would not have been so completely shielded from him as by that talismanic name – "Madame John Kárpáthy!"

It was impossible for him to have any relations whatever with Madame John Kárpáthy!

Every eye that had sated itself with gazing on the beautiful young bride, strayed back to him, and every look fixed upon him was full of scorn and ridicule. The dandy, who was celebrating his uncle's wedding! The outwitted suitor, whose adored one gave her hand – not to him, but to his uncle!

It almost did Abellino good to see someone in the company who seemed to be as hard hit as himself – namely, Monsieur Griffard, and true, even now, to his malicious nature, he turned towards the banker and inquired mockingly –

"Qu'en dites vous, M. Griffard?"

"C'est bien fatal!"

"Mon cher Abellino!" said Fennimore, who chanced to be standing by him, and never had his thin drawling voice seemed so offensive, "it looks very much as if you owed me a thousand ducats. Ha, ha, ha!"

Abellino turned furiously upon him, but at that instant his eyes met those of Squire John, who had just then reached the place where he was standing, with his wife under his arm, and introduced them to each other with the most benevolent smile in the world.

"My dear wife, this is my dear little brother Bélá Kárpáthy. My dear little brother, I recommend my dear wife to your kinsmanlike regard!"

Ah, this was the moment which he had so joyfully anticipated; this was the exquisite vengeance, the thought of which had grown up in the heart of the persecuted girl, and made the eyes of the gentle creature sparkle so brightly.

The hunter had fallen into the snare – the snare that he himself had laid. He had been hoodwinked, rejected, worsted utterly.

Abellino bowed stiffly, biting his lips hard all the time; he was as white as the wall.

Then Squire John passed on and had himself specially introduced to Monsieur Griffard, who expressed his intense gratification at finding the Nabob in the possession of such excellent health.

But Abellino, the moment they had passed by, stuck his thumbs into the corners of his vest, and humming a tune, and holding his head high, as if he were in the best of humors, strolled from one end of the large assembly room to the other, feigning ignorance of the fact that the whispering and tittering that resounded on every side was so much scorn and ridicule directed against him.

He hastened to the card-room.

As he passed through the door he heard how everybody there was laughing and sniggering. Fennimore's shrill voice resounded through the din. The moment they saw him the peals of laughter broke off suddenly, all signs of hilarity disappeared, everybody tried to put on a solemn and expectant look. Could anything in the world be more aggravating?

Abellino dragged a chair to the table and sat down among them. Why did they not go on laughing; why did they not continue their conversation? Why did Fennimore make such efforts to put on a solemn face, when his mouth was regularly twitching?

The cards were dealt.

It was now Abellino's turn to keep the bank.

He began to lose.

Fennimore was sitting at the other end of the table, and he won continually; he doubled, trebled, quadrupled his stakes; he doubled them again, and still he won. Abellino began to lose his *sang-froid* and get flurried. He did not keep a proper watch on the stakes, and often swept in the stakes of the winners and paid the losers. His mind was elsewhere.

And now Fennimore again won four times as much as he had staked.

He could not restrain a laugh of triumph.

"Ha! ha! Monsieur de Kárpáthy, the proverb ill applies to you also: you are unlucky at cards, and unlucky in love as well. Poor Abellino! Heaven help you! You owe me a thousand ducats."

"I?" asked Abellino, irritably.

"Yes, you. Did you not bet me that you would seduce Fanny? And how splendidly it has turned out! Abellino flies from the embraces of his uncle's wife like a new Joseph fleeing from a new Madame Potiphar! You had much better take care lest the lady takes a fancy to some other nice young man. Ah, ah, ah! Abellino as the protector of virtue! Abellino as a garde des dames! Why, it's sublime! You might make a capital farce out of it."

Every word was as venom to his ears, every word cut him to the quick, cut him to the very marrow. Abellino turned pale and shivered with rage. What Fennimore said was true. He must needs tremble now at the thought that this woman would find someone to love. Damnation! Damnation!

And still he kept on losing.

He scarce noticed now what he dealt. Fennimore again won four times the amount of his stakes. Abellino only paid him double.

"Oh, my friend, you have made a mistake! I laid as much again."

"I did not observe it."

"Why, this is pure filibustery!" cried Fennimore, with insolent indignation.

At this insulting word, Abellino instantly sprang to his feet, and flung the whole pack of cards right between Fennimore's eyes.

Fennimore's naturally pale face grew blue and green, and, seizing the chair on which he had been sitting, he made a rush at Abellino; but the company intervened, and dragged Fennimore back.

"Let me go – let me go! Give me a knife!" he roared, with foaming lips; while Abellino, breathing hard, regarded him with bloodshot eyes. Only with the greatest difficulty were they prevented from tearing each other to pieces.

At this unseemly disturbance, Mr. Kecskerey rushed in with a very alarmed expression of face, forced his way through the ranks of the wranglers, and, assuming his most imposing manner, exclaimed with a voice that rang out like a clarion, "Respect the sanctity of my house!"

This intervention brought the combatants to their senses. They began to recognize that this was not the place for adjusting affairs of honor. The appeal to the sanctity of Mr. Kecskerey's house also did something to restore the good-humor of the majority. Fennimore and Abellino were therefore advised by their friends to go home, and settle their little matter the next morning. They departed accordingly, and the company was disturbed no more. A few minutes afterwards everyone knew that Fennimore and Abellino had quarreled at cards, but everyone pretended that he knew nothing at all about it.

But the quarrel in the card-room of Mr. Kecskerey's establishment had serious consequences for both the principal disputants. There could be no thought of a reconciliation after such a deliberate and public affront as that inflicted upon Fennimore by Abellino; so they sent their seconds to each other, and it was arranged that they should fight the matter out in the large room of The Green Tree tavern. They met accordingly, and a stubborn contest ensued, marked on both sides by an altogether unprecedented display of vindictive temper. Finally, Fennimore, after treacherously wounding Abellino in the back during a suspension of hostilities, and again on the shoulder when the fight was resumed, was himself transfixed by his adversary's sword, and died without uttering a sigh or groan, or moving a muscle of his face. As for Abellino, he was confined to his bed for a whole month, and when he had partially recovered, he received a hint from his well-wishers to the effect that, until the affair had blown over a little, it would be as well if he took the air somewhere abroad; and that, too, not in any civilized kingdom, for there they would not be very long in nabbing a man like him who had so many creditors and loved to make a stir, but in some nice Oriental empire where he would be out of harm's way. So it ended in his setting off for Palestine, to visit the Holy Sepulchre, where, said the wags, he was going to do penance for his sins. Thither we need not follow him.

But Squire John Kárpáthy, the happy, the more than happy Nabob, set off with his fair consort for Kárpátfalva, there to spend their honeymoon.

Chapter X

POOR LADY!

Poor lady!

The poor lady I mean is Madame Kárpáthy. She had got a husband, and along with him enormous wealth and a monstrously grand name, both rather burdens than blessings as a rule.

The day does not dawn twice for the richest man, and all the treasures in the world cannot give their possessor peace, joy, love, contentment, and a good conscience.

And then that illustrious name; what was it after all?

The whole world knew who had inherited that name – an old gentleman with the reputation of a fool, who, to spite his nephew, had married a girl belonging to a family of ill-repute. The old gentleman was either very magnanimous or very foolish. The girl must necessarily be frivolous and forward. Everyone was ready to believe the worst of her beforehand.

Poor lady!

Fanny naturally felt miserable and lonely. There was nobody about her, no friend of her own age and sex in whom she could confide, and she knew not where to look for such a treasure. And yet one day she found a confidant where she least expected it. Her husband had resolved to have a house-warming in her honor, and had had a list made of the intended guests which he sent to her for her approval, by the hands of old Mr. Varga, the steward. This particular piece of attention showed, moreover, how polite and condescending Kárpáthy was towards his wife.

Mr. Varga took the list, and, as was his wont on his passage through the house, continued knocking at every door he came to till he was told to come in. On perceiving his mistress, he stood on the threshold in an attitude of the deepest respect, and would very much have liked to have had there and then an arm long enough to have reached from the door to the sofa.

Fanny was strangely attracted towards the old man. There are some persons whom Fortune endows with a cast of countenance which allows you to read right through their features into their pure and honest souls, so that you feel confidence in them at the very first glance. Fanny did not wait for Mr. Varga to come nearer to her, but arose and went to meet him, took his hand, and, despite the old man's strenuous efforts to bow low at every step he took, drew him forward, made him sit down in an armchair, and, in order that he might not get up again, threw her arms round him in childish fashion, which plunged the old fellow into the most unutterable confusion. Naturally, the moment Fanny let him go, and sat down herself, up he sprang again.

"Nay, my dear Mr. Varga, do sit down, or else I must stand up."

"I am not worthy of such an honor," stammered the old steward, very circumspectly letting himself down into the chair again, as if he were about to beg pardon for being so bold as to sit in it at all, and bending forward so that he might not lean upon it too heavily.

"What have you brought me, my dear, good Mr. Varga?" asked Fanny, with a smile. "If you have brought nothing but yourself, I should be all the better pleased. Now you can see how pleased I am to see you."

Varga murmured something to the effect that he did not know what he had done to deserve so much favor, and hastened to hand her the document, at the same time delivering Squire John's message; then he prepared to take his leave. But Fanny anticipated him.

"Pray remain," said she. "I have a few questions to put to you."

This was a command, so he felt bound to sit down again. He had never felt so bad before any other examination. What could her ladyship have to ask him? He devoutly wished that some other person was sitting there in his stead.

Fanny took the list and ran her eye down it, and as she did so, her heart sank within her. There were so many strange names, and all she knew about them was that they were all the names of great and illustrious men in high positions, and unexceptionable women. She had not a single acquaintance among all these women, and had no idea which of them she would find attractive, or which of them she might have cause to fear. How was she to comport herself in the society of all these high and haughty dames? If she put on a bold and confident air, they would snub her; if she humbled herself before them, they would ridicule her. They would not credit her with any good qualities. Her very beauty would make them suspicious of her; a hidden meaning, a secret insinuation, would lurk behind all the friendly words they addressed to her. Woe to her if she did not realize this, and woe to her also if she realized it and did not keep her feelings to herself! Woe to her if she did not give back as good as she got, and woe to her if she did! Poor lady!

So she ran her eyes down the long list of names before her from end to end.

How she longed to find among them some good-natured, generous, tender-hearted woman whom she might look upon as a dear mother – not another Mrs. Meyer, but a dear ideal mother such as all good people imagine every mother to be! how she longed, too, to find among them many a gentle girl, many a young sympathetic damsel whom she might love like sisters – though not such sisters as hers! But how was she to recognize; how was she to approach them? how was she to win their hearts, their confidence?

Again and again she read through the list of names aloud, as if she would have discovered from the *sound* of the names the disposition of their bearers; then she laid it down before her with a sigh, and turned an inquiring look upon the steward.

"My dear Mr. Varga, pardon me if I trouble you with a question."

Mr. Varga hastened to assure her that he was her most humble servant, and only awaited her commands.

"But this question is very, very important."

Mr. Varga assured her that he was ready for anything in the world; even if her ladyship should require him to leap through the window, he was prepared to do so.

"I am going to ask you a question, to which I require a perfectly sincere answer. You must be perfectly frank towards me. Fancy yourself for the moment my dear father, about to give to me, your daughter, good counsel on the eve of my entering into the world."

She said these words with so much feeling, and in a voice that seemed to come so directly from the bottom of her heart, that Mr. Varga, for the life of him, could not help drawing from the inside pocket of his dolman a checkered cotton pocket-handkerchief, with which he dried his eyes.

"What is it your ladyship deigns to command?" he inquired, in a voice that sounded as if every syllable he uttered were shod with as tight jackboots as the ones he was himself wearing.

"I want you to be so good as to go through all the names written on this list, one by one, and tell me quite frankly, quite openly, what your opinion is of each one of them, what their dispositions are, how the world regards them, which of them are likely to love one, and which are likely to give one the cold shoulder."

In all his life Mr. Varga had never had to face so rigorous an ordeal. If Lady Kárpáthy had charged him to call out five or six of the persons who were down on the list, or take a message to each one of them individually and to go on foot, or to work out the genealogy of everyone of them in the shortest conceivable space of time, he would have considered all such commissions as mere trifles compared with what was required of him now. What! he, the humblest of retainers in his own estimation, who regarded with such boundless respect every member of the higher circles that he would have considered himself the most miserable of men had he failed, in addressing them, to give them every tittle of their proper titles and designations – he, forsooth, was now to sit in judgment on these great gentlemen and ladies who did him too much honor in allowing him to address them at all?

In his despair Mr. Varga scoured the floor with his heel, and his forehead with the checkered handkerchief.

Fanny, perceiving the confusion of the good old man, turned towards him with a look of tender encouragement.

"My dear friend, look upon yourself as my father, as the one person whom I can ask for advice in this new and strange world, of which I know absolutely nothing. *I* cannot help looking upon you as my father. Why are you so good and kind to me?"

The good old man felt his heart fortified by the genuine and touching sincerity of these words, and, after coughing once more with uncommon vigor and resolution, by way of a parting adieu to the temptations of cowardice, and thereby steeling his mind the more, thus replied –

"My lady, you honor me far above my merits by your ladyship's boundless favor, and I feel myself inexpressibly happy and fortunate when I am able to do your ladyship any service, however small. And although it is a hateful thing for such an insignificant person as myself to give his judgment or opinion concerning such distinguished gentlemen and ladies as those whose names stand here before me, nevertheless the love – I beg pardon – the respect I bear towards your ladyship –"

"I like the first word better; let it stand, please!"

"And it is true. I only say what I feel. I also had a daughter once. It was long, very long ago. She was just of the same age as your ladyship; not so beautiful, but she was good, ah, so good! She died long ago, in her youth. And she loved me dearly. But I beg your pardon for making so bold as to speak of the poor thing. But to turn to the business in hand, your ladyship – before I proceed to answer the question before me, pray allow me to make one small remark, by way of advice, which proceeds, believe me, from the purest intention and the utmost good will. First of all, I do not consider it necessary that I should speak to your ladyship at all concerning those persons towards whom – how shall I put it? – towards whom your ladyship cannot feel the fullest confidence; for although God preserve me from taking any exception to anything in the lives of such distinguished gentlemen and ladies, yet, nevertheless, there may be reasons why it might not be quite desirable for your ladyship to have any intimate relations with them. On the other hand, I will pick out from this list such persons as will respond to your ladyship's goodness and tenderness of heart with equal tenderness of heart and goodness. Those, again, whom I shall humbly venture to pass over in silence – and I assume, of course, that they possess in their own honorable persons every recognized good quality – must be taken to be such persons as your ladyship would not care about knowing."

"Excellent, excellent, my good friend! You shall make me acquainted with those only whom I should like, and say nothing about the rest. Ah, you know the world well. That is indeed good advice."

Mr. Varga looked beseechingly at Fanny, as if to insist that she was not to praise him too much, or he should get confused again and forget what he wished to say.

Then he took up the long list, and began to go through it, running his finger along it, but so as not to touch the names, lest he might offend their owners by such ignoble contact. Now and then the conducting finger would pause at a name, and Mr. Varga would look up as if about to speak; but in the very act of coughing to give the proper shade of respect to his voice, he would look again at the name singled out by his finger, think better of it, and tacitly schedule it among those who, though blessed with all recognized good qualities, he did not think suitable for his purpose. But as he drew near to the end of the list, he was horror-stricken to observe how many names he had been obliged to pass over in silence, and drops of honest sweat began to congregate on his forehead as the index finger left ever more and more names behind it – the names of people whom he always treated with the most awful reverence, but not one of whom he would have recommended to the confidence of his daughter, if he had had one. And he had now begun to regard Fanny as his own daughter.

Ah! at last his long-drawn features grew round again with satisfaction, and his hand trembled on the paper when it reached a name that it had long been in search of.

"Look, my lady!" said he, extending the list towards her. "This admirable lady is certainly one of those in whom your ladyship can repose your confidence without running the risk of being deceived."

Fanny read the name indicated – "Flora Eszéky Szentirmay."

"What is this lady like?" she inquired of the old man.

"Verily, I should have need of very great eloquence to describe her to you worthily. She is rich in all the virtues one looks for in a woman. Gentleness and prudence go hand in hand with her. The oppressed and downtrodden find in her a secret protector; for she does her good deeds in secret, and forbids grateful tongues to talk about her. Not only is it the hungry, the naked, the sick, and the wretched among whom she distributes bread, garments, medicine, and kind words, who know what a good heart she has; not only is it those under legal sentence, for whom she pleads compassionately in high places: her benevolence goes much further than all that; for she takes the part of those who are spiritually poor and wretched, those whom the world condemns, poor betrayed girls who have tripped into endless misery, poor women bending beneath the crosses of a hard domestic life; and they all find in her a friend, a defender who can get to the bottom of their hearts. Pardon me for presuming so far. I know right well that there are many other exalted personages who also do a great deal of good to the poor; but they seem only to take thought for the bodily wants of the destitute, whereas this lady cares for their spiritual needs as well, and thus it comes about that she frequently finds poor sufferers in need of her assistance, not only in hovels, but in palaces. This lady brings a blessing into every house she enters, and scatters happiness and contentment all round about her. Indeed, I only know of one other lady who is worthy to stand beside her, and nothing would give me greater joy than to see them both at one with each other."

The emotion written on Fanny's face showed that she appreciated the tender insinuation.

"Is this lady young?"

"About your ladyship's own age."

"And is she happily married?" Fanny was rather speaking to herself than asking a question.

"That she is," replied Varga; "indeed, it would not be possible to find on the whole face of the earth a couple so exactly suited to each other as she and His Excellency Count Rudolf Szentirmay. Oh, that is a great man if you like! Everyone admires his intellect and his great qualities, and the whole kingdom praises and exalts him. They say that at one time he was a man disgusted with life, who troubled himself very little about his country; but from the moment when he met his future wife, Flora Eszéky, abroad, a great change came over him, and returning with her to Hungary, he became the benefactor not only of his country but of humanity. But even now God has rewarded him, for that greatest of blessings, domestic happiness, has fallen to his lot so lavishly that it has become a proverb, and anybody seeing them together would imagine that Paradise had already begun for them on this earth."

An involuntary, an unconscious sigh arose from Fanny's breast at these words.

At that moment the rumbling of a coach was audible in the courtyard; a chance guest had arrived. A great bustling about was heard outside, in the midst of which resounded Squire John's stentorian voice. He seemed to be joyfully welcoming someone, and immediately afterwards Martin entered and announced: "Her Excellency the Countess Flora Eszéky Szentirmay!"

Fanny, with the trepidation of joy and surprise, awaited the guest who had just been announced. She had tried to form an idea of her, but what would this imaginary figure be like in reality?

How the young lady's heart did beat as footsteps drew nearer and nearer to the door and she heard Kárpáthy cheerfully conversing with someone! And now the door opened, and in there came – not that face, not that figure which Fanny had imagined, but a tall, dry lady of uncertain age, with a false complexion, false teeth, and false eyes, dressed according to the latest fashion. A monstrous hat covered with whole bouquets of flowers, quite shut out the prospect of everything that was behind her back.

Her mantle was thrown back over her shoulders, which gave a martial, amazonic cast to her figure, and this impression was intensified by the low cut of her dress, which allowed one to catch a good glimpse of her scraggy shoulders and projecting breast-bone, an alarming spectacle. She had hands, moreover, of correspondingly extraordinary leanness, embellished, why I cannot tell, by monstrously big swanskin muffs, and as she was unable to move her arms without saying something at the same time, and as she could never speak without laughing, and as whenever she laughed she displayed not only the whole of her upper row of teeth (the best procurable at Dr. Legrieux's, No. 11, Rue Vivienne, Paris), but the whole of her gums as well, she continually kept the attention of whatever company she happened to be in riveted with a horrible fascination on her elbows, her gums, and her breast-bone.

She had come with her niece as a sort of guard of honor, and Flora had sent her on in front while she lingered behind to rally Squire John a little.

Kárpáthy hastened to make the ladies known to each other: "Dame Marion Countess Szentirmay – Countess Rudolf Szentirmay – my wife."

Dame Marion Szentirmay made the lady of the house the most perfect and unexceptionable curtsy, regarding her all the time with an air that seemed to say, "I wonder if she knows how to return it, poor little ignoramus?"

And, in fact, so confused and taken back was Fanny that she scarce knew what to say; moreover, she was so lost in the contemplation of Dame Marion's gums that she hardly had had time to observe Flora. But, indeed, there was no need for her or anybody else to try and find words; on the contrary, if anybody had had any to spare, he would have had to keep them to himself, for Dame Marion always brought with her sufficient conversation to keep a whole assembly going.

"Pray be seated, ladies! You, Lady Flora, sit down here, by my wife. Dame Marion, a hundred thousand pardons!"

A glance at the lady's face had suddenly convinced Squire John that she was quite well aware where she ought and meant to sit, without his telling her; and down she sat accordingly, in an armchair on the other side of the room.

"I must ask your pardon, my dear neighbor," began Dame Marion, in an artificial sort of style, belonging to none of the recognized categories of rhetoric, and which continually suggested the suspicion that the speaker was rolling something about in her mouth which she was too lazy to spit out – "I must ask your pardon, *chère voisine* – we live, you know, close to the Kárpáthy estate in these parts" (*i.e.* It belongs neither to you nor to your husband, but to the Kárpáthy family) – "for making so bold as to interrupt you in your occupations" (*i.e.* I should like to know what *you* can find to occupy yourself with, forsooth!), "for although, of course, we ought to have waited for Squire John Kárpáthy to have introduced us, in the first instance, to the wife so worthy of his love, which is the regular course" (*i.e.* Perhaps you don't know that: how could you?), "nevertheless, as we happened to be passing this way" (*i.e.* Don't imagine we came here on purpose!), "and I have a long-standing legal suit with Squire John Kárpáthy" (*i.e.* So, you see, you have to thank me and our suit, for our visit; not Countess Rudolf's kindness, as you may perhaps suppose) – "and a pretty old suit it is by this time! for I was young, a mere child, in fact, when it began, ha, ha! – By the way," she continued, flying off at a tangent, "they advised us to put an end to the suit by arranging a match between me and Kárpáthy. I was young then, as I have said – a mere child, ha, ha! – but I would not entertain the idea, ha, ha! I made a mistake, no doubt; for how rich should I not have been now, a good *partie*, eh!" (*i.e.* Squire John was already an old man when I was your age; but I did not sell myself for his wealth, as you have done!) "Well, you are a lucky fellow, Kárpáthy, *you*, at any rate, have nothing to complain of. A wife so worthy of your love as yours is, is a treasure you really do not deserve" (*i.e.* Don't give yourself airs, you little fool! Don't fancy people praise you for your beauty as if it were a merit! You ought to be ashamed that it is only your beauty that has made a lady of you!).

Here Dame Marion lost for a moment the thread of her discourse, which gave Flora an opportunity of bending over Fanny and whispering in her ear, in a gentle, confidential voice –

"I have long wished to meet you, and have been on the point of coming over every day."

Fanny gratefully pressed her hand.

A beneficent attack of coughing here prevented Dame Marion from resuming her conversation. Kárpáthy inquired after his friend Rudolf, Lady Flora's husband, expressing the hope that he would not forget his promise to honor Kárpátfalva with his presence on the occasion of the entertainment that was coming off there in honor of the young bride.

"Oh, he must be here by then," replied Flora; "he gave me his word that he would be back home in time for it."

Then turning towards Fanny, Flora continued, "I have been expecting to meet you everywhere. We country-folks about here are pretty lively, and are always delighted to see our circle increased; and now that we have met at last, we will conspire amiably together to make everyone around us feel happy."

Dame Marion, however, at once hastened to weaken any pleasant impression which these words might have produced.

"Kárpáthy naturally makes a mystery of his wife's whereabouts. The sly rogue would hide her away, so that nobody may catch a glance of her but himself" – (*i.e.* the old fool is afraid to show her, and with good reason).

"Oh, my husband is most kind and obliging," Fanny hastened to object; "but I must own to feeling a sort of hesitation – I might even call it fear – at the prospect of appearing in such lofty circles. I was brought up among quite simple folks, and I feel exceedingly obliged to your ladyships for giving me so much encouragement."

"Naturally, naturally!" returned Dame Marion. "It is most natural, and could not very well be otherwise. A young wife is in the most difficult position conceivable when she first makes her entry into the great world; especially when, from the nature of the case, she is obliged to do without what is most necessary for her, what should be her surest support – a mother's advice, a mother's guidance. Oh, a mother's watchful providence is of inestimable importance to a young wife!"

Fanny felt her eyes grow burning hot, and her face flushed purple; she could not help it. Alas! to speak of a mother before her was to cause her the most terrible torture, the most piercing shame!

Flora convulsively pressed the young lady's hand in her own, and, as if simply continuing the conversation, she said –

"Yes, indeed; nothing makes up for the loss of a mother."

Shortly afterwards old Kárpáthy and Dame Marion repaired to the family archives, where the family fiscal and Mr. Varga were awaiting them, in order to discuss their eternal lawsuit once again for the hundredth time or so, and the two young women were left alone.

The door had scarce closed behind Dame Marion when Fanny, with the most passionate impetuosity, suddenly seized Flora's hand with both her own, and before the latter had had time to prevent her, pressed the pretty little hand to her lips and covered it with kisses – kisses that came straight from her burning heart. Again and again she heaped her kisses upon it, but could not utter a word.

"Ah, my God! what are you doing?" said Flora; and thus, in order to prevent Fanny from repeating her action, she took her in her arms, kissed her face, and compelled her to do the same.

"Oh!" sobbed Fanny, "I know that you are the ministering angel of the whole countryside. As soon as I had arrived here, I heard them talking of you, and from what they said I could well picture to myself what you were. You must have already guessed that in me you would find a poor creature, who was also in need of your charity; but the greatness of that benefit only I could know, only I could feel. Say not that it is not so! Permit me to remain in that happy belief! Permit me to go on loving you as I loved you from the first moment I beheld you. Oh, let me hold fast to the thought: here is a blessed being who thinks of me, pities me, and has made me happy!"

"Oh, Fanny!" exclaimed Flora, in a gentle, tremulous voice. She really did pity the woman.

"Oh yes, yes! call me that!" cried Fanny, full of rapture, as she impetuously pressed Flora's hand to her heart. She had never released it for an instant, as if she feared that the moment she let it go the blissful vision would vanish.

By way of guarantee, Flora pressed her beautiful lips to Fanny's forehead, and gently bade her, from henceforth, call her Flora and nothing else. There was to be no more strangeness between them. They were now to be friends, firm friends.

Only with the greatest difficulty did Lady Szentirmay succeed in preventing Fanny from flinging herself at her feet; the poor girl had to be content with hiding her head in Flora's breast and sobbing; and when she had wept there to her heart's content, then only did she feel happy, oh so happy!

"Come, come, my dear Fanny!" said Flora at last, with a friendly smile; "don't you think we have had as much of this as will do us good? Listen to me! If you promise never to talk about this again, I will remain here with you a whole – a whole week."

On hearing this it was as much as Fanny could do to prevent herself from shedding fresh tears, tears of joy.

"And after that I will help you to make the necessary preparations for the coming housewarming which your husband has resolved to give. Oh, you would never imagine how much there is to be done, and how weary you would get over it; but if there are two of us, we shall be able to make quite a jest of it all, and how we shall both laugh at the many funny little mishaps which are sure to occur!"

And then the pair of them fell a laughing. Why, of course it would be one of the funniest, merriest affairs in the world – of course it would.

Meanwhile it afforded Fanny infinite delight to relieve Flora of her hat, mantle, and every other sort of impoundable article which it is the custom to deprive arriving guests of, as a greater security against their running away. Then they sat down together, and the conversation turned naturally upon women's dress, women's needlework, and other similar trifles which generally interest gentlewomen, so that by the time Dame Marion returned with old Kárpáthy from the family archives, there was no longer any trace of the passionate and touching scene that had taken place between the two ladies, but they were conversing with each other like old, like good old, acquaintances.

"Ah, ha!" said Dame Marion, wagging her head when she observed Flora without hat or mantle. "You are making yourself quite at home, I must say."

"Yes, aunt; I am going to stay here for a short time with Fanny."

Dame Marion, with an air of astonishment, looked around her into every corner of the room, and then up at the ceiling, as if she could not make out who Fanny was.

"Ah! mille pardons, madame. I recollect now, of course, of course – that is your Christian name. I am quite confused by all the family names with which Squire Kárpáthy's *director jurium* has been filling my ears. Really this Kárpáthy family has quite a frightful lot of connections. The female branch is united by marriage with all the most eminent families in the realm. I verily believe there's not a name in the calendar that it has not appropriated;" which meant, being interpreted, "*Your* family is not very likely to add fresh glory to the Kárpáthy family tree!"

But Flora only laughed good-naturedly, and said –

"Well, now, at any rate, Fanny is a very honorable name in the family records."

Dame Marion, however, kept standing there in amazement, with her long-handled parasol in her hand – like Diana might have looked if she had shot one of her dogs instead of a hare. She could not understand from whence these people derived so much good humor when she was so bent upon aggravating them.

"And how long, may I ask, will – this – short – time – be?" she inquired of Flora, with a biting, staccato sort of intonation, gazing vaguely into vacancy.

"Oh, a mere bagatelle – only a week, aunty."

"Only a week!" exclaimed Dame Marion, in horror; "only a week!"

"If only I am not kicked out in the meantime," retorted Lady Szentirmay, jocosely; whereupon Fanny immediately embraced her affectionately, by way of signifying that she would like to keep her forever.

"Ah, indeed!" remarked Dame Marion, petulantly. "Well, well! young women soon make friends with each other. I am so delighted you have got to love each other so much all at once – that shows how much your natures are alike, at which I am charmed. I hope, however, my dear niece, that you will permit *me* to return to Szentirma. I hope," continued she, "that I leave my niece in safe custody, though. I do not know whether Szentirmay is likely to trouble Kárpáthy Castle very much with his jealousy. Adieu, my dear neighbor, chère voisine! Adieu, chère nièce, adieu!"

This ambiguous farewell was capable of a double interpretation, each alternative of which was equally insulting, as it might be taken to mean, either that no sane person had any reason whatever to be jealous of old John Kárpáthy, or that Kárpáthy Castle had such a bad reputation that no woman's good name was likely to be improved by a residence within its walls.

No sooner had the old wet blanket disappeared than the two young women, in the exuberance of their high spirits, took possession of Squire John, and, singing and dancing, marched him up the stone staircase again into the castle. Squire John himself was in the best of humors; his face beamed, he laughed aloud, and he thought to himself what a fine thing it would have been if both these young women were his daughters and called him father.

The ancient rooms resounded with the hubbub and innocent frolics of these two merry young dames. It had been a long long time since those walls had rung with such a sound as that.

Chapter XI

THE FEMALE FRIEND

Lady Szentirmay gained her object. Her week's residence at Kárpáthy Castle had completely changed Fanny's position in the eyes of the great world. Even the most prejudiced became more favorably disposed towards the woman whom Lady Szentirmay freely admitted to her friendship. The proudest dowagers, who hitherto considered that they would be showing infinite condescension if they appeared at a festival where a *ci-devant* shopkeeper's daughter would play the part of mistress of the house, now began to think that their condescension might bear a little paring down. Rigorously virtuous ladies, who had doubted within themselves whether it were befitting to bring their youthful daughters to thread the labyrinths full of Eleusianian mysteries at Kárpáthy Castle, now ordered their dresses from the dressmakers without the slightest apprehension. The appearance of Lady Szentirmay was the surest guarantee of virtue and propriety. The mere fact that Fanny *had* gained Flora's friendship made her own domestics regard her with quite different eyes, and even Squire John himself began to understand what sort of a wife he had won; and so the nimbus of gentility began to shine around her.

The whole day the two ladies might have been seen together, engaged in their great and difficult labors. No smiling, please! The work was really great and difficult. It is easy enough for us menfolk to say, "I will give a great dinner-party tomorrow, or a month hence; and I will invite the whole countryside to it. I will invite not only those I know, but those I have never seen;" but it is our womenfolk who have to take thought for it. It is they who have to bear in mind everything necessary to make it all adequate and splendid; it is they who have to take into consideration the thousand and one pretensions, partialities, and caprices of a whole army of guests. It would not have been surprising if the new housewife had not known where to begin first; but under Flora's direction everything went along as smoothly as possible. She was used to such things. She remembered everything, and yet she always appealed so artfully to Fanny as to how this or that ought to be done, that, had not Fanny had the keenest appreciation of her friend's delicacy and tact, she might very easily have fancied that it was she herself who managed everything. At any rate Squire John henceforth lived in the conviction that his consort was as much at home in all these mighty matters as if she had lived all her life in the castles of countesses.

And when the evening came, and they were alone together, and had time to converse, how many sage and pleasant counsels Fanny listened to from her friend! She did nothing but listen to, nothing but look upon those delicate, eloquent lips, and those still more eloquent, sparkling eyes, from which she was beginning to learn happiness. At such times they would send away their ladies' maids, and help each other with their evening toilets, and then they would talk freely and merrily of the great world and its follies.

First of all, the list of names, which had caused Mr. Varga so much sweat and anguish, would be brought forth, and then they would sit down together and talk scandal of their neighbors, and a delightful joke it was too.

For there's a difference between scandal and scandal. To circulate false reports of the people you know, to lay hold upon their most recondite faults and carefully pass them on from hand to hand, to undermine the good name of your acquaintances, – that is certainly not a nice occupation, I call it ungentlemanly scandal. But to be acquainted with the vices of the world, and communicate them to innocent souls liable to err; to warn and call the attention of the sensitive and the tottering to the thorns, the flints, the vermin, and the pitfalls which beset their path, – that is a proper thing to do in season, and I call it gentlemanly scandal – although many who read these lines will perhaps prefer to call it nonsense.

We will therefore confine ourselves to gentlemanly scandal, and let us take the men first. It is not I who do it, remember, but these two young women who have got hold of such an interesting list. If I had a hand in it, I should certainly begin with the ladies.

"Here's one right at the top," said Lady Szentirmay, "let us begin with him. If he were an ordinary man instead of a nobleman, they would call him badly behaved. He thinks ill of every woman except his own wife, for of her he never thinks at all, and is violent and passionate besides. When he flies into a rage he does not pick his words, nor looks about to see whether women or only men are near. In the most mixed society, where two or three young girls at least must be present, he tells such queer stories that even the more sensitive of the men cannot but blush. Yet he is a great patriot, whose name is well known and admired; so he claims respect, and must not be blamed like other men. The respect in which he is held, however, is the best weapon to use against him. He will pay court to you impetuously, and you will not be able to avoid him; but all you have to do is to praise him for his political virtues. That always holds him in check. I have tried it, and never known it to fail."

"Let's tick him off," said Fanny. "Count Imre Szépkiesdy: that's his name, is it?" – and she underscored him with her lead pencil, and wrote underneath, "A great and very estimable man!"

"Here comes another high and mighty gentleman," resumed the Countess. "If he had not a title, I don't know that the world would recognize him at all. *I* have never been able to discover what qualities he possesses, though I have the privilege of meeting him once a month. One thing, however, I can label him with: he has a tremendous appetite, and yet is always complaining that he cannot eat. He is a very amiable man: before dinner he complains that he has no appetite, and after dinner that he has overeaten himself, and if you don't offer him anything he sulks and starves. He doesn't give much trouble therefore."

"Let us write after his name then: 'Baron George Málnay, an amiable man.'"

"Here is a dear silly, Count Gregory Erdey. He is the most delightful fellow in the world, and can keep the whole company in convulsions with his quips and cranks. He can imitate the absurdities of costume of every nation, and can present you with an Englishman, a Spaniard, a Frenchman, and a Jew by a mere twist of his hat. The very simplicity of his absurdity makes him the most harmless of men. You cannot imagine him giving offence to anyone. He would be incapable of deceiving a girl of sixteen. His whole ambition is to make people laugh, and all the lovers of laughter are on his side."

"Count Gregory Erdey," Fanny noted down, "a dear silly."

"Let us proceed. Count Karvay Louis, a true man of the world *à la Talleyrand.* He observes everyone, and is very particular that everyone should observe him. He only puts a question to you in order to discover how far you are unable to answer him – it is a positive trap, the consequences of which you cannot possibly foresee. Then he has a trick of sulking for a whole year without saying why; the merest trifle, a letter to him misdirected, is sufficient to upset him till his dying day. If anyone comes to see you when he is with you, and this somebody should be lower in rank than himself, and you should sin against the rules of etiquette by rising from your seat instead of merely bowing – Louis will lose his temper, and say that you have insulted him. And yet he will never give anyone a hint as to what is likely to offend him and what not."

"Well, let us write under his name, 'a prickly gentleman.'"

"And now comes Count Sárosdy, the *föispán.* He is a worthy, good-natured man, but a frightful aristocrat. It delights him to do good to the peasants and the poor, but don't ask him to make the acquaintance of his fellow-men. No tenantry in the whole of Hungary is better off than his, but he will not have a non-noble person in his service even as a clerk. You will find he will be a little stiff towards you at first, but fortunately he has a good heart, and there are always keys wherewith to open a good heart. It will be no easy matter to win him over to more liberal sentiments, but if we both combine against him, victory will be assured.

"And now we come to the young originals."

"Oh," said Fanny, "I shall understand that class better than you do! I know more about them already than I like."

"Last of all come the fine gentlemen. I need not tell you about them either; so we can pass on to the ladies."

"Oh yes, let us discuss the ladies by all means!"

"First of all comes the wife of the aristocratic *föispán.* She is a cockered, discontented dame, who has swooned as many times as other women have sighed. You might stand upon burning embers more comfortably than before her; for you may be sure that she will not approve of anything you may say, do, or even think. If anyone crosses his legs in her presence, she faints; if a cat strays into the room, she will have convulsions; if a knife is put across a fork, she will not sit down to table; if there are roses outside in the garden, she will perceive the smell through double windowpanes, and faint, so that no flowers can be kept in the room where she may happen to be. You must not let anybody in a blue dress sit down at the same table as herself, for that color is horrible to her, and she has convulsions the moment she sees it. Finally, you will do well to talk of nothing at all in her presence, for the slightest thing is likely to upset her nerves.

"Ah! next comes the Countess Kereszty. She is an excellent woman. She has a tall, muscular, masculine figure, with thick, broad eyebrows. She never speaks in a voice lower than what is usually required for commanding a regiment; while her gruffest voice is sufficient to utterly embarrass a nervous man, especially as she has a trick of perpetually interrupting the person talking to her with her 'How – why – wherefore's?' and, when she begins to laugh, the whole room trembles. She dragoons every assembly which she honors with her presence; and whomsoever she is angry with had much better have been born blind. Our very young men have a cold ague fit when they see her, for she inspires them with as much terror as any professor, and, besides that, can speak fluent Latin, has the code at her fingers' ends, can hold her own against the most astute of advocates, drinks like a fish, and revels in tobacco. It is true she does not drive her own horses; but, should the coachman drive badly, she is quite capable of snatching the whip from his hand and belaboring him with the handle. For the rest, she is the best-hearted creature in the world, and readily makes friends. Kiss her hand, and call her 'My lady sister,' and you need not have the slightest fear of her; for she will love you, make herself your champion, and woe betide whomsoever dares to disparage you behind your back when she is present, for she will make them stampede in every direction.

"And now we come to Lady Szépkiesdy. She is a quiet, silent woman, whom it is impossible to offend. Her husband has found out from experience that nothing pains her; but, on the other hand, there is nothing that can make her happy. And her whole face, her whole figure, seems to express but one wish, but one desire – the longing to be under the sod as soon as possible."

"Poor lady!"

"And she is also tormented by the knowledge that every pretty face she sees will cause her misery involuntarily; for her husband pays his court to everyone of them in her presence. She was esteemed a great beauty once upon a time; but care and sorrow have made her quite old within the last two years."

"Poor lady!" sighed Fanny.

"And now let me introduce you to Madame George Málnay. Beware of her. She will be eternally flattering you, in the hope that some secret, some unguarded word may escape you. She is a veritable Mephistopheles in female form. She is the enemy of everyone she knows; but whenever she meets you she will kiss and embrace you, till you fancy she is quite in love with you. It is of no use quarreling with her. The very next day she will embrace, kiss, and traduce you, as if nothing had happened. The best way is to keep clear of her. Receive her, therefore, with a cold, forbidding countenance. She'll requite you, perhaps, by calling you boorish and underbred behind your back; but that is the kindest thing you can expect from her."

Fanny gratefully pressed Lady Szentirmay's hand. What blunders she must have made but for her!

"And is there anyone really worth mentioning among so many?" she asked.

"Yes; Dame Marion."

"Really!"

"She is just as you saw her; she is always like that. And it is no affectation, but her natural character."

"Then what is her real character?"

"Well, she is – like the rest of them – a treacherous scandalmonger, with an ill word for everyone, who takes a delight in picking out people's most secret faults; but you need not fear her, for she loves you sincerely, and will never betray, disparage, or injure you behind your back. Have you not found that out already?"

Fanny, half-laughing half-weeping, hid her head in her friend's bosom, and embraced her tightly; and then they kissed each other, and laughed at the facility with which they also had fallen into the scandalizing ways of the world.

Chapter XII

THE HOUSE-WARMING

Carriage after carriage rumbled into the courtyard of Kárpáthy Castle. Every sort and kind of four-wheeled conveyance was visible that day within the gates of the crowded mansion.

There seemed to be no end to the continuous flow of guests, male and female, and Madame Kárpáthy won and captivated every heart. Of course she had the immense advantage of knowing them all beforehand, of knowing their weak and their strong points, their virtues and vices; but it is due to her to add that she had learnt her lesson excellently well, and turned it to the best advantage. She received Count Szépkiesdy with all the grave respect due to the most honorable of patriots, and assured him that she had long since learnt to admire him as a great orator and a noble-minded man. The Count inwardly cursed and swore at meeting with someone who regarded him as a hero. To Count Gregory Erdey she extended a smiling salutation from afar, which he requited by saluting her with his hat in one hand and his wig in another, which provoked a roar of Homeric laughter from the assembled guests. The young buffoon had had his head clean shaved in order that his hair might grow all the stronger, so that his bald pate quite scared the weak-nerved members of the company. The young housewife curtsied low in humble silence before the *Fõispán* Count Sárosdy and his wife, whereby she greatly pleased that aristocratic patriot. He admitted that middle-class girls are not so bad when they have been brought up in gentlemen's families. And Fanny completely won the favor of his consort by impressing upon her servants to be constantly in attendance on her ladyship, and fulfill all her wishes; for, although Countess Sárosdy had brought two of her own maids with her, she did not consider them sufficient. On the arrival of the Countess Kereszty, Fanny joyfully rushed forward, and kissed her hand before she could prevent it; whereupon the amazonian dame, first of all, seized her with both her muscular arms, and held her at arm's length, at the same time wrinkling her thick black eyebrows as if to scrutinize her the better, and then drew her towards her, patting her on the back all the time, and exclaiming in her bass-viollike voice, "We like each other, my little sister; we like each other, eh?" Yes, there could be no doubt about it, Fanny was a success. Her beauty won the hearts of the gentlemen, and her correct deportment the good opinions of the ladies.

Shortly afterwards the dinner-bell rang, and the company, with a great clatter and still greater good-humor, occupied the tables, from a description of which I conscientiously abstain – firstly and lastly because such things as dinner-tables are only diverting *in natura*, but infinitely tiresome in books. There was all the wealth, pomp, splendor and profusion that the occasion and the reputation of the Nabob demanded; there was everything procurable for man's enjoyment, from the native products of Hungarian cookery to the masterly creations of French gastronomic art, and of wines every sort imaginable. The dinner lasted far into the night, and towards the end of it the company began to grow uproarious. The great patriot, as usual, related his lubricous, equivocal anecdotes without troubling himself very much as to whether ladies were present or not. He was wont to say *Castis sunt omnia casta,* "To the pure all things are pure," and whoever blushed had, no doubt, a good reason for blushing, and was therefore corrupt enough already. The ladies, however, pretended not to hear, and began conversing with their neighbors without taking any notice of the hoarse laughter of the young bucks, who held it a point of honor to applaud the witticisms of the great patriot.

Nevertheless everyone did his best to enjoy himself as much as possible.

And who so happy as the Nabob?

It occurred to him that, scarce a year ago, he had sat in the same place where he was sitting now, and had seen a horrible sight; and now he saw by his side a young and enchanting wife, and around him a merry lively host of guests with cheerful, smiling faces.

And now from the adjoining chamber resounded, alternately grave and gay, the notes of the Bihari fiddlers; one or two of the young wags thereupon pushed their chairs away, went out among the gypsies, and fell a dancing with each other. The more loquacious of the patriots who remained behind began drinking the health of every fellow-guest present, in turn, especially toasting the host and hostess; thence proceeding to drink to the success of all manner of abstract objects, such as social unions, counties and colleges, and other contemporary institutions. Count Szépkiesdy made a long speech, into which he very neatly interwove every applauded phrase which he had uttered during the last twelve months at public assemblies. There were some present who had heard this speech at least four times already, but this did not prevent anybody from cheering him vociferously: we know, of course, that a good thing cannot be repeated too often. Squire John himself was invincible as a toast-responder, and if I were not obliged in this particular to give the pre-eminence to an honored lady, the amazonian Countess Kereszty, I should have said that, for witty sallies and the draining of bumpers, he was the hero of the evening.

In any case he deserves peculiar praise for one thing: in the midst of all this talking and toasting he it was who first of all bethought him of raising his glass in honor of two young men who were not actually present – to wit Count Stephen and Count Rudolf; and he so worthily extolled the superlative merits of these gentlemen, as to evoke an unprecedented burst of enthusiasm, the very ladies themselves seizing brimmers and clinking them with him.

While every face was still beaming with delight, a lackey entered, and delivered a letter to Lady Szentirmay which a rapid runner had brought from Szentirma.

Flora with a beating heart recognized her husband's writing on the cover, and she begged leave to retire and open it. This was the signal for release and departure, the whole company quitting the tables, and scattering in the adjoining rooms. Flora and Fanny flew off to their bedrooms unobserved, to read the precious letter in all peace and quietness; for Fanny, also, naturally wanted to know what was in the letter.

The lady broke the seal with a hand that trembled for joy, and, after pressing the letter to her heart, read its contents, which were as follows: –

"Tomorrow I shall be at Kárpátfalva. There we shall meet. Rudolf. 1000." This "thousand" signified a thousand kisses.

How delighted the beloved wife was! Again and again she kissed the place where her husband's name was written, as if to snatch beforehand at least a hundred of the consignment of kisses; and then she concealed it in her bosom, as if to preserve the remaining nine hundred till later on; then she drew it forth once more, and read it over again, as if she could not quite remember the whole contents of the letter, but must needs read it anew in order to understand it properly; and then she kissed it over and over again until, at last, she herself did not know how many kisses she had taken.

And Fanny fully shared the joy of her friend, joy is so contagious. Tomorrow Rudolf will arrive, and how nice it will then be for Flora! She will see the greatest joy that a loving heart can imagine, and will not be a bit jealous – no! she will rejoice in another's joy, rejoice in the happiness of her best friend, who possesses as her very own, so to speak, the man in whose honor everyone has spoken so well and made such pretty speeches. And tomorrow he will be here; and, to make his wife happy till he comes, he has notified the day of his arrival. He does not come surreptitiously, unawares, like one who is jealous; but he lets her know of his coming beforehand, like one who is well assured of how greatly, how very greatly he is loved. Oh what a joy it will be even to look upon such happiness!

The two ladies with radiantly happy faces returned to the company, which diverted itself till midnight, when everyone retired to his own room. Squire John helped his guests to their repose with a musical accompaniment, the gypsy band proceeding from window to window and intoning beneath each one a sleep-compelling symphony. Finally, the last note died away, and everybody dozed off, and dreamed beautiful dreams. The hunters dreamt of foxes (there was to be a hunt on the morrow), the orators dreamt of assemblies, Mr. Málnay dreamt of parties, Lady Szentirmay dreamt of her husband, and Fanny dreamt of that beautiful smiling countenance she had been thinking of so often, and which looked at her so kindly with its eloquent blue eyes and spoke to her with such a wondrously sweet voice. It is permissible, of course, to dream of anything.

Well, tomorrow!

Chapter XIII

THE HUNT

Early next morning the hunting-horns awoke the guests. Those who had gone to sleep thinking of hunting, and had dreamt of hunting, at once sprang to their feet at that joyous sound. The others, who would gladly have compounded with themselves for an extra half-hour and allowed their heavy eyelids just one more little snooze, were violently thwarted in their inclinations by the ever-increasing racket which suddenly dominated Kárpáthy Castle; for the bustling to and fro of heavy boots, the sound of familiar voices in the halls and parlors, the baying of dogs in the courtyard, the cracking of whips, and the neighing of horses would have sufficed to disturb the sweet slumbers of the Seven Sleepers themselves. But what is the use of expecting moderation or discretion from sportsmen? The most exquisite of drawing room dandies, when he prepares him for the chase, puts on quite another character with his hunting boots and cap, and considers himself justified in making as much row as possible, and bawls in a voice that is quite different to his own.

Day had scarcely dawned when the fully dressed guests came into the hall to show themselves and have a look at the weather. The more original young bucks were dressed in coats with large flapping sleeves, vests with broad flat buttons, and velvet caps with crane's feathers; the elegants, on the other hand, affected tightly fitting dolmans and spiral hats; only the buffoon, Count Gregory, was got up, *à l'Anglaise*, in a red cut-away coat, and piteously begged everyone to explain to the dogs that he was not the fox.

Most of the ladies were also in hunting attire, the close-clinging bodices exhibiting to admiration their amazonian figures; while the long trains had to be held up, lest the spurred and booted heroes around them should trample ruthlessly thereon. And who so beautiful amongst all these beauties as Flora and Fanny!

And now the bell rang inviting the guests to breakfast. Sausage and herb pottage, dishes *à la fourchette*, and corresponding drams of strong spirit awaited them in the dining room. There was no affectation or finnicking now: all alike were sportsmen. The sweetest, prettiest ladies did not refuse, at the request of their admirers, to moisten their rosy lips with a few drops of thirty-years old szilvorium: everything was permissible now, and, besides, they had need of strong hearts today. Even the elderly women meant to accompany the huntsmen in carriages.

It was a glorious summer morning when the imposing cavalcade issued from the courtyard of Kárpáthy Castle. First of all came the ladies, so many slim, supple amazons, on prancing steeds, in the midst of a circle of noisy youths, who made their own horses dance and curvet by the side of their chosen dames; behind them came the wags of the party, on splendidly caparisoned rustic nags; and, last of all, the elderly ladies and gentlemen in their carriages. Squire John himself was in the saddle, and showed all the world that he could hold his own with the smartest cavalier present, and every time he looked at his wife he seemed to be twenty years younger, and his face beamed at the thought that she was such a pretty woman and he was her husband.

Three prizes had been fixed for the best foxhound: the first was a golden goblet with an inscription on it, the second was a silver hunting-horn, and the third a beautiful bear-skin; and no doubt the victorious foxhound would, personally, have been most grateful for the last. Most of the competing dogs, tied together in couples, were led along by the men-servants; but each of the favorite foxhounds was brought on to the ground in a cart, lest any of the horses should kick it. Naturally none of the company carried fire-arms; it is not usual to have them at a fox-hunt.

As the whole merry company was approaching the end of the long avenue of Italian poplars, they perceived a solitary horseman trotting towards them from the opposite end of the avenue.

Even at a distance everyone recognized him at once from his mode of riding, and like quick fire the rumor spread amongst the company; ah, at last he has arrived!

Who was it, then, who had arrived at last? Why, who else but the most gallant of cavaliers, the most daring of courtiers, who had only to come, see, and conquer – Mike Kis, the Whitsun King!

In a moment he had reached the cavalcade, and was apologizing to the ladies for having remained away so long, conveying the impression, from slight allusions he let drop, that some serious business, a duel perhaps, had detained him; then he proceeded to make his excuses to the gentlemen, allowing it to be supposed that some tender affair, a private assignation for instance, was the cause of his delay. Then, shaking hands right and left, and even finding time to throw a word or two to each of the foxhounds by name, he politely begged those who thronged him to make way, as he wished to pay his respects immediately to Madame Kárpáthy, whom, without the slightest embarrassment, he began to call a goddess, an angel on horseback, and other pretty names.

Unfortunately Fanny misunderstood him, and, regarding everything he said as so many capital jokes, rewarded them with far more laughter than their merits deserved.

"Squire John, Squire John!" cried Dame Marion, in a shrill, pointed sort of tone, to Kárpáthy, who was trotting beside her carriage, "if I were you I would not have a bosom friend who has the reputation of being irresistible."

"I am not jealous, your ladyship; that is the one little wheel which is wanting in my mechanism. I suppose it was left out of me when I was made – ha, ha, ha!"

"Then, if I were you, I would not come to a fox-hunt, lest my dogs should regard me as an Actæon."

"To give your ladyship cause to conduct yourself towards me like Diana, eh?"

Dame Marion pouted, and turned her head aside; the man was such a blockhead that he absolutely could not understand any attempt to aggravate him.

And now the company trotted merrily on again.

The course had been chosen outside a village, and in front of it a pleasure-house had been erected. Here the prizes were to be distributed. Here those of the gentlemen and ladies who were not on horseback alighted, and ascended to a terrace, in shape like a lofty tower, which rose from the midst of the pleasure-house, and from whence the whole plain was visible. Only here and there was a dot of forest to be seen; everywhere else stretched a waste expanse covered with broom, coarse grass, and sedges, – a true realm of foxes. Thus from the tower of the pleasure-house the best possible view of the whole competition was obtainable, and there were field-glasses provided for those who wanted them.

A whole army of foxhounds had followed the hunters. It was a fine sight to see how, at a single familiar whistle, the various packs of hounds were separated from each other; how the dogs crowded round their respective masters, for the favorites were now let down from the carts and the rest were unleashed; and how, barking and yelping, they leaped in the air, to reach and lick their masters' uplifted hands.

It is curious how human passions prove contagious to the very beasts.

Squire John selected from among the rest two pure snow-white hounds, and, whistling to them between his two fingers, led them to his wife.

"They are the finest and the boldest foxhounds in the whole pack."

"I know them: one is Cziczke, and the other Rajkó."

The two dogs, hearing their names mentioned, joyously leaped and bounded in their efforts to lick their mistress's hand as she sat on horseback.

It was very pleasant to Squire John to find that his wife knew his dogs by name, he was equally pleased to see that the dogs knew their mistress – ah! everyone did her homage, both man and beast.

"But where, then, is Matyi?" inquired Fanny, looking about her.

"I am taking him with me."

"What, sir, are you going to take part in the race? Pray do not!"

"Why not? Don't you think me a good enough horseman?"

"I readily believe that you are; but pray, for my sake, do not proceed to prove it!"

"For your sake I will immediately dismount."

Flora whispered to Count Gregory, who was riding by her side, "I should like to know how many of the husbands present would give up hunting for the sake of their wives?"

And, indeed, Squire John's affection must have been something altogether out of the way to make him renounce his favorite pastime in the joyful anticipation of which he had been living for months beforehand, simply to please his wife. Fanny, deeply touched, held out her hands towards him.

"You are not angry with me, I hope," said she; "but I feel so frightened on your account."

John Kárpáthy pressed the extended hand to his lips, and, holding it in his palm some little time, asked –

"And ought *I* not to be afraid on your account also?"

Fanny involuntarily glanced at her friend, as if to ask whether she also ought not to remain here.

Kárpáthy guessed the meaning of the look.

"No, no; I don't want you to remain here. Go and enjoy yourself! But take care of yourself. And you young fellows there, watch over my wife as if she were the light of your eyes."

"Oh, we'll look after her!" replied Mike Kis, twirling his moustache.

"And *I,* also, will look after her," cried Lady Szentirmay, with a strong emphasis on the word *I*; for she had observed that Kárpáthy's good-natured appeal had somewhat confused his wife.

And now the horns began to sound and the whips to crack, and both dogs and horses grew unruly and impatient. The company divided into three parts, forming a center and rings like an army, and advanced into the bushy plain, sending the dogs on in front. The ladies waved their handkerchiefs, the gentlemen their caps, to the friends they had left behind on the tower who responded in like manner, whereupon the galloping groups scattered in every direction, disappearing here and there among the thick brushwood. Only the heads of most of the riders were now visible above the bushes, but the fluttering veils of the two ladies could be plainly seen by everyone, and every eye was fixed upon them with delight. And now they came to a ditch. Lady Szentirmay boldly raced towards it, and was over it in a trice; a moment later, Madame Kárpáthy also leaped the ditch, her slender figure swayed and danced during the leap; after her plunged her escort, Count Gregory, the Whitsun King, and some other horsemen. The people on the balcony applauded.

Only Kárpáthy felt uneasy, and did not know where to bestow himself. He descended among the grooms, and finding old Paul there, said to him, anxiously –

"I can't help feeling anxious lest some accident should happen to my wife. Isn't that horse rather shy?"

"The steadiest goer in the world; but perhaps you would like me to go after her?"

"Well, I should. You have just hit it. Mount my horse. Take care they do not go astray near the swamp; call their attention to the fact that they might easily come to grief there."

Palko immediately mounted Squire John's horse, and Kárpáthy returned to the balcony to see whether he would manage to overtake them.

The hunt sped onwards tempestuously. The hounds had now started a fox, but they were still a long way off, and the field was so scattered that the artful beast seemed likely to throw them off his track. He kept plunging into the bushes while his pursuers dashed past, and then, all of a sudden, darted off side-ways. But fruitless was all his craftiness; he only rushed into a fresh foe, and tried vainly to hide or double: there was no refuge to be found anywhere, and the quick cracking of whips on every side of him told him that a war of extirpation against his whole race was on foot, so he resolved on flight, and gained the very first hillock, where he stopped for a moment, looked round to see from what direction the enemy was coming, and then made for the reeds with all his might.

"Look! the fox, the fox!" cried his pursuers, when they perceived him on the hillock: the next moment he had disappeared from it.

But they had seen enough of him to perceive that he was a splendid beast. He was evidently an old stager, who would give the best dogs something to do.

After him!

Off galloped the whole party in the track of the hounds, the faces of the two ladies were aglow with the passionate ardor of the chase, and at that instant there occurred to the mind of Fanny her vision of long ago: what if he, her nameless ideal, were now galloping beside her on his swift-footed steed, and could see her impetuously heading the chase till she threw herself down before him, and died there, without anybody knowing why! But Flora thought: "Suppose Rudolf were now to come face to face with me, and see me" – and then she felt again how much she loved him.

And now the fox suddenly emerged again on the open. A newly mown field, of a thousand acres or so in extent, covered with rows of haycocks, lay right before the huntsmen; and here the really interesting part of the hunt began. The fox was a fine specimen, about as big as a young wolf, but much longer in the body, and carrying behind him a provokingly big brush. He trotted leisurely in front, not because he could not go quicker, but because he wanted to economize his strength, and all the time he kept dodging to and fro, backwards and forwards, in the endeavor to tire his enemies out, and ceaselessly threw glances behind him at his pursuers, out of half an eye, keeping about a hundred paces in front of them, and accelerating his pace whenever he perceived that the distance between him and them was diminishing.

And yet the very best hounds of Squire John's – Cziczke, the two white ones, and Rajkó, Matyi, big Ordas, Michael Kis's Fecske, and Count Gregory's Armida, to say nothing of the whole canine army behind them, were hard upon his traces.

The fox began to go slower and slower. He seemed to regret the brushwood from which he had leaped forth, and kept flying towards one haycock after another; as if he fancied he could find a shelter beside it, and then, snarling savagely, cantered on again. Even from afar he could be seen gnashing his teeth together when he looked back.

And indeed he was in evil case, cooped up on that level ground, where there was neither stream nor hiding place which might shelter him from his pursuers. Sideways, indeed, lay an arm of the river Berettyo, well-known to crayfish catchers and summer-bathers as a broad and deep stream, and well would it be for him now to have that water between him and the hounds, for the foxhound will not swim if he can help it, but it looked very much as if they would surround him, and tear his skin off his back before he could reach it.

And now it was easy to perceive that his pace was diminishing, as he ran in and out among the haycocks; soon he must be completely surrounded.

"Seize him, Fecske! seize him, Rajkó! seize him, Armida!" resounded from all sides.

The dogs rushed after him with all their might.

The two white dogs were nearest to him; like the wind they rushed after him, their long slender necks straining forward as if to let the fox know that a few more minutes and they, would be upon him.

Suddenly the fox stood still. Sweeping his tail beneath him, and gnashing his teeth, he faced round upon the hounds, who, taken unawares, stopped in front of him, snarling viciously, and wagging their upturned tails. The hunted beast took advantage of this momentary respite, and with a side spring slipped between the two white dogs, and tried to find a refuge more to the right.

Again they were all after him.

Now Count Gregory's Armida got nearest to him.

"Bravo Armida! The victory is yours."

Another leap. The fox suddenly crouched down, and Armida bounded over him, only perceiving when she had run twenty paces further that the fox had remained behind.

And now they all suddenly turned to the right.

"Seize him, Fecske!" cried Mike Kis.

And Fecske really did seize the fox; but the fox in his turn seized Fecske, and bit his ear so savagely that the dog immediately let go again: so that was all poor Fecske got.

And now the fox, with all his might, made straight for the Berettyo. The crafty old fellow had succeeded in checkmating all his pursuers and reaching his lurking-place. The hounds were now far behind him.

But now old Matyi, the wolf-grey, solitary foxhound, came to the front, and showed what he could do. Hitherto he had not very much exerted himself, but had let the others do what they could. He knew very well that a single dog would never catch this fox – nay, two and even three would be no match for him. It was an old fox, and they knew each other, for they had often come across each other here and there. Now then, let him show his enemy what he was made of.

Again the fox practiced his old wiles, darting aside, crouching down, gnashing his teeth: all in vain – he had now to do with a practiced foe. If only Squire John could now have seen it all! Ask an enthusiastic fox-hunter how much he would have given for such a sight?

And now the fox stopped short again in mid career, and crouched down; but Matyi did not leap over him as the flighty Armida had done, but, as the fox turned towards him with gnashing teeth, he snapped suddenly at him from the opposite side like lightning, and in that instant all that one could see was the fox turning a somersault in the air. Matyi, seizing him by the neck had, in fact, tossed him up, and scarcely had he reached the ground again when he was seized again by the skin of his back, well shaken, and then released. Let him run a little bit longer, if he likes!

"Bravo, Matyi! bravo!" shouted everybody present.

This exclamation encouraged Matyi to show the spectators fresh specimens of his skill. By a series of masterly manœuvres he turned the fox back towards the hunters, in order that they might the better see him mount head over heels into the air again. He never held the dangerous beast in his jaws for more than one moment, for he knew that in the next the fox could seize him, and dogs have their own peculiar ideas of a fox's grip, for it is the bite of all other bites they like the least. He contented himself therefore with harrying and worrying him as much as possible without coming to too close quarters till he should have succeeded in wearing him out. The fox no longer defended himself, but simply ran straight on, limping and stumbling on three legs. Everyone fancied that it was now all up with him, when, suddenly, he made another dart sideways, and perceiving a herd of oxen on the high-road, made straight towards them.

Here a pretty high fence confronted the hunters, which they were obliged to take, and which gave both the ladies another opportunity of showing their agility; both of them successfully cleared it. At that moment they perceived a horseman coming towards them on the high-road, whom, owing partly to the high bushes and partly to their attention being directed elsewhere, they had not observed before.

"'Tis he!"

Flora's face that instant grew redder than ever, while Fanny's turned as pale as death.

"'Tis he!"

Both of them recognized him at the same time. 'Tis he, the loving husband of the one, the beloved ideal of the other.

Flora rushed towards him with a cry of joy. "Rudolf! Rudolf!" she cried.

Fanny, in dumb despair, turned her horse's head, and began to gallop back again.

"Good God!" cried Rudolf, whose face still burned with the kisses of his loving wife, "that lady's horse has run away with her!"

"That is Madame Kárpáthy!" cried Flora in alarm; and she whipped up her horse in the hope of overtaking her friend.

The lady was galloping helter-skelter across the plain. Everyone fancied that her stallion had run away with her. Flora, old Palko, Mike Kis, and Count Gregory vainly sped after her; they could not get near her: only Rudolf was beginning to catch her up.

And now the stallion had reached the narrow dyke, and was galloping along it; on the other side of it, six fathoms in depth, were the waters of the Berettyo. A single stumble, and all would be over. But now Rudolf was catching her up, and he was the best horseman of them all. And now he was level with her. It was the first time in his life that he had seen this woman. He had no idea that he had met her many and many a time before, for he had never noticed her. The stallion, with foaming mouth, rushed on, with the lady clinging to him. Her face was pale and her bosom heaved. It was just at this moment that the young man came abreast of her; her flying locks flapped his face: and she had a hundredfold more reasons now than ever for wishing to die at that moment. This youth, this ideal of her romantic dreams, was the husband of her dearest, her noblest, her loveliest friend.

Rudolf was obliged to give up all idea of stopping the maddened steed. Instead of that, and, just as Fanny fell back half-swooning from her saddle, he swiftly seized her in his muscular grip, and pulled her right on to his own saddle. The lady fainted away over his shoulder, and the horse dashed wildly onwards.

Chapter XIV

MARTYRDOM

After this event Lady Kárpáthy was very seriously ill; for a long time her life was even despaired of. Kárpáthy summoned the most famous doctors in the world to attend to her, and they consulted and prescribed for her, but none of them could tell what was the matter. It is a great pity that nobody knows how to prescribe for the heart.

For a long time she was delirious, and talked a lot of nonsense, as sick people generally do whose fevered brains are full of phantoms.

A soft smooth hand stroked her burning forehead from time to time. It was the hand of Flora, who watched by the sick-bed night and day, denying herself sleep, denying herself even the sight of her husband, despite the terrifying suggestions of Dame Marion, who maintained that Madame Kárpáthy was sickening for smallpox.

If that had been all the poor woman was suffering from, how little it would have been!

At last Nature triumphed. A young constitution usually struggles more severely with Death than an old one, and throws him off more quickly. Fanny was delivered from death. When first she was able to look around her with an unclouded mind, she perceived two persons sitting by her side; one was Flora, the other – Teresa.

Though nothing in the world would have induced Teresa to call upon Fanny as a visitor, the very first rumor of her severe illness brought her to her side. She arrived on the very day when a change for the better had set in, and relieved Flora by taking her turn in the nursing.

Nevertheless, Lady Szentirmay would not depart till she knew for certain that her friend was out of danger, and therefore resolved to wait a few days longer.

So Fanny regained life and consciousness; she no longer chattered oddly and unintelligibly, but lay very still and quiet. She was cured, the doctors said.

And now she could coldly review the whole course of her life. What was he, what had she become now, and what would become of her in the future?

She was the scion of a wretched and shameful family, from whose fate she had only been snatched by hands which, wont to lift themselves in prayer to God, had shielded and defended her against every danger, and prepared for her a peaceful and quiet refuge, where she might have lived like a bird of the forest in its hidden nest.

This refuge she had been forced to quit, in order to take her place in the great world – that great world which had so much in it that was terrifying to her.

Then she had sought a woman's heart that could understand her, and a manly face that might serve her for an ideal.

And she had found them both – the noble-hearted friend, who had been so good, so kind to her, far better and kinder than she had dared to hope; and the idolized youth, of whose heart and mind the world itself had even grander and finer things to say than she herself had ever lavished upon him. And this woman, and this idol of a man were spouses – and he happiest of spouses too!

What must her portion be now?

She must be the dumb witness of that very bliss which she pictured to herself so vividly. Every day she must see the happy face of her friend, and listen to the sweet secrets of her rapture. She must listen while *his* name is magnified by another; she must look upon the majestic countenance of the youth whom she may not worship – nay, she must not even dare to speak of him, lest her blushes and the tremor of her voice should betray what no man must ever know!

How happy she would have been now, had she never learnt to know this passion, if she had never allowed her soul to fly away after unattainable desires! If only she had listened to that honest old woman she would now be sitting at home in her quiet peaceful cottage among the meadows, with nothing to think of but her flowers!

That was all, all over now!

She was no longer able to go either backwards or forwards. Only to live on, live on, one day after another, and, as every day came round, to sigh, as she got up to face it: "Yet another day!"

But her husband, that good old fellow, what of him?

Only now did Kárpáthy feel how much he loved his wife! Perhaps if she had died he would not have survived her. Sometimes the doctors would allow him to see his wife, and at such times he would stand with streaming eyes at the foot of the sick woman's bed, kissing her hand, and weeping like a child. At last his wife was out of danger. On her departure, Lady Szentirmay impressed upon Kárpáthy the necessity of taking great care of Fanny, of not letting her get up too soon and take cold, of rigorously carrying out the doctor's directions, of not letting her read too long at a time, of allowing her, in a week's time or so, to go out for a drive, if the weather was fine, and she was well wrapped up, and much more to the same effect. Women understand these things so much better than men.

Kárpáthy called down endless blessings on the head of his kind neighbor as he bade her adieu, and promised to come and see her as soon as possible.

"It is now your turn to come and see us," said she. "In a month's time, I hope Fanny will be able to redeem the promise she made to come and see me and my husband at home. I don't think, however, that I'll say good-bye to her now, for fear of disturbing her; it will be better if you will tell her of my departure."

Armed with this commission, and ascertaining first of all from Teresa that Fanny was now awake, and might be seen without harm, he stole softly to her room on the tips of his toes, went up to the bed, gently smoothed down her hair, took her hand in his, and asked how she was.

"Quite well," replied the invalid, and she tried to smile.

The smile was but a poor success, but it did Squire John good to see the attempt, at any rate.

"Lady Szentirmay sends her love; she has just gone."

Fanny made no reply to this, but she drew his hand across her forehead, as if she wished to drive from thence the thought which arose within it.

Kárpáthy fancied that his hand was cooling, perhaps, to the poor hot forehead, so he pressed it tenderly.

Then Fanny seized his hand with both her own, and drew it to her lips. How happy Kárpáthy felt at that moment! He turned aside for a moment, lest she should see the tears in his eyes.

Fanny fancied he would have gone away, and drew him still closer to her.

"Don't go away," she said – "stay here; let us talk!"

"You see," continued she, "that I am quite myself again now. In a short time I shall be able to get up. Don't be angry with me if I ask you to do me a favor?"

"Ask not one favor, but a thousand favors!" cried Kárpáthy, rejoicing that his wife asked anything of him at all.

"Are you not getting ready a new mansion at Pest?" asked Fanny.

"You wish to live there, perhaps?" cried Kárpáthy, hastening to anticipate his wife's wishes. "You can take possession of it at a moment's notice, and, if you don't like it, and want something more handsome, I'll have another built for you this winter."

"Thanks, but I shall be quite satisfied with the one at Pest. I have been thinking to myself what an entirely new life we'll begin to live there together."

"Yes, indeed; we will have lots of company, and of the merriest, – splendid parties –"

"I did not mean that. I am thinking of serious things, of charitable objects. Oh! we who are rich have so many obligations towards the suffering, towards the community, towards humanity."

Poor woman! how she would have escaped from her own burning heart amidst coldly sublime ideas!

"As you please. Seek your joy, then, in drying the eyes of the tearful. Be happy in the blessings which Gratitude will shower upon your name."

"Then you promise me this?"

"I am happy in being able to do anything that pleases you."

"Nay, be not too indulgent. I warn you that will only make me more exacting."

"Speak, speak! would that there were no end to your wishes! Believe me, only then am I unhappy, when I see that nothing delights you, when you are sorrowful, when there's nothing you feel a liking for – then, indeed, I am very, very unhappy! Would you like to go to a watering-place this summer? Where would you like to go? Command me, where would you feel most happy?"

Fanny began reflecting. Whither away? Anywhere, if it only were far enough! Away from the neighborhood of the Szentirmays, and never come back again!

"Mehadia, I think, would be the nicest place. That is far enough away anyhow," thought she.

"I'll engage for you beforehand the best quarters procurable for the coming summer: it really is a very pleasant place."

"And I have something else to ask."

Kárpáthy could scarce contain himself for joy.

"But it is a greater and more serious wish than all the rest."

"All the better. What is it?"

"I should like you to come with me everywhere, and to be with me always, and never leave me."

Ah, this was more than a human heart could bear! The foolish old man went down on his knees beside the bed of his wife, and covered her hands with his tears and kisses.

"How have I deserved this happiness, this goodness from you!" he cried.

The lady smiled sadly, and for a long, long time she did not release her husband's hand from her own. Kárpáthy spent half the day by her bedside in gentle prattle, listening to the modest wishes of his dear sick little wife, and happy beyond expression at being allowed to give her her tonics from time to time.

A few days afterwards Fanny was able to leave her bed, and, leaning against her husband's shoulder, walked up and down the room. Day by day her health returned, and she grew more and more like her old self. And then she would spend whole days with her husband, and bring her embroidery or her book into his room; or she would invite him into her room, when she played the piano; or would drive about with him, in fact, she never left him. She did not wish for any other society. She directed the servants that if any of her old visitors came to see her, they were to be told she was not feeling well, and all the time she would be sitting inside with her husband, and forcing herself to make him happy and load him with joy.

During these days she had very little to do even with Teresa, and very shortly her worthy kinswoman took her leave. Fanny parted from her without tears or sorrow, yet Teresa saw into her soul. When she had kissed the silent lips, and was sitting in the carriage on her way home, she sighed involuntarily, "Poor girl! poor girl!"

Chapter XV

THE SPY

And now we are in Mr. Kecskerey's quarters again. It would be a great mistake on our part to leave him out of sight. An individual like him, once seen, may not be forgotten. He was now living at Pest, where he had elegant chambers and all his old renown, carrying on his old business of amalgamating the various elements of society.

It was still early, and the worthy man was not yet half dressed. When I say not yet half dressed, I mean the expression to be taken in the literal sense of the word. He was sitting in the middle of the room on a rich purple ottoman, enfolded in a red burnoose, sucking away at a huge chibook, puffing smoke all round him, and contemplating himself in a large mirror exactly opposite to him. At the opposite end of the ottoman sat a huge orangutan of about his own size, in a similarly charming position, wrapped in a similar burnoose, also smoking a chibook, and regarding himself in the mirror.

Scattered all about were heaps of scented *billet-doux*, verses, musical notes, and other perishable articles of the same sort. Round about the walls hung all kinds of select pictures, which would certainly have been very much ashamed if they could have seen each other. On the table, in a vase of genuine Herculanean bronze, were the visiting-cards of a number of notable men and women of the smartest set. The carpets were all woven by delicate feminine hands, and bore the figures of dogs, horses, and huntsmen. The tapestried walls revealed the presence of small hidden doors, and the windows were covered by double curtains close drawn.

In the antechamber outside, a small Negro groom was scratching his ear for sheer *ennui*. He had orders not to admit any gentleman visitor till after twelve o'clock, from which he drew the temerarious conclusion that he was free to admit ladies up to that hour.

Despite this prohibition, however, it chanced that Jussuf, in reply to a determined pull at the bell, did admit a gentleman; and Mr. Kecskerey heard the nigger lad talking in his Kaffir tongue to the new arrival, and was furious with him in consequence.

"Who is it, Jussuf?" cried Mr. Kecskerey, in such a sharp voice that the baboon on the sofa behind his back began to hiss for fright.

By way of answer the new arrival himself rushed through the door. "These privileged friends of mine are vastly impertinent," murmured Mr. Kecskerey to himself, as he perceived the intruder in the doorway; and it seemed to give him great satisfaction when the visitor fell back at the sight of his peculiar costume. But a moment later he recognized who it was, and, with a determined effort at gaiety, exclaimed, stretching out his long dry hand towards him –

"Ah, Abellino! 'tis you, eh? We fancied you had mediatized yourself in India. Come and sit down by me. Have you brought back with you some of those famous pastilles which you mentioned in your genial letters?"

"Go to the devil, and take your baboon with you," cursed the new arrival. "You resemble one another so closely that I did not know which was the master of the house."

"Ah, this monkey belongs to the species most fashionable at the Egyptian court. Besides, my baboon is under an obligation to be polite. Joko, show your good breeding by giving a pipe to my guest."

Joko did as he was told, and brought the pipe.

"And now sit down by me and make yourself comfortable," continued Kecskerey. "Jussuf, fill my guest's pipe for him. I regret I cannot oblige you with a narghilly."

Abellino took off the huge mantle which covered his shoulders, sat down face to face with Mr. Kecskerey, and amused himself in the meantime by throwing paper pellets at the baboon.

"And what, then, has brought you back into this realm, my hero, my troubadour?" inquired Mr. Kecskerey. "Some love-adventure, some notable affair, I'll be bound. I'll dare to guess that you have abducted some Hindu vestal from Budhur?"

"Answer me first of all; is there still any rumor abroad about my former affair?"

Kecskerey made an angry grimace.

"My dear friend," said he, "you ask too much of me. You seem to expect that folks will talk of nothing but your beggarly duel for a whole twelve-month. Why, it is as much forgotten as if it had never been. Look now! you killed Fennimore, and Fennimore had a younger brother who by his death succeeded to the family estates. They asked him a little time ago why he did not pursue the action brought against you. 'I am not so mad,' said he, 'as to take action against my benefactor.' You can meet him at my place this very evening. He is a much finer fellow than his brother, and he'll be very glad to see you."

"The luck's on my side then, but let us talk of other things. It looks as if Pest were now becoming the nest of the elegant world, or you would not have established yourself in it. What are you doing here?"

"We are spreading civilization. It is a somewhat poorer diversion than spending the season at Paris, but a few Hungarian magnates have taken it into their heads to live henceforth at Pest, and for their sake others, and for these others' sake others still have pitched their tents in this little town, in which there is as much pleasure as you'll find at London, and as many illusions as you'll find anywhere."

"That's all right. And what do you know about the Kárpáthys?"

Mr. Kecskerey blew himself out haughtily like a frog, and grunted in a strangulated sort of voice, "My friend, for what do you take me, pray?

Am I your spy, that I should go ferreting into family secrets in order to betray them to you? What sort of an opinion can you have of me?"

Abellino, with a feeling of satisfaction, launched the remainder of the crumpled-up visiting-cards in his fist at Joko's head. He knew the manners and customs of Mr. Kecskerey thoroughly. He was wont to fling back every dishonorable commission and query with the utmost indignation, into the face of their proposer, but he executed them all the same, and reported accordingly.

"What business is it of mine what the Kárpáthys are doing? The world says, however, that Madame Kárpáthy has a fresh lover every day. At one time 'tis Count Erdey, at another 'tis Mike Kis. It says, too, that old Squire John himself invites his cronies to Kárpátfalva, and is quite delighted if his wife finds any among them worthy to be loved. He lets her go visiting at the neighboring villages with Mike Kis hundreds of times, and much more is said to the same effect. But what has it all got to do with me? I think as little of such things as of the dreams of my baboon."

After this, Kecskerey, with the assistance of his little Negro servant, slowly proceeded with his dressing.

"Well, my dear friend," he resumed after a while, "so you have come back from India, eh? I suppose you'll be a fixture in our little circle now, and will honor my assemblies with your distinguished presence?"

"I am much obliged to you for the invitation, but I am no longer rich enough to take part in them. Griffard refuses to lend me another sou, and I am obliged to learn the science of economy like any other Philistine."

"Ah, that's a pity for you, for you cannot find it very amusing. You would do more wisely if you made it up with your uncle."

"I would rather be a bandit than a beggar."

"Take care you don't fall into a snare."

"What snare can you possibly imagine?"

"Your uncle is as much enamored of his wife as ever, or I am greatly mistaken."

"I rather incline to think that someone else may be enamored of her."

"That would be somewhat singular."

"Why should you think so?"

"That old man has completely changed. He looks twenty years younger; one scarcely recognizes him. He leads a regular life, and no doubt his doctors are clever. Besides, it is a tradition in your family that the ladies find the gentlemen amiable even in advanced old age. The day that I encountered your kinswoman at Szolnok, I thought she looked happier and more contented than I had ever seen her before."

"Hell and devils!" exclaimed Abellino, mad with rage. "What can be the reason why this woman is so happy and contented? Her husband is incapable, I'll swear, of making her so. There's falsehood, there's fraud somehow."

"There *may* be falsehood and fraud, my friend," replied Kecskerey, coolly clasping one of his knees with both his hands, and swaying himself to and fro in a rocking-chair.

"If I could only prove that that woman was in love with someone; if anyone were able to show the world in the clearest, the most sensational manner that she had secret relations with anybody —"

"But, as a member of the family, that would naturally bring disgrace upon you also."

"They are playing a game against me."

"It may be so. The old man is quite capable of overlooking his wife's infidelity in order to do you out of the inheritance."

"But it cannot be, it cannot be! Our laws would not allow such a scandal."

Kecskerey burst out laughing.

"My friend, if our laws were disposed to make very conscientious investigations concerning the proper descent of all our great families, endless confusion would arise in the making out of our family trees."

"But I tell you I will not allow a downtrodden beggar-woman to force her way into an illustrious family, and rob the rightful heirs of their inheritance by saddling her decrepit husband with brats that are the fruit of her base amours."

At these words Kecskerey laughed louder than ever.

"Since your return you have become quite a moral man, I see. You would have been glad to have had one of these same base-born brats yourself a year ago."

"Joking apart, my friend, you see that I am a ruined man, a man whom infernal intrigues have sent to the devil. If what I fear really happens, I shall blow my brains out. I must find out at any price something that will compromise Madame Kárpáthy before the law, and if something of the sort cannot be discovered, it must be invented."

Kecskerey pulled a wry face.

"My dear friend, I know not why you say such things to me. Do I look like a person competent to give advice in such matters? It is a serious business, I assure you. I am very sorry, but you must do what you want yourself. The Kárpáthys will reside here this winter. Do as you please, corrupt their servants, set your creatures to their work, and get them to lead the young woman astray and then betray her; plant your spies about her, watch every step she takes, and put the affair in the hands of sharp practitioners; but leave me in peace, I am a gentleman, I will *not* be a spy, or a well-feed Mephistopheles, or a hired Cicisbeo."

So the worthy gentleman hastened to wash from off him the least suspicion of such a shady transaction, but nevertheless he showed Abellino what to do. He protested against every attempt to draw an opinion from him, but for all that he did his best to give an exhaustive answer.

Abellino was very well pleased with him. New projects began to spring up in his brain; he took up his hat and bade his friend a grateful adieu, and so they parted with mutual assurances of a speedy *au revoir.*

Chapter XVI

LIGHT WITHOUT AND NIGHT WITHIN

Yet it had to be.

Madame Kárpáthy had promised her friend to share her labors as hostess on the occasion of the feast in honor of her husband's installation as Lord-Lieutenant, just as Lady Szentirmay had shared hers before the fox-hunt. She had vainly tortured her brain for a whole fortnight in order that she might find an excuse to release her from her promise, and not one could she find. Unfortunately, she was so well that she could not even complain on that score. What she feared above all happened. Flora did not forget the promise that had been made, and when the great day was only a week off, she wrote to her friend that she should rely upon her at the end of that time. And so for a whole week Fanny, resigned to her fate, but with the torment of her secret passion in her bosom, suffered in silence at the thought of going to the house of him whom she loved as her soul's ideal, but who would not have been too far away from her, so she thought, if he had lived in another planet.

Flora welcomed her friend with great joy, her satisfaction was unmistakably visible on her honest, lovely face as she pressed Fanny between her arms. Rudolf's manner was kindly and courtly, but nothing more. He was glad to see his pretty neighbor in his house and anxious to make her comfortable, but she did not interest him in the very least.

And indeed Fanny herself found the situation much less dangerous than she had imagined. Ideals, especially ideals of the masculine gender, in their domestic circles lose very much of the nimbus which they carry about with them elsewhere. At home you hear them whistle and shout, and bully their servants and domestics, and see them immersed in everyday household affairs. You see them eat and drink and look bored. You see them with imperfect or unaccomplished toilets, and often with muddy boots, especially when they look after their own horses. You begin to realize that ideals also are as much subject to the petty necessities of life as ordinary men, and do not always preserve the precise postures you are wont to see them in when their portraits adorn the picture-galleries. With women it is quite different. Woman is born to beautify the domestic circle, woman is always fascinating whether she be dressed up or domestically dowdy, but man is least of all fascinating at home.

In a word, Fanny felt the danger to be much less when it was actually before her than it had seemed to be when seen from afar, and she looked at Rudolf much more calmly with her bodily eyes than she had been wont to do with the eyes of her imagination.

Thus the first week which Fanny spent at Szentirmay Castle was by no means so very painful, and after that Rudolf had to go to the capital from whence he was only to return on the day before the installation.

Meanwhile the two ladies, with the utmost forethought, were arranging everything for the approaching festivities, and whatever one of them forgot was sure to occur to the other. Fanny began to find her position more and more natural; every day she began to gain a greater command over her tender emotions, and indeed life, practical life, makes possible and comprehensible much which poetical logic and the imagination label – absurd.

On the day of the installation, Lady Szentirmay and Madame Kárpáthy drove over to the county town where lodgings had been provided for the former's husband as Governor-General, at the town-hall.

Szentirmay wished his installation to be conducted with as little pomp and ceremony as possible. The most eminent ladies of the county watched the procession from the balcony, and Madame Kárpáthy also was among them. It was difficult to recognize anyone in particular among all those holiday faces, such a different aspect did their Oriental gravity and splendid Oriental *Köntöses* give them. Several of the younger cavaliers saluted the ladies with their swords.

At length the carriage of the *Fõispán* came in sight with a clattering escort of twelve knightly horsemen. He himself was sitting bareheaded in the open carriage, and something like emotion was visible on his handsome noble face. Loud cries of "Éljen! éljen!" announced his approach. Everyone knew of him by hearsay as the noblest of men, and everyone rejoiced that the best of patriots and the most excellent of citizens should have attained the highest dignity in the county. Madame Kárpáthy looked at him tremblingly, better for her if she had never seen him like this.

The procession passed across the square to the gate of the town-hall, and half an hour later Rudolf was standing in the large assembly-room filling it with his sublime impassioned words, till all who heard felt their hearts leap towards him. Madame Kárpáthy also heard him, she was in the gallery. Ah, it would have been better had she neither seen nor heard him there. Now she not merely loved, she adored him.

All at once she began to notice that somebody in the assembly-hall below was making frantic signs to her with hands and head, and using every available limb to attract her attention; nay, he even got upon a chair in order to be able to see her better. At first she did not recognize the man, but presently the disagreeable recollection thrilled through her that she had seen him before somewhere, and she regarded him more closely with a look of aversion – it was Mr. Kecskerey.

Why, what could have brought that worthy man thither, for it was not his way to put himself to any inconvenience without very good reason.

The sight of this man made a very disagreeable impression upon Fanny, and jarred upon her nerves. Every time she looked at him she perceived, much to her indignation, that his eyes were fixed constantly upon her.

The official ceremonies were generally terminated by a magnificent banquet during which the assembly-room with magical rapidity was converted into a dancing-room, to which the guests then returned.

The best and bonniest of the whole countryside were together, the most illustrious of the men and the loveliest of the women.

Rudolf opened the ball with the Princess * * * who was considered the most important personage present amongst the ladies, and then danced with all the other women in turn, according to rank. How Fanny trembled, and how her heart began to beat, when she saw him approaching her. Lady Szentirmay had just been carried off by some young cavalier for a waltz, and she was sitting there alone.

Rudolf politely walked up to her, and with a deep bow invited her to dance. Oh, how beautiful he was! Fanny durst not regard him at that moment. Rudolf bending half over her, offered her his arm.

Poor lady, she was scarce able to utter these few words: "I am not allowed to dance, my lord. I have been very ill."

He could not but believe what she said, as she was as pale at that moment as if she were about to descend into the tomb.

Rudolf expressed his regret in a few courtly words, and then retired.

For some time afterwards Fanny durst not raise her eyes, as if she fancied he was still standing before her. At last, however, she did look up, and the eyes that met her gaze were – Mr. Kecskerey's.

"The Madonna of Mount Carmel, for all the world!" said that worthy cavalier, saluting her *chapeau-bas*, and confidently drawing still nearer.

Fanny hastily pulled herself together. She had the foreboding that she must hide her very soul from the scrutiny of this man; so she accepted his salutation with a cold smile, and made as if she were not afraid of him.

"What a loss it is to the company that your ladyship does not dance, but what a gain to me who, also, do not dance," said the hero, with impertinent familiarity. And he sat down beside Lady Kárpáthy as if he were an intimate friend, throwing back his dress-coat on both sides, and nursing one of his legs in both hands. "Will it bore your ladyship if we have a little talk together?"

"I am a good listener."

"During the last few days a joyous rumor has flashed through our capital which has made everyone happy who has heard it."

"What rumor is that?"

"That your ladyship intends to spend the coming winter in the capital."

"It is not yet certain."

"You drive me to despair. Surely, my friend Kárpáthy is not such an ungallant husband? Why, he should fly to execute his wife's wishes!"

"I have never told anybody that I wanted to reside at Pest."

"The lady is secretive," thought Kecskerey. "I know that they are making their palace at Pest habitable. We shall get to the bottom of it presently."

"Yet the Pest saloons will be very attractive this winter, and we shall form some very elegant sets. The Szépkiesdys are coming up, and we may also expect to see there Count Gergely with his mother, young Eugene Darvay, the handsome Rezsö Csendey, and that genial prince of buffoons, Mike Kis."

Fanny toyed indifferently with her fan; not one of all these persons interested her in the least.

"And I know it as a fact, that our fêted friend Rudolf is also going to spend the winter there, with his handsome wife."

Hah! what impression will that make? Will she be able to conceal the smarting pain she felt at that moment? But no, she did not betray herself; she merely said, "I don't fancy we shall go to Pest."

With that she rose from her seat. The dance was over, and Flora, hastening to her friend, passed her arm round her waist, and they took a turn together round the room.

Mr. Kecskerey began to rock himself gently to and fro on the sofa and draw conclusions.

"Why did she sigh so deeply when she said, 'I don't fancy we shall go to Pest'?"

Just then Rudolf drew near, and Mr. Kecskerey seizing his opportunity, put his arm through Rudolf's, and paced with him up and down the splendid saloon, as if they had been the very best friends in the world. And here we should do well to remember that Mr. Kecskerey was a personage of remarkable consideration in the highest circles, and enjoyed a position of distinction there peculiarly his own.

The worthy cavalier – I mean Mr. Kecskerey – had just drawn Rudolf underneath a chandelier, whether that people might see them together there, or whether he himself might see Rudolf better, I cannot say. The two young belles, the queens of the ball, were walking in front of them, arm-in-arm. How beautiful they both were!

"What a pair!" cried Kecskerey, rapturously. "To which of them would that wretched mythological Paris have given the apple of Eris, if he had had to choose between two such goddesses? And how they walk, arm-in-arm. A true *belle alliance!* Nay, I express myself badly, I ought to say *affreuse alliance!* Why, separately they are capable of subjugating the world! Why need they combine their charms? My friend, beware of this dangerous alliance; Madame Kárpáthy is a splendid woman."

"My wife is the prettier," replied Rudolf, with mild self-satisfaction.

"I honor you for that word, Rudolf. You are indeed a tender husband! But your wife really is an angel. Madame Kárpáthy pales before her. Hers is not the beauty which can interest men of genius, she is too sensitive."

"Nay, nay; I will not have you depreciate her in order to cry up my wife. On the contrary, I admit that Madame Kárpáthy is a very beautiful woman; indeed to some person's tastes, she might appear the ideal of loveliness."

"Yes, true; poor Abellino, for instance, at one time, would scarce allow that a more beautiful woman had been born into the world since Helen of Troy or Ninon d'Enclos. He was quite mad about her; ruined himself, in fact, because of her. He spent sixty thousand florins upon her."

"What do you mean by that?" inquired Rudolf, much offended.

Kecskerey laughed good-humoredly. "Ma foi! that is a vain question from you, Rudolf. As if you did not know that it is usual to spend something on young women."

"But I know exactly what happened to Abellino when he forced six hundred florins into the girl's hand, and the manner in which she flung them back in his face was equivalent, among friends, to at least three boxes on the ears. I remember it well, because it led to a duel, and I was one of the seconds of Abellino's opponent."

"Ah ça, that's true! But you know how often it happens that when one has flung back a paltry five or six hundred florins between the eyes of the giver, one does not do the same with sixty thousand florins, when offered afterwards. I do not say this from any wish to injure Madame Kárpáthy, for, of course, nothing happened between them. But it is true, nevertheless, that she accepted the offer, and promised her dear mother, worthy Mrs. Meyer, that she would listen to Abellino's words, or to his sixty thousand florins, which is the same thing; and when luck unexpectedly suggested to old Jock that he should sue for her hand, in order to spite his nephew, the girl had sense enough to choose the better of two good offers, and accepted him. But not for all the world would I say anything ill of her. She is a lady of position and altogether blameless; but, for that very reason, I do not see why one or other of us might not have tried his luck with her."

At that moment several other acquaintances came up to Rudolf, and claimed him; so he parted from Kecskerey. But henceforward an unusual air of disquietude was visible on his face, and as often as he encountered his wife, who never left Madame Kárpáthy for an instant, an unpleasant feeling took possession of him, and he thought to himself, "That is a woman who might have been won with sixty thousand florins."

And then he reflected that, in the course of the evening, Kecskerey would tell the same pretty story to a dozen or more other men; so that within an hour's time the whole company would know all about it, and at the same time see his wife walking about with this woman, and talking and whispering to her familiarly. What cared he for Madame Kárpáthy? She might be as beautiful again as she really was, for aught that he cared; but he reflected that she might cast a shadow on his own wife, his adored, his idolized wife, and this reflection disturbed him. Why had he ever allowed her to make this woman's acquaintance? Flora was so kind-hearted that she would have raised this woman up to her own level; but she never reflected that this woman had a shady past, and that her own good name might be soiled by contact with her.

Of course he knew that it was Kecskerey's habit to run down everyone unmercifully, but he also knew that he vouched for everything he said. Whatever he said of anybody was never actually false. He did not circulate downright libels, but he had the knack of probing down into the deepest hidden secret shame of everyone he knew.

As soon as the ball was over, Rudolf hastened to seek out his wife. His servants told him that she had already retired to her bedroom. He knocked at the door, and, hearing her voice, entered.

Flora was still in full ball-dress; her maid was doing up her hair.

"May I have a word with you?" inquired Rudolf, peeping through the door.

Flora, with a smile, dismissed the maid; and Rudolf embraced his wife, and impressed a burning, a lover's kiss on her radiant face.

"Ah, stop!" cried Flora, hastily, disengaging herself from the encircling arms. "Are you not aware that I am very angry with you?"

Well, at any rate, it was very amiable of the dear wife to allow herself to be kissed first, and then only to recollect that she was angry.

"May I know how I have offended?"

"You have been very discourteous to me today. The whole evening you have not deigned to speak to me. Ten times, at least, I have purposely passed by where Rudolf was standing, and Rudolf took not the slightest notice of me."

While she was saying these words Rudolf succeeded in securing one of the threatening little hands, and, placing it first to his lips and then to his breast, compelled his beloved wife to sit down beside him again on the sofa.

"Let me make good my fault," said he. "For three hours I have not been near you, therefore for three days I will not quit your side, although I know that in that case it will be the innocent party who bears the punishment."

"Ah, Rudolf, that was but a poor jest, I don't like such witticisms. I want you to give an account of yourself. Why are you in such a bad humor?"

"There was something unpleasant in the installation speeches."

"Ah, my friend, that won't do; you don't deceive me. You would tell me a falsehood, eh? You would lie in despite of that honest open face of yours, in spite of those transparent eyes? And you would lie to me, who exchanged souls with you? It cannot be so; tell me the truth!"

Rudolf's face grew serious, he fell a-thinking, but presently he replied –

"Don't let us talk about it now."

"Why not?"

"It would take too long."

"Ah, Rudolf is sleepy! Poor Rudolf is afraid the conversation would go on forever. Well, good night, dear Rudolf. If you want to go and sleep, send in my maid again!"

At these words Rudolf arose, bowed, and prepared to go in real earnest.

Then, naturally, it was the wife's turn to give way.

"Well, remain then, I was only joking," said she. "Even now, you see, you are inclined to be ill-tempered – one may not even jest with you. Come here now, and we will play at guessing riddles. Let us lay a wager that I find out what is the matter with you?"

"Let us see," replied Rudolf, making himself comfortable on the sofa, while Flora leaned her head on his breast, and began counting off her guesses on her fingers.

"You have been listening to gossip?"

"Something of the sort."

"About whom?"

"Oh, if I were to tell, the riddle would be at an end. You must guess."

"About me?"

"Anybody who would circulate gossip about you would have to be endowed with a very lively imagination."

"About whom then?"

"Don't worry me. I will tell you. I came here, indeed, resolved to tell you; but then I thought it might disturb you, and I take you to witness that I only come out with it after the most rigorous inquisition on your part. It does not please me, nay – more than that, it disquiets me to see you so very friendly with Madame Kárpáthy."

"Ah!" So astounded was Flora, that that was all she could say. It was the last thing in the world she had expected to hear. "This really is surprising!" she exclaimed at last. "Another husband would only have been afraid of his wife's intercourse with men: you present the very first example of a husband who is afraid of his wife's women-friends likewise."

"It is because I love you so. My love of you is so devoted, so idolatrous, that I would have everyone who sees and knows you approach you with a reverence, a homage equal to mine own. Not even in thought must anyone dare to sin against you."

"And do I give cause to the contrary?"

"You do not, but your surroundings do; and this Kárpáthy woman has a very equivocal reputation."

"Rudolf, my good Rudolf, why are you so incensed against this poor woman? If you only knew her, you would say there was not a more honorable woman in the whole world."

"I know all about her; and you, from sheer compassion, have made her a present of your heart. Your sympathy does you honor, but the world has an opinion of this woman very different from yours: in the world's opinion she is frivolous enough."

"The world is unjust."

"Not altogether, perhaps. This woman has a past, and there is much in that past which justifies the world's judgment."

"But in her present there is much which contradicts that judgment. This woman's present conduct is worthy of all respect."

Rudolf tenderly stroked the head of his consort.

"My dear Flora, you are a child; there is much you do not understand, and will not understand. In the world there are ideas, ugly, extraordinary ideas, of which your pure, childlike mind can form no notion."

"Oh, don't suppose me so simple! I know everything. I know that Fanny's sisters were very bad, unprincipled women, and that only the energy of good kinsfolk saved Fanny herself from being betrayed and ruined. I know that in the eyes of the world hers is a very dubious record; but I also know that, so long as I hold that woman's hand in mine, the world will not dare to reproach, will not dare to condemn her; and the thought of it makes me proud and well pleased."

"And suppose you are attacked?"

"I don't understand."

"Suppose they say of you what they say of her, that you are a frivolous, flighty woman?"

"Without cause?"

"Not without cause. She lives in the midst of a band of empty-headed men, who certainly have no particular regard for a woman's reputation. And you, in consequence of your intimacy with Madame Kárpáthy, rub shoulders every day with her acquaintances, and will also be taken for a light, frivolous, frail sort of woman."

"I a light, frail, frivolous woman!" cried Flora, visibly wounded; but the moment afterwards she shrugged her shoulders. "It matters not. Rather let the whole world be unjust to me, than that I should be unjust to anyone. And, after all, why should I care about the world, when you are the whole world to me? Let everybody regard me as a light woman for Madame Kárpáthy's sake; so long as you do not, I care nothing about the others."

"And if I, also, considered you as much?"

Flora sprang up from Rudolf's side in amazement.

"Rudolf! think what you are saying. Are you serious?"

"Yes, I am serious."

Flora reflected for an instant, then she said decidedly –

"Very well, Rudolf, I assure you that I am neither frivolous nor weak – weak not even in respect to you." And with that she sprang to the bell-rope and pulled it violently three times.

The maid entered.

"Netti, you will sleep in here with me tonight."

Rudolf looked at his wife with the greatest surprise.

"This is a sentence of banishment, eh?"

"It is."

"For how long?"

"Until you withdraw your words."

Rudolf smilingly kissed her hand and quitted the room; but he lay down in a very bad humor, and it was a long time before he could go to sleep. Often he was on the point of starting up, hastening to her room, begging her pardon, and giving her a written assurance under his hand and seal that women are the strongest, the most determined creatures in the world, and that there never was and never will be such a thing as a frivolous, frail young woman – but the self-respect of a husband always restrained him. It was not right that he should surrender so soon. He must show that if his wife had strength of mind enough to dismiss him, his strength of mind was not less than hers. On the morrow she would certainly be the first to plead guilty of contumacy; and with thoughts like these he went to sleep.

Chapter XVII

A DANGEROUS EXPERIMENT

The next day Rudolf only met his wife at dinner before a numerous company. There was no trace of displeasure on the lady's handsome face; she was as captivating, as fascinating as ever, and nothing could exceed her tenderness, her amiability towards her husband.

Late in the evening, when all the guests had dispersed, they found themselves alone with each other again, and Rudolf had a grateful recollection of the German proverb, which says that lovers ought to quarrel occasionally in order to love each other all the better afterwards. He fancied that he was enjoying to the full the victory won in yesterday's warfare, and he felt magnanimous and would not reproach his wife with her defeat in that sweet hour. But when he embraced Flora with both arms as if he were going to hold her fast forever, the lady gently disentangled herself, and, leaning on his shoulder, whispered in his ear –

"And now, my dear Rudolf, God be with you! Let us wish each other good night."

Rudolf was dumfounded.

"You see I am not so flighty as you fancied. I am not weak even where you are concerned; but I can love, and nobody shall forbid me to love whom I will." And with that she blew him a kiss from the threshold of her bedroom, and Rudolf heard her double-lock the door behind her.

Now this of itself was more than enough to make any man angry.

Rudolf tore at least two buttons off his coat in the act of undressing, and in his wrath took down Hugo Grotius, read steadily away at it till midnight, and then dashed Hugo Grotius to the ground, for he did not understand a word that he had been reading. His thoughts were elsewhere.

And the following day passed away with the same peculiar variations.

His wife was captivatingly amiable. Like a seductive siren, she immeshed her husband in the magic charms of her caresses, was kindness, tenderness personified, loaded him with every little attention which one can look for from a gracious lady, right up to her bedroom door, which she again locked in his face.

Now this was the most exquisite torture conceivable to which a man can be submitted. Compared with this little fairy, a Nero, a Caligula was a veritable philanthropist.

"But how long is this obstinacy to last?" burst forth Rudolf one day, in spite of himself.

"Until you withdraw your disparaging opinion of women."

Well, a single word would have been enough, but that single word was too precious for the pride of a husband to part with. Such a word meant submission, unconditional surrender; only at the very last extremity could it be resorted to.

No, instead of that, he will compel his wife to surrender, and he had plenty of time in those lonely, sleepless nights to hatch a plan of action. He would leave home for a week, and not tell his wife where he was going. The Kárpáthys were now at their castle at Nagy Kun Madaras; he would spend the week with them. That young woman would be certain to welcome him most gladly, and he would pay his court to her. Success was certain. He was sure to triumph over women of a much more obstinate character, if only he made up his mind to conquer. Old Kárpáthy would not trouble himself about it; he would only be too glad if his wife had plenty of amusement. There was not even any necessity for using any particular charm or seduction, the young woman was so avid of pleasure, that she was pretty sure to show favor to anyone. She herself would be his best ally.

With such ideas in his head, he prepared, on the following day, for his journey. Flora was as kind, as tender as ever as she parted from him, and it was impossible to suspect her of any pretence.

Rudolf whispered lovingly in her ear, "Come now, shall there be an end to our warfare?"

"I require an unconditional surrender," said Flora, with an unappeasable smile.

"Good! there shall be an end to it when I return, but then I shall *dictate* peace."

Flora shook her pretty head dubiously, and kissed her husband again and again; and when he was actually sitting in the coach, she ran after him to kiss him once more, and then went out on the balcony and followed him with her eyes, whilst Rudolf leaned out of the coach, and so they kept on bidding each other adieu with hat and handkerchief till the coach was out of sight.

And thus an honest husband quitted his house with the fixed resolve to deceive another man's wife, simply in order that he might thereby win back his own.

If only he had known what he was doing!

Since the day of the installation, the Kárpáthys had been residing at their castle at Madaras. Old Kárpáthy had yielded to his wife's wishes in that respect. She had begged that they might live there for a short time, although it was by no means so pleasantly situated as Kárpátfalva. Fanny wished, in fact, to be far away from Szentirma, and had no longer the slightest desire to go to Pest since hearing from Kecskerey that the Szentirmays intended living there during the winter.

Squire John and his wife were just then walking in the newly-laid-out English garden. The gentle fallow deer already knew their mistress well. Her pockets were always full of sugar almonds, and they drew near to eat the dainty morsels out of her hand, and accompanied her up and down the walk. Suddenly the rumble of a carriage was audible on the high-road, and Kárpáthy, looking over the fence, exclaimed –

"Look, look! those are the Szentirmay horses!"

Fanny almost collapsed. The Squire felt her arm tremble.

"I trod on a snail," said his wife, turning pale.

"You silly thing, what's there to be afraid of? I knew that Flora would come here to seek you out. Oh, how greatly that lady loves you! But, indeed, who would not love you?"

But Fanny could see very well, from afar, that in the carriage which was approaching sat not a woman but a man. Kárpáthy's eyes were weak. He could recognize a horse even at a distance, but he could not distinguish people.

"Come, we will go and meet her," said he to his wife as the carriage swept into the park.

Fanny stood still as if her feet were rooted to the ground.

"Come, come, don't you want to meet your friend?" insisted the good old man.

"It is not Flora," stammered Fanny, with frightened, embarrassed eyes.

"Then who else can it be?" asked the Squire. He must have been somewhat surprised at the conduct of his wife, but there was not a grain of suspicion in his composition, so he simply asked again, "Then who else can it be?"

"It is Flora's husband," said Fanny, withdrawing her hand from her husband's arm.

Squire John began to laugh.

"Why, what a silly the girl is! Why, you must welcome him too, of course. Are you not the mistress of the house?"

Not another word did Fanny speak, but she hardened her face as well as her heart, and hastened towards the coming guest on her husband's arm.

By the time they reached the forecourt of the castle, Rudolf's carriage was rumbling into the courtyard. The young nobleman perceived and hastened towards them. Kárpáthy held out his hand while he was still some way off, and Rudolf pressed it warmly.

"Well, and won't you hold out your hand too?" said the Squire to his wife; "he's the husband of your dear friend, is he not? Why do you look at him as if you had never seen him before?"

Fanny fancied that the ground beneath her must open, and the columns and stone statues of the old castle seemed to be dancing round her. She felt the pressure of a warm hand in hers, and she involuntarily leaned her dizzy head on her husband's shoulder.

Rudolf regarded her fixedly, and his ideas concerning this woman were peculiar: he took this pallor for faint-heartedness, this veiled regard for coquetry, and he believed it would be no difficult matter to win her.

As they ascended the staircase together, he told Kárpáthy the cause of his coming: he had, he said, to settle a boundary dispute between two counties, which would detain him for some days.

The two men spent the hours of the afternoon together; only at the dinner-table did they all three meet again.

Kárpáthy himself was struck by the paleness of his wife; all through dinner the lady was speechless.

The conversation naturally turned on general subjects. Rudolf had little opportunity of speaking to Dame Kárpáthy by herself. After dinner Kárpáthy used generally to have a nap, and it had now become such an indispensable habit with him that he would not have given up his after-dinner repose for the sake of all the potentates of the Orient.

"And meanwhile, little brother," said he to Rudolf, "amuse yourself as you please. Have a chat with my wife, or, if you think it more prudent, make use of my library."

The choice was not difficult.

Fanny, as soon as dinner was over, withdrew to the garden. Presently, hearing footsteps approaching, she looked up and beheld Rudolf.

The unexpected apparition of a tiger just escaped from his cage would not have terrified her so. There was no escape from him. They stood face to face.

The young man approached her with friendly courtesy, and a conversation on some general topic began. Rudolf remarked that the flowers in the garden around them were as wondrously beautiful, as if they were sensible of the close proximity of their mistress, and did not wish to be inferior to her in beauty.

"I love flowers," stammered Fanny, as if she felt obliged to answer something.

"Ah, if only your ladyship were acquainted with them!"

Fanny looked at him inquiringly.

"Yes, if only your ladyship knew the flowers, not merely by name, but through the medium of that world of fancy which is bound up with the life of the flowers! Every flower has its own life, desires, inclinations, grief and sorrows, love and anguish, just as much as we have. The imaginations of our poets give to each of them its own characteristics, and associates little fables with them, some of which are very pretty. Indeed, you will find much that is interesting in the ideal lives of the flowers."

Here Rudolf broke off an iris from a side-bed.

"Look, here is a happy family, three husbands and three wives, each husband close beside his wife. They bloom together, they wither together; not one of them is inconstant. This is the bliss of flowers. These are all happy lovers."

Then Rudolf threw away the iris, and plucked an amaranth.

"Now, here we have the aristocrats. In the higher compartment is the husband, in the lower the wife – upper-class married life. Nevertheless, the ashen-purple color of the flower shows that its life is happy."

Here Rudolf rubbed the amaranth between his fingers, and innumerable little dark seeds fell into the palm of his hand.

"As black as pearls, you see," said Rudolf.

"Yes, as pearls," lisped Fanny, thinking it quite natural that they should pour out of the youth's hand into her own, for it was a shame to lose them. There was not a pure pearl in the Indies that she would have exchanged for these little seeds. And now Rudolf threw the amaranth away too.

Fanny glanced in the direction of the rejected flower, as if to make sure of the place where it had fallen.

"And now will your ladyship look at those two maples standing side by side? What handsome trees they are! One of them seems to be of a brighter green than the other: that, therefore, is the wife; the darker one is the husband. They also are happy lovers. But now look over yonder! There stands a majestic maple tree all by itself. How yellow its foliage is! Poor thing! it has not found a husband. Some pitiless gardener has planted it beside a nut tree, and that is no mate for it. How pale, how yellow it looks, poor thing! But, good Heavens! how pale you are! What is the matter?"

"Nothing, nothing, sir," said Fanny, "only a little giddiness," and without the slightest hesitation she leant on Rudolf's arm.

He fancied he understood, but he was very far from understanding.

And now they reached the richly furnished conservatory in which a splendid snow-white dahlia with a scarce perceptible rosy tinge in its innermost petals was just then beginning to bloom. It was a great rarity in Europe at that time. Rudolf thought this specimen very beautiful, and maintained that only at Schönbrunn was a more beautiful one to be seen.

And again they fell a-talking about trifling general topics, walking as they talked up and down the garden; and Rudolf fancied that now he had conquered this woman, and the woman fancied that she had already sinned sufficiently to be condemned forever. It is true she had only been walking arm-in-arm with Rudolf throughout one long hour, and they had only been talking of insignificant, comical, general topics. But oh, through it all she had felt a sinful pleasure in her heart. And what did it matter that nobody knew, she herself felt that that happiness was a stolen treasure.

At last they returned to the Castle again.

When Rudolf went to bed that night, he found on a table in the antechamber of his bedroom a bouquet of flowers in a handsome china vase, in the midst of which he immediately distinguished the unique and magnificent dahlia.

And he thought he understood.

Next day the men were occupied all the morning with so-called official business, and who would think of a woman in the midst of such grave matters?

In the afternoon, rainy weather set in, whence arose the double disadvantage that Squire John was doubly as sleepy as usual, and that Fanny was unable to seek refuge in the garden where, beneath the protection of the open air, she was better protected against the threatened danger.

She felt the fever in every limb. She knew, she felt that the man whom already she madly adored wanted to make her love him. If this was sport on his part, what a terrible sport! and if it were reality, how much more terrible still!

When there was a knock at the door she was scarce able to say, "Come in." The door opened, and Rudolf entered.

Fanny was not pale now, but her face burned like fire when she perceived Rudolf. She immediately arose from her recumbent position and confusedly begged him to excuse her for a moment; she would be back in a short time, and in the meantime would he occupy her place, and with that she fled from the room. She wanted to speak to her lady-companion, she said. She traversed three or four rooms without perceiving a soul. God only knew where everybody had gone. Not a domestic was near. And with this disquieting knowledge she was obliged to return.

At the very moment when she returned, Rudolf noticed that Fanny had hastily concealed a book which she evidently had hitherto been reading, and flung a handkerchief over it in order that he might not see it.

Rudolf was interested, he felt he must take a deeper glance into the character of this woman. What book could it be that she was so anxious to hide from him? These modern women read risky books in private, and love to be rigid moralists in public at the same time.

He raised the handkerchief from the book, and he opened the book – it was a Prayer-book. And as the book opened wide of its own accord in two places, he perceived two pressed flowers between its leaves – an iris and an amaranth.

Rudolf suddenly grew grave. His heart felt heavy. Only now did he begin to reflect what sort of a game he was playing. These two flowers so fascinated him, so engrossed his attention, that he only perceived that the lady had returned when she stood feverishly trembling before him.

Each of them shrank back from the other.

The secret was revealed.

Rudolf gazed speechlessly at the woman and she at him. How beautiful, how bewitchingly beautiful she was in her dumb misery as slowly, unconsciously, she folded her hands together and pressed them against her bosom, to stifle by force the tempest of her tears!

Rudolf forgot his part, and, deeply moved, exclaimed, "My God!"

Now, for the first time, he really understood everything.

The sorrow in his voice broke down the energy with which Fanny had hitherto restrained her tears, and they began to flow in streams down her beautiful face as she sank into an armchair.

Taking tenderly one of her pretty hands, Rudolf asked compassionately, "Why do you weep?"

But he knew well enough now why she wept.

"Why did you come here," inquired the lady in a voice trembling with emotion – she could control herself no longer – "when, day after day, I have been praying God that I might never see you again? When I avoided every place where I might chance to meet you, why did you seek me out here? I am lost, for God has abandoned me. In all my life, no man's image has been in my heart save yours alone. Yet I had buried that away too, far out of sight. Why, why did you make it come to life again? Have you not observed that I fled every spot where you appeared? Did not your very arms prevent me from seeking death when we met together again! Ah, how much I suffered then because of you? Oh, why did you come hither to see me in my misery, in my despair?"

And she covered her face with her hands, and wept.

Rudolf was vexed to the soul at what he had done.

Presently Fanny withdrew the handkerchief from the Prayer-book, dried her streaming eyes, and resumed, in a stronger voice –

"And now what does it profit you to know that I am a senseless creature struggling with despair when I think of you? Can you be the happier for it? I shall be all the unhappier, for now I must deny myself even the very thought of you."

What could he say to her? What words could he find wherewith to comfort her? What could he do but extend his hand to her and allow her to cover it with her tears and kisses? What could he do but allow her in her passionate despair to fall upon his breast, and, sobbing and moaning, hold him embraced betwixt unspeakable agony and unspeakable joy?

And when she had wept herself out on his breast, the poor lady grew calmer, and ceasing her sobbing, said in a determined voice –

"And now I swear to you before that God who will one day judge me for my sins, that if ever I see you again, that same hour shall be the hour of my death. If, then, you have any compassion, avoid me! I beg of you not your love but your pity; I shall know how to get over it somehow in time."

Rudolf's fine eyes sparkled with tears. This poor lady had deserved to be happy, and yet she had only been happy a single moment all her life, and that moment was when she had hung sobbing on his breast.

How long and weary life must be to her from henceforth!

Rudolf quitted the woman, and scarce waiting until Kárpáthy had awoke, he took his leave and returned to Szentirma. He was very sad and ill at ease all the way.

On reaching home, his merry, vivacious, affectionate wife flew towards him, and dried the traces of the bitter tears with her loving kisses.

"Ah, ha! so you were at Madaras, eh?" said Flora, roguishly; "a little bird whispered me that you would go a-spying. Well, what have you discovered?"

"That you are right," said Rudolf, tenderly – "women are not weak."

"Then there is peace between us. And what news of Fanny?"

"God help the poor lady, for she is very, very unhappy!"

Chapter XVIII

UNPLEASANT DISCOVERIES

It was the winter season at Pest. The Szentirmays had also arrived there, and the beautiful countess and her worthy husband were the ideals of the highest circles, and everybody tried hard to make their acquaintance. But the greatest commotion of all was made by the arrival of Mr. Kecskerey. Without him the whole winter season would have been abominably dull. There was no mention even of balls and assemblies until he came back again. Some men have a peculiar talent, a special faculty, for arranging such things, and it was "our friend" Kecskerey's specialty. The whole world of fashion called Kecskerey "our friend," so it is only proper that we should give him the same title.

His first business was to get together a sufficient number of gentlemen to form a club where only eminent and distinguished members of society would assemble. Kecskerey himself was a singularly interesting person, and when he had dressed himself for the evening, and laid himself out to be agreeable, he had such a store of piquant anecdotes to draw upon, all more or less personal experiences during his artistic ramblings, that even the tea-tables were deserted and the witty gentleman was surrounded by merry crowds of eager listeners.

Something particular was in the wind now, for there was a considerable whispering among Kecskerey's *habitués,* and they let it be known that should he be seen conversing with Abellino, it would be as well to be within earshot, as something unusually interesting would be going on.

"Why, what great misfortune can have befallen Abellino that our friend Kecskerey can speak of him so lightly?" inquired Livius, turning towards Rudolf. "Generally speaking, he is in the habit of treating him with greater respect in view of his ultimate claims to the Kárpáthy estates."

Rudolf shrugged his shoulders. What did it matter to him what befell Abellino?

Look; now he is coming in! He had still that defiant, devil-may-care step, that haughty, insolent look, as if the whole world were full of his lackeys, that repellent beauty, for his features were as vacant as they were handsome.

"Ah, good evening, Bélá; good evening, Bélá!" screeched our friend Kecskerey, while Abellino was still some distance off; he did not move from his place, but sat there with his arms embracing his legs like the two of clubs as it is painted on old Hungarian cards.

Abellino went towards Kecskerey. He attributed the fact that he drew after him a whole group of gentlemen, who quitted the tea-tables and the whist-tables to crowd around him, to the particular respect of the present company to himself personally.

"I congratulate you," cried Kecskerey, in a shrill nasal voice, waving his hands towards Abellino.

"What for, you false club?"

Thus it was clear that Abellino also was struck by Kecskerey's great resemblance to the historical playing-card already mentioned, and this sally brought the laughter over to his side.

"Don't you know that I have just come from nunky, my dear?"

"Ah, that's another matter," said Abellino, in a somewhat softer voice. "And what, pray, is the dear old gentleman up to now?"

"That's just where my congratulations come in. All at home send you their best greetings, kisses, and embraces. The old gentleman is as sound as an acorn, or as a ripe apple freshly plucked from the tree. Don't be in the least concerned on his account; your uncle feels remarkably well. But your aunt is sick, very sick, and to all appearance she will be sicker still."

"Poor auntie!" said Abellino. "No doubt," thought he to himself, "that is why he congratulates me; and good news, too. No wonder he congratulates me. Perhaps she'll even die – who knows? – And what's the matter with her?" he asked aloud.

"Ah, she is in great danger. I assure you, my friend, that when last I saw her, the doctors had prohibited both riding and driving."

Even now the real state of things would not have occurred to Abellino's mind, had not a couple of quicker-witted gentlemen, who had come there for the express purpose of laughing, and were therefore on the alert for the point of the jest, suddenly laughed aloud. Then, all at once, light flashed into his brain.

"A thousand devils! You are speaking the truth now, I suppose?"

His face could not hide the fury which boiled up within him.

"Why, how else should I have cause to congratulate you?" said Kecskerey, laughing.

"Oh, it is infamous!" exclaimed Abellino, beside himself.

The bystanders began to pity him, and the softer-hearted among them quietly dispersed. It was a horrible thought that this man, who on entering the room had believed himself to be the master of millions, should have been plunged back into poverty by a few words.

Kecskerey alone had no pity for him. He never pitied anyone who was unfortunate; he reserved all his sympathy for the prosperous.

"Then there's nothing more to be done," murmured Abellino, between his teeth, "unless it be to kill myself or that woman."

Kecskerey's strident rasping voice seemed to cut clean through that desperate murmur.

"If you want to kill or be killed, my friend, I should advise you to read Pitaval,* wherein you will find all sorts and kinds of tips for murderers, including lists of poisons both vegetable and mineral, a liberal choice of weapons of every description, and the best means of disposing of the *corpus delecti* afterwards, either by submersion, combustion, dissection, or inhumation. The whole twelve volumes is a little library of itself, and a man who reads it patiently through to the end will easily persuade himself that he is a born murderer. I recommend the matter to your attention. Ho, ho, ho!"

To all this Abellino paid no attention. "Who can be this woman's lover?" said he.

"Look around you, my friend, and choose for yourself."

"At least I should like to recognize and kill him."

"I am absolutely sure I know who her lover is," remarked Kecskerey.

"Who?" asked Abellino, with sparkling eyes. "Oh, that man I *should* like to know!"

Kecskerey, who was having rare sport with him, drew his neck down between his shoulders, and continued – "How many times have I not seen you fall upon his neck, and kiss and embrace him!"

---

* The allusion, no doubt, is to F. G. de Pitaval's "Causes célèbres et intéressantes." – Tr.

"Who is it, who is it?" cried Abellino, catching hold of Kecskerey's arm.

"Would you like to know?"

"I should."

"Then it is – her husband."

"This is a stupid jest," cried Abellino, quite forgetting himself; "and nobody will believe it. That woman loves somebody, loves someone with shameful self-abandonment. And that old scoundrel, her husband, knows and suffers it in order to gratify his vengeance on me. But I will find out who he is, I will find out who it is if it be the devil himself, and I will bring a scandalous action against this woman, the like of which the world has never yet seen."

At that moment a loud manly voice rang out amidst the group of listeners who were beginning to rally Abellino, and ironically beg him not to suspect them as they were quite innocent, and could not lay claim to the honor of making Madame Kárpáthy happy.

"Gentlemen," it said, "you forget that it is not becoming in men of breeding to make ribald jests about the name of a lady whom nobody in the world has any cause or any right to traduce."

"What, Rudolf! Why, what interest have you in the matter?" inquired the astonished Kecskerey.

"This much – I am a man and will not allow a woman whom I respect to be vilified in my presence."

That was saying a great deal, and there was no blinking it, not only because Rudolf was right and enjoyed the best of reputations, but also because he was known to be the best shot and swordsman in the place, and cool-headed and lucky to boot.

So from henceforth Madame Kárpáthy's name ceased to be alluded to in the club.

Chapter XIX

ZOLTÁN KÁRPÁTHY

What Abellino had cause to tremble at had really happened. Madame John Kárpáthy had become a mother. A son was born to her.

Early one morning the family doctor invaded the sanctum of the Nabob with the joyful intelligence – "Your wife has borne you a son!"

Who can describe the joy of Squire John thereat? What he had hitherto only ventured to hope, to imagine, his hardiest, most ardent desire was gratified: his wife had a son! A son who would be his heir and perpetuate his name! who was born in happier times, who would make good the faults of his father, and by means of his youthful virtues fulfill the obligations which the Kárpáthy family owed to its country and to humanity.

If only he might live long enough to hear the child speak, to read a meaning in his sweet babblings, to speak words to him that he might understand and never forget, so that in the days to come, when he was the *fêted* hero of all great and noble ideas, he might say, "I first heard of these things from that good old fellow, John Kárpáthy."

What should be the child's name? It should be the name of one of those princes who drank out of the same wine-cup with the primal ancestor of the House of Kárpáthy on the fair plains of Hunnia. It should be Zoltán – Zoltán Kárpáthy – how beautifully that would sound!

Presently they brought to him this new citizen of the world, and he held him in his arms and kissed and embraced him. He could scarce see him for the tears of joy that streamed from his eyes, and yet how greatly he longed to see him! With twinkling eyes he regarded the child, and a fine, vigorous little lad it was, like a little rosy-cheeked angel; his little hands and neck were regularly wrinkled everywhere from very plumpness, his mouth was hardly larger than a strawberry, but his sparkling eyes, than which no precious stone was ever of a purer azure, were all the larger by contrast, and whenever he drooped them the long lashes lay conspicuous on his chubby cheeks. He did not cry, he was quite serious, just as if he knew that it would be a great shame to be weak now, and when Squire John, in his rapture, raised him to a level with his lips and kissed his little red face again and again with his stiff, bristly moustache, he began to smile and utter a merry little gurgle, which those who were standing round Squire John were quite positive was an attempt to speak.

"Talk away, my darling little soul," stammered Squire John, perceiving that the child was screwing up his little round lips all sorts of ways, as if he knew very well what he wanted to say but could not find the right words, "talk away, talk away! Don't be afraid, we understand you. Say it again."

But the doctor and the nurses thought well to interpret the little suckling's discourse as a desire to go back to his mother. Enough of caresses then, for the present, they said, and, taking him out of Squire John's arms, they brought him back to his mother, whereupon the good gentleman could not but steal softly into the adjoining room and listen whether the child was crying, and every time anybody came out he would ask what was going on or what had happened since, and every time anybody went in he sent a message along with him.

Towards the afternoon the doctor emerged again, and asked him to retire with him to another room.

"Why? I prefer being here; at least I can hear what they are talking about."

"Yes; but I don't want you to hear what they are talking about in there."

John stared at him. He began to feel bad as he met the doctor's cold look; and he followed him mechanically into the adjoining room.

"Well, sir, what is it you wish to say to me that others may not hear?"

"Your worship, a great joy has this day befallen your house."

"I know it. I understand it. God be praised!"

"God has indeed blessed your worship with a great joy, but it has also seemed good to Him to prove you with affliction."

"What do you mean by that?" thundered the terrified Kárpáthy, and his face turned blue.

"Look now, your worship, this is just what I feared, and that is why I called you aside into an adjoining room; show yourself a Christian, and learn to bear the hand of God."

"Don't torture me; say exactly what has happened."

"Your honor's wife will die."

After hearing this Kárpáthy stood there without uttering a word.

"If there was any help for her in this world," continued the doctor, "I would say there is hope, but it is my duty to tell you that her hours, her moments, are numbered, therefore your honor must play the man, and go to her and bid her good-bye, for ere long she will be unable to speak."

Kárpáthy allowed himself to be led into the dying woman's chamber. The whole world was blurred before him, he saw nobody, he heard nothing; he saw *her* only lying there pale, faded, with the sweat of death upon her glorious face, with the pallor of death around her dear lips, with the refracted gleam of death in her beautiful inspired eyes.

There he stood, beside the bed, unable to speak a word. His eyes were tearless. The room was full of serving-maids and nurses. Here and there a stifled sob was to be heard. He neither saw nor heard anything. He only gazed dumbly, stonily, at the dying woman. On each side of the bed a familiar form was kneeling – Flora and Teresa.

The good old aunt, with clasped hands, was praying, her face concealed among the pillows. Flora held the little boy in her arms; he was sleeping with his head upon her bosom.

The sick woman raised her breaking eyes towards her husband, stretched out her trembling, fevered hand, and, grasping the hand of her husband, drew it towards her panting lips, and gasped, in a scarcely audible voice, "Remember me!"

Squire John did not hear, he did not understand what she said to him, he only held his wife's hand in both his own as if he believed that he could thereby draw her away from Death.

After an hour's heavy struggle, the feverish delirium of the sick woman began to subside, her blood circulated less fiercely, her hands were no longer so burning hot, her breathing grew easier.

She began to look about her calmly and recognize everyone. She spoke to those about her in a quiet, gentle voice; the tormenting sweat had vanished from her face.

"My husband, my dear husband!" she said, casting a look full of feeling upon Squire John.

Her husband rejoiced within himself, thinking it a sign of amendment; but the doctor shook his head, he knew it was a sign of death.

Next, the sick woman turned towards Flora. Her friend guessed the meaning of her inquiring look, and held the little child nestling on her bosom to the sick woman's lips. Fanny tenderly strained it to her heaving breast, and kissed the face of the sleeping child, who at every kiss opened its dark-blue eyes, and then drooped them and went on sleeping again.

The mother put it back on Flora's breast, and, pressing the lady's hand, whispered to her –

"Be a mother to my child."

Flora could not reply, but she nodded her head. Not a sound would come to her lips, and she turned her head aside, lest the dying woman should see the tears in her eyes.

Then Fanny folded her hands together on her breast, and murmured the single prayer which she had been taught to say in her childhood –

"O God, my God, be merciful to me, poor sinful girl, now and forevermore. Amen."

Then she cast down her eyes gently, and fell asleep.

"She has gone to sleep," murmured the husband, softly.

"She is dead," faltered the doctor, with a look of pity.

And the good old Nabob fell down on his knees beside the bed, and, burying his head in the dead woman's pillows, sobbed bitterly, oh, so bitterly!

Chapter XX

SECRET VISITORS

Soon came winter. The cold, frosty, snow-laden season began; nothing but white forests, white fields, are to be seen in every quarter of the level *Alföld*, and as early as four o'clock in the afternoon the dark-grey, lilac-colored atmosphere begins to envelope the horizon all round about, rising higher and higher every moment, till at last the very vault of heaven is reached, and it is night. Only the snowy whiteness of the plain preserves some gleam of light to the landscape.

Pale fallow stripes appear to have been drawn across the snowy expanse; they are the tracks of the sledges, stretching from one village to another.

Kárpáthy Castle seemed to make the uniform monotonous landscape still more melancholy. At other times the windows, of an evening, shed their light far and wide, and merry groups of sportsmen bustled about the well-filled courtyard; but now, scarcely more than a gleam of light was to be seen in two or three of the windows, and only the blue smoke of the chimneys showed that it was still inhabited.

Alone on these dun-colored roads, in the fall of the long winter evening, a peasant's sledge, without bells, might have been seen gliding along through that featureless, semi-obscure wilderness towards Kárpáthy Castle.

In the rear of the sledge sat a man wrapped in a simple mantle; in front, a peasant, in a sheepskin *bunda,* was driving the two lean horses.

The sitter behind frequently stood up in the sledge, and swept the plain on every side, as if he were in search of something. The preserves of the Kárpáthy estate loomed darkly before him, and by the time they reached a ramshackle old wooden bridge, the visitor perceived what he sought.

"Those are pine trees, are they not?" he inquired of the coachman.

"Yes, young sir; one can recognize them from a distance, for they are still green when the others have shed their leaves."

They were the only trees of the sort in the whole region. They had all been planted in Squire John's time.

"Here we will stop, old comrade. You return to the wayside *csárda*; I will take a turn about here alone. I shall not be longer than an hour away."

"It would be as well were I to accompany you, young sir, if you mean to take a stroll, for wolves are wont to wander hither."

"It is not necessary, my good friend, I am not afraid."

And with that the stranger dismounted from the sledge, and, taking his axe in his hand, directed his way through the snowy field to the spot where the pines stood out darkly against the snow-white plain.

What was beneath those pines?

The family vault of the Kárpáthys, and he who came to visit it at that hour was Alexander Boltay.

The young artisan had heard from Teresa on her return home that Fanny was dead. The great lady had been lowered into her tomb for the worms just as the wife of the poorest artisan might have been, and her tomb was perhaps still more neglected than the tomb of the artisan's wife would have been.

Then Alexander opened his heart to the old people. He meant, he said, to make a pilgrimage to the tomb of the dead dear one whom he worshipped both in life and in death, and to whom, now that she was under the ground, he might confess his love, he had as much right now to her death-cold heart as anybody else in the world. The two old people did not attempt to dissuade him; let him go, they thought; let him take his sorrow there and bury it; perchance he will be lighter of heart when he has wept himself out there.

In the ice-bound season the young man set out, and from the description which Teresa gave him, he recognized the funereal pine-grove which John Kárpáthy had had planted round the family vault, in order that there it might be green when everything else was white and dead.

He quitted the sledge, and cut across the plain, while the driver returned to the wayside *csárda.*

Meanwhile a pair of horsemen might have been seen slowly approaching from the opposite direction. One of them was a little in the rear of the other, and led four hardy hounds in a long leash.

"I see the trail of a fox, Martin," said the foremost horseman, calling the attention of the one behind to the trail. "We can easily track him through the fresh snow if we look sharp, and can catch him up before we reach Kárpátfalva."

The groom appeared to confirm his master's assertion.

"Follow the trail as straight as you can, and hand over two of the hounds to me while I make a circuit of the wood yonder."

With that he took over two of the dogs, and sending his escort on in front, turned aside, slowly wading through the snow. But the moment his man was out of sight, he suddenly changed his direction, and strode rapidly towards the pine grove.

On reaching the trench which surrounded it, he dismounted, tied his horse to a bush and the dogs to his saddle bow and waded across the narrow ditch. By the light of the snow it was easy to find his goal.

A large white marble monument arose by the side of a green tree, on the top of it was the sad emblem of death, an angel with an inverted torch.

The horseman stood alone before the monument – this visitor was Rudolf.

Thus both of them had come at the same time, and it was the will of Fate that they should meet there before the tomb.

Rudolf hastened confidently towards the white colonnaded monument and stood rooted to the ground with amazement on perceiving the figure of a man, apparently in a state of collapse, half sitting, half kneeling on the pedestal. But the man was equally amazed to see him there.

Neither recognized the other.

"What are you doing here, sir?" asked Rudolf, who was the first to recover his composure, drawing nearer to the pedestal.

Alexander recognized the voice, he knew that it was Rudolf, and could not understand why he should have come to that place at that hour.

"Count Szentirmay," he said gently, "I am that artisan to whom you showed a kindness once upon a time; be so good as to show yet another kindness to me by leaving me here alone and asking no questions."

Then Rudolf recognized the young man, and it suddenly flashed across his mind that the dead woman before she became Dame Kárpáthy had been engaged to a poor young artisan who had so bravely, so chivalrously, exposed himself to death for her sake.

Now he understood everything.

He took the young man's hand and pressed it.

"You loved this lady? You have come hither to mourn over her?"

"Yes, sir. There's nothing to be ashamed of in that. One may love the dead. I loved that woman, I love her now, and I shall never love another."

Rudolf's heart went out to the young man.

"You remain here," he said, "I will leave you to yourself. I will wait in the cemetery outside, and if I can be of any service to you command me."

"Thank you, sir, I will go too; I have done what I came here to do."

The name of the dear departed was inscribed on the tomb in golden letters, and these letters gleamed forth in the light of the snow: "Madame Kárpáthy, *née* Fanny Meyer."

The young artisan removed his cap, and with the same respect, the same reverence with which one touches the lips of the dead, he kissed every letter of the word "Fanny."

"I am not ashamed of this weakness before you," said Alexander, standing up again, "for you have a noble heart, and will not laugh at me."

Rudolf answered nothing, but he turned his head aside. God knows why, but he could not have met the young man's eyes at that moment.

"And now, sir, we can go."

"Where will you spend the night? Come with me to Szentirma!"

"Thank you; you are very good to me, but I must return this very hour. The moon will soon be up, and there will be light enough to see my way by. I must make haste, for there's lots for me to do at home."

He could not prevail upon him; a man's sorrow has no desire to be comforted.

Rudolf accompanied him to the wayside *csárda,* where the sledge was awaiting him. He could not restrain himself from warmly pressing the artisan's hand and even embracing him.

And Alexander did not guess the meaning of that warm grasp, or why this great nobleman was so good to him.

Shortly afterwards the sledge disappeared in the darkness of the night by the same road by which it had come. Rudolf returned to the pine trees, and paid another visit to the white monument. There he stood and thought of the woman who had suffered so much, and who, perhaps, was thinking of him there below. Her face stood before him now as it had looked when she had followed with her eyes the rejected amaranth; as it had looked when she galloped past him on her wild charger; as it had looked when she had hidden it on his bosom in an agony of despairing love, in order that there she might weep out her woe, amidst sweet torture and painful joy, that secret woe which she had carried about with her for years. And when he thought on these things, his fine eyes filled with tears.

He noticed the imprints of the knees of the departed youth, where he had knelt on the pedestal of the monument in the snow, and he fell a-thinking.

Did not this woman, who had so suffered, lived and died, deserve as much? And he himself bent his knee before the monument.

And he read the name. Like a spectral invitation, those five letters, F-a-n-n-y, gleamed before him so seductively.

For a long time he remained immersed in his own reflections, and thought – and thought –

At last he bent down and kissed the five letters one after another, just as the other young fellow had done.

Then he flung himself on his horse. His errant groom, not finding his master, was impatiently blowing his horn in every direction. Rudolf soon came up with him, and half an hour later they were in the courtyard of John Kárpáthy's castle. Kárpáthy had invited Rudolf to hasten to him that very night.

Chapter XXI

THE LAST WILL AND TESTAMENT

They already expected Rudolf at the Castle. The moment he dismounted, Paul, who was awaiting him in the hall, led him straight to Kárpáthy.

The servants all wore black since their mistress had been buried, and all the mirrors and escutcheons in the rooms were still covered with the black crape with which they had been enveloped on the day of the funeral.

Squire John was waiting for Rudolf in his private room, and as soon as he saw him enter, he rose from his seat, hastened to meet him, and warmly pressed his hand.

"Many thanks, Rudolf, many thanks for coming. Pardon me for sending for you at such an hour and in such hot haste. God has brought you. Thank you very much for coming. Rudolf, a peculiar feeling has come over me. Three days ago, a strange sort of sensation, not unpleasant, took possession of my limbs, and when I awoke from my sleep in the night it was with a odd sort of joy, I know not how to express it, as if my soul had quitted me. I take it as an omen of my death. Do not gainsay me, I beg. I am not afraid of death; I long for it. At such times a quick current of air brushes past my ear, as if someone were about to fly away from close beside me. I know what that means. Twice I have had a similar sensation, and on each occasion a current of air has struck me. I fancy this will be the last of them. I think of it with joy, and have not the slightest fear of it. I have sent for you in order that I may make my last will, while I still have the possession of all my faculties, and I wish you to be my executor. Will you accept the trust?"

Rudolf indicated his willingness in silence.

"Then come with me to my library. The other witnesses are waiting there now. I have got them together as rapidly as I could, and they are all honest fellows."

As they were passing through the suite of rooms, Squire John suddenly stopped Rudolf, and said –

"Look! in this room I heard her laugh for the last time. On that chair yonder she lost her shawl – it is there still. On that table is a pair of gloves, the last she ever wore. Here she used to sit when she sketched. There's the piano, still open – a *fantasia* lies, you see, on the music-stand. If she should come back again, eh?"

And now he opened the door of a room illuminated by candles – Rudolf shrunk back.

"Old friend, that's not a fit place to enter. Surely you have lost yourself in your own house! That is your wife's bedroom."

"I know, but I can never pass it without going in. And now I mean to have a last look at it, for tomorrow I shall have it walled up. Look, everything remains just as she left it. She did not die in this room – don't be alarmed! That door yonder leads to the garden. Look, everything is in its old place – there the lamp by which she used to read, on the table a half-written letter, which nobody has read. A hundred times have I entered the room, and not a word of that letter have I read. To me it is holy. In front of the bed are her two little embroidered slippers, so tiny that they look as if they had been made for a child. On the table is an open prayer-book, between the open leaves of which are an iris and an amaranth and a maple leaf. She greatly loved those flowers."

"Let us go away from hence, let us go away," urged Rudolf. "It pains me to hear you talk so."

"It pains you, eh? – it does me good. I have sat here for days together, and have called to mind every word she said. I see her before me everywhere, asleep, awake, smiling, sorrowful – I see her resting her pretty head on the pillows, I see her sleeping, I see her dying –"

"Oh! come, come away!"

"We will go, Rudolf. And I shall never come back again. Tomorrow a smooth wall will be here in the place of the door, and iron shutters will cover all the windows. I feel that I ought not to seek her here anymore. Elsewhere, elsewhere I will seek her: we will dwell together in another room. Let us go, let us go!"

And smilingly, without a tear, like one who is preparing for his bridal day, he quitted the room, casting one more look around upon it from the threshold, and a dumb kiss into the darkness, as if he were taking leave for a last time of a beloved object visible only to himself.

"Let us come, let us come!"

In the large library the witnesses were awaiting them.

They were four – the local notary, a stoutish young man, with his back planted against the warm stove; the estate agent, benevolent Peter

Varga, who had asked, as a favor, that he might wear black like the other family servants; the parish priest, and Mike Kis. That worthy youth had quitted the brilliant saloons whose hero he was, to comfort his old friend in the days of his tribulation. The fiscal was there also, cutting quills for everyone present, and sticking them into the inkstands, which were placed all round the round table in front of the witnesses.

When Squire John and Rudolf entered the room, everyone present saluted them with the grave solemnity befitting the occasion.

The Squire beckoned to everybody to be seated – Rudolf on his right, Mike Kis on his left, the fiscal opposite to him, that they might the better hear what he was going to say.

At the furthest end of the table sat Mr. Varga, with all the candles piled in front of him. *He* knew why.

"My dear friends and good neighbors," began the Nabob, while everyone listened with the deepest attention, "God has numbered my days, and is about to call me from this transitory life to His glory, and therefore I call you all to witness that what I am going to say now is said clearly, deliberately, and while I am in the full possession of all my faculties. I find that the estates which God, of His goodness, has entrusted to my hands, now yield over a million of florins more of clear income than when I came into possession of them. God grant that they may be more productive of blessings in the hands of others than they have been in mine! I begin my last will and testament with a reference to her who was dearest to me in the world and now slumbers in her tomb. This tomb is the beginning and the end of my arrangements in this life; it has been my first thought when I rose up, and my last thought when I lay down, and will last on when I rise up no more. My first bequest, then, is 50,000 florins, the interest on which is to go to that gardener on my domains whose duty it shall be, in return therefore, to cultivate from early spring to late autumn, irises and amaranths, – flowers which 'she' loved so much, – and have them planted regularly round the grave of my unforgettable wife. Furthermore I bequeath the interest of 10,000 florins to the gardeners of the Castle of Madaras, from father to son, whose corresponding obligation it shall be to maintain a conservatory near to the maple tree, beneath which is a white bench." Here the Squire sighed, half to himself, "That was her favorite seat; there she used to sit all through the afternoons. And the gardener is to plant another maple tree beside it, that it may not stand so solitarily there. If at any time the tree should wither, or if any careless descendant of mine should ever cut it down, the whole amount reserved for this purpose shall go to the poor."

Rudolf sat there with a cold, immovable face while all this was being said; nobody guessed what he felt while these words were being spoken.

"'How foolish the old man must have grown in his latter years,' his descendants will one day say, when they read these dispositions, 'leaving legacies to trees and shrubs!'"

"Furthermore," pursued Squire John, "I bequeath 50,000 florins to form a fund for dowering girls of good behavior on their marriage. On every anniversary of the day on which my unforgettable wife fell asleep, all the young maids on my estate shall meet together in the church to pray to God for the souls of those that have died; then the three among these virgins whom the priest shall judge to be the most meritorious shall be presented with bridal wreaths in the presence of the congregation, and the sum of money set apart for them; and then they shall proceed to the tomb and deck it with flowers, and pray that God may make her who lies there happier in the other world than she was in this. And that is my desire."

Here he stopped, waiting till the lawyer had written down all his words, during which time a mournful silence prevailed in the room, interrupted only by the scratching and spluttering of the pen on the paper.

When the lawyer looked up from his parchment by way of signifying that he had written everything down, the Squire sighed, and hung his head.

"When it pleases God to bring upon me the hour in which I shall quit this transitory life, when I am dead, I desire to be buried in the dress in which I was married to her; my faithful servant, old Paul, will know which it is. The coffin, in which I am to be put, stands all ready in my bedroom; every day I look at it, and accustom myself to the thought of it; often I lay me down in it, and bethink me how good it would be were I never to rise from it again. It is quite ready. I took some trouble about it; it is just like hers. My name has already been driven into it with nice silver nails, only the date of my death has to be added. That priest is to pray over me who prayed over her, and how beautiful that will be!"

"Sir, sir!" interrupted the priest, "who can read in the book of life and death, or tell which of us twain will live longest, or die first?"

The Squire beckoned to the priest to bear with him – he himself knew best.

"Further, remove none of the mourning draperies from the rooms, let everything remain as it was at the time of her burial. Let the selfsame cantors come from Debreczen and sing over me the same chants, and no other. Just what they sang over her, and the selfsame youths must do it. All those chants were so dear to me."

"Oh, sir," said the priest, "perchance everyone of these students may be grown-up men by then."

The Squire only shook his head, and thus proceeded –

"And when they have opened the vault, they are to break down the partition wall between the two niches, so that there may be nothing between her coffin and mine, and I may descend into the grave with the comfortable thought that I shall sleep beside her till the day of that joyful resurrection which God grants to every true believer. Amen!"

And all those big grave men sitting round the table there fell a-weeping, and not one of them felt ashamed of himself before the others. Even the matter-of-fact lawyer spoilt his nib, and could not see the letters he was writing. Only on the Squire's face was there no sign of sadness. He spoke like one bent on preparing his bridal chamber.

"When I am buried, my funeral monument – it is standing all ready in my museum – must be placed beside hers. The date of death is alone wanting, and I want nothing added to the inscription: it must remain just as it is – my name and nothing more. Beneath it are inscribed these lines: 'He lived but one year, the rest he slept away.' One of my treasures is beneath the ground, and in no long time I shall be alone with it. My second treasure, my joy, the hope of my soul, remains here. I mean my son."

At these words the first tear he had shed appeared in Kárpáthy's eyes. He dried it hastily, but it was a tear of joy.

"May he never resemble me in anything! may he be better, wiser than his father was! Mr. Lawyer, write down what I say in as many words. Why should I make any mystery of it? I am standing before the presence of God. I want my son to be better than I was. Perchance God will forgive me for the sake of his virtues. May my country, too, forgive me, and my ancestors who have led lives like mine, for our sins against her! May his life make manifest what ours ought to have been! May his wealth never spoil his heart, so that in his old age he may not repent him of his youth. I would have my son a happy man. But what is happiness? Money? possessions? power? No, none of these. I possessed them all, and yet I was not happy. Let his soul be rich, and then he will be happy. Let him be an honorable, wise, courageous citizen, a good patriot, a nobleman not merely by name, but in heart and soul, and then he will be happy.

"I am well aware," pursued Kárpáthy, "that if I left my son in the guardianship of his nearest relative – I allude to my nephew Bélá – it would mean his utter ruin. I charge that kinsman of mine before God's judgment-seat with being a bad man, a bad relative, a bad patriot, who would be even worse than he is if he were not as mad as he is bad. No! I will not have the heart of my boy ruined by such a man as that. I would place him in the hands of those who would inspire him with all noble ideas; who would guide him along the paths of honor and virtue; who would cherish and defend him better than I could do were I able to stretch forth my hand from the tomb in his defense. I would place him in the hands of a man who will be a better father to him than I could ever be, and who, if he cannot love him better than I love him, will, at least, love him more wisely. The man whom I appoint the legal guardian of my son is Count Rudolf Szentirmay."

The good old man warmly pressed the hands of the youth sitting on his right, who thereupon arose from his chair and embraced the Nabob with tears of emotion. On resuming his seat, he whispered, in a husky voice, of which he was scarce the master, that he accepted the trust.

"'She' also wished it," said the Nabob. "In her last hour, as she placed my child in the arms of your wife, she said these words: 'Be a mother to my child!' I have not forgotten it; and now I say to you, 'Be a father to my child!' Happy child! What a good father, what a good mother, you will inherit!

"And now," continued the Nabob, "a word or two concerning him who was the cause of the bitterest moments of my life. I mean my nephew, who was christened Bélá, but who calls himself Abellino. I will not reckon up the sins he has committed against God, his country, and myself. God and his country forgive him, as I have forgiven him; but I should be a liar and a hypocrite before God if I said, at this hour, that I loved him. I feel as cold towards him as towards one whom I have never seen. And now he is reduced to the beggar's staff; now he has more debts than the hairs of his head. What will become of him? He cannot work – he has never earned a penny; he has never learnt anything: he is bankrupt both in body and mind. He is not likely to take his own life, for libertines do not readily become suicides. And far be the thought of such a thing from him. I desire it not. Let him live. Let him have time to turn to God! Nor do I wish him to be a beggar, to feel want, to beg his bread at other men's doors. I order, therefore, that my agent at Pest shall pay him a gold ducat down every day. I fancy that will be quite enough to keep anybody from suffering want. But this ducat he himself must come and fetch day by day, and it must be paid to nobody but himself personally. But every time he fails to come for such ducat it shall be forfeited to the lawyer, and it must in no case be attached for debt, or paid to him in advance. But every time my birthday, John Baptist's Day, comes round, he shall receive a lump sum of one hundred ducats down extra. It is my wish that he should rejoice beforehand at the coming of that day every year, and that he should thus remember me from year to year.

"And now my business with the world is over. I have no other kinsmen to remember. My friends I can easily count up. I only know of three to whom I can really give that name. The first is Rudolf, to him I have left my child. The second is Mike Kis. He, also, was always a good fellow, who loved me right well. Whenever misfortune came, he was always to be found by my side. To him I leave my favorite horse and my favorite dog. I could not leave them a better master, or him a more pleasant keepsake. My third good friend is my steward, Peter Varga."

"Oh, sir!" the other old man would have murmured; but his tongue refused to move.

"To him I leave my old servant Paul, and old Vidra the jester, and the Lapayi property. May he live there happily with my two faithful servants.

"All my agents now employed upon the estate are to go on receiving their usual salaries, and they are not to lose their pay if they have to be discharged from old age or infirmity. The general management of my estate I leave to the wise discretion of Count Rudolf Szentirmay.

"And now, committing my soul to God and my body to the earth, I await with resignation my dissolution, and, putting my whole trust in God, I look forward to the hour when I shall turn to dust."

These last words were also written down. The lawyer then read the will; and then, first Kárpáthy and then all the witnesses present subscribed and sealed it. And the same night a fair copy of it was made and sent to Rudolf, as the chief magistrate of the county.

Then Kárpáthy bade the priest send in the sexton.

He entered accordingly, and a golden goblet with wine in it and a golden patten with a thin slice of bread on it were placed on a little round ebony table. It was the Holy Sacrament of the Lord's Supper, the last supper such as the sick unto death partake of.

The priest stood in front of the table on which the wine and the bread were. Kárpáthy, with Christian humility, approached the sacred elements, the others stood around in silence. Then the priest communicated him in their presence, and, after the simple ceremony was over, the old man said to the priest –

"In no very long time, I shall see the happier country face to face. If you hear that I am sick, say no prayers in church for my recovery, – it would be useless; pray rather for my new life. And now let us go to my son."

"To my son!" What feeling, what pathos was in that one phrase: "To my son!"

All who were present followed him, and surrounded the child's cradle. The little thing looked gravely at all those serious manly faces, as if it also would have made one of them. The squire lifted him in his arms. The child looked at him with such big wise eyes, as if he were taking it all in; and the old man kissed his little lips again and again.

Then he was passed round among all the other old fellows, and he looked at them all so gravely, as if he knew very well that they were all of them honorable men; but when Rudolf took him in his arms the child began to kick and crow, and fight with his little hands, and make a great fuss, as children are wont to do when they are in a good humor – who knows why? – and Rudolf kissed the child's forehead.

"How glad he is," said the Nabob, "just as if he knew that from henceforth you will be his father."

A few hours later the whole company sat down to supper.

They noticed that the Squire ate and drank nothing, but he explained that, after taking the holy bread and wine, he would not sit down to ordinary food, and meant to eat nothing till the morrow.

And the old servant waiting upon them whispered to Rudolf that his master had not touched a thing since yesterday evening.

Chapter XXII

LEAVE-TAKING

Everyone in the castle retired to rest early except Rudolf, who remained up for a long time. The fire burned cozily on the hearth, and there he sat before the fire till past midnight, reflecting on the past and on the future. To speak of his thoughts would be treachery. There are secrets which are better left at the bottom of men's hearts.

Towards midnight a great hubbub arose in the castle, and servants began rushing up and down stairs. Rudolf, who was still half dressed, went out into the corridor, and came face to face with old Paul.

"What is the matter?" said he.

The old servant would have spoken, but his lips were sealed; he shivered convulsively, like one who would fain cry and cannot. At last he came out with it, and there were tears on his cheek and in his eyes –

"He is dead!"

"Impossible!" cried Rudolf; and he hastened to the Squire's bedroom.

There lay the Nabob with closed eyes, his hands folded across his breast, in front of him his wife's portrait that he might gaze upon it to the last. That countenance looked so venerable after death, it seemed to have been purified from all disturbing passions, only the old ancestral dignity was visible in every feature.

He had died so quietly that even the faithful old servant, who slept in the same room with him, had not been aware of it: only when, struck by the extraordinary stillness, he had gone to see if his master wanted anything, did he perceive that he was dead.

Rudolf at once sent for the doctor, although one glance at the quiet face assured him that there was no need of doctors here.

By the time everything was ready for the funeral – for indeed everything necessary therefore was already at hand in the bedroom, the coffin, the pall, the escutcheons, the torches – he had no longer had that fear of a coffin which he had felt on his birthday. Everything was done as he had planned it.

They attired him in his wedding garments, and so placed him in the coffin. They sent for the very same youths who had sung the dirges over his wife so sweetly, and they sang the selfsame hymns for the dead over his coffin likewise.

The news of his death had spread all over the county, and the courtyard of Kárpátfalva was thronged once more with the bizarre mob which had filled it before on that day of rejoicing, except that sad faces came now instead of merry ones. Not one of his old acquaintances remained away; everyone hastened to see him once more, and everyone said that they could not recognize him, so greatly had death changed him.

A tremendous crowd followed the coffin to the grave. The most eminent men in the kingdom carried torches before it, the most distinguished ladies in the land were among the mourners that followed after it. Custom demanded that the heir, the eldest son, should accompany his father's coffin. But as the heir was only six months old, he had to be carried, and it was Lady Szentirmay who carried him in her bosom. And everyone who saw it maintained that she embraced and protected the child as tenderly as if she were really its mother.

Happy child!

The good old Nabob was committed to his last resting-place by the selfsame priest who had spoken such consolatory words over the body of his wife. There was much weeping, but the one who wept the most was the priest himself, who ought to have comforted the others.

Then they lowered him down into those silent mansions where the dead have their habitation, and they laid him by the side of his departed wife as he had desired. The last hymns sounded so ghostly down in the vault there as the wailing chant ascended up through the earth, even those who wept made haste to depart from thence and get into the light of day once more. And the heavy iron door clanged thunderously on its hinges behind them.

And the Nabob? Ah, now he is happy indeed, happy forevermore!

The End

List of the Hungarian Words Used in This Version

ALFÖLD, the great Hungarian plain.
ATTILA, the short, fringed pelisse of the Hungarian national costume.
BÁCSI, uncle, a term of familiarity between a young and an old man.
BETYÁR, a vagabond, a loafer.
BUNDA, a mantle.
CSÁRDA, a country inn.
CSIKÓS, a guard or keeper of horses in the steppe.
CSIZMA, a boot
EGRI, a red wine of the claret kind produced near Eger.
ÉLJEN, *vivat!* hurrah!
FÖISPÁN, a lord-lieutenant.
FOKOS, a hand-axe.
FRISS-MAGYAR, an Hungarian country-dance.
GUBA, a shaggy mantle of coarse wool.
GULYÁS, a herdsman.
GUNYA, a peasant's jacket.
HEGYALJA, the Tokay district.
KACZAGÁNY, a fur overmantle.
KALPAG, the Hungarian tall fur cap, mostly plumed, part of the national costume.
KANTUS, a short under-garment.
KÖNTÖS, a gown, or robe.
MÉNES, a stud of horses.
MENTE, a short fur pelisse.
MESZELY, a white Hungarian wine.
PÁLINKA, Hungarian brandy.
PRIMÁS, the conductor of a gypsy band.
PUSZTA, the wilderness, a wide-spreading heath.
SZILVORIUM, a spirit made from plums.

www.ingramcontent.com/pod-product-compliance
Lightning Source LLC
Chambersburg PA
CBHW020926310726
48980CB00005B/405

* 9 7 8 1 6 0 3 1 2 6 9 6 0 *